NS

E14

5.00

Florence Rutter
Dec 1946

Thieves in the Night

Books by Arthur Koestler

SPANISH TESTAMENT (1937)
THE GLADIATORS (1939)
DARKNESS AT NOON (1940)
SCUM OF THE EARTH (1941)
ARRIVAL AND DEPARTURE (1943)
THE YOGI AND THE COMMISSAR (1945)
TWILIGHT BAR (1945)

Thieves in the Night

CHRONICLE OF AN EXPERIMENT

BY

ARTHUR KOESTLER

But the day of the Lord will come as a thief in the night.

(II Peter iii, 10)

THE MACMILLAN COMPANY · NEW YORK

1946

PRINTED IN THE UNITED STATES OF AMERICA

First Printing

The characters in this chronicle are fictitious; the happenings are not. It is dedicated to the memory of Vladimir Jabotinsky, and to my friends in the Hebrew Communes of Galilee: Jonah and Sarah of Ain Hashofeth; Loebl and Guetig of Khefzibah; Teddy and Tamar of Ain Geb.

Jerusalem, 1945

CONTENTS

THE FIRST DAY

(1937)

"We shake off the old life which has grown rancid on us, and start from the beginning. We don't want to change and we don't want to improve, we want to begin from the beginning."

A. D. GORDON, Galilean pioneer

THE FIRST DAY (1937)

1

"If I get killed to-day, it won't be by falling off the top of a truck," Joseph thought, digging his fingers into the tarred canvas cover of the swaying and lurching vehicle. He lay on his back, with arms spread out, a horizontally crucified figure on a rocking hearse under the stars. The truck's load was piled so high that Joseph and his friends travelled about five yards above ground, heaving from one side to the other on the bumpy rock-bed of the wadi; it felt as if the whole black mammoth of a truck might topple over at any minute.

As he peered down over the edge of the canvas, Joseph was reminded of the sensation of dizzy height he had experienced as a small child when, for the first time, he had been lifted to the back of a horse. The engine roared and the top-heavy truck jolted in first gear over the rocks of the dried-up stream-bed; it stalled; it started again with a plaintive whine. In front of them the long, stretched-out line of the other trucks in the convoy crept haltingly forward on the twisted course of the wadi, a caravan of swaying, dark clumsy giants on wheels. The moon was not due to rise for another hour, but there was a brilliant display of stars; the Great Bear curiously sprawling on its back and the Milky Way clustered into one broad luminous scar across the dark sky-tissue. All the trucks in the convoy had dimmed their headlights. The pallid rocks lay quiet in their archaic slumber. The rear of the convoy, spread over a mile, followed behind them as a moving garland of sparks in the hostile night.

The truck heeled over at almost thirty degrees and from the

other end of the canvas came a delighted squeak from Dina. Joseph could only see her by either twisting his neck until his vertebrae seemed to crack, or by heaving his body into an arch pivoting on the top of his head, so that he looked at the world upside down. But to see Dina profiled against the starlight was worth the effort. She laughed, clutching the canvas with both hands.

"Like that you look even more comic than usual."

Her Hebrew had the right guttural inflection which Joseph envied and could not imitate. From the front came Simeon's dry authoritative voice:

"Be silent, you two."

"And why?" cried Dina. "Is this a funeral?"

"Yell your head off if you like," said Simeon impatiently. He was sitting stiffly upright on the front edge of the canvas, with his knees pulled up in front.

"I will," cried Dina. "Let them know that we are coming. They will know by now anyway. Let them know. We—are—off to—Gal-i-lee."

Her voice rose and slipped into the familiar tune, the song of the Galilean pioneers:

El yivneh ha-galil,
An'u yivn'u ha-galil. . . .

God will rebuild Galilee,
We shall rebuild Galilee,
We are off to Galilee,
We will rebuild Galilee. . . .

Joseph joined in, singing with his head still upside down, but a vicious jolt of the truck threw him on one side and made him grab at the canvas. Dina's voice too had broken off.

"Are you all right?" he asked.

"Yes," she said, slightly subdued by the shock. But a moment later she cried excitedly:

"Look! Oh look! Are they ours?"

Far off ahead of them and slightly to the left a spark had

begun to blink at regular intervals. It was only slightly brighter than the biggest stars, but its colour was red and its flashes and effacements had an unmistakable rhythm and meaning. It seemed suspended in the air, but by straining one's eyes one could make out the pallid, almost transparent silhouette of the hill.

"Let me see about the direction," said Joseph. "Where is the Polar Star?"

"You have to draw a straight line through the last two stars of the Bear," said Dina.

"Be silent," came Simeon's voice. "I am reading the message."

They held their breath and stared at the distant red spark, flash and darkness, flash fiash and darkness, long flash and even longer darkness, an interminable and disappointing pause, then flash again, flash and flash, dot and dash. The truck gave a jolt and came to a standstill: the driver, deep down underneath them, was probably also reading the message. Suddenly he began hooting wildly into the night, and simultaneously the truck started moving again with a jerk that nearly threw them off the canvas.

"Well?" Dina cried. "Tell us for God's sake."

Simeon's figure in front of them seemed to become even more rigid and erect; with a flick of thumb and forefinger he jerked his trousers up an inch over his ankles. They recognised the familiar gesture even in the dark. He spoke in his usual aggressive voice, but a deep, hoarse undertone had crept into it:

"The fellows of the Defence Squad have occupied the Place. So far no interference. They have put out sentries and started ploughing up around the site."

"Halle-lu-yah!" Dina shouted and, stumbling to her feet, for a precarious second kept her upright balance, then plunged headlong across Joseph's chest. They rolled over towards the centre of the canvas. Joseph saw that the girl's face was wet with tears; for a moment he felt the wild hope that she had got over it—the Thing to Forget. Then she sat up and drew away, shivering.

"I am sorry, Joseph," she said.

"You need not be," he said gently.

"Oh shut up, you two," said Simeon.

For a while none of them spoke. The engine roared; now and then the truck took a sudden forward leap, slowed down groaning, got stuck with wheels desperately milling and grinding the sand, then lunged forward again. Joseph lay down in his former position with arms spread out, face to face with the Milky Way. His thoughts circled round Dina, abandoned her in resignation, fastened on Simeon's slim and rigid shoulders, his hoarse, strangled voice of a minute before. The words announcing the occupation of the Place had come out of him like a jet through the crack of a high-pressure chamber. Joseph wondered how a man could live under such constant emotional tension. He himself in moments of emotion always felt like a cheap actor, even if there was no audience present; even now.

The lorry behind had closed in on them and had turned its headlights full on. The sharp beam lit up Simeon's face and projected their three shadows onto the rugged slope of the wadi. Only their heads and shoulders were silhouetted out; they rose and dived on the rocks like the grotesque giant-shadows of a punch-and-judy show. Then the lorry switched its lights off and there was peace again.

—But why, thought Joseph, should one analyse things on this of all nights? If ever one had a right to take oneself seriously, as others saw one and not as one knew oneself, this was the hour. This was the hour of the deed, and not of its malicious inward echo. The world will know only about the deed—the echo shall be effaced. . . .

Some jackals, invisibly escorting the convoy behind the rocks, howled pointlessly and without conviction. The truck turned a bend in the wadi and below them, in the plain, they could again see the luminous dots of dimmed headlights moving forward silently, stealthily with slow, indomitable purpose.

—Yes, thought Joseph, we shall rebuild Galilee, whether God takes a personal interest in the matter or not. The trouble is that I cannot take part in a drama without being conscious of taking part in a drama. The Arabs are in revolt, the British are washing their hands of us, but the Place is waiting: fifteen hundred acres of stones of all sizes on top of a hill, surrounded by Arab villages, with no other Hebrew settlement for miles and a malaria swamp thrown in into the bargain. But when a Jew returns to this land and sees a stone and says, This stone is mine, then something snaps in him which has been tense for two thousand years.

He found that his right arm had gone to sleep and began to wave it wildly through the air.

'Oh, rot,' he told himself. 'Perhaps this whole idea of the Return is a romantic stunt. If I am killed I shall not even know whether I die in a tragedy or in a farce. . . . But whichever it is, that feeling about the Place is real; it is the most real thing I have ever felt. Funny. We shall have to think this out, if there is time left.'

He twisted his head to look at Dina. Dina too was lying on her back, at right angles to him, some distance away. She had folded her arms under her neck; her profile had softened in the starlight, with lips slightly parted in an unconscious smile. She too was thinking of the Place. She had only seen it once, more than a year ago, before it had been bought from the Arab villagers by the National Fund. She did not even remember exactly which hill it was—they all looked so much alike, the hills of Galilee, softly curved like hips or breasts, but with their stone-ribs sticking out since the flesh, the fat red earth, had been carried away by rain and wind during the centuries of neglect. No, she could not remember it very clearly, but anyway it was a lovely hill and they were going to restore it to its ancient abundance. They would feed the starved earth with phosphates and lime, and remove the festering sore of the swamp, and cover the hill's nakedness with a fur of trees and a lace-work of terraces. There will be figs and olives, and pepper and laurel. And poppies and cyclamen, sunflowers and roses of Sharon. First we will build the stockade, the watch-tower and the tents, the shower-bath, the dining-hut and the kitchen. Then the metal road, the cowshed, the sheep's pen and the children's house. Then the living quarters for ourselves. In two years from now we shall have a dining-hall in concrete, a library, reading-room, swimming-pool and open-air stage. It will be a lovely place and it will be called Ezra's Tower and it will efface the thing to forget, and I shall get over it and have a child and another child and they will have no things to forget. And maybe they will be Reuben's and maybe they will be Joseph's; and maybe they will be Abel's and maybe they will be Joseph's. . . . Oh I love them all, even Simeon, I love them all, I love the Place, I love the stones, I love the stars. . . .

Simeon sat erect on the foremost edge of the canvas, his elbows on his knees; he was thinking of a passage in Isaiah he had come across by one of those hazards which he believed not to be hazards, the night before: *The wilderness and the solitary place shall be glad for them; and the desert shall rejoice.* We are coming, he whispered to himself; we are coming, we are back.

Joseph began to chuckle.

"What is the matter, you fool?" asked Dina, sitting up.

"I'll tell you when we arrive."

"Tell me now."

"It might upset you," said Joseph, giggling irrepressibly.

"Nothing can upset me if this truck doesn't turn over."

"But that is just the point! Look . . ."

He grabbed her hand and led it with his own to the edge of the canvas. "Do you feel something?"

"Wood. Crates."

"Yes, but I know these particular crates, I have only to feel round their edge. They are those with our home-made eggs."

Dina too began to giggle, though somewhat forcedly. Nobody had great confidence in their self-made illegal hand grenades; they had a reputation of going off at the wrong moment. "Typically Jewish grenades, over-sensitive and neurotic," an English Police officer had called them.

"You know," said Joseph mirthfully, "they are packed in sawdust like real eggs. And you are brooding over them like a hen waiting for the chicks to come out."

A jolt of the truck bumped their heads together. "Oh, Moses our Rabbi," said Dina, "I wish you hadn't told me."

The invisible driver underneath them had turned the headlights full on. The white beams quivered on the desolate, stone-littered earth.

"I wish you two could be quiet for a minute," said Simeon, without turning his head. "We are almost there."

2

So far, in a seemingly leisurely, almost casual way, everything had gone according to plan.

Three hours earlier, at 1 A.M., the forty boys of the Defence Squad, who were to form the vanguard, had assembled in the communal dining-hut of Gan Tamar, the old settlement from which the expedition was to start. In the large, vaulted, empty dining-hall the boys looked very young, awkward and sleepy. They were mostly under nineteen, born in the country, sons and grandsons of the first settlers from Petakh Tikwah, Rishon le Zion, Metullah, Nahalal. Hebrew for them was the native tongue, not a precariously acquired art; the Country their country, neither promise nor fulfilment. Europe for them was a legend of glamour and frightfulness, the new Babylon, land of exile where their elders sat by the rivers and wept. They were mostly blond, freckled, broad-featured, heavy-boned and clumsy; farmers' sons, peasant lads, unjewish-looking and slightly dull. They were haunted by no memories and had nothing to forget. They had no ancient curse upon them and no hysterical hopes; they had the peasant's love for the land, the schoolboy's patriotism, the self-righteousness of a very young nation. They were Sabras—nicknamed after the thorny, rather tasteless fruit of the cactus, grown on arid earth, tough, hard-living, scant.

There was a sprinkling of Europeans among them, new immigrants from Babylon. They had gone through the hard, ascetic training of Hekhaluz and Hashomer Hatzair, youth movements which united the fervour of a religious order with the dogmatism of a socialist debating club. Their faces were darker, narrower, keener; already they bore the stigma of the things to forget. It was there in the sharper bend of the nasal bone, the bitter sensuousness of fleshier lips, the knowing look in moister eyes. They looked nervous and overstrung amidst the phlegmatic and sturdy Sabras; more enthusiastic and less reliable.

They all sat round the raw deal tables of the dining-hall, heavy with sleep and silent. The naked bulbs suspended on wires from the ceiling gave a bleak, cheerless light; the chipped salt-cellars and oil cruets formed pointless little oases on the empty communal tables. About half of them wore the uniform of the Auxiliary Settlement Police—khaki tunics which were mostly too big for them, and picturesque Bersaglieri hats which made their faces look even more adolescent. The others, who wore no uniform, were a section of the *Haganah*—the illegal self-defence organisation whose members, when caught defending a Hebrew settlement, were sent to jail together with the aggressors.

At last Bauman, the leader of the detachment, arrived. He wore riding breeches and a black leather jacket—a relic from the street-fighting in Vienna in 1934, when the malignant dwarf Dollfuss had ordered his field guns to fire point-blank into the balconies, lined with geranium-boxes and drying linen, of the workers' tenements in Floridsdorf, crossing himself after each salvo. Bauman had received his leather jacket and his illegal but thorough military training in the ranks of the Schutzbund; he had the round, jovial face of a Viennese baker's boy; only in the rare moments when he was tired or angry did it reveal the imprint of the things to forget. In his case there were two: the fact that his people had happened to live behind one of those little balconies with the geranium-boxes; and the warm, moist feeling on his face of the spittle of a humorous jailer in the prison of Graz every morning at six o'clock when breakfast was doled out in the cells.

"Well, you lazy bums," Bauman said, "get up; attention, stand over there."

His Hebrew was rather bumpy. He lined them up along the wall dividing the dining-hall from the kitchen.

"The lorries will be here in twenty minutes," he said, rolling himself a cigarette. "Most of you know what it's all about. The land which we are going to occupy, about fifteen hundred acres, was bought by our National Fund several years ago from an absentee Arab landowner named Zaid Effendi el Mussa, who lives in Beirut and has never seen it. It consists of a hill on which the new settlement, Ezra's Tower, will be erected, of the valley surrounding it and some pastures on nearby slopes. The hill is a mess of rocks and has not seen a plough for the last thousand years, but there are traces of ancient terracing dating back to our days. In the valley a few fields were worked by Arab tenants of Zaid Effendi's, who live in the neighbouring village of Kfar Tabiyeh. They have been paid compensation amounting to about three times the value of the land so that they were able to buy better plots on the other side of their village; one of them has even built himself an ice factory in Jaffa.

"Then there is a Beduin tribe which, without Zaid Effendi's knowledge, used to graze their camels and sheep each spring on the pastures. Their Sheikh has been paid compensation. When all this was settled, the villagers of Kfar Tabiyeh suddenly remembered that part of the hill did not belong to Zaid, but was *masha'a* land, that is communal property of the village. This part consists of a strip about eighty yards in width running straight to the top of the hill and cutting it in two. According to law *masha'a* land can only be sold with the consent of all members of the village. Kfar Tabiyeh has 563 souls distributed over eleven *hamulles* or clans. The elders of each clan had to be bribed separately, and the thumb-prints of each of the 563 members obtained, including the babes' and village idiot's. Three villagers had emigrated years ago to Syria; they had to be traced and bribed. Two were in prison, two had died abroad, but there was no documentary proof of their death; it had to be obtained. When all was finished, each square foot of arid rock had cost the National Fund about the price of a square foot in the business centres of London or New York. . . ."

He threw his cigarette away and wiped his right cheek with the palm of his hand. It was a habit which originated from his experience with the humorous jailer in Graz.

"It took two years to finish these little formalities. When they were finished, the Arab rebellion broke out. The first attempt to take possession of the place failed. The prospective settlers were received with a hail of stones from the villagers of Kfar Tabiyeh and had to give up. At the second attempt, undertaken in greater strength, they were shot at and lost two men. That was three months ago. You are making to-day the third attempt, and this time we shall succeed. By to-night the stockade, the watch-tower and the first living-huts will have been erected on the hill.

"Our detachment is going to occupy the site before dawn. A second detachment will accompany the convoy of the settlers which will start two hours later. The Arabs will not know before daybreak. Trouble during the day is unlikely. The critical time will be the first few nights. But by then the Place will be fortified.

"Some of our cautious big-heads in Jerusalem wanted us to wait for quieter times. The place is isolated, the next Hebrew settlement eleven miles away and there is no road; it is surrounded by Arab villages; it is close to the Syrian frontier from which the rebels infiltrate. These are precisely the reasons why we have decided not to wait. Once the Arabs understand that they cannot prevent us from exercising our rights, they will come to terms with us. If they see signs of weakness and hesitation, they will first fleece us and then drown us in the sea. This is why Ezra's Tower has to stand by to-night.—That's all. We have five minutes left; single file into the kitchen for coffee."

At 1.20 A.M. Bauman and the forty boys got into three lorries and drove with dimmed headlights out through the gates of the settlement.

3

For a while the huge dining-hall remained empty in the blaze of its electric lights. Lazy night insects flew from the darkness into the close wire-netting of the windows. Cockroaches crept busily over the cement flooring, and now and then a rat made a dash across the white surface.

About 2 A.M. Misha, the night watchman, came in to fetch hot water from the kitchen boiler for a glass of tea. Then he went off to wake the cooks and dining-hall orderlies. They began to drift in about a quarter of an hour later, their faces still swollen with sleep but nervously alert from the shock of the cold shower-bath. They had got up almost three hours before their usual time to provide breakfast for the new settlers who were to depart in an hour. The cooks disappeared into the kitchen; the orderly girls, in shorts and khaki shirts, began methodically to lay the tables.

At 2.30 A.M. Dov and Jonah stamped in in their rubber

gumboots. They were in charge of the cowshed and started work half an hour before milking began. Leah, one of the orderlies, put a big wooden bowl of salad before them, mixed of tomatoes, radishes, cucumber, spring onions and olives, the whole seasoned with lemon and olive oil. They chewed it in silence, between bites from thick chunks of bread. Dov was blond, with a narrow face and blue, short-sighted eyes; his frail figure looked lost in the heavy oilskin overalls like a diving suit. He was twenty-five, came from Prague, and was one of the founders of the Commune of Gan Tamar. Though he had been in charge of the cowshed for the last three years, he still couldn't get accustomed to getting up before dawn; it was torture crystallised into routine. To go to bed at nine in the evening, as he was supposed to do, would have meant exclusion from the Commune's social life—the meetings, lectures, discussions and the orchestra in which he played the 'cello. He also reviewed once a fortnight modern poetry for the *Jerusalem Mail,* and was translating Rilke into Hebrew.

"Listen," he said to Jonah after five minutes of silent chewing, "I would like to go out with the convoy of the new ones."

"*Tov,*" said Jonah, "All right."

"I shall be back to-night."

"*Tov.*"

"Do you think you can manage alone?"

"Yes."

"Miriam is due to calve some time to-day."

"Yes."

Jonah was not yet a member of the Commune; he had arrived three months ago from Latvia and worked as a probationer. He was a good worker, slow and reliable. He beat all records in taciturnity; Dov could not remember having heard him utter one complete sentence. He was rather a puzzle to the community of Gan Tamar, who couldn't make up their minds whether to regard him as a philosopher or a moron.

Leah brought them white cheese, porridge and tea. She lingered at the table, trying to catch Dov's veiled, sleepy eyes.

"Going out with them to the new place?" she asked, propping her elbows on the table beside him.

Dov nodded.

"They are quite nice kids, the new ones," she said, in a tone which implied: But we, the old-timers, were of course of a different sort. Leah too had lived in the Commune of Gan Tamar ever since its beginnings seven years ago. She was about Dov's age but looked older. Her dark, sharp-featured semitic face was not without beauty, but it had matured precociously and wilted early, as happened to many of the girls in the Communes. She wore tight khaki shorts and socks like all the others, and her athletic thighs were curiously dissonant with her unyoung face.

"They will have a hard time at first," she said, and added with a little shudder: "God, I wouldn't start again at the beginning."

"I don't know," said Dov, considering the matter while he went on chewing bread thickly spread with cheese. Leah was always fascinated by the contrast between his dreamy look and enormous appetite. They both thought of the hardships of the first years—the physical exhaustion caused by the unaccustomed work, the malaria and typhus; the heat, the irksome discomfort of tent life with no water, no lavatories, no sanitation; the dirt, the mud, the mosquitoes and sand-flies. . . . Looking back from the relative comforts of Gan Tamar in its seventh year of existence, those early pioneer days appeared like a heroic nightmare.

"I don't know," said Dov in his slow way. "We were all different then. We used to dance a lot of horra. . . ."

"There was always something to celebrate," said Leah. "The first calf. The first crop. The first tractor. The first baby. The water pump. The diesel. The electric light. . . ."

Her mood, always narrowly balanced between extremes, had already transformed the nightmare into romance. She leaned with her elbow on Dov's shoulder. "Shall I get you another plate of porridge?" she asked.

He shook his head. "I must be going," he said, rising from the table. Followed by Jonah, he tramped out of the dining-hall and towards the cowshed, his flapping oilskin overalls enveloping him in stable-smell and rusticity.

There was an interlude of a few minutes which gave the orderlies time to finish their preparations. The long deal tables became a more cheerful sight as they were covered with bowls of salad, heaps of thick-sliced bread, stone mugs, bakelite plates and cutlery. The first people arrived at a quarter to three, and a few minutes later the hundred and fifty men and women who were to leave with the convoy had occupied their seats.

There were eight seats to each table, four on each of the wooden forms alongside; according to custom they were filled up in order of arrival from the kitchen end of the hall towards the entrance, without preference to place or company; a custom which eased the work of the orderlies and at the same time served as a kind of social cement-mixer, reshuffling the members of the Commune three times a day.

This, however, was an unusual crowd: the twenty-five young people who were to become the future settlers of Ezra's Tower, and the hundred and twenty Helpers who were to assist them in erecting the fortified camp before sunset, and to return by the end of the first day. The Helpers were volunteers who had come from the older Communes of Judaea, the Samarian coast, the Valley of Jezreel and Upper Galilee; most of them were well known, and some quite legendary figures of the early pioneer days. The new settlers, among their silent and hard-eating elders, felt awe-stricken like debutantes. Though theoretically they were the centre of the show, they had shrunk to timid insignificance; they sat on the deal forms jammed between the massive Helpers who paid little attention to them—too excited to eat and with a vague nervous feeling of being cheated out of the pathos and solemnity of this nocturnal hour to which they had looked forward through months and years.

Dina, to her delight, found herself placed next to old Wabash from K'vuzah Dagánia, oldest of the Hebrew Communes. Dagánia stood in the Jordan Valley at the southern tip of the Lake of Tiberias. It had been founded in 1911 by ten boys and two girls from Romni in Poland, who had decided to put theory into practice and embarked on the first experiment in rural communism. They shared everything—earnings, food, clothes, the Arab mud huts which were their first living quarters, the mosquitoes and bugs, the night-watches against Beduins and robbers, malaria, typhoid and sand-fly fever; everything except their beds, for, true to romantic tradition, they lived for a number of years in self-imposed chastity. They refused to employ hired labour, to handle money except in their dealings with the outside world, and even to mark their shirts before they went to the communal laundry for fear that the bug of individual possessiveness might start breeding in them. They regarded themselves as the spiritual heirs of the Essenes, who, fleeing from the shallow glamour of Jerusalem, had founded in the desert their communities based on the sharing of labour and its fruits. They had studied the Bible, Marx and Herzl, and knew neither how to plant a tree nor how to milk a cow. The Arabs thought they were madmen, and the old Jewish planters in Judaea thought the Commune of the Twelve a bad joke and a heresy. Yet to-day Dagánia's third generation was being brought up in the communal nurseries on the same mad Essene principles, while more than a hundred other Hebrew communal villages had spread all over the country, from the Mediterranean to the Dead Sea and from Dan to Beersheba. Some, like Yagur and Herod's Well, had over a thousand members, and some only fifty; the older ones were prosperous, with parks, swimming-pools and amphitheatres, and the new ones poor, hard-living, squalid and ugly. Some did mixed farming, others specialised in exotic fruit or artificial fishponds; but all of them had the same basic features: the communal dining-hall, workshops and children's house; the prohibition of hired labour; the abolition of money, barter and private property; the sharing of the work according to everyone's capacity and of its produce according to his needs.

Dagánia, which the twelve founders had named with self-conscious under-statement after the modest blue cornflower of the Jordan Valley, was their common ancestor; its members were regarded as a kind of collective aristocracy; and with its giant palm trees and shaded valleys the ancient Commune of the Twelve had indeed an air of exclusiveness and patrician prosperity.

Old Wabash, sitting next to Dina and paying no attention to her, looked in her opinion exactly like an oil print of a biblical patriarch. His white, frizzled beard grew all round his face and even out of his nostrils and ears. He had blue eyes and wore a blue, open-necked cotton shirt and brown corduroy trousers, held up by a worn leather belt around his voluminous stomach. He ate his porridge with great application, and as the beard got in his way he kept tucking it back absentmindedly into his shirt. Dina felt thrilled by her close contact with one of the three survivors of the legendary Twelve. As he paid no attention to her, she nudged him after a while with her elbow:

"Comrade Wabash? I wonder what you are thinking about."

He turned to her in mild surprise, his spoon suspended in the air.

"Thinking, my dear?"

Joseph, who sat opposite Dina, drew his intelligent monkey face into a grimace. At this moment she disliked Joseph. She laid her hand on Wabash's arm.

"It was kind of you to come and help us, Comrade Wabash."

He again turned to her and she couldn't help noticing that his eyes were watery and that his round, childish face looked rather weak and insignificant if one imagined the beard away.

It was Joseph's stare that always made her realise such things; that was why she disliked him sometimes.

"So you are one of the new pioneers, my dear?" old Wabash said. "Good, very good. The youth carries on. You will continue the work that we began. . . ."

Dina wished she had never spoken to old Wabash. She avoided looking in Joseph's direction and concentrated on picking out the olives in her salad-bowl. But old Wabash, having finished his porridge, became talkative. He spoke in a mild, rabbinical voice, his Hebrew betraying a strong Yiddish accent, of the national renaissance and socialist ideal, the joy of rebuilding the twice-promised land and the tragedy of the unredeemed millions in exile. He dwelt repeatedly and sorrowfully on the "masses" and the "millions" and seemed to derive a grievous satisfaction from words like "tragedy" and "persecution." But as they came mildly spouting out from among the oil-print curls of the white beard, those words seemed to Dina to lose all reality and meaning, to have no connection with that ulcerous tissue of her memory, the thing to forget.

At last a sharp whistle signalled that the lorries were ready, and caused a great shuffling of boots as they all rose simultaneously from the tables. Dina walked in the crowd towards the door, leaving old Wabash without a word. In the centre passage Joseph caught up with her; she looked as if she were going to cry.

"The trouble was," he said to her with a grin, "that he had to keep on saying 'milliohnim, milliohnim.' Has it occurred to you that there is no word in Hebrew for million? Thousand is the highest figure we can name. Hence he had to use the modern numeral with the old Hebrew plural; that is what makes it so jarring. We should banish the millions from our vocabulary. Thousand is the upper limit of the imaginable; above that one enters the sphere of abstractions."

They had been carried out by the crowd through the open door into the darkness, and waited with the others for their turn to embark. The trucks drove up one after another, their blinding headlights full on, took their load of passengers and jogged off on the bumpy road, across the sleeping settlement and out through the open gate. Each truck, as it departed, made the darkness appear vaster and deeper. As they stood waiting for their turn, they felt the cool morning breeze from the sea and the insistent silence of the starry sky.

Next to Dina stood Simeon. He stood still, as if to attention, wrapped in his loneliness as in a scarf. She laid her hand on his arm:

"Let's all climb on top of a truck. It will be lovely to travel on the top. . . ."

It was just past 3 A.M. when the last truck of the convoy set out for the distant hill basking in the starlight, undisturbed for the last thousand years, which was to become the Commune of Ezra's Tower.

4

The Mukhtar of Kfar Tabiyeh was the only man in the village who slept in pyjamas. The other Mukhtar, who lived at the other end of the village, slept in his clothes on a mat, Beduin fashion.

At 6.30 A.M. the Mukhtar was woken by Issa, his eldest son. Issa had been standing for quite a while next to the bed not daring to touch his father; his close-set, slightly squinting eyes in the pale, pock-marked face were anxiously fixed on the enormous bulk in the blue-and-yellow striped pyjamas. The Mukhtar had thrown the blanket off in his sleep; his crumpled pyjama-jacket had slipped upward, revealing a strip of brownish skin covered with black fluff just above the navel. Issa averted his eyes from his father's nakedness. He held a small cup of bitter coffee in his hand which would soon get cold and thus lead to violent unpleasantness. His eyes shifted nervously round the whitewashed room, bare except for the bed, the straw mat, some low wicker stools and a fly-paper hanging from the ceiling. The wall opposite the bed was adorned with a coloured paper fan and portrait prints of General Allenby and of a smirking person in striped trousers with a carnation in his buttonhole, who looked like a ladies' hairdresser from Leeds and at closer scrutiny proved to be Mr. Neville Chamberlain. The portraits were each decorated with a bunch of dry cornflower stalks as a token of the Mukhtar's loyalty, and a chain of blue glass beads to protect Mr. Chamberlain against the Evil Eye.

The coffee was getting cold. Issa cleared his throat. "Father," he called. "Welcome, Father."

The Mukhtar woke at once, and with one sudden heave got himself into an erect sitting position.

"Welcome twice," he said, reaching for the coffee. He knew that they would not dare to wake him without urgent reason and waited to be told, his heavy bloodshot eyes on his son's insipid face, gulping the bitter coffee with noisy sips.

"Father, they have occupied the Hill of Dogs," said Issa. Hill of Dogs was the name by which the villagers of Kfar Tabiyeh called the Place, derived from some old legendary event which they had forgotten.

The Mukhtar heaved himself out of bed, ignored the slippers which his son held out for him and, barefooted, walked out to the balcony. The sun had risen about an hour ago, and already the air was hot. He leaned heavily with his palms on the parapet of red bricks which, with gaps left between each adjoining pair, made a kind of horizontal lattice. Beyond the Mukhtar's house there were only a few clay huts which formed the outposts of the village, then the sparsely terraced slope down to the valley. The valley was arid and stony with a few patches of black, ploughed-up earth; on its further side rose the equally arid Hill of Dogs. The top of the hill seemed to swarm with tiny black crawling figures. In the midst of that busy antheap something like a vertical match-stick could be made out: the watch-tower.

With slow, deliberate chewing movements the Mukhtar

gathered the saliva in his mouth, masticated it and spat over the parapet. He cursed softly and savagely under his breath, then turned to Issa:

"Why are you standing about, you pock-marked mule? Get my war glass."

The youth jumped and returned a moment later with a heavy and impressive telescope of brass. It was a relic of the Turkish Army, in which the Mukhtar had fought as an officer against General Allenby's forces in the first world war. He adjusted the glass and the Hill of Dogs jumped from a distance of two miles to one of two hundred yards. The panelled frame of the watch-tower, now visible in detail, dominated the scene; on its top one could see the cyclopean reflector-eye which at night would blink its messages to the intruders' confederates, defiling the peaceful darkness of the hills. Around the tower there were the messy beginnings of a camp with tangled barbed wire, trenches and dug-outs, several tents and the first wall of a pre-fabricated wooden hut in the process of erection. And all around bustling figures, digging, hammering and running about in undignified, alien hurry in their loathsome clothes, bareheaded in open shirts; and their loathsome shameless women with naked bulging calves and thighs, and nipples bursting through tight shirts—whores, harlots, bitches and daughters of bitches. . . .

The Mukhtar let the glass sink. His face had become a greyish yellow, as in an attack of malaria, and his eyes were bloodshot. His stomach almost turned over at the thought that henceforth every morning when he got up the first thing to meet his eyes would be this abomination, this defilement, this brazen challenge of the intruders. Dogs on the Hill of Dogs, dropping their filth, wallowing in it, building their citadel of filth. . . . It was finished. The whole landscape was spoilt. Never again would he, the Mukhtar of Kfar Tabiyeh, be allowed to enjoy the use of his own balcony. His eyes would no longer rest in peace on God's creation, watch the fellaheen in the valley walking behind their wooden ploughs in dignified leisure, watch the sheep flocking over the slopes—they would be drawn to that one spot in which the whole landscape had become focused, that poisoned fountain of evil, the well of blasphemy and temptation. . . .

From inside the house he heard the slow clop-clop of the old man's stick on the stone floor. Issa, who had also heard it, quickly brought his father's clothes. The Mukhtar got into his long wide skirts, pulled the striped vest over his pyjamas, wrapped the kefiyeh round his head, lifted the coiled agál with both hands into the air like a crown and adjusted it on top of the kefiyeh. He had just finished dressing when the old man, stick in front, emerged on the balcony. Disregarding his son's and grandson's greetings, he advanced with small firm steps to the parapet, rested his stick on its top and lifted his blind face towards the hills. "Where?" he asked with a curt, commanding bellow. His sparse white goat's-beard stuck out in front, and his bony nose with the hawk's bend seemed to sniff the air for the smell of the intruders.

"Over there, on the Dogs' Hill," the Mukhtar said submissively, guiding the stick in the old man's hand towards the spot.

The old man gave no answer; he stood erect and motionless at the parapet, his face lifted to the hills. Issa, avoiding the Mukhtar's eye, had disappeared into the house. The Mukhtar stood behind his father like a waiter in attendance, his big, heavy body slumped into guilty shapelessness. At last he could bear the old man's silence no longer.

"It is not my fault," he said in a throaty, plaintively bumptious voice. "The whole village wanted to sell. They would have sold even against my will, the dogs, and we would have got nothing."

The old man made no answer and no move.

"I only got eight hundred," said the Mukhtar, "and they would have sold anyway. I could do nothing. They cheated us, the swine. In Khubeira they paid six pounds for the dunum and another five hundred to the Mukhtar."

The old man again said nothing and after a while turned

round and hobbled back into the house, his stick stepping in front.

The Mukhtar listened to the receding clop-clop on the tiles. By God, he thought, what does he know? He sees nothing and understands nothing of the world. By God. . . .

He retreated into his bedroom without turning again towards the hill; but in the centre of his back, between the shoulder-blades, he felt its contemptuous stare like the stare of the Evil Eye.

On his morning walk through the village the Mukhtar felt lonely and weighed down by the decisions he had to take within the next few hours; in fact he knew that he should have decided at once when Issa woke him with the news. He would have cancelled the walk but for the inferences which the villagers and the other Mukhtar would have drawn from such an omission. So he marched as usual along the one cobbled street which wound its way serpent-like through the village, stately in his bulk, unapproachable with his dark, morose face, dignified and awe-inspiring. Despite the holes and bumps in the street he never had to look down at his feet, which knew every gap between the cobbles and each turn of the gutter-canal that ran along the middle of the street as the serpent's inverted spine—its lay-out had not changed since the time of the Romans. The fellaheen who were not out in the fields greeted him with their usual deference in front of the clay huts, while the women on the doorsteps withdrew with their usual modesty into the semi-darkness inside. At the sight of their shapeless, slatternly black widow-gear, of their faces which were withered and dumb at twenty, and of the eternal infant with the fly-ridden slimy face which they carried on their sagging breast or in a sling on their back, the Mukhtar thought with renewed fury of the shameless bitches on the Hill of Dogs and their naked arms and thighs. Yes, everything was as usual, and when he stopped to honour some elder of prominent family or other man of consequence, by inquiring after his health and the health of his sons and the state of his fields and of his cattle, the Mukhtar got the usual answer that thanks to God all was well and nothing to complain about. Not one referred, by word or implication, not even by a questioning glance, to the impending events; and yet their shadow lay on every face, and they all knew of the decision which the Mukhtar had to take—and washed their hands of it, the cowardly swine, so that afterwards they could say that they had heard nothing, known nothing, of the events of the coming night—provided, that is, that such events were to take place at all. . . .

So now his thoughts had already embarked on the problem which he had tried to shelve or at least to postpone, yet from which there was no escape. It was a fateful dilemma which he ought to be able to discuss with other wise and experienced men, but which by its very nature precluded discussion. Not even with his own family could he share the burden. His father, whom may God grant still many years, had lost his understanding for the ways of this world, and his eldest son was a pock-marked hyena with nothing in his head but dreams of money to visit the whore-houses in Syria—waiting with glee for his own father to fall into the trap this way or the other: to get either hanged by the Government or shot by the Arab Patriots in the hills.

For these, indeed, were the alternatives in store for the Mukhtar if he did not act with extreme wisdom and caution. The Patriots were everywhere around in the hills, led by the famous Syrian revolutionary Fawzi el Din Kawki, whom may God grant still many years of glory, though as far away as possible from the peaceful village of Kfar Tabiyeh. The trouble, however, was that Fawzi's secret headquarters happened to be at the moment not more than three hours' horse-ride away at a certain hidden spot in the hills, and that his men came regularly every other night to Kfar Tabiyeh to fetch the village's tribute to the Cause in sheep, flour and durrha. Not for nothing had Fawzi served in the Turkish Army and under King Ibn Saud; he knew how to organise his supplies and live on the fat of the land. Of these nightly goings-on the Mukhtar was officially as ignorant as the rest of the village; and during the occasional visits of Assistant District Commissioner Newton, after the greetings and courtesies had been exchanged, the health and prosperity of both families mutually ascertained, after coffee had been served, the weather and the prospective crops discussed, his innocence became established clearer than daylight for everybody concerned. The recent increase in nocturnal thefts was of course admitted and deplored with deep sighs and mournful reflection on these godless and lawless times; but what could a poor village Mukhtar do against these sneaking, invisible thieves? One could not expect each sheep or hen to be fastened by a lock and chain round its legs—and this joke, though often repeated, always gave rise to great and protracted hilarity, the slapping of one's knees and the wiping of tears from one's eyes—except for Newton Effendi who would continue to sip his coffee in absent-minded silence. So far, so good—but the Mukhtar had a premonition that it couldn't be carried much further, and that the joke was losing its flavour. At his last visit Newton Effendi had been more absent-minded than ever and, talking of sheep and cattle, had mentioned in his mumbling way the impending arrival of a pack of bloodhounds capable of tracing any trail of thieves to the very end of this hilly world. They could of course prove nothing definite against the Mukhtar; but what if they searched the village and found some of Fawzi's men, who had the regrettable habit of staying overnight in one hut or another—a service which hospitality couldn't refuse; or if some dirty rat from the other Mukhtar's family gave evidence and swore to some invented pack of lies? There was danger everywhere, and who knew Newton Effendi's game? It was evident that he wanted to avoid trouble; but on the other hand it was undeniable that the Patriots had gone too far by killing not only Hebrews but Englishmen as well, and turning against the Government itself. The whole situation had changed and a man knew no longer where he was, not even with Assistant District Commissioner Newton. And then there were the Military; they had lately started to blow up houses to punish peaceful villages like Kfar Tabiyeh against whom nothing could be proved; and they always selected the best houses in the village to be blown up, the Mukhtar's first. . . . There was of course the Arab Bank which was quite generous in granting credit for the rebuilding of the victims' houses, and some people in Lydda and Ramleh had fared quite well by getting a handsome stone house built to replace a clay hut or some decrepit ruin; it was even said that some clever ones had found the means of having their mud huts blown to glory though the English forgot to bother about them. Still, one's house was one's house, and if it happened to be a good house one did not like to take risks with it; and even less with one's neck, which no generosity of the Arab Bank could replace. . . .

Pursuing his thoughts, the Mukhtar had completed his circular walk and arrived home; he put on his slippers, ordered his water pipe and sat down under Mr. Chamberlain's portrait to continue his lonely meditation. The quiet bubbling of the pipe soothed his mind, while his hands were engaged in pushing the yellow amber beads of his rosary.

His thoughts turned to the other horn of the dilemma. It had been the expressed wish of Fawzi el Din that a messenger should be sent to him at once if the Hebrews tried to take possession of the Dogs' Hill. It was easy to guess the reasons for the Patriot leader's keen interest in the matter. He wanted to set an example. An example which would prove to the world once and for all that the Arab nation had decided to put a stop to the building of new settlements by the Hebrews. If Fawzi succeeded, the dogs would never dare to try it again, and the piecemeal slipping away of the land into their hands would be ended.

Yes, Fawzi's intention was obvious, and there was every chance of his succeeding in wiping the dogs of the Dogs' Hill from the face of the earth. The Mukhtar took a deep breath, and the bubbles in the pipe increased as if the water had started to boil. Oh, to wake up in the morning and to look at the hill and to see the watch-tower gone and those creeping insects vanished like jinn in the night; and to breathe the pure air and behold the peaceful country with its silent hills. . . . By God, it shall be.

The Mukhtar got up and called for Issa. He had made up his mind. He had given a promise to Fawzi el Din and he was going to keep it, whatever the consequences might be. The English might blow up the village, they might even blow up his house—they would soon find out that no threats and no brutality could prevail against a nation united in its will, decided to defend its soil against the foreign intruder. Besides, they couldn't prove anything. Kfar Tabiyeh was a peaceful village whose peasants slept the sleep of the just and knew nothing of the happenings of the night.

Issa received the Mukhtar's instructions with frightened, shifting eyes but in respectful silence. He bowed, touched his forehead, kissed his father's hand and went to saddle his horse. After all, the Mukhtar thought, he is a good boy. And in a warm surge of generosity he decided to buy Issa a good wife, regardless of cost; a strapping girl as firm-fleshed and round as any of the bitches on the hill in their tight-bottomed pants.

Now that he had made up his mind, he felt relaxed and at peace with himself. For beneath the surface of his boisterousness he knew himself to be a weak, corrupt and greedy man; but he also knew that his love for the hills and his country was genuine, and that he would defend it against the intruders with cunning, courage and ruse, with smiles and treachery, and was quite prepared, at least as long as his present mood lasted, to get himself hanged and not even to twitch when they slipped the coiled rope over his head.

5

The convoy had arrived at its destination just before sunrise.

Only the lighter trucks were able to drive up nearly to the top of the hill. Their engines roared and their radiators spouted steam as they crept at two miles an hour up the pathless incline covered with rubble and patches of dry; crumbling earth. The heavier trucks had to stop half-way up where the dirt track ended.

Bauman and his boys awaited the convoy at the top. They had arrived two hours earlier and seemed already much at home among those inhospitable starlit rocks. Bauman had dispersed the boys along the undulating saddle of the hill and on the edge of rocks protruding over the slope; there they stood or squatted in dark clusters, the glowing sparks of their cigarettes suspended in the air, their rifles sharply silhouetted against the stars.

On the very top of the hill, in the most advantageous position, a rectangle of a hundred by sixty yards was neatly pegged out, marking the site for the camp. A tractor with a plough rattled slowly and painfully around this rectangle drawing the first symbolical furrow, which, according to Arab custom, signified that the new settlers had effectively taken possession of the land.

About half-past five a slight inflammation over the hills to the east showed that the sky was preparing for the rise of day; a grey pallor expanded overhead in which the stars dissolved one by one, and soon afterwards the sun rose with brisk abruptness, as if in a hurry. Within a quarter of an hour the cloudless sky had changed from light grey into a transparent greenish blue, and all around the hills emerged in their normal day-shape, arid and desolate and yet soft and gently curved. They were reddish brown at close range, chalk-grey in the distance, and became of an unreal tender violet pastel shade as they receded towards the horizon. The new settlers found themselves in the centre of a landscape of gentle desolation, a barrenness mellowed by age. The rocks had settled down for eternity; the sparse scrubs and olive trees exhaled a silent and contented resignation. A few vultures sailed round the hill-top; the curves they described seemed to paraphrase the smooth curvature of the hills.

On the slope across the valley to the east stood the village of Kfar Tabiyeh, silent and apparently deserted. Its houses were the colour of the hill, built from the clay and stone of the hill; they hugged the slope out of which they were carved and into which they seemed to dissolve by natural mimicry. Their walls were blind with only the smallest square window-hole or no windows at all. The terraces below the village were protected by loose stone walls, demolished in parts by last year's rain. Some of the houses carried spherical domes of baked clay; others had flat mud roofs with grass and weeds growing out of them. The whole of the village looked like an ancient ruin spread over the slope and gently crumbling away into the dust out of which it had arisen in some timeless past; it basked peacefully under the early but already hardening rays of the Galilean sun.

The people who had arrived in the convoy clustered round a truck from the top of which Reuben, the leader of the new settlers, read out the roll and the task allotted to each man and woman. He was a tall, bony fellow with sparse gestures and a way of commanding silence without raising his voice. After some initial muddle the groups sorted themselves out, and by 6 A.M. everybody was at his job. The largest group, of about fifty people, was engaged in clearing a path for the heavy trucks from the end of the dirt track to the camp on the hill-top, a distance of about two hundred yards. The stones they picked up were thrown into baskets; the baskets travelled from hand to hand along a chain to the top, where a second group, skilled men from the *Haganah*, used them for the building of parapets.

These parapets protected five dug-outs, two of them facing north, and one each towards the east, south and west. A third group was digging zigzag trenches to connect the dug-outs; owing to the shallowness of the earth over the rocky ground these connecting trenches could only provide protection for men creeping on all fours. Another group rammed iron posts into the earth for the barbed-wire fence which was to surround the camp in front of the trenches.

Meanwhile the erection of the watch-tower and of the living quarters within the fortified area had started. The watch-tower, a panelled wooden frame thirty-five feet high and weighing over three tons, had travelled on a specially constructed caterpillar carrier; its erection was a delicate job tackled by specialists who had done it before in other settlements. Their method was primitive and ingenious. They made a heap of stones and drove the front part of the carrier over it, until the base of the tower which was jutting out over the rear of the carrier, touched ground. Then they fixed a steel cable with one end to the top of the tower; the other end was attached to a drum worked by the engine of a tractor. They also fixed two ropes to the head of the tower and held them tight at right angles to the cable, a dozen hands pulling on each side to prevent the tower toppling over sideways. The tower now lay on the carrier like a giant figure, the ropes forming its outstretched arms; then the engine of the tractor started to work, the drum turned and the cable began to pull the giant by its forehead, forcing it to rise slowly into the air. There was something solemn and stirring about the tower's slow, majestic erection, and while it lasted all work stopped. Silent and breathless the crowd watched the tower rise to an angle of thirty degrees, then forty-five, then sixty. When it had almost reached the vertical position the engine was stopped, and in the sudden silence the tower continued to swing forward, very slowly, under its own gravity, like a man balancing on his heels; while the men at the end of the two ropes hung anxiously on to them to ensure the tower's smooth alighting. At last, with a slight bump, the whole base touched ground;

the tower quivered once and stood on the earth, firm and erect. A spontaneous yell burst forth from the crowd, hoarse and inarticulate. All the tension of the previous night seemed to explode in that one gasping shout, a long-drawn a-a-ah, a roar of savage release. For a moment it looked as if they were all going to start dancing round the tower some pagan roundelay of priapic worship; then, with an awkward hesitation, they picked up their tools and went back to their work.

At 6.30 A.M., the moment when the Mukhtar of Kfar Tabiyeh was woken from his sleep, two tents had been roped to the ground, the unloading of the trucks was in full swing, the first pre-fabricated section of the first living-hut was being carried to its site, and Ezra's Tower had an air about it of having stood there from time immemorial. On the small platform on top of the tower stood Bauman in his black leather jacket, armed with a telescope; at his side stood a boy with a red signalling flag. Soon after sunrise Bauman had sent out mounted patrols to the surrounding hills, and the first of these had just emerged on the hill across the wadi to the west. The three riders moved slowly in single file along the crest; they wore Arab headgear and fitted quite convincingly into the landscape. Presently the first rider lifted his red flag with a wide, sweeping gesture over his head.

"Signal," Bauman said to the boy, without taking the glass from his eye.

The boy swept the flag round in a semicircle, held it for a second stiffly over his head, and dropped it abruptly. His arm moved in swift, precise movements like a mechanical doll's, and the flag gave a faint rustling sound each time it swished through the air.

Now it was the turn of the rider on the hill. His flag was to the naked eye a tiny red dot jumping about in the air in vertical, horizontal and circular lines with beautiful precision.

"All quiet," Bauman read through his glass. "Too quiet for my liking," he said to the boy. "Tell them to hang on."

By 9 A.M. the rough path from the dirt track to the site had been sufficiently cleared for the heavy trucks to move up. Their unloading started at once. The empty trucks were formed into a convoy and sent back to Gan Tamar to fetch the rest of the materials. At that time three walls of the first living-hut were already standing, the hole for the latrine was dug, the water-tank installed on its ramshackle temporary base, and the pipes for the shower-bath were unloaded. Some of the Helpers were beginning to think of a break, but there was to be none until twelve o'clock.

At 10.45 the watch-post reported the approach of Arabs from the direction of Kfar Tabiyeh. Bauman had already spotted them from the tower. They were a strange procession. In front walked two barefooted children in their loose, striped kaftans which looked like nightgowns. Behind them three or four women in black, also barefooted. Behind these the men, about ten of them, in striped skirts and European jackets, their naked feet in string-laced shoes. They were unarmed except for some shepherds' sticks. They came unhurriedly up the slope; the children's faces looked scared, the women's vacant, the men's watchful and blank.

As they approached the barbed wire, the Hebrews working on the site lifted their heads, gave them a short look and went on working, pretending to ignore their presence. Their faces had become taut and shut; the quiet elation of the work had gone. Bauman and Reuben met the Arabs at the barbed wire. The Arabs came slowly up to them, the women and children falling back, the men approaching the fence with a negligent stroll. They saw the symbolic furrow, and their eyes followed the furrow's course around the site.

"Marhaba," said one of them, "Welcome."

"Welcome twice," Reuben said.

The Arabs started moving along the fence towards the end which was not yet fenced in. But where the barbed wire ended the boys of the *Haganah* stood leaning on their rifles, wooden-faced, barring their way.

"We want to come in," one of the Arabs said. He looked more like a Turk and smiled blandly.

"Two of you are welcome to come in," said Reuben. His Arabic, as his Hebrew, was fluent and businesslike.

"God," cried another Arab, an excitable little man with one eye, "can't we even walk on the land of our fathers and of our own?"

"The land is ours," said Reuben, "and there are people working who should not be disturbed. But if you come in a few days' time you are welcome to share our meal."

"We came to talk," said the Turk, smiling over the stumps of some decaying teeth.

"Then come in and be welcome—the two of you."

"Don't go," said the excitable one. "Who knows what will happen? God, and on our own land. . . ."

"Come, ya Abu Tafidi. We shall go in and talk to them," said the Turk.

"Don't go, ya Abu Tafidi," cried the excitable one. "These men are bad, otherwise they would let us all in."

The Arabs parleyed loudly among themselves, while the Hebrews watched them with expressionless faces. Finally the Turk and Abu Tafidi walked into the camp, while the others squatted down outside the barbed wire. Abu Tafidi was a member of the Mukhtar's clan; in fact he was his cousin, great-uncle and son-in-law all at the same time; and yet, owing to the caprices of heredity, he belonged to a different type. He was a tall and bony old man with a distinguished stoop about his shoulder and a quiet, pensive way of speech. The Turk was fattish, smooth-mannered and jaunty. They exchanged compliments with Bauman and Reuben, sat down at the foot of the tower and started earnestly to discuss the weather and the crops. Then in due course the Turk came to the point. Smiling, emphatic and with every sign of sincerity, he explained that the settlers—nice, strong young people to whom he wished every good in the world—were victims of a cruel mistake in starting to build on this hill, for the land was not theirs and shortly of course they would have to evacuate it, according to the law. So why not go in peace at once, to avoid unpleasantness and remain friends?—He spoke with great simplicity, in a rapid and friendly way, while his hands milled round in smooth swift gestures as in a deaf-mute pantomime.

Reuben interrupted him. "What is this nonsense about the land not being ours?" he asked evenly.

The Turk laughed as if at an excellent joke. But surely, he explained, they all knew the law—the law of 1935 about the protection of tenants in cases of transfer of land? Of course the settlers knew it, they only played the innocents, ha-ha—and he winked his eye and slapped his knees and shook his finger at Reuben and Bauman, while the old man looked on, silent and impassive. Of course, the Turk went on, the settlers had offered some compensation to the dispossessed tenants, but was it enough? Was it fair? Of course it was not. The law guaranteed protection to dispossessed tenants, and the law was sacred. And if some of the tenants, poor, ignorant, uneducated fools, had in momentary confusion agreed to take some compensation money and signed some paper which they did not understand—what did that mean, and who was to prove that such an agreement was valid? "Oh, come, come," the Turk said with paternal affability, "you are educated young people, you have been to schools and universities, surely you know all this? Surely you want to act according to the law, and avoid trouble and bloodshed?"

Bauman and Reuben both rose at the same time, without having exchanged a glance. "We must get on with our work," said Bauman. "This land has been lawfully acquired, and there is nothing more to be said about it."

The Turk's face had grown a shade darker; it looked as if he had never smiled.

"You young fools and children of death," he said quietly. "You don't know what may happen to you."

"We are prepared," Bauman said curtly.

There was a moment's silence. One of Bauman's boys came

up to them, carrying a copper tray with four small cups of unsweetened coffee. The Turk, after a short hesitation, took his cup; the old man refused. They sipped their coffee standing. Then the old man spoke for the first time.

"I know not much about the law," he said; his voice was gentle, almost soft. "A man who is rich and cunning may offer money to another one who is poor and ignorant, and this other man may sell him his cattle and his hut. There is no justice in this. This hill belonged to our fathers and our fathers' fathers."

"And before that, it belonged to our fathers' fathers," said Bauman.

"So the books say. But your ancestors lost it. A country which one has lost one cannot buy back with money."

"This hill has borne no crop since our ancestors left it," said Reuben. "You have neglected the land. You let the terraces fall to ruin, and the rain carried the earth away. We shall clean the hill of the stones and bring tractors and fertilisers."

"What the valley bears is enough for us," said the old man. "Where God put stones, man should not carry them away. We shall live as our fathers lived and we do not want your money and your tractors and your fertilisers, and we do not want your women whose sight offends the eye."

He had spoken angrily, but without raising his voice, as one accustomed to see young men take his words reverently and in blind obedience.

"Our ideas differ," Bauman said with polite finality. "And now I believe we have said all that is to be said."

The old man turned silently on his heels and walked out of the camp. The Turk hesitated, then said with a certain reluctance:

"The fellaheen of Kfar Tabiyeh are peaceful men. There are Arabs in the hills around who are not so peaceful. You have been warned." He lowered his voice and added in a confidential tone: ". . . This warning our Mukhtar charged me to transmit to you, as a sign of his goodwill, although the Patriots would pay him ill if they knew about it."

Bauman chuckled softly. "Your Mukhtar is a wise man," he said. "Nobody likes to see his house blown up by soldiers. Your Mukhtar is like a fox who lives in a hole with two escapes, one to sunrise and one to sunset."

The Turk shrugged. "Peace with you," he said, turning to catch up with the old man.

The Arabs outside the barbed wire rose to their feet. At first they had sat there in tense silence and watched the proceedings under the tower. As the minutes had passed and they saw the Turk laugh and slap his knees in animated talk, they had relaxed. When they were offered coffee on trays, which they refused twice and accepted the third time as is befitting, they had relaxed even more. The children had munched oranges and the women, sitting huddled together at a little distance from the men, had started giggling and pointing at the girls with naked legs. Then the men had started chatting with some of the *Haganah* boys who knew Arabic; the boys, leaning on their rifles, had answered condescendingly and treated them to cigarettes. When the parley at the tower broke up, the excitable one-eyed villager had just started inquiring whether the new settlers would bring a doctor and open a dispensary as the other settlements had done, and whether the doctor would be able to cure his blind eye. Now, as their speakers returned and they saw their dark faces, they surrounded them with the guilty look of children who had been naughty in their parents' absence. The Turk and the old man walked silently through the group. The others formed into pairs behind them, and the procession slowly descended the slope without turning their heads.

The Turk and the old man did not speak until they had almost reached the valley. Then the Turk said:

"The devil may take them away, but he could leave their tractors. They are dogs and sons of bitches but they know how to work. They will grow tomatoes and melons and God knows what out of that stony hill. . . ." He sighed. "We are too lazy, ya Abu; by God . . ."

The old man turned on him with a hard look.

"You speak like a fool," he said. "Is the hill here for me, or am I here for the hill?"

After the villagers left, Joseph, who had watched the parley with curiosity from the top of a truck which he was helping to unload, came up to Bauman. "Listen," he said, "why did you not let them all come in? It was very rude."

Bauman looked at him with a faint smile.

"We are too weak to afford to be polite," he said. "By keeping them out we established ourselves in their eyes as masters of the place. By now they have all unconsciously accepted the fact."

Joseph grinned. "Where did you learn all this psychology, Bauman?" he said.

"Intuition," said Bauman.

"I thought one only had intuitions about people one liked."

"Who told you that I don't like them?" said Bauman.

"I wish my Arabic was as good as yours," said Joseph. "What was the old Sheikh explaining so solemnly?"

"He explained that every nation has the right to live according to its own fashion, right or wrong, without outside interference. He explained that money corrupts, fertilisers stink and tractors make a noise, all of which he dislikes."

"And what did you answer?"

"Nothing."

"But you saw his point?"

Bauman looked at him steadily:

"We cannot afford to see the other man's point."

6

During the half-hour's break at noon, two private cars came jolting up the wadi, escorted by a Bren carrier and followed by a cloud of dust. The first car carried the Assistant District Commissioner and Mrs. Newton, accompanied by a Major of the Police Force. Mr. Newton was a thin, tired-looking middle-aged man with a sparse and untidy moustache. He had been transferred to this country after eight years of service as an Assistant Commissioner in Roonah, North-West India. In the club in Roonah he had always been referred to by the men as a Decent old chap and by the women as Such a dear, followed by an imperceptible pause and a change of conversation. During his term of office in Roonah he had been involved in no scandal and acquired no distinction; he had vanished out of the colony as unobtrusively as he had entered it eight years before, leaving no memory-trace except for an occasional mild joke about his only known hobby, chess, and a compassionate reference to the only major blunder he had ever committed, the marrying of his wife.

Mrs. Newton was the daughter of a Sergeant-Major in the Indian Army. An intimate analysis of the motives which had attracted timid Mr. Newton to that tall, bony and virginal female would have produced embarrassing results by unearthing Mr. Newton's steady, stealthy and fervent loathing for Roonah, the Club, the Indian Civil Service and Army; and his oblique sense of humour which the first time led him to visualise the Sergeant-Major's chaste and angular daughter in a series of those preposterous attitudes which the act of procreation entails. It started as a grotesque private joke and grew until it became an obsession of Mr. Newton's starved and chess-trained mind, accustomed to visualising positions after both partners' various moves. What he did not foresee—for he was a kindly man with no more repressed nastiness than the average—was the stalemate which followed the first few opening moves almost immediately after their marriage. The real situation had none of the humour and mystery which made the imagined one so fascinating; but it was too late by then. A stalemate cannot be undone.

The third passenger in the car, copper-faced Police Major Edwards, was in a bad temper because Mr. Newton, pretending to be polite, had taken the seat next to the driver which the Major liked; while Mrs. Newton vaguely thought, as always when in the company of a man in uniform, how much happier she would be had she married into the Forces.

In the second car sat Mr. Glickstein and Mr. Winter, both members of the Zionist Executive in Jerusalem, and wedged in between them an American newspaper man named Dick Matthews who was on a ten days' tour through the country. On the front seat next to the driver sat the Zionist Executive's official photographer, Dr. phil. Emil Lustig. The photographer and the driver were discussing in German Nietzsche's influence on Fascist ideology. The journalist was listening with one ear to their conversation, looking bored. Glickstein noticed it.

"Do you understand German?" he asked.

"A little," said Matthews.

"We are a funny country, what?" said Glickstein. He had put on his propaganda smile, baring his gold teeth. "Our driver was a graphological expert at the Criminal Court of Karlsruhe before he became a pioneer."

"They are all great guys," said Matthews, bored.

"The photographer," Glickstein continued, "was a lecturer of philosophy at Heidelberg."

"Yeah," said Matthews, who had stood two hours of propaganda in Glickstein's bumpy English. "It reminds me of the taxi-drivers in Paris after the last war who were all Russian Grand Dukes."

Glickstein's smile became pinched. "Allow me," he said. "Those people were thrown out of Russia. But most of our pioneers came to our country of their own free will, long before Hitlerism began."

"You win—as usual," said Matthews. His sense of fairness compelled him to admit that Glickstein was right and that all these admirable guys were doing an admirable job about this National Home of theirs. But he wished to God Glickstein would talk less about it, and with less of that intensity which sprayed the moisture from his lips into one's face, and that all these clever and admirable guys would relax sometimes and offer a guy a drink instead of statistics and heroics, and would get drunk sometimes themselves. He had now spent almost five days touring the country and had collected a lot of stuff for his story, but somehow the story didn't come off—or came off the wrong way, with a twist in it which he hadn't intended to put in, and which would have been unfair to these guys whom, the more he was with them, the more he admired and disliked.

Matthews sighed and rather embarrassedly pulled a flat bottle from his hip pocket. These people didn't drink, and he did not wish to shock them, but sometimes a guy got fed up. He offered the bottle to Glickstein and to Winter and then gave it up and fiercely took a deep gulp, almost blushing. He saw Glickstein's indulgent, gold-flashing smile, and he wished to God Glickstein were a Fascist and that he had an excuse for a good, straight punch at his nose.

Winter, sitting on the other side of Matthews, had not said a word for the last hour. He was filled with a quiet, aching bitterness which each remark of Matthews' increased. A goy remains a goy, he thought, well-meaning or not. Here he travels through a country where our people are doing something more fantastic and difficult than their famous conquest of the West, and all he can think of is to compare us with Paris taxi-drivers and night-club whores; and all the emotion he is capable of working up comes out of his bottle;—look how he tilts it up and how his lips form a disgusting ring of flesh round its neck. Ay, don't we know the Bottle and what it does to the goy—the songs at the top, the sentimentality in the middle, and the pogrom at the bottom. . . .

Joseph and Dina lay resting side by side in the narrow strip of shadow next to the still roofless dining-hut. Behind their heads sat Simeon with his back against the wall, knees drawn up against his body and trousers pulled up neatly over his ankles. He was reading last night's *Davar,* the Labour evening paper which a lorry had just brought up from Gan Tamar. Next to him sat Dasha, a good-natured fattish girl with a pretty face already coarsening under the influence of climate and work.

"There come the big-heads," said Joseph, as the two cars and their escort came in sight, struggling up the last stretch towards the top.

No one answered. They were all exhausted, fearful of the moment, twenty minutes ahead, when they would have to start work again. Except for the watch-posts the whole camp lay prostrate, dazed by the blazing sun, immobile like lizards on a hot rock. As the cars pulled up near the tower, they lifted their heads and let them fall back again on their arms. Only Reuben and Bauman got up to greet the guests.

Mrs. Newton got out first; she viewed the scene in disapproval, taking it as a personal insult that nobody seemed to get up or take any notice of their arrival. The Major climbed out next from the car. "Good morning," he shouted with bluff heartiness, turning to Reuben and Bauman. "Are you the leaders of this happy gang?" His voice exploded like a shell in the heavy, dazed silence.

They all shook hands, except Mrs. Newton. The travellers from the other car joined them. They stood about in a group in the shadow of the tower. Dr. phil. Lustig took informal snapshots of them, prowling around the group with self-conscious unobtrusiveness, a permanent smile on his lips and behind his rimless, sharp-lensed glasses, which meant to convey that he was Only a Photographer. Then he strolled off with his Leica to photograph the hill with its stones and the camp *in statu nascendi.* Each time he clicked the shutter, he saw in his mind's eye the caption to the picture just exposed, as it would appear in some future propaganda album: "FIVE YEARS AGO EZRA'S TOWER WAS NOTHING BUT A STONY DESERT . . ." while underneath would be the photograph of a modern communal village, with white concrete houses, shady eucalyptus alleys, lawns, orchards and laughing children: ". . . AND THIS IS HOW IT LOOKS NOW."

He took a snapshot of one of Bauman's boys with his rifle, in profile, from a low angle, so that the figure became toweringly silhouetted against the sky: ". . . EVEN AS IN THE TIMES OF EZRA, WHEN THE MEN WHO RETURNED FROM THE BABYLONIAN EXILE WITH ONE OF THEIR HANDS WROUGHT IN THE WORK AND WITH THE OTHER HELD A WEAPON . . ."

Dr. Lustig was moved. The sun shone hard, sweat from his forehead trickled down under his glasses and stung his eyes. He rubbed them with the handkerchief from his breast pocket, wiped his glasses, and took a shot of Joseph and Dina, squatting on his heels behind their heads, at a refined angle which would make their horizontal faces appear hard and sculpted like partisans in a Russian film. His imagination, trained to see everything in patterns of "BEFORE" and "AFTER," like advertisements for a face powder or nerve tonic, had already surrounded them with a bunch of children happily eating home-grown oranges, while Dina played on some vague string instrument, a harp or lute, as Bath Sheba had played for David.—He tiptoed on, smiling to himself, lost in his daydream of the resurrected Hebrew State, elated and quite forgetful of the fact that he was Only a Photographer.

Reuben was meanwhile showing the guests round the site. He made only a few matter-of-fact comments and Matthews thought that he liked this guy much better than those big-heads from Jerusalem. Mr. Newton listened absent-mindedly; he had a feeling of bewildered admiration for all these young people who started on these ventures against such heavy odds, driven on by a sentimental fanaticism which was entirely alien to him; at the same time he resented the bother which would arise if the Arab terrorist gangs started some monkey-business which they certainly would, though this was, thank God, the Major's business and not his. He also disliked all this messiness which went with the building of the camp. It was sure to become one more of those ugly, uncouth, modern settlements which were an offence to the landscape. What a contrast to the melancholy beauty of Arab villages, like the one across the valley, peacefully dormant in the hot, trembling air. . . .

Mrs. Newton, who walked in front at the Major's side, had similar thoughts, though they were less clearly defined and lacked aesthetic appreciation of the beauty of Arab villages. But at least with those Arabs one knew where one stood; they were natives and knew their place. Their notables were polite and dignified, the mob picturesque and obsequious. If occasionally they did some rioting or shooting that was only natural, for what else could one expect from them? But the Jews were different. They had no notables and no dignity and they were not picturesque. Instead of being grateful to the British for letting them in, they behaved as if the country belonged to them. Look how they lie about on their backs and stomachs, ignoring one, instead of jumping to attention when a Major and the A.D.C.'s wife inspect them. Good heavens, if they dared to behave like this in Roonah! . . . The trouble of course was that they were white—white natives, who has ever heard of such a thing? And on top of it they were all university professors or whatnots. Thought they were cleverer than oneself, and yet couldn't even offer one a decent cup of tea at their parties, or carry on a really nice conversation. Had to show off all the time with their bookishness and the languages they knew and what clever-clever fellows they were. . . .

The Police Major, walking by her side, followed his own trend of thoughts. The dry heat reminded him, as it always did, of the Sudan from where he had been transferred only a few months before; and how much simpler everything had been there. Meanwhile he observed, with a curious and expert eye, the dug-outs and trenches those Jew-boys had made. They had some pluck to come up here just now, and if it was true that Fawzi's band had moved into the vicinity they were in for a hot time. When all was said, the twelve rifles they had been allowed did not amount to much—but then they had their blasted defence organisation, the *Haganah,* with its illegal arms. . . .

Anyway, they had been warned, and if they wanted to play the dare-devils and insisted on getting their wretched hill—like that famous pound of flesh—well, it was their funeral. As to Fawzi and his gang, that was the concern of the Military, bless their souls. . . .

"Look!" Mrs. Newton exclaimed, and with sudden animation pointed at Simeon, buried in his Hebrew newspaper. "Look—he *does* read from right to left, isn't it funny?"

It was the first comment she had made since they had got out of the car, and it was made in her sharp, loud voice. Simeon slowly dropped his newspaper. The Major turned his head, and his blue, slightly goggling eyes plunged all of a sudden into a pair of burning black ones with an expression of such calm, concentrated hatred that the Major experienced something like a faint electric shock. He saw with bewilderment a lean young man sitting rigidly erect with his back to the hut, with a dark, gaunt face dominated by those fanatic eyes which quickly made him avert his own. "Christ," the Major whispered to Mrs. Newton, "that fellow looks daggers. . . ."

He had the weird feeling that he had met the fellow before under almost exactly the same circumstances and had received, equally undeservedly, the same dirty look. "Nonsense," thought the Major, as he walked on at the abruptly silenced Mrs. Newton's side. "But by jove, what a country, what a country!—it's as if everybody was walking about with sunstroke."

At 12.30 P.M. Reuben's whistle sounded the end of the break, and out of the narrow strips of shadow behind the tents and huts the workers emerged and scrambled to their feet, tottering with fatigue. Soon afterwards the official visitors took their leave. As he shook hands with Reuben and Bauman—Mr. and Mrs. Newton were already inside the car—the Major expressed in a hearty and slightly embarrassed voice the hope that all would go well.

"We share your hopes," said Reuben with a faintly sarcastic

smile. "The more so, as we have learnt to look after ourselves."

The Major said nothing and closed the door of the car with a bang. They slowly jolted down the new track, followed by the Bren carrier. The party which had come with the second car decided to stay for the afternoon and go back with the convoy of the returning Helpers, before sunset.

Matthews had succeeded in getting rid of Glickstein and Co., as he called them to himself—they were animatedly conversing in Hebrew with old Wabash—and strolled alone through the camp. The barbed-wire fence was almost completed, and so were the five main dug-outs; but the trenches connecting them were in places still very shallow, and the sweat-glistening faces of the people working at them—mainly young and sturdy Sabras—became more dogged and sullen as the afternoon advanced. In contrast to them the carpenters who were fixing the plywood panelling of the dining- and living-huts whistled cheerfully, and the boys hammering away at the roof-girders and laths were in equally high spirits. The two huts stood at right angles to each other and, together with the watch-tower, formed a square in the middle of the site. The outward-facing walls of the huts were reinforced by a stockade of timber, block-house fashion, which had arrived in pre-fabricated segments; the gap between the stockade and the hut walls was partly filled up with gravel. Only partly, for there had been a hitch: the amount needed had apparently been calculated too low, and in addition one of the lorries carrying the gravel had broken down. They had signalled from the watch-tower to Gan Tamar for further supplies, but it was doubtful whether they would arrive before sunset; to Matthews' surprise nobody seemed to worry about it.

In the centre of the square stood three tents, huddled together between the protecting walls of the tower and the two huts. Outside the square, near the barbed wire, was the latrine, screened by a fence of pales and divided into two by a wooden partition; a few yards further they were fixing the pipes of the shower-bath, also surrounded by a fence but as yet with no partition inside. Matthews made a mental note of this; he also wondered why these people bothered about a shower-bath before they had finished digging trenches. True, there were as many people digging as space permitted without getting into each other's way; but still . . .

The chap with the black leather jacket smiled at him from the platform of the watch-tower and Matthews climbed up, awkwardly lifting his heavy body up the ladder whose steps were set too wide apart. He noticed that even this slight effort drove at once the sweat through his pores and made the blood pulsate in his temples; and his respect increased for these fellows who had been working since sunrise—and who had chosen to live and work in this God-forsaken spot to the end of their days, provided they were not kicked out or bumped off.

"Why don't you take that bloody jacket off?" he asked as he arrived puffing on the platform. "Got the shivers?"

"It doesn't matter," said Bauman with his broad smile.

Matthews divined that for Bauman his leather jacket was a kind of uniform and that he regarded it as a symbol of his authority as an officer of their famous illegal *Haganah*. Below them, at the foot of the tower, Glickstein and Co. were still talking in Hebrew to old Wabash, who, leaning on a spade which served him mainly for ornamental purposes, looked more than ever like a biblical prophet. "What is he saying?" Matthews asked Bauman.

"He is excited about the roofs," said Bauman. "He would like to see them finished. According to Ottoman Law once a house had a roof on it nobody had a right to tear it down, even if it was built without the landowner's permission."

"But is that law still in force?"

"No."

"So what?"

"It was in old Wabash's time. In this country traditions have a thousand lives, like cats."

"Do you believe the Arabs really care whether there is a roof or not?"

"No. But old Wabash does," said Bauman, and his smile broadened.

Matthews let his eyes wander and take in the landscape from the height of the tower: all those arid and yet softly undulating hills, now ochre-coloured under the flaming sky; a silent landscape which bore the hallmark of eternity. With a sigh of regret he turned again to the messy camp. Twenty yards to their left, they were unloading the last truck; it contained slates for the roofs and some bales of barbed wire which were urgently needed to complete the fence. They were all slightly nervous and in a hurry now; some had torn their fingers in handling the heavy barbed-wire rolls without even noticing it. On the top of the truck stood Dina, in her khaki shorts and blue open-necked shirt, legs apart, handing down slates. Her palms were torn by the wire and from time to time she lifted them absently to her mouth, licking the blood off them. Her face, trickling with sweat, glistened like metal in the sun; her smooth brown hair was all over her face and shoulders. Bauman too was looking at Dina.

"That kid's a knock-out," Matthews said. "To which one is she married . . . does she live with?" he corrected himself awkwardly.

"She lives with nobody," said Bauman.

"But I guess most of them do?" Matthews had to force himself to go on. He hated nosing into these people's privacy, but after all it was his job to find out about the ways and habits of their community.

"Most of them do," said Bauman laconically.

"Look," said Matthews, "I guess you wish me to hell, but I would like to get this whole business straight."

"It is quite straight," said Bauman with his amused smile. Then, to avoid being impolite, he added:

"Dina is a special case. She comes from Central Europe and didn't get away in time. They did certain things to her. She hasn't quite got over them yet. . . ."

He left it at that, rubbing his cheek. Matthews did not press him further; Bauman had a quality of being frank and elusive at the same time. They all had it, these youngsters; they gave the impression of having nothing to hide, but lots of things they refused to talk about to outsiders. As long as they talked to you they did it with complete sincerity; but when they shut up, there was an air of finality about them.

The group which had been standing at the foot of the ladder was no longer there; Glickstein and old Wabash had climbed into one of the dug-outs and were explaining something to each other with sweeping gestures, squatting on their heels. Winter had disappeared, but after a while Matthews discovered him hanging on precariously with one hand to the roof of the dining-hut and with the other driving nails into the girders. "He will fall down in a minute," said Matthews, pointing at him.

"Winter is all right," said Bauman. "He used to be a slater in Tel Aviv before he became a Labour leader and member of the Executive."

"And Glickstein?"

"Oh—he is in the Political Department. . . ." He again left it at that and lifted the field-glasses to his eyes: they were signalling from the opposite hill-top. Matthews had a feeling of being unwanted and climbed down the ladder. He wandered about rather aimlessly for a while, then stopped near one of the trenches. The boys were working in the same dogged, sullen silence as an hour before. Dasha, the nice fattish girl, was walking along the row, handing them mugs of cool water from an Arab clay jug. They swilled the water round their palates before swallowing it and spilled the last drops over their handkerchiefs which they wore nightcap-fashion on their heads. Their faces were smeared with sweat and dirt, their lips dry and cracked; they worked with slow, automatic movements.

After a while something in the expression of one of the workers—a thin, narrow-chested, short-sighted boy with pimples on his face—caught Matthews' attention. He had slowed down in his work; presently his movements became vague and tottering, as if he were drunk or asleep. Suddenly he stopped altogether, leaning on the swaying handle of his spade; his neighbour was just in time to catch him in his arms before the boy crashed into the trench. There was only a slight commotion while the boy was carried into the first-aid tent; and without quite knowing how it came about, Matthews had taken over his spade and place, and was shovelling earth and rubble out of the trench. His neighbours made no comment; they carried on steadily as if nothing had happened. The next time Dasha passed with her jar, he removed his cork helmet and replaced it by his handkerchief which Dasha wetted for him, her thick lips smiling pleasantly in her pretty and rather dumb face. Matthews felt elated and a fool. He worked on steadily, trying to be economical in his movements and to get into the rhythm of his neighbours. After a while he saw Dr. Lustig prowl with his Leica towards the trench, manœuvring himself into position. Matthews managed to catch the right second to stick his tongue out and pull a face just before the camera clicked. Dr. Lustig put on a rather strained smile, but the boys in the trench grinned approval and Matthews felt that at that moment he had passed a kind of test in this tough and elusive community of Jew-boys.

By 5 P.M. the shower installation was finished; half an hour later the roof of the living-hut was completed, and a few minutes afterwards that of the dining-hut too. The putting in of the furniture took less than an hour. There were ten deal tables with forms for the dining-hall, providing accommodation for sixty people, and four mattresses for each of the six cubicles in the living-hut; the rest had to sleep in the tents.

At 6 P.M., shortly before sunset, the truck with the gravel arrived. The relief with which it was greeted betrayed in retrospect the anxiety which all had felt about its arriving too late. The gravel was dumped in two heaps in front of the stockades; and while the new settlers, who were going to stay, began filling the gravel into the gaps, the Helpers stacked their tools at the tower and took their places in the waiting lorries of the homeward convoy. There had been some suggestion about speeches to be made before they went back, but they had worked on the trenches till the last possible moment and now they had to hurry if they did not want to be caught in the wadi by the darkness. Old Wabash looked disappointed; he had prepared a beautiful speech full of the suffering milliohnim. The boy who had fainted at the trench sat fast asleep in the seat next to the driver of one of the trucks. Matthews sat once more with his broad back squeezed in between Glickstein and Winter; the small private car looked like a toy in the file of heavy lorries. The farewells were hurried and, on the part of those who left, of a rather forced cheerfulness. They felt sleepy and exhausted; as they stood tightly crammed in their lorries while the engines started up, and bent down for a last handshake with the new settlers, they already looked like strangers to the place.

The first truck started with an abrupt jerk; after a few moments' interval the second followed; soon the whole convoy moved with painful jolts down the new track and vanished at the foot of the slope. After a while they came into sight again, considerably diminished in size, down in the wadi. By then it was already growing dark, and one after another the lorries switched their headlights on as they receded into the dusk. The hum of their engines and the farewell greetings of their horns could be heard until the last truck had disappeared round the wadi's bend, this time for good; and then the silence fell, and with it, the night.

7

There were five and twenty of them; twenty men and five women. The rest of the Commune, twelve more women and three babies, were to join them after the first week.

As a group, they had been in existence for five years—years of training and preparation. They came mostly from the youth movements of Central Europe, with a sprinkling of Russians, Poles and Balkanese, and one young Englishman. The core of the group had been formed on the immigrants' ship from Trieste to Haifa. On arrival they had registered the group at the Hebrew Trade Unions' Agricultural Department. The Agricultural Department had entered them into the list of other groups waiting to be settled on land purchased by the National Fund. The funds of the National Fund came from the blue collecting-boxes in synagogues and Jewish meeting-places all over the world, and from private donations. Most of the land bought by the National Fund was derelict and consisted of swamps, sand dunes, waterless desert and fields of stone. All land acquired by the Fund became unalienable property of the nation and was leased to the settlers for forty-nine years, to be renewed in subsequent generations. The settlers drained the swamps, planted trees on the dunes, dug irrigation channels, carried the stones from the fields, built terraces and resurrected the land. They had no capital and needed none; they received equipment and credit from public funds and repaid them when the land bore fruit; while the rent for the ground went back to their landlord, the nation.

While waiting for their turn to be settled, the members of the group had worked as hired labourers; but already during that period of preparation they had paid their wages into the communal purse and had lived in common household. At times the group had had to split up: some of them went to work in the potash factory on the Dead Sea, while others found seasonal employment in the orange plantations of Samaria and a third batch went through vocational training in one of the older Communes of the Valley of Jezreel. At other times the whole group had been reunited; but whether together or not, they had regarded themselves as members of one family or order, with as yet no settled domicile. Their average age when they had come to the Land had been eighteen; now it was three and twenty. Couples had formed and re-formed during these years of preparation, and some of them had become stable unions. A few had found partners from outside who had been accepted as members, a few others had left the group. At present the group consisted of twenty men and seventeen women, two-thirds of whom were regarded as living in stable unions; and of three children, all under the age of two.

They had been adolescents when they arrived, and now they were men and women hardened by experience. They had undergone certain transformations during those years, but as the change had been gradual and simultaneous, they were not aware of it. The men had become less talkative, their movements slower and more deliberate; the women's faces had grown coarser under the hard climate and work, and they had a tendency to develop strong hips and breasts. But though they had aged in experience and changed in appearance twice the value of that time, they still regarded those five years as nothing but a prelude, a prehistoric era, the embryonic stage in the life of the Commune, which was really to start on the Day of Settlement. For five long and hard years they had waited for that day, dreamed of that day, schemed and prepared for it; and now the day had come—and after the day, the night.

8

The silence which fell when the last lorry had turned its back on them and was swallowed up by the dusk had only been a short one, for they recovered quickly and went on shovelling gravel into the stockade. But during that short moment or two they had felt like children who, after being told to be brave, were left alone in an empty house where the silent shadows crept in through the windows and reflections in mirrors froze into horrible masks. In that moment most of them would gladly have jumped onto the crowded trucks to be carried back, out of the horror of these archaic hills and their savage tribesmen, back to the safety of their own race and kin.

The night came quickly. The searchlight on the top of

the watch-tower was on; its sharp white beam was directed in an acute angle downward onto the stockade. They went on filling in the gravel under a shower of dazzling light which made the outer darkness even thicker and more impenetrable.

By 7 P.M. the work was finished. The reflector lifted its beam into the air, and slowly lowered it again as it began its patient revolutions round and round, sweeping the terrain beyond the barbed-wire fence with its white broom of light. The dugouts and the observation post on the watch-tower were manned; there was nothing else to be done. Those not on guard duty filed silently into the dining-room for the first hot meal in their new home.

The dining-room had as yet no electric light; there were candles on the tables and a single oil-lamp near the door. The kitchen was behind a wooden partition, and the food came out through a hatch in it, with a counter in front. They had onion soup, bully beef and oranges; and, to mark the occasion, a cupful each of sweet white Carmel wine. Apart from the twenty-five settlers, only Bauman and ten of the *Haganah* boys had stayed behind, and if all went well these too would go in a few days, to wherever they were needed next. Thirty men were enough to man the trenches, and they only had twenty rifles and two automatics to go round anyway. It was a principle that each Commune had to be self-supporting from the beginning, and that included defence as well.

Joseph had as usual succeeded in sitting next to Dina; on her other side sat Reuben and opposite them Dasha and Simeon. All five held responsible positions in the Commune, and though strictly speaking places were to be occupied in the order of arrival, they usually sat together at meals.

Joseph looked across the dim, stuffy dining-hall. There were no candlesticks, and the cheap candles were stuck on the deal tables in little pools of frozen tallow. Hardly anybody talked; the men slouched on the forms like exhausted animals. At the table next to theirs a boy with a round, puffed, vacant face sat with his cheek propped against his left hand, while the right half-consciously spooned soup into his mouth. His neighbour slept with his chin on his arms. Everywhere Joseph saw the same slumping figures, their jaws in slow grinding movement as they chewed their food.

So this was their bridal night with the earth. At regular intervals the beam of the searchlight passed over the roof of the hut; its lower fringe swept through the upper part of the windows and through the room, forcing the diners to avert their faces or close their eyes. They might as well have been on an island with a lighthouse in the middle of the ocean. The darkness outside was complete and the wind whined and whistled in protest at the unexpected obstacle on its ancient course through the hills.

Joseph was struck by the ugliness of the faces around him as they were lit up in the intermittent ghastly flash of the searchlight. It was not the first time that he had noticed it, but tonight his revulsion against this assembly of thick, curbed noses, fleshy lips and liquid eyes was particularly strong. At moments it seemed to him that he was surrounded by masks of archaic reptiles. Perhaps he was over-tired and the one cup of sweet wine had gone straight to his head. But it was no good denying to himself that he disliked them, and that he hated even more the streak of the over-ripe race in himself. The only oasis was Dina; but then Dina only half belonged to them like himself, though in a different way. The other girls made him shudder in incestuous revulsion. Their flesh had lost its innocence from birth or before. They might be chaste and prim, and yet some acrid spice of their intellect permeated the very pores of their bodies. That knowingness expanded over the nervous surface of their skin, destroyed their capacity for self-forgetfulness. They were saturated with the long experience of the race which lingered in their eyes and on their skin like the heat of the former occupant in a chair.

"You can have the rest of this," he heard Dina say, pushing her cup of wine to him. "It's too sweet for me."

"Blessed be the grape," said Joseph, lifting the cup and

emptying it. And blessed be Dina, my oasis, he thought. Without her it would be the desert. But alas, she is the mirage, not the well.

"What has happened to the searchlight?" asked Dasha. The periodic flashes had stopped for the last minute.

"Signalling," said Reuben with his mouth full. "Bauman is talking to Gan Tamar."

Reuben is all right, thought Joseph. He liked Reuben's laconic matter-of-factness, his unvarying even temper. Reuben was neither witty nor brilliant; he completely lacked vanity and ambition. His leadership was based mainly on his lack of negative qualities, on a kind of neutral personality which offered no points for attack and made him the socially ideal type for collective life.

"I hope Bauman won't forget to tell them to send up my carrots to-morrow," said Dasha. Dasha was in charge of the communal kitchen and a stickler about the right vitamin diet; she had been through a training course.

"Bauman never forgets anything," said Dina—a remark which Joseph disliked. His mood, when he was near her, was like a precision barometer on an April day; everything she said, however apparently remote from personal implications, produced a change.

"What did you think of our guests?" he asked. "That female walked about the camp as if she were inspecting a zoo."

"She was the typical English aristocrat," said Dasha, who was a fervent socialist and had never spoken to a live Englishman.

"Aristocrat my foot," said Joseph. "She is what they call at home the lower middle class, and what in the colonies becomes the ruling class. It is a kind of Pygmalion-miracle which is automatically performed each time a P. & O. liner passes Gibraltar. The whole Empire is a kind of glorified suburbia."

" 'Pygmalion' was written by G. B. Shaw," stated Dasha.

"Look," cried Dina, mimicking Mrs. Newton and pointing at Simeon. "He reads his paper from right to left. Isn't it funny?" In Europe Dina had studied for the stage. By sucking in her lips and pushing out her chin and drawing in her nostrils she managed to give her face a pinched, hag-like expression. They all laughed, except Simeon who had not spoken a word during the whole meal. Now that he had become the target of Dina's act, he lifted his gaze from his plate.

"There was no need for Bauman to be polite to that Police officer," he said. "Nor for you, Reuben."

"We were correct to them, that's all," said Reuben.

"Precisely," said Simeon. He put his fork down. "We keep on being correct and the Arabs keep on shooting. Result: the Arabs are appeased and we pay the bill."

"We have had that out before," said Reuben, whose mind was on to-morrow's tasks: the reinforcement of the trenches, the installation of electric light, the laying of the foundations for the cowshed.

"But Simeon is right," said Dina. The barometer rose: if Dina supported Simeon, then her previous praise of Bauman had also to be seen in a purely objective light.

"Pressure demands counter-pressure," said Simeon. "Otherwise we shall continue to lose ground. The only answer to violence is retaliation."

"An eye for an eye and a tooth for a tooth," said Dasha with her rather silly laugh.

"No," said Simeon. "It has nothing to do with ethics. The concept of revenge is archaic and absurd. We have to counter terror by terror for purely logical reasons."

The discussion had attracted some people from other tables. They lingered around them, with one foot on the bench and elbows propped on the table.

"I don't believe in terror," said Dasha. She had the stubborn aggressiveness of the female arguing against an intellectually superior partner.

"No, you don't," said Simeon with trenchant sarcasm, "but you believe in carrots because of vitamin A. What you mean to say is that you don't *like* terror. It disagrees with your conditioning. I dislike carrots. They disagree with my conditioning. But I eat them—because they contain vitamin A."

"So what?" said Dasha, who had been unable to follow.

"So we shall eat no more carrots," said Reuben with his conciliatory smile.

"Talking of logic," said Joseph. "Arab terrorism is directed partly against us, partly against the Government. So to restore your equilibrium we would not only have to retaliate against the Arabs, but also to terrorise the Government."

"It will depend on their attitude," said Simeon with deliberate elusiveness, after a moment's silence.

"But we know their attitude," Dina burst out. "They hate us; they all hate us like that female to-day. I saw it in her eyes, that look of suburban hatred. I bet she has a photograph of the sweet little Fuehrer. She must—all suburban haters adore him. Because he tells them what a noble feeling their pet hatred is and because he wears his hair plastered down like the hairdresser's assistant of their dreams. . . ."

Her full, violent mouth dropped at the corners, and for a moment it looked as if she was going to cry.

"All right, Dina," said Joseph gently, "all this we know. But Simeon has not answered my question."

"We have to force them to change their attitude," said Simeon.

"Force them—how?"

"By our achievements," said Reuben quietly.

"By whatever means we find expedient," said Simeon.

It had become quiet around them. There was now quite a crowd round their table. Joseph, while following the argument with one half of his mind, observed with the other how Simeon grew in stature when he had an audience. Practically everybody here was opposed to the views he held, but they listened to him with a reluctant admiration, and the longer they listened the stronger became his spell over them. They followed the argument with an inward-turned look, as if searching for an answer which they did not quite dare to face.

"Let us get this quite clear," said Joseph, who had grown pale. "Assuming they don't change their policy towards us. And assuming there is further persecution in Europe which leads to a mass exodus——"

"Why assuming?" Simeon interrupted with cold irony. "The synagogues in Europe are burning and our girls are walked through their towns with sandwich-boards round their necks inviting passers-by to spit into their faces."

"Oh, shut up," said Dasha with a note of hysteria in her voice.

"Why shut up?" Simeon continued in the same acid manner. "As it happens, it happened to my sister. Don't look like that; why does it make any difference whether it's my sister or somebody else's? She was just a fat, dumb girl like Dasha, name of Rose. She studied chemistry."

There was a silence, then Dina said in a constrained voice: "Why did you never speak about it before?"

"Why should I speak about it? I came to be a peasant in my country, not to the wailing wall. I only mentioned it because of Joseph's 'assuming.' Well, let's go on with our assumptions. I assume that the British won't change their policy unless we force them to. I have studied their history, their traditions, their methods. If the *autos-da-fé* are resurrected in Europe and our people burnt alive, they will be very indignant about it. They will write letters to their newspapers, ask questions in their Parliament and their Bishops will pray for our souls. But if some wretched survivors ask to be let into this our promised land, they will talk of economic difficulties and the poor dispossessed Arabs. And if the wretches won't listen to reason and come swimming for their lives across the sea, they will put barbed wire on our beaches and let them drown. . . ."

He closed his eyes for a moment. Something extraordinary was happening to him, something which he had never experienced before. He saw the drowning people before his eyes.

It was a sharp, short flash which lasted only a split second but was fantastically clear. There were hundreds of them, with arms and legs sticking out of the water, but there was no sound and the whole scene was laid out on a calm and peaceful sea basking in the hot sun.

There was a heavy silence, in which Reuben said drily:

"I think Simeon is exaggerating. At any rate I don't think we can gain anything by imitating Fascist methods."

Unnoticed by most of them, Bauman had entered the hut a few minutes before, and had remained standing at the door, listening to Simeon's speech. Dina saw him; in the prolonged silence she asked:

"And what do you think, Bauman?"

They all turned their heads.

"I share Simeon's opinion," Bauman said curtly. "By the way, Dasha, your carrots will be here first thing in the morning."

Bauman's entry broke the spell. Naphtali, a short dark boy with a squint who had so far restrained himself with some effort, began savagely to attack Simeon, but nobody listened to him. They all crowded round Bauman to hear the latest news from the outside world. Simeon too wanted to get up, but Naphtali didn't let him. "I don't believe in violence," he cried. "I hate violence. We have to come to an understanding with the Arabs. . . ."

"But if they don't wish to come to an understanding with you?" said Simeon, who had regained his calm and his caustic tone.

"We have to educate them. We must get them to join our trade unions. We have to emancipate the fellaheen and break the influence of their priests and replace their chauvinism by class-consciousness."

"And how long will this modest programme take to be carried out?"

"I don't know. It doesn't matter."

"No, it doesn't. Our people will wait on the burning stakes until we have finished."

He pushed past the excited youth and walked out into the darkness. They paid no attention to him. They were listening to Bauman's news, passed on by heliograph from Gan Tamar where they had a wireless. But there wasn't much in it. The Spanish rebels had occupied most of the Basque country and were closing in on Bilbao. The Council of the League had discussed the planned partition of the country into a Hebrew and an Arab state, proposed by the Royal Commission a few months ago, but there were as yet no details. . . .

They did not comment on this last item; they had discussed the question of partition, its pros and cons, till they had become sick of it. Besides, nobody really believed that the Government would have the determination to carry the idea out. Joseph quoted a joke he had seen in an English paper: the best partition would be to let the Arabs have the country during the summer and the Jews during the winter;—but only Dina and Bauman smiled. They all stood about irresolutely, wondering whether they should snatch a few hours' sleep before they were called for guard duty, but a vague feeling of despondency, of a disappointing anticlimax, made them linger on.

In the midst of this indecision the thin voice of a mouth-organ filtered in from the darkness outside, grew stronger as it approached, and a moment later Mendl burst in through the door, blowing with puffed cheeks his mouth-organ and lifting his knees high into the air, in the marching pose of the Pied Piper. He seemed unconscious of the crowd, stalked straight into the centre of the hut, and broke into the tune of "God will rebuild Galilee", swaying and squirming with his hunchbacked body to the swift vigorous rhythm of the tune. He gave the impression of being drunk, but they knew that he was merely seized by one of his sudden moods, when the otherwise quiet and rather silent little Mendl became possessed by a kind of craze, spontaneous and irresistible. Like fog under a violent gust of wind, the stupor which had lain on them burst into shreds. They kicked the forms aside and ran the tables against the wall, clearing an open space in the centre of the hut where already the dark squinting boy and two others had formed the first ring of the horra, the stamping and swaying round-dance, a savage ring-polka. Others joined in; with arms interlaced round each other's shoulders and heads thrown back, they formed a wheel which now spun round as they all raced clockwise to the left, now halted, swaying in and outward as they stamped their feet shouting the refrain of the song, their bodies leaning back almost to the horizontal. The wheel broke and re-formed as more dancers joined in and threw their arms round their neighbours' shoulders, thus welding it again. Soon the circle became too large for the hut; part of it tore itself off and formed a second, smaller ring inside the first, spinning in the opposite sense; and then a third concentric ring, of five dancers only, formed inside the second, spinning again in the reverse direction. The whole horra was like a whirling eddy, giddy and rapturous; and in its centre stood, all by himself, Mendl with his mouth-organ, swaying and squirming like an ecstatic dervish.

Joseph stood by the door, watching the dancers. Their faces, thrown back and turned towards the ceiling, were covered with sweat; many of them had closed their eyes. When they stopped racing round to shout out the refrain, the three magic syllables of *hag-al-il* burst from their lips like savage barks. When they resumed their circular race their mouths remained half open in a self-forgetful, panting rapture. Thus transfigured, they no longer appeared to Joseph ugly and reptilious, but like some stylised Assyrian or Sumerian carving come to life in the flickering light of the candles. His feet had begun to stamp out the torrential rhythm of the dance, his body to sway, he longed to be swallowed up in the whirling eddy. He glanced at Dina who stood next to him. She shook her head. "But *you* go," she said, trying to sound casual. He hesitated for a second, then took a short run, leapt into the air with outstretched arms and broke into the chain. Before the drunkenness of the dance got complete hold of him he saw Dina walk out of the hut; but at that moment he did not care.

Dina walked quickly across the dark square to the living-hut and entered the cubicle which she shared with Dasha and two other girls. Fortunately there was nobody in yet. For a second she stood still in the dark, stuffy little room, listening to the sound of the mouth-organ, the shouts and stamping of feet from the dining-hut. Then the tension in her snapped and she threw herself face down on her bunk. Her shoulders shook and her teeth bit into the straw mattress to stifle the sound of her gulping sobs. After a while she fell asleep, fully dressed, and was only woken two hours later by the crash of the first volley fired against the palisades.

9

The trouble with Dina was that she could not bear to be touched. It was curious to watch, when somebody touched her, a coarse gooseflesh spread on her skin and her face begin to quiver. She could put her hand on a man's, or lay her arm around his shoulder, but winced in suppressed panic if he tried to do the same to her. She would sit on a form at the dining-table and suddenly become conscious of her shoulder or hip touching her neighbour's; she would shrink into herself and make herself small and try to control her trembling so as not to offend the other; and after a while she would get up and slink unobtrusively out of the room, with her meal unfinished. Doctors had been consulted and had asked her questions which she refused to answer; they had suggested drugs, hypnosis, psychotherapy, but it all pointed in one direction, and she refused to let anybody touch upon the thing to forget.

Dina's father had been editor of a distinguished Liberal daily newspaper in the town of Frankfurt-on-Main. It was a patrician paper in a patrician town. She remembered her father as a frail, middle-aged man with gout-bent fingers, a very soft voice and a pointed greyish beard, pacing up and down the worn path on the carpet in the library which one could only enter on tiptoe, or writing with his back to the room at an old-fashioned standing-desk. He had published books on Federal Union, Pan-Europa, against militarism in general, and in his own country in particular; he had been a delegate at various disarmament conferences and a candidate for the Nobel Prize for Peace. He fought nationalism in every form and disguise, adhered to no Church or religious community, and regarded his race as an accident of birth. When the National Socialists came into power he refused to go abroad, but was persuaded by his friends to hide. Dina, then seventeen, was to join her mother, who lived, separated from her husband, in the south of France. She was arrested at the frontier and kept for six months, during which they tried to find out from her her father's whereabouts. When they let her out she was told that her father had given himself up to obtain her release and had died shortly afterwards in a non-specified way.—During those six months, when they kept on trying, methodically, scientifically, ingeniously, to make her betray her father's hide-out, happened the things to forget.

On the whole she was gay and composed. Somewhere inside her the memory of those things lay encrusted, like a bullet which had not been extracted, in its cocoon of insulating tissue. Normally the injured is unconscious of it except when touched near the scar; and Dina's scar expanded over the whole immaculate surface of her body.

10

The first volley came shortly after midnight. It found them mentally unprepared. Although the probability of an attack had been the whole day at the back of their minds, the tension had gradually relaxed as the night wore on. The horra had come to an end about an hour earlier, as abruptly as it had started, and those not on guard duty had tottered to their palliasses in complete exhaustion. When the shooting woke them, they had the feeling of having closed their eyes only a minute ago.

They ran towards their assigned posts, still dazed by sleep but automatically keeping their heads down. After the first salvo it had become quiet again; the men in the dug-outs had orders to fire only when they saw the attackers, and for the time being they could see nothing. The trouble was that the hill had the wrong shape. It was shaped rather like the back of a camel, but with three instead of two humps. They sat on top of the southern or rear hump with the two others in front of them, the camel's head pointing north as it were. For this reason they had built two dug-outs facing north side by side, and only one each facing in the other three directions. The northern communicating trench was also the deepest.

In front of the northern trench ran the barbed wire, and immediately beyond it the ground sloped down into a hollow, and beyond that hollow came the second hump less than a hundred yards away; and another hundred yards further the third. The height of each hillock was only about fifty feet, but this was quite enough to hide and protect the raiders. Bauman had thought of putting observation posts on each of the other two humps, but he had dropped the idea. There had been no time to fortify them, and the outposts, exposed from all directions, would have been bumped off at once.

As was to be expected, the salvo had been fired from the north, either from behind the second or the third hump.

The moon was due to rise in about an hour, and the sky was heavily clouded. The beam of the searchlight crept slowly along the top of the second hillock, then swept with equal care through the hollow, stopping here and there at a suspect bush of thistle or camel-thorn which grew in clusters out of the rock like ugly tufts of hair from a wart. But it could not penetrate through the rock and could not even expose the chinks and holes behind the stones, filling them instead with sharp, ink-black trembling shadows which acted rather unpleasantly on the defenders' imagination. Bauman and the other leaders of the *Haganah* had known for some time that these famous watch-tower reflectors were not much good for the task of spotting snipers who knew how to exploit each nook and cranny of the terrain; they kept them up mainly for the sake of their psychological effect on both the raiders and defenders.

The lull lasted about a minute. Then the searchlight performed one of its periodic quick sweeps round the hill to make sure that no surprise threatened from the flanks or rear; and during these few seconds of darkness the second volley came crashing in from the north. This time the trench and the two dug-outs facing north were fully manned, and the defenders could see the gun-flashes like sparks of St. Elmo's fire all round the next hillock. Bauman ordered fire and presently about twenty rifles spat out a rather ragged volley, most of the men firing for the first time in their lives at human targets.

Joseph, who also belonged to this category, stood in the left northern dug-out. His heart drummed, he felt an annoying pressure in the bladder and after the second volley of the attackers he lost a few drops of his water. At the same time he was in a way enjoying himself. 'That happens to everybody the first time in battle,' he told himself serenely. A bullet whined past, quite close so it seemed. 'A hail of bullets round my bloody head,' he explained to himself. Then he heard Bauman's voice from the other dug-out to the right, giving the command to fire. 'Now then,' he thought, 'hold your breath, close your left eye, aim slightly low on the target at six o'clock.' But there was no target. He pulled the trigger and was deafened by the crash. 'At night it sounds louder,' he thought. 'Now we must wait for a gun-flash and fire at it immediately.' He did so, and would have given a lot to know whether he had hit something. 'Ha,' he told himself, 'that's the hunting passion awakening.' He began positively to enjoy himself.

For a while there were only isolated shots from both sides. Then Bauman yelled, "Hold it for a minute." Bauman had so far not fired a single shot, only waited for the gun-flashes. Now he lifted his Lewis and gave a long burst, methodically sweeping round the dark contours of the hump in front. Joseph saw the flaming muzzle slowly move round in an arc and thought it was a beautiful curve. He regretted that they had no red tracer bullets for fireworks.

To his right stood the squinting youngster Naphtali, and beyond him Reuben, who had the second Lewis gun and was in charge of their dug-out. Naphtali was fumbling about with his rifle, trying to put a new magazine in, but his hands shook and in the end Reuben took the rifle and pressed the magazine in for him. "Don't waste your ammunition," he said in his usual businesslike voice. "And don't get rattled. This isn't serious. There are no more than sixty or eighty of them." Joseph thought resentfully that the youngster had already wasted a full magazine while he had only fired thrice and regarded each pull on the trigger as a special treat.

This went on for about half an hour and Joseph began to feel bored. Once or twice he thought of Dina who, together with little Mendl and another girl, was in charge of the first-aid tent, but he knew that she was reasonably safe behind the stockade. Only Naphtali at his side irritated him. The boy was very nervous and apparently obsessed by the idea that the attackers might have sneaked unobserved into the hollow in front of the barbed wire, and might pounce on them at any moment. Twice he had exposed his head over the parapet to peer down the incline in front, and had stammered some confused apology when Reuben sharply ordered him to take cover.

About 1 A.M. a gale sprang up, with the suddenness and ferocity peculiar to these hills. Towards the east the clouds tore apart and for a minute the moon appeared, travelling rapidly across drifts of black steam; then the gap was filled up again with low, heavy clouds and an instant later the rain came down in torrents, its hard, blinding jets lashing at the defenders' faces almost horizontally.

Since the first sharp gust of wind Joseph had felt by instinct that things were going wrong. The density of the rain made the searchlight practically useless. The glitter of the beam on the streaks of falling water produced a strangely theatrical effect, but behind this wavering curtain of white threads anything might indeed happen now. The youngster at Joseph's side became increasingly fidgety; Joseph had just pulled his head down with a hard grip on the back of his neck when the light suddenly went out. There was some confused shouting from the other dug-out and for a second Joseph felt touched by panic; he had the sensation of an icy jet injected into his veins. He fired three shots as a special treat aimlessly into the rain and regained his self-control. It took some time until his eyes became adjusted to the darkness; in the now total night around them the splash and splutter of the rain sounded louder while the firing of the enemy seemed more remote. He heard Reuben shout: "Cable short-circuited—nothing serious—pass it on," and he passed the message on to the Auxiliary crouching in the connecting trench to his left. He thought that the ancient tongue never sounded more melodious than when shouted through wind and rain in the night; it was a wild and tragic language unfit for small talk. The cloudburst seemed on the point of exhausting its power, the rush of water sounded thinner, and Joseph became aware that for some time already the noise of the enemy's firing had changed in character: instead of single shots one could now hear the steady rattle of an automatic, a Lewis or a Bren. Apparently they had received reinforcements.

He was still digesting this when a dull explosion made them all jump. It had come from behind them, from the direction of the square. Reuben yelled a command over Joseph's head which Joseph did not catch, but he saw the Auxiliary jump out of the trench and run with his head bent towards the square. "The others stay," Reuben yelled, and Joseph turned once again towards the attackers. In all his anxiety he thought that Reuben was a brick, and that it was a great comfort to obey blindly instead of having to decide what to do. The enemy's firing now sounded much nearer, and Joseph wondered whether they had really got into the hollow. In a surprisingly short time he heard the splashing footsteps of the Auxiliary running back through the mud. "Nothing," he shouted while jumping back into the trench. "Only tent B collapsed. Pass it on." Joseph passed it on, and for the next few minutes he was busy shooting at a great number of gun-flashes which now were definitely nearer on this side of the hump; the enemy was obviously advancing towards the hollow, and both Reuben and Bauman were now using their automatics practically without pause. The noise became deafening, the squall had once more increased to its maximum strength, everything was dark and hellish. Joseph aimed and fired in quick succession at target-flashes which now seemed only a few yards away; he felt his head swim and yet his fingers worked with smooth precision; somewhere at the back of his mind a last spark of self-consciousness marvelled at the nimble automaton which his body had become. He was aware of two sharp explosions in quick succession only a few yards ahead of him; in the reddish bengal flashes which accompanied the detonations the silhouette of the barbed wire emerged like a vision of a delicate etching, and vanished again; then he realised that Reuben was throwing hand grenades at the barbed wire, his long dark arm swinging forward and back like a flail. Judging by the frequency of the explosions, Bauman and somebody on the other side were also throwing grenades. "Give, give!" he yelled at Reuben, but Reuben bent over him across the crouching Naphtali and said quite calmly: "No need. It was only to make sure they haven't crept up to the barbed wire."

Joseph took that to mean that they hadn't, and felt relieved, though he did not understand how Reuben could tell. But his intellectual curiosity had left him entirely, and his only desire was to be an automaton and obey. The shooting calmed down a little, and then Joseph saw a vicious gun-flash directly in the line of his aim, and almost simultaneously he fired. He could not say why, but this time the act of pulling the trigger and the report seemed to be different from all the previous occasions and the wild idea crossed his brain that, just as some women were supposed to know by instinct the moment when they conceived, so a man might know the moment when he has killed. In fact, he was convinced of having hit; he had the almost physical sensation of his bullet having been stopped by, and buried in, some dully and elastically resisting matter. A moment later the searchlight was on again.

A wild cheer went up from the trench and Joseph felt the conviction sweep through his whole body that from now on they were safe. It was a sensation like drinking something hot and sugary when very tired; its sweet warmth seemed to penetrate into all his tissues. Only now did he realise that his feet were all a-tremble and his knees on the point of giving way. He pulled a drenched cigarette out of his pocket but it disintegrated between his fingers.

The return of the light seemed to have a demoralising effect on the raiders. Their fire became rather desultory and more distant. Doubtless they were retreating behind the farther slope of their hillock. That white, dazzling eye staring at them from its height like a watchful giant's, and its majestic, slow movement must be an uncanny sensation for them.

Joseph badly wanted a cigarette and asked Naphtali whether he had a dry one, but the youngster gave no answer. He crouched in a curiously huddled-up position against the back of the parapet, and Joseph thought he had perhaps fainted. He went down on his knees by Naphtali's side, reproaching himself for not having looked after him better, and groped for his face. Instead of a face his fingers found a soft, dripping mess and his forefinger went straight into some slushy cavity. He withdrew his hand with a cry and began shaking it wildly through the air as if he had burnt it. Reuben flashed his torch on the youngster and Joseph saw what he had touched, but only for a second. He turned to the other side and vomited.

The youngster by the name of Naphtali had kept some hold on himself until the light went out. From that moment he had been a shaking, teeth-chattering bundle of horror. His brain, paralysed by toxic fear, held only one idea: that the killers had got into the hollow and would in the next second burst through the barbed wire. When Reuben started throwing his hand grenades, Naphtali finally went off his head. He jumped up and down on one spot, gurgling inarticulate sounds and biting his clenched fists. His neighbours were too busy to pay any attention to him. He went on leaping into the air like a joyful child, gurgling and whimpering, until something hit him massively in the eye. He thought it was Reuben, angry because he had not kept his head down; and that Reuben did not have to hit him so hard. He saw great coloured circles spinning and crossing each other like flaming hoops that jugglers throw into the air, and everything became rather quiet; only one last fiery wheel kept turning and expanding, until it too faded and only darkness and peace remained.

11

About 4 A.M. it became clear that the attack had been beaten off. No shot had been fired during the last half-hour; the raiders must have returned to their own hills, anxious to reach their hide-outs before daybreak. Bauman sent the men to sleep, keeping only those on guard duty in the dug-outs.

Joseph felt that he would be unable to sleep and decided to look in at the first-aid tent, hoping that Dina might still be on duty. He had learned that, besides Naphtali who was dead, two men had been wounded at the height of the attack: one of the Auxiliaries had been shot through the chest, and Mendl had received a bullet in his arm while repairing the electric cable, but had gone on until he had finished the job. Stamping through the mud with his torch, Joseph thought that his feet had never in his life felt so heavy. His mind was in a dreamy, floating haze, while his whole body seemed imbued with the consciousness of gravity. This, he thought, is what people on Jupiter must feel like, where every object weighs three times heavier than on the Earth. I wonder whether Jupiter too has its Jews. . . . No doubt it has; no species would be complete without its Jews; they are the exposed nerve, an extreme condition of life. . . . There was light showing from the first-aid tent; he lifted the flap and saw Dina making Turkish coffee over a spirit-lamp as if she were waiting for him. On a stretcher on the floor lay the wounded Auxiliary, covered with a rug, asleep. Dina had put the bright acetylene lamp out and lit candles instead. She seemed pleased to see him. He leaned his rifle carefully against the canvas and with a feeling of bliss squatted down on the floor. "Where is Mendl?" he asked in a whisper.

"He is all right," she said. "It was only a flesh wound and he went to sleep in his own bed with his mouth-organ under the pillow.—You need not whisper; he's had a shot of morphia." She spoke in a low murmur which sounded less strained than whispering, and more intimate. "They are going to send the ambulance car from Gan Tamar first thing to-morrow morning."

"It is to-morrow already," said Joseph.

She let a drop of cold water fall on the thick brown liquid in the shiny copper pot and poured it out into two small cups. Joseph sipped it voluptuously, leaning his back against the foot of the chair.

Dina had a leather jacket wrapped round her shoulders, with its empty sleeves hanging down. She seemed to be shivering. There were dark-blue shadows under the lighter blue of her eyes and her hair kept falling into her face as if it were too tired to remain in its proper place.

"Would you like to wash your face?" she asked after a while. He touched his face with his fingers; it was all grimy. He grinned, slowly shaking his head. "Too lazy," he said. "Just let me sit for a while. You need not look at me."

He closed his eyes and after a while opened them again and saw that she was looking at him with a kind of approval.

"Reuben looked in before you came," she said. "He mentioned that you had done quite well."

So Dina had specially inquired after him, Joseph thought happily. And Reuben had approved of him. He suddenly felt the tears shoot into his eyes. Oh, it was good to be approved of. There was nothing better than to be approved of—to like and be liked. In that moment he was so full of a warm, simple certainty about everything that he felt no shame and no need to pose. He leaned his head against the foot of her chair, closed his eyes and let the tears run down his face. He felt that in this moment of abandon he lost his last chance of ever winning her. But the bliss of surrender, of shedding all pretence, was stronger than his desire. It is finished, he thought, for it is I who am giving myself, not she. . . .

The next time he opened his eyes he knew that he must have slept though he could not remember it. The candle had grown short and old, covered with knobs of tallow like a warted gnome. Dina had slumped down in her chair and was resting with her cheek on his shoulder, asleep. At a slight movement of his she woke and moved her head away. "It will soon be day," she said in a murmur.

"Another hour," said Joseph.

She lay back in her chair, shivering. The Auxiliary on the stretcher moved in his sleep. "How did Naphtali die?" she asked after a while.

"I don't know. We should have watched him. . . ." He remembered the unutterable contact of his hand with the slushy mass, and remained silent.

"Poor Naphtali," said Dina. "I never liked him."

Joseph said nothing; he felt no desire to speak or to move;

he only wished he could remain there for a while, leaning against the chair, limp and desireless.

"You know," said Dina, "I have never understood why you joined us. You don't really fit in here."

"Do you?" he said.

"That's different. . . . But even by race you only half belong to us."

"I have opted for the belonging half."

"But why? You would be happier among the others. Why won't you tell?"

"There was some incident."

"What incident?"

"Is this a confessional?" he asked tiredly.

They remained silent for a while; he could feel through the chair, acting as a conductor, that she shivered. The Auxiliary on the stretcher moaned. Dina got up and smoothed his blanket. Her teeth were chattering.

"It is cold," she said. "I must lie down."

"All right," said Joseph. "I will go." He started wearily to scramble to his feet.

"But you needn't," said Dina. She slid down to the floor and touched his face with her lips. "Will you let me sleep with my head on your arm?" she asked, lying down at a little distance from him and pulling the blanket over both of them. "But please don't do anything."

"No," he said, lying stiff and frozen with the soft warm weight on his arm. "Sleep, Dina, you are safe; we are both safe here."

She breathed quietly against his head. After a while she asked:

"Was it very bad—the shooting?"

"No," he said. "It was all bluff and bluster, like everything these Arabs do."

After another while she said timidly:

"Is it very beastly of me to lie on your arm and ask you to keep still?"

He did not answer at once. Then he swallowed and said huskily:

"Anything you like, darling. Darling, anything you like."

12

He could not go to sleep again. Instead his thoughts travelled once more back the worn path to the Incident. He wished he could bring himself to tell Dina about it, but shame and the fear of ridicule always held him back. It was such a squalid and grotesque story that he could not expect even her to understand its influence on his life.

He had been eleven when his father died. His father had been a Russian-Jewish pianist of some renown. His mother was English and a gentile. Her people had never approved of her marriage. After her husband's death she went back to live with them in their house in Oxfordshire. Joseph was an only child; he grew up in the large country house, played cricket and tennis, went to church, rode a pony and later a horse. His father was rarely mentioned and Joseph at eleven accepted this as one of the many paragraphs in the sacred code of "don'ts".

In due course he was sent up to Oxford, and during the summer vacation after his second term fell in love with a woman from the neighbourhood whom he met at a local tennis tournament. Lily was five years older than Joseph, blonde, slim, pretty and divorced. She was generally liked among the neighbours, and sometimes teased by them on account of her enthusiasm for a new political movement which organised demonstrations through the London East End, and whose members wore black shirts and had fights with policemen. But Joseph at that time was not interested in politics.

After his third term Joseph proposed to Lily and was told not to be an ass. After his fourth term they went to a hunt ball where they drank several cocktails and a good deal of champagne. During the last dance he caught a peculiar smile in her eye; while the band played God Save the King she asked him in a whisper where his room was, and told him how to find hers.

He had known Lily for almost two years, was humbly in love with her, had talked to her poetry, sex and eternity, and had never kissed her lips. After the ball, without transition, he became the lover for a wildly unreal and elusive hour, of a woman so completely transformed that he kept stammering her name aloud to convince himself of her identity. Then came the awakening and the crash. Even now, years later, he grew hot with humiliation as he thought of it. In her dark room she had switched the bedside lamp on to look for a cigarette. The sudden light had revealed their nudity, and with it the sign of the Covenant on his body, the stigma of the race incised into his flesh. The horror in her face made him at first think that she had discovered in him the symptoms of some repulsive disease; then, in a voice icy with contempt she had accused him of infamy and deception, cross-examined him about his ancestry, ordered him to get dressed and clear out of her room. At last the reason dawned on him.

It was indeed a squalid little incident, impossible to tell Dina or anybody else. Even less could he explain to them that it had changed the course of his life. Not because of Lily—that aspect of it he got over after a while. Lily had merely been an instrument, and perhaps without her some other incident would have produced the same result. The result was a kind of shell-shock. Everything was changed. He began making inquiries about his father. He made a cult of his memory, to atone for his own cowardly part in the conspiracy of silence about him. This led to a breach with his mother's family. He took rooms in London and frequented the people whom he was henceforth to regard as his own. At first he did not like them, but he read the newspapers and learned that Incidents were the rule in their lives. He read books and learned that it had been the same in the past. He read more books and learned about the movement of the Return and its founder, the Viennese journalist Dr. Herzl, whose story reminded him of his own. He too had thought that the stigma was buried in the past, until he had met with his Incident: the trial of Captain Dreyfus which he had been sent out to report. Towards the end of his life he had summed up his philosophy to a friend:

"If you are faced with a fence and can't creep through under it, your only choice is to jump. For twenty centuries we have tried to creep through under the fence. They wouldn't let us. Now we are taking the jump."

Once Joseph had taken the jump the rest became easy. He forgot about Lily and the shell-shock. He no longer ran away from something, but ran forward towards an aim. It had the lure of an exotic country, the fascination of a romantic revival and the appeal of a social utopia, all in one—almost too good to be true. It had been a curious journey—from Lily's bed to Ezra's Tower in Galilee. Whether it was a pilgrim's progress or a wild-goose chase he did not know; and at the moment he did not care to know.

He felt the soft weight of Dina's face on his arm, and the quiet rhythm of her breathing carried him off to sleep.

13

They woke at daybreak both at the same time. Neither of them had changed position or moved in their sleep. Both of them were fully awake at once.

"Come," said Dina. "Let us see the sun rise."

They walked out of the tent into the light grey morning mist and the fresh dewy smell of the air. To the east, behind the hill with the sleeping Arab village, the sky was pink and yellow, rapidly changing colour. Dina threw her hair back and shook herself like a puppy getting out of the water.

"I talked a lot of nonsense last night," she said.

"Did you? I slept," said Joseph. "Look at the sheep."

A flock of tiny light woolly specks were zigzagging down the slope beyond the wadi.

"We shall have a bigger flock," said Dina. "And cows. What shall we call the first calf?"

"Dr. Karl Marx," said Joseph. "Let's climb on top of the tower."

They climbed up the wooden ladder, Dina first. Her legs were over his head and he saw the muscles play in her calves and had to restrain himself not to bite into the smooth, brown skin. Well, he thought, that will never be; but there are other things. To approve and be approved of, to like and be liked. . . .

They stood on the platform of Ezra's Tower, surrounded by the gently undulating silver-grey hills of Galilee. They saw Dasha emerge from the living-hut, a towel round her neck and a big sponge in her hand, on her way to the showers.

"To-day we shall start building the cowshed," said Dina.

The sparkling tip of the sun had pierced the yellow mist. It was 5.30 A.M.; and the evening and the morning were the first day.

MORE DAYS

(1938)

MORE DAYS (1938)

1

Extract from the Constitution of Communal Settlements, in Compliance with the Standard Rules under the Co-operative Societies Ordinance, Government of Palestine, 1933:

SECTION A: NAME, ADDRESS, OBJECT, POWERS AND AFFILIATIONS

The general objects of the Society are to organise and promote the economic and social interests of its members in accordance with co-operative principles and in particular to—

(*a*) *Manage and develop a collective farm;*

(*d*) *Dispose of products of the settlement and purchase its requirements;*

(*e*) *Maintain a common purse into which all the earnings of their members shall be paid and from which all their requirements shall be provided;*

(*f*) *To assist members in raising their economic, cultural and social level by mutual aid, to care for their sick, to support the old and feeble . . . and to maintain and educate the children of the members;*

(*h*) *To supply all the social, cultural and economic requirements in the settlement and to undertake all steps which may be deemed necessary for improving these conditions, and in particular to establish and maintain crèches, kindergartens and schools for the education and bringing-up of the children;*

(*i*) *To establish and maintain in the settlement public institutions and services and generally undertake all activities which are customarily undertaken by village authorities.*

SECTION D: SPECIAL PROVISIONS RELATING TO THE BUSINESS OF THE SOCIETY

(3) *Rights and Duties of Members:*

(*a*) *The members have equal rights to receive from the common purse of the Society food, drink, clothing, housing and other necessities and amenities of life.*

SECTION C: FINANCIAL PROVISIONS

(1) *Capital:*

The Society has no capital.

2

Pages from the chronicle of Joseph, a member of the Commune of Ezra's Tower

Friday, October . . . 1938

To-day it is a year since young Naphtali was shot through his eye and brains because he couldn't keep his head down. He has since become a hero and our local patron saint. Particularly as the poor, squinting little fool did not believe in violence and had so much set his heart on educating our Neighbours. However, heroes should be looked at through the telescope, not through the microscope.

History is a series of futilities with grandeur as their cumulative effect. That, I suppose, is another example of the dialectical change of quantity into quality. . . .

Anyway we have waxed and expanded during this first year and are beginning to look more or less like a village—or rather a cross between a fortified camp and a life-size model from a town-planner's drawing-board. The Watch-tower is our parish church, the Dining Hut our club, town-hall and forum romanum, all in one. So far the living quarters are still of wood, but the first concrete buildings are completed and look most impressive—they are the cowshed, dairy and the Children's House. The latter has up to date five inmates who are quite fun. Two of them were born since we have settled and there are more on the way. The female comrades all seem to walk about with big bellies, terribly pleased with themselves for improving the national birth-rate and looking even less attractive than usual. I suppose they sing the Anthem during the act of procreation.

We also have our graveyard with so far five concrete slabs. One died of typhus and three more were sent Naphtali's way by our Neighbours: two during night attacks, the third ambushed while walking alone through the wadi and killed with particular beastliness—castrated, eyes out and all. And the people of Kfar Tabiyeh still have the cheek to come to our dispensary with their boils and belly-aches and fly-ridden children.

The height of this tragi-comedy was the visit the Mukhtar paid us to-day to congratulate us on our first anniversary. He came on a white stallion, accompanied by his eldest son, Issa. The son is a pock-marked, shifty-eyed lout, but the Mukhtar looked magnificent. Reuben showed them the library, tractor-shed, Children's House, tree-nursery, etcetera; the Mukhtar praised everything with clickings of the tongue and avuncular beams, while Issa looked like a fellow with jaundice in a delicatessen shop.

Reuben asked them to stay on for the midday meal, and the Mukhtar started with gusto the ceremonial game of protest. He protested with both hands pushing an imaginary dish away into the air and clasping them to his chest as if to assert his innocence of any intention of robbing his hosts of so delicious a dish; and after this had been repeated three times we went into the Dining Hall. He looked quaintly out of place at the communal table with his checked head-cloth floating round his shoulders and his enormous behind bulging over the narrow form; while his cunning eyes scanned with curiosity the informal coming and going of the comrades, particularly the girls. I thought the meal appallingly poor after so much ado and felt rather ashamed of it, though I knew that Reuben was right not to make any fuss about the Mukhtar and, by making him eat according to our custom and not theirs, to show him that we are here in our own right. The Mukhtar felt it too and didn't like it, though he kept up his jovial tone, while Issa sulkily munched his food without saying a word, and cast his furtive eyes down whenever a bare-thighed girl brushed past him in her shorts. The four of us were left alone at our table, only Max and Sarah from our extreme Arab-liberating anti-Imperialist wing kept casting loving glances at Mukhtar and son, itching to explain to them that Allah is opium for the people and that their women should use birth-control; fortunately they can't talk Arabic.

When we got to the coffee which, as a concession, was made the native way, the Mukhtar let the cat out of the bag. He lowered his voice to confidential intimacy and asked whether we knew what boundary between the Arab and Jewish states the Partition Commission is going to propose. Reuben said truthfully that he knew nothing about it except that the report of the Commission is supposed to be published shortly; besides, in his opinion the whole idea of partition is going to be dropped. The Mukhtar then started nudging both of us with his elbows, with tremendous laughs and slappings of knees, pretending that we knew everything and were trying to hold back the secret from him. Finally he came out with it himself: according to rumour, the boundary is to cut Galilee into halves, with the village of Kfar Tabiyeh falling into the Jewish State. . . .

Reuben merely shrugged and repeated that in his opinion the partition scheme is going to be abandoned. I asked the Mukhtar where he got his information from; he put on a secretive air and said he got it from a very high and important personality. Probably it was the travelling cloth-merchant whom we saw the day before yesterday ride into Kfar Tabiyeh on his donkey; but the Mukhtar seemed firmly convinced that it's true. Reuben was bored, but I enjoyed the situation. I asked the Mukhtar whether he did not think that they would be much better off in the Hebrew State, reciting to him the whole stock-in-trade of arguments: how the Arab living-standard has risen and the death-rate fallen since our coming; how the country was nothing but swamps and desert twenty years ago, while to-day the Arabs of Palestine are envied for their prosperity by all those in the neighbouring states. Hamdulillah, the Mukhtar said solemnly, Thank God. I told him that we were paying all the taxes out of which the Government built the roads and Arab schools; Hamdulillah, he said, nodding his head. I told him that the Arab labourer in this country earned about five times more than in Egypt and ten times more than in Iraq thanks to the capital we have brought in, and that Arab infant mortality had dropped to less than one-third thanks to our hospitals; Hamdulillah, he said with emphatic vigour. I told him that the great Feisal himself, son of the Kalif Hussein and King of Iraq, had after the last war officially welcomed the rebuilding of the Hebrew State and that after all the Kalif's son knew better what was good for the Arabs than the assassins hired by the godless Germans; "Aywa," said the Mukhtar, "God how true you speak! I have always held the same opinions but there are fools who will not listen to wisdom and even send a bullet into its seat." He fell again into a conspiratorial whisper and revealed to us that he had always been a follower of the moderate Nashashibi clan, but since the extremist Husseinis were backed by the English and had got the upper hand; and since their leader, the Great Mufti Hadj Amin, was directing the terrorists from Damascus;

and since most of the moderate Nashashibi leaders had been bumped off by the Husseinis for wanting to come to terms with the Jews; and since the other Mukhtar of Kfar Tabiyeh was a Husseini-man and had a blood-feud with our Mukhtar;—and so on. In short, it was clearer than daylight that we never had a better and truer friend than the Mukhtar of Kfar Tabiyeh, and that the least we could do to repay our debt to him was to give him, once the Hebrew State was established, a nice, remunerative function like Collector of Taxes or Inspector of Road Transport; and of course to hang the other Mukhtar with his whole family. . . .

At last he was off, with protestations of eternal friendship and good-neighbourhood. Though his charm was wasted on Reuben, I couldn't help liking the old brigand. How convincing he was even when he lied, and how unconvincing our Glicksteins are even when they speak the truth! That's one of the reasons why the English like them and loathe us. We keep on demonstrating our loyalty to them, and the Arabs keep on double-crossing them. But the point is that the English don't for a minute expect the Arabs not to double-cross them; it's part of the game. They have an old and subtle tradition of dealing with Natives; they are attracted and amused by them, they exploit them as a matter of course and expect to be stabbed by them as soon as they turn their back, as an equal matter of course. Whereas with us they don't know where they are. They regard us not as Natives but as Foreigners, and that is quite a different matter. There is no superiority complex without an inferiority complex; and while the native appeals mainly to the first, the foreigner appeals mainly to the second. Our protestations of loyalty make us only the more suspect.

Sunday

Thank God, Moshe our Treasurer is coming back from Hospital, so after the General Meeting next week I shall be relieved from deputising for him and go back to my own work. But first I have to prepare the annual Balance Sheet for the meeting, which is a rather unpleasant job. Though it is understood that for the first three years we shall work with a deficit, and shall only start paying ground rent and repaying our investment loans to the National Fund after the fifth year, it is nevertheless depressing to have to produce a balance-sheet which starts:

INCOME

Produce	*Pal. Pounds*
Olive groves	0 : 0 : 0
Other fruit trees	0 : 0 : 0
Woodland	0 : 0 : 0
Tree nurseries	0 : 0 : 0
Goats and sheep	0 : 0 : 0

So far our only sources of income were the first crops of about three acres of wheat and barley, milk and butter from our dairy, a few pounds from the chicken farm and vegetable garden, the cash earnings of six of our members who work as day-labourers in the Haifa cement factory, and under the item "Miscellaneous" the sale of a gold watch which Max's aunt in New York sent him as a birthday present.

However, communal bookkeeping has its fascinating side. The basic unit of our arithmetic is not the pound but the "Work Day" and the "Maintenance Day". A Work Day is the amount of work done by one member in one eight-hour day. The value of the Work Day varies according to production branch. It is calculated by dividing our total annual income from *e.g.* milk and butter by the number of Work Days expended in dairy and cowshed. This is what the cow boys and dairy workers theoretically earn per day; but of course they are not paid, the money remains in the communal purse. The fewer the Work Days spent on each pound's worth of produce, the more profitable is that branch of production and (taking amortisation and depreciation into account) we thus obtain a check on rentability. As in all new settlements the average value of our Work Day is still very low: three shillings and sixpence is what we theoretically earn per head per day.

But this of course applies only to the "earners", *i.e.* to those who are engaged in income-producing work. The work of the cooks, orderlies, seamstresses, laundresses, etc., produces no income. A little under half of the members of the Commune are employed on such non-productive household work. Thus the income from a Work Day should be at least twice the expenditure per Maintenance Day (that is the cost of feeding, clothing, and social services per head and day). Alas, it is not. The cost of a Maintenance Day is still two shillings and ninepence.

What really fascinates me is the quaint statistical picture of how the average civilised human being in a rationally organised society spends his or her time to satisfy the basic human needs. There are now 36 adults in Ezra's Tower (37 founding members minus 5 dead plus 4 new probationers). There are 365 days in the year, so the theoretical total of working days is 36 x 365 = 13,140. Of these, 6,624 Work Days were spent on income-earning labour (that is in the fields, orchards, olive groves, dairy, poultry farm, vegetable garden, tending the sheep, and maintenance work). If we divide this total by the number of members we find that the average member spent 196 days in the year to earn his keep. By the same method we find that he (or she—the statistical average is always a hermaphrodite) spent 28.5 days on cooking, washing up and serving meals; 12.6 days on dressmaking and repairing; 3 days on shoe-making, 3.5 on laundering, 3.5 on cleaning his/her living quarters, 4 on tending the lawn and other embellishments of the Commune, 6.5 on travelling, 1.5 on looking after the Library and Stores, 3 on dispensing medical care, 21 on running the Children's House, 20 on being ill, 5.6 in childbed and suckling, 4 on leave, 56 on Shabbaths and Holydays and 2.2 on doing nothing because of heavy rains.

Now according to this time-table about one-eighteenth of

the total working days of the Commune are spent in running the Children's House—in other words two people are employed full time to look after our five children—quite apart from the time which the parents spend with the children in their leisure hours. Whence follows that the children are much better looked after in the Commune than in the family. The wife of an individual farmer with five children not only looks after them alone, but has also to cook, do the housework, and at times to help in the fields and with the cattle. Her time-table would show about 700 Work Days in the year to do all these jobs—and less well than in our case. She can only manage it by squeezing two eight-hour days into each day of her life; and the same goes for the man.

The revolutionary thing about the Commune is that it makes farming possible on an eight-hour basis and turns it into a civilised occupation. From 5 P.M. onward my time is my own. And when all is said, what is the final aim of socialism if not the conquest of leisure?

Saturday

Yesterday at the weekly stores distribution I played Father Christmas for the last time before Moshe's return. "Shopping hour" on Shabbath eve is one of the highlights of the week, and to be salesman in a free-for-all shop one of the most gratifying occupations. The queuing-up in front of the stores is a kind of social occasion; everybody comes fresh from the showers, in clean linen and Shabbath-gear, looking his or her best, cheered by the prospect of to-night's meat dinner and to-morrow's long sleep and rest. Then they file with their shopping-lists into my decrepit shack with an air of looking for a fur coat in Bond Street. The standard allowance is fifteen cigarettes, one cake of soap and one razor-blade a week, one tube of toothpaste and boot polish a fortnight, one toothbrush a month; furthermore note-paper, envelopes, stamps, bootlaces, contraceptives, electric bulbs, torch-batteries, combs, hairclips and so on, by special order according to need. All of us get one complete issue of working clothes and one Shabbath-outfit each year. The working clothes are bought from wholesalers ready-made, the Saturday clothes for the women are made in our own workshop according to taste, so as to provide variety. It is surprising how few basic needs people have once competition and hoarding are abolished.

In a couple of years we shall have our own furniture workshop and start going in for luxuries. For the time being our luxury-budget for the whole Commune is twelve pounds a year —the equivalent of two Work Days per head per year. . . .

Moshe has a trick of handing out the goods with some terrific sales-talk in a mixture of three languages, giving each item a fantastic imaginary price and carrying on a bitter mock-haggling with the customers. It is a performance one never gets tired of. Perhaps because it tickles our conceit, our feelings of superiority towards the capitalist world;—or because it comforts us by deriding the fleshpots of Egypt which we have left so irretrievably behind, and enhances the virtue of our appalling poverty?

For, when all is said, ours is a hard and drab existence, and one has to do a lot of sales-talk to oneself to stick it. Even so there are days . . .

However, they are only days. Remember Joseph, remember. Hast thou forgotten Pharaoh's hosts?

Powder and cosmetics are banned from our stores as attributes of "bourgeois decay." I wish they weren't. I wish we were now and then visited by some charitable scarlet woman of Babylon.

Sunday

Yesterday being Shabbath a bunch of us went down in the truck to Gan Tamar to listen to a concert by the Philharmonic Orchestra which is touring the settlements. Although Gan Tamar played the rôle of god-father to us, relations have been steadily deteriorating since we became solidly established on our own. There were the usual minor frictions about a truck they once borrowed and returned with a broken spring, and so on, but the root of the trouble is of course political. I wonder whether any other race has the same capacity for doctrinaire fanaticism as ours. It has, I suppose, to do with the Exile; *émigrés* always have cliques and quarrels, and we have been *émigrés* for two thousand years. The exiled have nothing to hang on to except doctrines and convictions; hence they fight over ideas like dogs over bones. The others call it politely our semitic intensity.

Anyhow, at the last municipal elections in Tel Aviv they had thirty-two competing party lists, and each party was convinced of being the only true prophets of the kingdom of heaven.

But the real fun only starts when the Hebrew prophetic streak cross-breeds with socialist sectarianism. Then dots on I's and crosses on T's become a matter of life and death and deviations from the party line are castigated with all the wrath of Amos and Isaiah. This is what turned Marx into such a quarrelsome old bully; and we the disciples have inherited, if not his grandeur, at least his cantankerousness. Thus even our rural Communes, though they are all built on the same principle, are split up between three rival Federations. Ezra's Tower is affiliated to the "United Group of Communes" which supports the Hebrew Labour Party; whereas Gan Tamar belongs to "Hashomer Hazair" ("The Young Guardian") which stands on the extreme left of our Labour movement and corresponds to the British I.L.P. They have strong sympathies for Russia, whereas we are rather critical of the Soviet system. So after the concert there was the usual argument in the Reading Room of Gan Tamar—passionate, venomous and futile, as is proper and befitting in the socialist fraternity.

It started as usual with Russia—the one-party system, the inequality of pay, the Purges, the let-down of Spain, etc. The Gan Tamar crowd had a ready excuse for everything, and our radicals Max and Sarah supported them. It is depressing to watch how these two gradually drift into a position where political grudges and personal discord fuse into one. Sarah feels frustrated, among other things because she believes that she should be in charge of the Children's House instead of Dina. Sarah is an Adlerian juvenile-individual-psychologist cum vegetarian-dietarian; she has a pale, pinched little face with large starved-virgin eyes. Max, who has an enormous, sniffing tapir-nose and an unkempt I.L.P.-name, feels that he should be a member of the Secretariat—which indeed he should according to his brains, but being quarrelsome and unpopular he ends up in all elections as an also-ran—a member of the Committee for Culture or such like. Both are unmarried.

So the argument on Russia took its usual course, rather like a game of chess where at the opening stages both partners know the other's answer in advance, and once it gets really going throw the chessmen at each other's head. This time the throwing was started by Moshe our Treasurer. We had already got through the opening, to wit:

White (Queen's pawn 4): Obvious untruth of the accusations against the Trotskyite opposition.

Black (Queen's pawn 4): All opposition in a Workers' State is *a priori* counter-revolutionary.

White (Queen's Bishop pawn 4): Growing inequality of pay and privileges for the Bureaucracy.

Black (King's Bishop pawn 3): Necessity to stimulate production by temporary expedients.

White (King's Knight Bp. 3): Chauvinistic education, boosting of leadership, religious revival, etc.

Black (Queen's Knight Bp. 3): Necessity of preparing backward masses for imperialist war and fascist aggression.

White (*Dasha,* pawn takes pawn): "They even encourage bourgeois decadence like lipstick, rouge and powder."

Black (*Sarah,* retakes pawn, blushes with rage): "The dialectics of proletarian sex-appeal as opposed to the prostitution of bourgeois matrimony . . ."

It was at this stage that Moshe lost patience and upset the game. Moshe is a heavy-weight, in every respect. He is short and stocky like a bull; he sits on our Communal purse like the Lord Chancellor on the Woolsack; he is a financial genius capable, like the other Moses, of drawing water from rock; and he has a way, with his slow speech and heavy common sense, of trampling through the thick of an argument like an elephant through the jungle. So Moshe told the Gan Tamar crowd that if they wanted to imitate Russia they would first of all have to abolish the Common Purse as a left deviation and start paying out salaries, it being understood that members of the Secretariat would be entitled to draw about three hundred times the amount paid to the average worker and to keep a secret police authorised to deport or shoot anybody without trial. As the next step they would have to build a separate dining hut for the skilled Stakhanovites, and a third one for the comrades of the Secretariat; they would have to abolish co-education, introduce school-fees and so on. . . .

There was a terrific uproar. When it had subsided, Felix's sharp academic voice made itself heard. Felix is an expert in timing; he can wait patiently behind his complicated lenses for the psychological moment, the short lull when everybody is off his guard; and before the others have recovered, he is in the middle of a lecture. Felix is the pocket-Lenin of Gan Tamar and one of the leading theoreticians of the Hebrew I.L.P. Among other things he is the inventor of the system, practised in some of the Hashomer Hatzair settlements, according to which up to the age of eighteen boys and girls take their shower-baths together but are bound by vows of chastity. For all that he looks like a male spinster practising the solitary vice every other Shabbath according to plan, with an extra go on the anniversary of the October Revolution. So now Felix set out to analyse, dissect, split, twist, turn and re-turn Moshe's arguments, and everybody, friend and foe, sat back to let the inevitable take its course. Felix's lectures have a quality of making one realise how hard the chair is on which one sits. He spoke for a quarter of an hour in complicated abstractions; the upshot of it all was that the Russian kolkhoz should not be compared with our Communes, because in Russia Socialism had to be imposed upon a backward population whereas our Communes were built by a picked élite of volunteers.

"All right, we know all this," puffed Moshe. "But if we are allowed to experiment in pure rural communism on territory ruled by capitalistic Britain, why could not a similar élite of Russian volunteers carry out similar experiments on Soviet Russian territory?"

Because, Felix explained, quoting various speeches by Stalin, conditions in Russia were different from conditions everywhere else, and methods employed by the proletarian state could not be compared to the methods of capitalistic states, and vice versa. Felix was fighting a battle of attrition, but one cannot wear down an elephant.

"You are all maniacs," puffed Moshe. "Our Communes are the only place in the world where individual property is completely vested in the community, where all men are really equal, and where you can live and die without ever having touched money. In these hundred-odd settlements of ours we have now been practising pure rural communism for over thirty years, have survived all trials without sacrificing a single basic principle, and have transformed a seemingly utopian idea into a small-scale but significant working concern. Now I ask you: why do the Russians not send delegations and experts to study experimental communism on the only spot on the earth where it is really practised? They send commissions to study American factories, English football and German police methods. Would you not expect them to be equally interested in the economic and social phenomena which applied rural communism produces? But they haven't sent a commission yet, not even a single journalist; every reference to us is banned in their Press, the Hebrew language is illegal in Russia and our comrades are shot. I see no reason why we should get excited about Russia, and every reason why they should get excited about us."

"Typical chauvinistic conceit," sniffed Max. The Gan Tamar crowd seconded. The curious thing is that their papers keep on boosting the "shining socialistic example of the Hebrew Communes" until one gets sick of it and begins to doubt whether we really exist or are merely an invention of our own propaganda; but when they talk about Russia they suddenly get self-deprecating and humble as if in church.

Felix had withdrawn into silence, and the discussion petered out in the usual stalemate. We all went into the kitchen and Ruth made us coffee. The cosiest place in all our settlements is the deserted kitchen around midnight, when the others are asleep and one starts cooking coffee and pinching biscuits from the larder with a feeling of being on a spree. It is called a "cumsitz"—a corruption of the German "come and sit down." During the cumsitz we all became quite jolly again. There were the usual bits of gossip about the other Communes: the snobs of Commune Khefziba (where practically each member has an academic degree) have started building a swimming-pool although they had a deficit last year. In Kfar Gileadi, one of the oldest Communes in Upper Galilee, the younger generation captured the Secretariat at the last election and the patriarchs of old Wabash's time are all very bitter about it. In Tirat Z'wi, a new Commune in the Jordan Valley run by the Orthodox party, they had a terrible quarrel about milking the cows on the Shabbath; they submitted the question to the Chief Rabbinate which ruled that the cows should be milked but that vinegar should be put into the pails to prevent Shabbath-milk being used for commercial purposes.

It was all very jolly—and would have been even jollier with a bottle of brandy or Scotch. I wonder when we shall get over this puritanism in our Communes. Sometimes I feel that I must get drunk or I can't stand our virtues any longer. But the new generation doesn't seem to miss anything; these Sabra-boys regard a glass of wine as something like opium or hashish, and the girls look upon lipstick as an invention of the devil, who dwells in the Babel of Tel Aviv and wears a dinner jacket with a white carnation.

Thursday

Mendl the Pied Piper is back from Jerusalem, and he's got the cello. I saw the cello advertised for sale by its refugee owner in the *Jerusalem Mail* a week ago. It was only five pounds—dirt-cheap; and luckily Moshe wasn't yet back. So in my capacity as Temporary Treasurer I decided to buy it for us—from next year's luxury budget, as this year's twelve pounds are already exhausted. I should of course have consulted at least the other members of the Secretariat, but I didn't. When Moshe heard about it he was puffing with fury and promised that the Annual Meeting would come down on me like a ton of bricks. I certainly let myself in for something—but what matters is that we now have our string quartet complete.

I asked Mendl whether he had picked up any political gossip in Jerusalem, about Partition and so on, but he hadn't. He is completely unpolitical—self-contained, silent and rather dreamy. He is our tractor-driver and mechanic and loves tinkering so much that I am sure he is secretly happy whenever something goes wrong with our electricity plant. His shyness prevented him from showing his excitement about the cello. He is always shy and restrained about music—until he gets going and becomes transformed into the Pied Piper. Each passion has its own chastity.

Monday

One of our periodic financial crises, which even Moshe's genius is unable to prevent. For the last three days we have been feeding on bread, olives, noodles and milk. Dasha says the vitamin balance is all right but we walk about with a hungry look, and whenever I meet anybody's eyes, I see in them a cello crossed by a dagger. We haven't had meat for a fortnight and Arieh refuses to sacrifice any of his sheep; it isn't the season—it apparently never is. We have sold our late vegetable crop and all our cheese and butter, and there we are, high and dry. We have seven working people on the sick-list—three with malaria, two with typhoid and two with dysentery—which in itself is only slightly higher than the norm, but unfortunately four out of our five cash-earners are among them. Usually they bring home about ten to fifteen pounds each Friday from the cement factory (not to mention the tools, soap and sundry items which they pinch from the factory for the common good). This sum is the mainstay of our weekly cash-budget—the rest of the turnover consists in a series of complicated credit operations with the Workers' Bank and the National Cooperatives who buy our produce and supply most of our needs; but a minimum amount of cash is needed to keep the concern going.

Fortunately our great friend the Mukhtar of Kfar Tabiyeh turned up this morning, and after the usual nerve-racking bigtalk about God's blessings and the Universe in general, came out with the proposal to hire our tractor for the ploughing-up of his falha fields. I ran to fetch Moshe, and he and Reuben haggled with the Mukhtar for an hour and a half, plying him with the last of our coffee and sugar, and finally agreed to do the ploughing for ninety piaster per dunum. Moshe and the Mukhtar both swore that they were ruining themselves and that they were only doing it out of pure love for the other, and both were highly satisfied; the Mukhtar because he had already tried to hire the tractor of our dear neighbours of Gan Tamar who had asked ten piasters more per dunum; and Moshe, because he has found a heaven-sent fifteen to twenty pounds ready cash. (Mendl who is going to work the tractor is to collect the cash after each couple of dunums ploughed.)

Anyway, Moshe promised that the crisis will be over by Friday and that on Shabbath we shall have a solid meal including sugared coffee; also an extra issue of pipe tobacco on shopping day. But these rosy prospects did not save me from having to go down to Gan Tamar to borrow some urgently needed items, including petrol for the tractor and two sheets of sole-leather for my shoe-shop. To borrow from Gan Tamar is never a pleasant job—they are eight years old and we only one; they are rich and we are poor; they have three hundred souls and we forty-one; they are patronising and we are arrogant. Besides, we all have a bad conscience for under-cutting them in this tractor business, and on top of it all I had to borrow not only the goods but also a truck of theirs to bring them up, as we have run out of the last drop of petrol.

So I took the donkey, and as I trotted down the wadi I felt like riding to Canossa. This kind of unpleasant mission always seems to fall to my lot; for instance if Moshe has to land a shady credit transaction with the Workers' Bank in Haifa, Reuben usually sends me along to give Moshe moral support by using what he calls "the exotic charm of my gentile streak." It is Reuben's favourite joke.—He hasn't many.

Au fond of course I enjoy this kind of crook-mission; besides, I had to atone for the cello. It is always a change to get away from the old place, and I trotted along the wadi serenely whistling to myself. It was a glorious day, not too hot; last night we had our first rain and everything around, including the sky, looked freshly polished and glistening as after a spring-cleaning. I also like riding a donkey. I like the solid, dusty touch of its hide with its sun-heated dry stiff hair. Sitting on its back one feels one is riding not an animal but a stuffed rocking-horse. I admire the donkey's head-strong pride and self-sufficiency, its complete lack of horsy or doggy sloppiness. If the camel is the ship of the desert, the donkey is a rowing boat: the oars are one's legs. I have seen Arabs on donkeys doing with their legs seventy-five strokes a minute. Our Garbo is a perfect specimen; if one stops rowing her she comes to a standstill at once. For all her unsentimentality she has the gluey, long-lashed eyes of her namesake.

In Gan Tamar I found another guest-donkey tied to the post in front of the Secretariat, but this one was a fat white and solemn animal which made our hide-bound Garbo look like Cinderella. On entering the Secretariat I learned that it belonged to old Rabbi Greenfeld who had come on his bi-annual visit, complete with *khupah* and other sacred paraphernalia to marry those willing to undergo the ceremony. Thanks to this circumstance I found Felix in one of his mellower moods (he had obviously not yet heard of our shady transaction with the Mukhtar). His awe-inspiring glasses lay in front of him on the table, and his suddenly defenceless eyes made me feel almost mean for swindling the leather and petrol out of him which God alone knows when they will get back. But after all, they are rich and we are poor (they have just bought polished hardwood tables for their dining-hall with chairs instead of forms!). Felix granted, with a sourish smile, all my requests, and then suggested that we should go and see the "monkey-business" which was just being transacted in front of the dining-hall. On our way he apologetically referred to the fact that of course the couples only submitted to the "monkey-business" when a child was born or on the way, as the handicap of illegitimate birth would be "dialectically unfair" to the offspring in this prejudice-ridden world. At the entrance to the dining-hut we found old Rabbi Greenfeld officiating in front of a couple who stood in their working clothes under the *khupah,* the ritual canopy. Its four poles were held up by four boys in khaki shorts and cartwheel hats of straw with ragged fringes. It looked like a scene from a comic opera and they were all frankly grinning. The old Rabbi did his best not to notice it, burying his nose in his prayer-book. As I looked closer, I saw that the bride was fat Peninah who has been happily married for years and has three children; Samuel, her husband, stood next to me among the spectators, grinning. Seeing my surprise he whispered:

"Hallo, Joseph. The real bride is eight months gone and didn't want to hurt old Greenfeld's feelings, so my Peninah is deputising for her. She's done it three times in the last two years. Old Greenfeld's short-sighted and Peninah loves to get married."

With some difficulty the bridegroom got the ring halfway up Peninah's fat finger, and the ceremony was over. The next couple was already waiting. Before they walked under the canopy Peninah and the bridegroom discreetly passed the wedding ring on to them; they have only one in Gan Tamar which has to serve for all.

I like old Greenfeld, so when it was all over I went up to shake hands with him. He looked at me over his gold-rimmed spectacles, trying to place me in his memory. I told him I was the cobbler from Ezra's Tower, and he said:

"Oh yes, yes—the new ones. A hard life up there, a hard life. *Nu,* how are things?"

I told him there were three couples who wanted to get married. He took out his grimy pocket-book, licked his thumb, turned the pages forward and back, and said that according to his schedule he was to visit us in about three weeks' time. At that moment Felix came up to me to say that if I wanted to go the truck was ready for me. "What, what?" said old Greenfeld, "you are going in the automobile, young man? Then I will come with you at once, it will save me a journey on the donkey and it will rest my piles."

So we set out for home, I driving the truck and old Greenfeld sitting beside me with an air of bliss and reading his Bible in spite of the bumps, while the *khupah* and other paraphernalia were stowed with the petrol and my precious leather sheets. In my hurry—for Felix wanted the truck returned before the night—I had forgotten to borrow their wedding ring as we had done on previous occasions; and on top of it I remembered that one of our prospective bridegrooms was in hospital with dysentery. That didn't matter much as we could find a deputy (the only thing that mattered was old Greenfeld's seal on the marriage licence); but the ring was rather embarrassing. So I coughed and told the Rabbi that as we had not counted on his visit so soon we had not yet bought the rings. He put the Bible down and looked at me over his glasses; he has little red veins in his eyes and yellow nicotine-stains in his beard. "I can sell you some rings," he said. He fumbled in the pocket of his black silk kaftan and produced three rings. He held them on the palm of his soft white hand as though on a jeweller's cushion. "Pure eighteen carat gold," he said. "I will sell them to you for a shilling each. After the ceremony I shall buy them back from the young couples for a shilling each. *Nu,* will you make business?"

"This is very kind of you, Rabbi," I said.

"You must give me the three shillings, young man," he said. "It must be transacted properly."

"But I haven't got them. You know that we never carry money—we don't own any, individually."

"*Betakh,*" he said. "Of course. I always forget the ways of you lunatics."

"Moshe, our Treasurer, will pay you for the rings when we arrive," I said.

"We shall see," he said doubtfully, putting the rings away in his pocket. "But don't forget: no money no rings, no rings no wedding." He spoke in earnest, pushed his glasses down and reverted to his Bible. Old Greenfeld lives in a world petrified into symbols and make-believe; but the rules of the make-believe have to be strictly adhered to. For the last two thousand years the believers left their doors open on Passover-eve for Messiah to walk in, and laid a cover for him to partake of their meal, and assured each other that "next year we shall celebrate in Jerusalem". They also sold all their plates and cutlery which had been in touch with leaven to their gentile neighbours, and bought them back when the festival of the unleavened bread was over. It was all make-believe, but this stubborn ritual alone held them together during the centuries of dispersion. There was cunning behind this naïveté and shrewdness behind their mysticism;—I wondered whether old Greenfeld was really so unaware of the farcicality of these marriage ceremonies as he pretended to be.

As if he had followed the trend of my thought, he suddenly turned to me:

"You speak the Tongue very fluently," he said.

"You know that we speak nothing else among ourselves," I said. (Old Greenfeld's Hebrew is fluent too, but he speaks in the traditional sing-song voice of the prayer; he sounds like a

Catholic priest alighting from Wells' Time Machine in the Roman Suburra on a market day, addressing the fish-wives in Church Latin).

"But what is the good of the language if you do not read the Book?" he said. "Do you know for example what Rabbi Eliezer of Safet said with reference to Jochanan the Cobbler?"

I confessed that I didn't, while watching the bumps on the road, for we were just turning into the wadi.

"Oi," cried old Greenfeld, shaken by a jolt and adjusting his fur-rimmed hat. "Drive slowly, what is the hurry? We shall arrive in time, blessed be the Name. . . . Now about Rabbi Eliezer of Safet. Whenever his way led him past the shop of Jochanan the Cobbler, he used to go in and read to him the day's chapter from the Book. Jochanan was highly pleased and honoured, though he couldn't hear a word as it had pleased the Lord to create him stone-deaf. So some of his disciples asked Rabbi Eliezer about this matter. And Rabbi Eliezer said: 'There is of course a difference whether he can hear or not, but it is a small difference. The sacrament of the Name acts upon the person even if he is unaware of it.' . . ." He looked at me with his red-veined eyes from under the brim of his fur hat. "*Nu*, does this story convey a meaning to you?"

I smiled and nodded, keeping my eyes on the road.

"Then come and visit me when you come to Safet. I live in the house next to the Synagogue of the Ari. Have you been in Safet before?"

"No, but I always wanted to go."

"Shame upon you," said the Rabbi. "There he lives for I don't know how many years in the Land and has not been to Safet. It is like living in an attic and having never been to the cellar."

In a way old Greenfeld is right. It is a shame never to have seen the cradle of Hebrew mysticism and poetry, the town of the mediaeval kabbalists and centre of Hebraism after the exodus from Spain. I promised old Greenfeld to visit him in Safet.

"From what country do you come?"

"From England."

"England? Very few come from England," he said. "What made you come?"

I gave an evasive answer and he pushed his glasses up to look at me.

"*Nu,* come, come, tell me," he said impatiently. "It is written: who can withhold himself from speaking?"

And suddenly I was itching to tell old Greenfeld about the Incident. "I am waiting," he said peremptorily.

So I told him the whole thing, choosing my words as tactfully as I could. Old Greenfeld shook his head meditatively.

"Oi, the stories one hears from you young people," he said. "You want to tell me that you left everything because of this stupid woman?" he asked with a sly twinkle in his eye.

"Oh, not because of her. But it was a kind of shock, you know. From that moment I saw everything in a different light."

"I understand, you must not talk so much," old Greenfeld cried excitedly. "His tongue is like a ready pen but he understands nothing."

"I don't often tell this story, you know."

"I know, I know. You are frightened that the other heathens will laugh at you, instead of praising the Name for Its cunning ways to teach a fool a lesson. And what is the lesson?"

"I don't know."

"Then let old Greenfeld tell you. Because you were a traitor in disguise, He showed you up in the nakedness of your flesh. . . ."

He pushed his glasses down again and turned back to his Bible, with an air of having settled the matter definitely and to everybody's satisfaction.

The arrival home with truck, rabbi, petrol and *khupah* was a triumph. Everything went smoothly. We bought the rings and married all three couples with Max deputising for the bridegroom with dysentery, and sold the rings back to old Greenfeld, and fed him on onions and noodles which he took quite nicely. Then I drove him to Gan Tamar and came back rowing Garbo.

It was a highly enjoyable day. In the evening I took Ellen out into the fields.

Wednesday

The annual meeting is over and I was not even lynched. I was saved by the news that we are going to receive a new batch of 30-40 people next month, and that within a year or so we are going to be brought up to our full establishment of 200 adults. The new wave of persecution in Central Europe has led to a speeding-up of the programme; all Communes are to be brought in the quickest time to their maximum absorptive capacity, according to the amount of land they hold.

This means that we are getting credits for urgent building and investments, and that the whole budget for the next year is changed. Most of the building programme is laid down according to the standard plans of the Fund, so that our opposition, led by Max and Sarah, had not much to argue about. Their opportunity came with the non-specific items of "general improvements" and "miscellaneous" (the latter including the so-called luxury budget). Having said all there was to be said about the wretched cello ("Joseph fiddles while Rome burns"), Max brought in a resolution according to which all not specifically allocated sums should be spent to the last penny on the Children's House. This was the signal for starting one more of the interminable debates about the children which have been going on in all Communes for the last twenty years. Everybody agrees that the children are the most important "produce" of the Communes and that their care and education should come before everything else. Accordingly the first stone or concrete building in any Commune is the Children's House; the second is usually the cowshed. The children first; then the cattle; then the workers, is the fundamental principle, the iron hierarchy of priorities according to which all our settlements are built. Even in a new pariah-settlement like ours, with up to now only five children, the Children's House is a little marvel of luxury, with tiled shower-baths and lavatories, and a separate kitchen, while the majority of the adult workers still live in wooden block-huts—icy in winter, baking-hot in summer—and some even in tents. We bring up our children like princes, while their elders live like pigs. It is one of the unhealthy extremes to which semitic intensity crossed with Left radicalism is so inclined. The new generation is becoming a fetish, the old one is mere "manure for the future" as they used to put it in the early puritan days of the Russian Revolution. Result: the high illness-rate among the adults, and the frequency of physical and mental crack-ups.

Another paradoxical result of communal upbringing is that, instead of eliminating, it increases the parents' sentimental addiction to their offspring which I always found one of the most tiresome attributes of our race. The children live in the House almost from birth, which means that they are brought up by trained nurses instead of untrained dilettanti (parenthood, the most responsible job in society, is the only one for which no licence is required). Our system has the further advantage of freeing both parents for work during the day, guaranteeing them uninterrupted sleep at night, and protecting the infant against old papa Oedipus and other plagues. I believe our children grow up in better physical and mental health than others, and the parents are even more devoted to them than in the normal family. As soon as they knock off work they rush to the Children's House, and from five o'clock until dinner-time one sees in all settlements nothing but proud parents taking their little angels for a walk. Most people find this charming, I think it is a bore; but then, I have always liked or disliked children according to their personality and not as a separate kind of species as most people seem to do.

The discussion ended after midnight because of general exhaustion. A few, as usual, were asleep, others dozing. But we all would rather sleep through a whole meeting than be for a minute absent from it; and rather lose a finger than the right to vote on the question of where the next chicken-house should be built.

Thursday

The night-job didn't progress to-night; the snoring of Max, with whom I share a room, suddenly began to irritate me. I gave it up. I went out of the hut and over to Ellen's room. But Ellen was already asleep; and as Dasha, with whom she shares the room, was also there, nothing could be done about it. In a sense I was quite glad, for I had caught a peculiar look of Ellen's during old Greenfeld's performance, and I was in no mood to-night for explanations and "talking-things-over".

I strolled across the Square in the dark. The tower at night always looks enormous against the stars: a friendly colossus watching over us. The searchlight has not been on for the last two months, since things have quietened down in our district. I walked up to the northern fence. All was silence and majesty in the great starry illumination. After a while Herman, one of our two Auxiliaries, walked quietly up to me and offered me a cigarette. He looked picturesque with his rifle and Bersaglieri hat; but he complained about the boredom of being tied down here where there hadn't been a raid for almost three months, while his colleagues in Wingate's Special Night Squads were having a great time hunting down Arab terrorists. He spoke with admiration of Wingate whose name is quickly becoming a legend throughout the country—a kind of Lawrence of the Hebrews. He explained to me in some detail the tactics of the counter-ambush which Wingate invented, with apparently unarmed working parties serving as decoy. I thought it must take some guts to act as a decoy, but since our heroic period is over, playing at war has lost its attraction for me. And even while it lasted and we had two to three raids every week and random sniping almost every night, it had soon all become a tedious routine and the main worry was lack of sleep. (For all that we have killed about thirty terrorists and injured a lot more, according to the police reports and the blood-tracks we used to find the following morning. But the corpses had always vanished as the Arabs invariably carried them away.)

How quickly one forgets if the present is absorbing and each day brings new excitements and fulfilments. But to start the bloody game all over again would be rather trying.

I left poor Herman to his martial frustrations and strolled back towards the Children's House. It is a pleasant white cubic concrete block with the beginnings of a garden in front. I looked in through the mosquito-grating of the open window of the nursery, and saw in the faint blue light of the night lamp the three toddlers deeply absorbed in the business of sleeping. One of them lay with its face to the window, its mouth half-open and its clenched fist curiously sticking up in the air, in a miniature anti-fascist salute.

I wandered on, across the Square, to the cowshed. It is also made of concrete and our main pride after the Children's House. For some reason the electric light is left on all night. The brightly illuminated interior with its two rows of sleeping beasts on both sides of the concrete gangway has something stage-like and enchanting. One black cow, name of Tirza, who is due to calve to-morrow, was standing upright alone among her sleeping neighbours. From under her tail the foetal bag was already hanging down—a clean, membranous globe filled with transparent liquid and suspended on what looked a thin tubular thread. She turned her head as I walked in at the end of the passage and followed me with her eyes as I came closer. I always think a cow's eyes have a particularly soft look before she calves, but it may be imagination. I rubbed her with my knuckles on her bony forehead and she pressed her head against my fist; and then I suddenly remembered the wretched tragedy of our cowshed. We cross Syrian cows with Dutch bulls, as this gives the best results in our climate. But as the Dutch race is bigger than the Syrian, the head of the foetus frequently gets stuck; and as there is as yet no technique for performing the Caesarean on cattle, one has in such cases to kill the cow in order to save the calf. At one of our weekly meetings Sarah actually made a hysterical fuss about it, accusing us of premeditated murder and bringing in Tolstoy, Buddha and the Bible. But we have to get through with the wretched business, and once we have our crossbreed established it won't have to be done again. However, as Tirza looked at me with her soft, sloppy eyes, rubbing her head trustingly against my knuckles, I felt rather like Raskolnikow. I also wondered whether Tirza had a premonition in her cloudy and floating inward awareness that she was going to die. Then her neighbour woke with a low, dumb moo, and the spell broke. I gave Tirza a pat and walked out of the shed.

In the Dining Hut the string quartet was rehearsing a movement of Beethoven. I listened for a while, then went back to my room in a pacified mood. My restlessness seemed to have evaporated in the cool night air. Max had turned with his face to the wall and had stopped snoring. I felt that my taste for the night job had returned and put about three hundred words of Pepys into Hebrew, complete with footnotes and annotations. Seventeenth Century English lends itself admirably to translation into biblical language. Turns of phrases presented themselves, bowing like willing brides. I read over the last chapter, very pleased with myself; smoked my last cigarette (until the next weekly issue to-morrow afternoon); *w'az la'mittà*—and so to bed.

Shabbath

Old David, the truck-driver of the milk-cooperative who often drops in to my workshop for a chat, brought yesterday the first news that Bauman has split the *Haganah*. He has walked out of it with about three thousand of his followers and a considerable amount of illegal arms, and has gone over to the extremists. Old David who is himself a member of the Regional Command of the *Haganah* was stammering with indignation. "Just imagine," he shouted at me, "to join those hooligans, those fascist cut-throats who walk about throwing bombs into Arab market-places, killing women and children. And Bauman of all people!" But he didn't know any details.

I am still unable to understand what happened. If the split had been caused by some romantic hothead, it would be just another episode in our internal quarrels. But Bauman is one of the most balanced and responsible fellows I know. He has grown up in the traditions of Austrian Social-Democracy and is a Socialist to his bones, by instinct and conviction. If he has decided to throw in his lot with Jabotinski's right-wing extremists, then the situation must be more critical than we in our isolation know. After all we live here on an island—Ezra's Ivory Tower. I haven't been to Jerusalem or Tel Aviv for more than a year. And we are so absorbed in our problems that we lost contact with reality. The egotism of a collective is no less narrowing than the individual's.

I became quite excited and alarmed. *Aux armes, citoyens!* The only person here with whom one can talk about these things is Simeon, so I left my shop in the middle of the working hours and went out to see him. He was in the tree-nursery, planting a row of saplings. That is *his* passion. He did not see me coming and I watched him. He was absorbed in his work. He knelt with his back to me, patting with his hands the hole into which the sapling was to go. He closed one eye, gauging whether the centre of the hole was exactly in line with the row. His violent, unhappy profile was softened up; it had the self-abandon of a child muttering to himself in play. He put the sapling in and heaped the earth round it with his fingers; then he remained looking at it quite still on his knees. When he noticed me standing a few steps behind him, he blushed; I had violated the chastity of his passion.

It is curious how most of us develop our specific passions here. They are not hobbies, for they are directly connected with the job. There is Dasha with her vitamin-and-calory mania running the kitchen; there is Arieh who is so intimate with his sheep that I suspect him of committing sodomy in the true bucolic tradition; there is Dina with her Children's House, and Moshe, our Communal Shylock. This fusing of job and hobby among the more skilled workers is partly of course a consequence of the freer choice of occupation which the Commune provides compared with town life or individual farming. But only partly. There is an additional something in Simeon's relationship to the trees or Dina's to the children who are not hers. It has to do with a new kind of possessive, proprietary feeling which the Commune breeds. I feel it in myself, but it is difficult to express. Last Shabbath, when we came back after the concert from Gan Tamar, this sensation was particularly vivid. As we turned late at night from the wadi into the dirt-track leading up to the Place, I remembered our first night here, my journey with Dina and Simeon on top of the swaying truck; and how we built that dirt-track at dawn, sweating and full of vague fears—I seemed to remember the imprint of each stone we cleared from the path. It was my path, more intimately mine than anything I ever possessed, wrist-watch or cigarette-case. And it is more mine because this mineness is shared by Dina and Simeon whose memories echo my own; for after all the feeling of possessiveness towards an object is the reflection of the memories it represents; its value is crystallised memory. And the same applies to the Tower which we all saw going up into the air like a dead colossus coming to life, and to every building we built, to every engine and tool and head of cattle we bought. This intimate feeling of possession is common to all peasants, but in our case there is more to it. Take an individual farmer who has built up his small farm with his wife. The value of each shed they have built is enhanced for him by sharing it with her, because he shares his memories with her, because there is more crystallised memory in it. When she dies he feels impoverished—a partnership of memories has been dissolved. The Commune is a great, dense, tight-woven partnership of memories. Thus by sharing everything in the Place with all the others, my feeling of mineness is not diminished but increased—and this is not a theoretical deduction but the analysis of an intimate experience. It could also be applied to analyse patriotic emotions—but the Race and Nation are more heterogeneous and diffuse bodies than the Commune.

Later

I am digressing as usual; though this time it might be an unconscious evasion of the issues which arose in my talk with Simeon. I said that he blushed when he became aware of my presence. He got to his feet and brushed the dust from the knees of his canvas trousers. His tidiness is fantastic. He never wears shorts and his trousers, though faded and patched like those of the rest of us, are meticulously clean and even have a hint of creases—he probably puts them under his mattress at night.

I told him the news old David had brought, though by now it seemed to me rather pointless that I had specially come to talk to him about it in the middle of working hours. There is always a certain embarrassment in the air when one talks alone with Simeon. His gaze has a thrusting and aggressive quality; he doesn't seem to know what to do with his eyes while he talks, like an adolescent with his awkward hands; one gets the impression that he would like to put his eyes into his pockets. Then, after a minute or so, his gaze gets suddenly locked with one's own and there results the same curious awkwardness as when two strangers get stuck with their glances in a tram-car or lift.

"I know," he said when I had finished speaking, "I have kept in touch with Bauman."

This was news to me; and yet I had expected that Simeon would know more than anybody about this business. I also remembered the scene on our first night when Simeon was preaching terrorism and Bauman's curiously dry voice when, asked his opinion, he had said: "I agree with Simeon."

"Then will you tell me what prompted Bauman to his decision?" I asked.

Simeon paused for a moment, then he said:

"How seriously are you interested in this business?"

"I think we are all equally interested," I said.

"No," he said slowly. "The majority are blind and dumb. They cultivate our little collective garden and close their eyes to reality."

"You were quite happy cultivating your little trees when I came," I said. I had become aggressive because already I was on the defensive, because already I knew what was coming; and wanted to escape it; and still want to escape it. But Simeon was no longer embarrassed by my having surprised him off his guard; he said with a kind of sadness:

"It won't be for long. . . ." He looked at his row of saplings and said bitterly:

"In two, three years there will be the beginnings of a forest. . . ."

"Will you talk to me straight, or not?" I said.

This was when the awkwardness happened and our eyes got stuck. But I was wrong in comparing it to the accidental embarrassment that occurs in a lift; there is nothing accidental about the stark black directness of Simeon's gaze. It is impossible not to avert one's eyes when confronted with such nudity of expression; and Simeon knows it and that's why he tries to put his eyes into his pocket. He seemed to measure the degree of my reliability but there was not much need for it—in Ezra's Tower everybody knows everything about everybody.

"If you want to talk, let's sit down for a minute," said Simeon. (I am slightly taller than Simeon and he doesn't like to talk uphill.) We sat down, Simeon jerking up his trousers between thumb and forefinger. He came at once to the point.

"The English are preparing to sell out on us. They have practically stopped immigration already, and shortly they are going to stop it altogether and for good. In Germany the night of the long knives has begun; our people stand lined up facing a bolted door while the knife penetrates inch by inch into their backs. Most of us here have relations among them; and what are we doing about it?—arguing about Russia and cultivating our little gardens."

He spoke quietly, only his hands were rubbing his knee as if trying to soothe a rheumatic pain.

"*Tov,*" he went on. "That is what the closing of the gates means to those outside the walls. To us, who are inside, it means that we are caught in a death-trap. We are to-day in minority of one to three, and the Arab birth-rate is about twice as high as ours. Cut off from the outside world our small community will become a stagnant pool, will have to adjust its living standards to the native level, become levantinised, submerged in the Arab sea. We came on the solemn promise that this would be our national home, and find ourselves sentenced to live in an oriental ghetto and finally to be wiped out, as the Armenians were. . . ."

He suddenly turned his embarrassing eyes on me, full beam. "Do you think I exaggerate?" he asked.

"No," I said. "Provided that they really intend to stop further immigration and to sell out on us, of which I am not yet convinced."

"They do. Look how they sold out on the Czechs."

"That's different. Germany is a real threat, while the Arabs are not."

"They'll do it nevertheless."

"How do you know with such certainty?"

"We have our information."

"Who is 'we'?"

"About that we may talk another time—perhaps."

We sat in the hot sun, side by side. On the slope opposite us, about half a mile away, Arieh was grazing his sheep; in the clear, transparent air we could see him lying on his back, his hat pulled over his face. Simeon was chewing a blade of dry grass and I was doing the same. I felt no emotion, only the dull awareness of some fatality slowly, smoothly, inescapably closing in on me.

"So now," I said, "assuming that your political weather forecast is correct, what will Bauman and his people do?"

"Fight."

"Whom? How? With what?"

Simeon repeated his previous phrase:

"About that we may talk another time."

"What are you waiting for?"

"For things to ripen inside you."

"How will you know when I am 'ripe'?" I asked.

"You will come to me," he answered with such simple, complete conviction that I had nothing more to say.

Monday

Tirza had to be killed; the calf is all right, wobbling on its thin legs. It's a heifer; we have called it Electra.

Dina is in hospital with sand-fly fever and won't be back for another fortnight.

Tuesday

Old Greenfeld's show has done something to our girls. It isn't exactly the mystic force of the Name working on the deaf, but something more prosaic and earthbound; a stirring of ingrained tradition which they thought they had overcome. They don't talk about it, but if one has lived for years in an intimate community, one feels the slightest changes in the atmosphere. Some of them walk about with a definitely wistful look, which came into their eyes while watching the performance under the faded velvet canopy and hasn't left them since. It will pass after a few days as it did after old Greenfeld's last visit, but for the moment the air is full of the stale ghosts of the past.

When, during the noon-break to-day, Ellen came into my workshop, I knew that the hour of "talking things over" had struck. Her eyes bore that expression of dull hurt and reproach which has lately become a permanent feature with her. And yet it had all started in such a nice, enlightened and businesslike manner. No nonsense about love—no—agreed. Sympathy —yes—moderate, agreed. Mutual need, give and take, agreed. No obligations, no entries on the credit or debit columns, quits. The perfect barter system on the Schacht model. Christ, were we enlightened.

She lingered and loitered and hovered round the shop and finally leant with her back against my working bench, and with each moment the shop became more saturated with the silent reproach of the wounded but proud female who keeps her sufferings to herself, yes, all to herself—unless of course you press the button which opens the sluices and drowns you in the rushing cataract; but then it was you who started it, was it not? On the other hand if you refrain from pressing the button you are an insensitive brute, and the silent reproach will increase in tension until your nerves vibrate like a chord. I decided to be a brute and to avoid touching off anything. "How is the veg-garden?" I asked, hammering away on the boot in hand.

"All right," she said, but her tone signified "so what?" Ellen works in the veg-garden. She is a good and conscientious worker, held in high esteem by the community, which all goes to make me feel the more a cad. For it must be admitted that the situation is, according to our standards, irregular. The regular and simple procedure would be to inform the Secretariat of our decision to share a room together. There would be a congratulatory party, Moshe would have to fork out twenty piasters for three bottles of wine and a cake, and everything would be all right. Old Greenfeld would not have to appear on the scene unless and until a child was on the way; and theoretically each of us could break up the union and move back to bachelor quarters at any time and without giving any reasons; the children, if any, would go on living in the Children's House as before, and there would be no financial or other obligations whatsoever.

Yes, theoretically. But in practice . . .

"Joseph," said Ellen.

"Yes?"

"What is the matter with you?"

"With me?"

"Yes."

"Nothing is the matter with me."

"Really?"

"Really."

Stage dialogue between two enlightened people living in a communistic society. . . . I began to sweat with the effort to remain a brute and not to touch the button. In the hard light of the noonday Ellen looked hefty, robust and sexless like any farm-wench at work. She had come in straight from the veg-garden on her way to the showers. In moonlight, the fragrance of a girl's armpits is an aphrodisiac; in the morning it is a deterrent. Particularly when mixed with the smell of cobbler's glue. But then I also knew that if I brought this thing with Ellen to an end, within three days I would start running about like a rat poisoned with sex hormones. There is no escape from the feminine blackmail. Of course if I refused to be blackmailed Ellen would suffer the same privation. But the essential difference is that a sex-starved woman is compensated by a feeling of virtue and moral satisfaction, while the sex-starved male feels in addition ridiculous and humiliated. . . .

Oh, the specious over-simplifications of enlightened theorists! Papa Marx and Uncle Engels made fun of the bourgeois family, but had nothing to propose instead; as for the Russians, they have established a code of Proletarian Morality compared to which our Victorian grandparents were wild libertines.

"Joseph . . ."

"Yes?"

"I would like to talk things over with you. . . ."

Bang! There we go; there was no escape. And Ellen had started biting her nails—the short, square nails of a competent veg-gardener and responsible comrade. Well then, if we must have it out, let's have it out; I put the shoe down and gave up pretending.

"*Tov,*" I said. "We will talk it over on condition that you stop biting your nails."

She suddenly burst into tears.

"Why are you so beastly to me? At the beginning you were quite different."

The trite stereotypy of the scene made me indeed feel beastly. It is another kind of chess: King's pawn four, Queen's pawn four—helpless, I knew beforehand the answer to everything she or I might say.

" 'The present pleasure,' " I quoted, " 'by revolution lowering, does become the opposite of itself.' "

"What's that?" Ellen asked, interrupting her snivels.

" 'Antony and Cleopatra,' my own translation. In the English original it doesn't sound much better either."

"Oh please, Joseph, don't mock me," she said, starting once more to bite her nails and crying helplessly.

And there it was—pity, the poisonous adhesive plaster, which one can't tear off without plucking one's own skin.

"I am not mocking," I said. "The translation comes in by right. It is my night-job and half of my life. If we lived together in one room I couldn't work."

"But why? If you can work with Max there, why not with me?"

"Max doesn't mind my leaving the light on and trampling up and down the room and going for a walk in the middle of the night; he turns to the wall and snores. But you wouldn't be able to sleep, and knowing that I am disturbing you, I couldn't work."

I knew it sounded a laboured excuse though it was true; but only half the truth. The other half—that Max's presence in the room was a neutral one whereas hers would be a constant impingement, a saturation of the room's space which would make all privacy and work impossible; that, in short, I wanted at intervals the amenities of her body but not her constant company—how on earth could one say this without horribly wounding a fellow-creature whom one likes and respects? So this "talking-things-over" must always remain a farce. Our enlightened three-quarter truths are sometimes worse than the Victorian half-truth. They frankly oppressed the flesh by the tyranny of sacramental consent; we grant it a certain autonomy but are still far from recognising its full, sovereign right of independence. And it is easier to rebel against tyranny than against an unctuous, hypocritically liberal compromise. It would be easier for me to refuse to marry Ellen if she were a conventional middle-class prude, than to deny her claims on intimate companionship beyond the purely sexual.

Ellen was sobbing and biting her nails in complete misery. "I promise I won't disturb you," she sobbed. It was a promise as futile as humiliating to make; and this self-abasement of a proud and strapping girl made me ache inside and made the adhesive poison the more effective.

"Why," I asked in despair, "why do you insist on a thing which we both know won't work?" But I knew that my arguments made no difference; and suddenly I had a suspicion.

"Or are you going to have a baby?"

She shook her head, and violently blew her nose.

"Look, Ellen. In the capitalistic world girls want to get married for reasons of prestige and economic security. Among us here there exists no such thing. Even if you have a baby it doesn't make the slightest difference whether we live in one room or not. Our huts are at a distance of twenty yards and we can see each other as often as we like. So why do you torture us both and spoil everything?"

Ellen swallowed hard to control her sobs, and started hiccuping instead. It was pathetic. With a small, timid voice, and looking the other way, she said between two hiccups:

"Don't you ever want to sleep with me—I mean really to sleep, all night, side by side, and wake up in the morning together?"

(That is precisely what I do not want.)

"But darling, of course, I want it very much. But don't you understand? . . ."

"To grant the Crown Colonies of the Flesh full sovereignty and independence, as the Honorable Member for Ezra's Tower proposes, would inevitably lead to chaos and anarchy." —"Hear, hear."

"If we don't like it," Ellen interrupted, "we can always separate again, can't we?"

"The Crown Colonies of the Flesh have, however, the constitutional means to appeal against any alleged infringement of their rights and may be assured that a sympathetic hearing will be given to their case."—"Hear, hear."

"Well, you know, Ellen," I said, "you know as well as I do that it isn't quite so easy to divorce here, although theoretically there is no obstacle. So far we have had only one case, and you remember all that hue and cry about poor Gaby's 'unsocial behaviour' and 'disruptive tendencies' because she got fed up with Max and went to live with Mendl. . . ."

There was a silence; then abruptly Ellen jumped down from the bench. She had realised the futility and humiliating nature of our discussion.

"All right," she said. "Save your arguments. Anyway, I know what, or who, is the cause of it all. . . ."

I knew it too; but I didn't ask her, and she had the decency not to mention Dina. She walked out, slamming the door behind her.

Damn old Greenfeld.

Haven't seen Simeon the whole day.

Wednesday

The Assistant District Commissioner and his wife were here yesterday to pay us their annual visit. This time they came without the Major. Newton seemed to be impressed by what we have made of the Place—which, when he saw it the first time a year ago, was just a fenced-off quadrangle in the desert. He didn't say much, only hummed and hawed in his absent-minded way that makes one think that he is always trying to work out some chess-problem (which he probably is), but nevertheless one could see that he was impressed. We took them over the fields, veg-garden, tree-nursery, laundry, etc. etc., and didn't miss a single chicken to show off with. I suppose he sees much the same thing in all the Settlements; it will take some time until we get accustomed to the idea that our cows and chickens are just like other cows and chickens, and stop boring visitors with our childish pride about each tomato we grow.

Looking across to Kfar Tabiyeh, Newton mentioned that they are going to assist next week at the great peacemaking ceremony which is to end the twenty-year-old blood feud between the families of the two Mukhtars. When I said that several of us are also invited to the ceremony, Mrs. Newton pulled a face as if we had been gate-crashing into the Club at Roonah. She looked more pinched than ever and seemed surprised that we had not been wiped out by the Arabs, and were still alive and kicking. According to custom they had lunch with us in the Dining Hut, and as usual the food was poor—onion soup and noodles with gravy. "Is that what you eat every day?" she asked, apparently implying that we had cooked a specially filthy lunch for them on purpose. Had we given them a rich meal she would have remarked afterwards on poor Arabs and guzzling Hebrews. To ease the tension I told them the story of Sir Arthur Wauchope's famous lunch at Khefziba. When Wauchope was appointed High Commissioner of Palestine, he paid a formal visit to Khefziba, one of the oldest Communes in the Valley of Jezreel. It was a rather ceremonious and political occasion, and the Khefziba people gave the new High Commissioner a princely meal. "Do you eat every day like this?" Wauchope asked; whereupon Lederer, the Secretary of Khefziba, said:

"Your Excellency, when we heard about your proposed visit we called a meeting to discuss whether you should eat as we eat every day, or whether we should eat as you eat every day; and we decided to adopt the latter course."

Newton tittered. When we showed them the Children's House, Mrs. Newton said:

"Do you know to whom they belong?—I mean who the fathers are?"

There was a dreadful silence, poor Newton coughing and humming, and then Moshe said with a poker face:

"No, Madame. You know, we draw lots."

"Oh, do you? How interesting," said Mrs. Newton, whereupon several of our girls started to giggle and the unfortunate female went crimson. God, how she must hate us.

Simeon was invisible as long as the visit lasted.

Thursday

Worked all day in the shop, repairing shoes. Without the two sheets of leather from Gan Tamar half the Commune would have to run bare-foot in the coming rains. Repairing shoes is a very gratifying job, almost more so than making new ones. One has the surgeon's satisfaction in healing, without the risks; not even the oldest boot gets internal haemorrhage under my knife. I like the smell of fresh leather and of the glue; I always have to whistle when I drive the tags into a heel—it's a conditioned reflex. The work is never monotonous; there are no boring preliminary stages, as for instance in carpentry preparing the wood with sand-paper. The transformation under my hands of a mud-caked, punctured, twisted, wrinkled relic into a shining, re-born, as-good-as-new boot is quick and exhilarating; I feel like a benevolent magician.

There is no other trade which provides the same intense contentment. A patch on a suit is a blemish; hence repair-tailors are a meek, diffident race with a look of secret guilt in their eyes. Or, if you are a garage-mechanic, you are always liable to come up against some nasty hitch on a job; a big rusty bolt which has got stuck somewhere where you can't get at it with the spanner, or a broken part for which there is no spare at hand. Hence garage-mechanics always look grumpy and reserved, and if asked how long the job will take they answer with wary and depressing you-never-can-tells; whereas I can always tell and have no fear of committing myself. My tags go in like a knife into butter and give me a sensation of effortless power. To cut a fresh leather sheet with a sharp knife following the curved contour of the heel gives me a clean, sensuous pleasure.

Take my opposite number, the hairdresser. He plays about with flimsy and futile embellishments on the top, whereas I provide the indispensable foundations for men walking the earth. Hence the hairdresser is a chatty, scatter-brained figaro, whereas the cobbler appears in all popular lore as a dignified and serene philosopher, full of contentment and benevolence. I can imagine myself at no other permanent manual task; the monotony of digging in a field would drive me crazy in a fortnight. I can't understand that the others don't all covet my job. But then Dasha and Moshe and Mendl and the other maniacs probably feel the same. . . . Why do people babble about the Red Scare, when it stands to reason that in a poor agrarian country nothing but a communal type of organisation can give a man sufficient scope to work only eight hours and to make his hobby his job?

Oh God, why can't I stay as I am? I was a fairly exacting chap, and yet, You see, here I have found peace—or as much peace as I am capable of holding. I have asked for much and yet, You see, I am content with little if given in the right way. I love these hills, and my day-job and my night-job; I am approved of and I approve; I like and am liked. Sometimes, lying on my back in the sun, I whisper the words of the Song: "and his banner over me was love. . . ."

Oh, let me stay as I am. You have twice expelled us from the Land and driven us from Spain and turned us into a race of eternal tramps; and however we try to disguise ourselves they smell us out and hold us up to derision in the nakedness of our flesh; now that the wheel is coming back full circle, with dry blood on each of its spokes, can't You make it stand still at last, at last . . . ?

I seem to be getting hysterical. I thought there was not much selfishness in coming here to live as a cobbler in the barren hills of Galilee; and now according to Simeon it is pure egotism and escape.

I wish Dina were back and I could talk to her.

To-morrow our string quartet will give its first concert. . . .

3

The peace-making ceremony in Kfar Tabiyeh was the most important event of its kind for many years in the district. Preparations for the great reconciliation meal had begun several days beforehand and a number of guests had been invited, among them a party of English people from Jerusalem, which was to include the wife of the Assistant Chief Commissioner, Lady Joyce Gordon-Smith.

The blood feud between the two leading clans of the village, the Hamdans and the Abu Shauish, went back to Turkish days. To keep the balance, the Turkish and later the British rulers had always appointed the most distinguished member of each of the two clans to dual mukhtarship. Fifteen years ago Issa's great-grandfather, Hadj Saade el Hamdan, had been murdered by a member of the Abu Shaouish clan. An *atwa* or truce had been arranged, but the negotiations on the blood-money had broken down, and after biding his time for eight full years, Issa's grandfather had killed the murderer, who had meanwhile been appointed Mukhtar on the Abu Shaouish side.

The reasons why Issa's grandfather had waited so long before he avenged the family's honour were two. First, the murderer was a cautious man, well aware of the constant danger in which he lived, and it was therefore necessary to wait for an opportunity and lay a carefully prepared trap. Secondly, Issa's grandfather had preferred to wait until the murderer had attained the same age and dignity as his victim at the time of his death, to make the act of revenge more impressive and satisfactory. Issa's grandfather enjoyed a wide reputation for his strict observance of tradition and etiquette, and the way he had killed his victim was to this day held up as an example of *savoir-faire* in the whole district. When, at the price of patience and cunning, he had at last succeeded in surprising the Abu Shaouish Mukhtar alone in his sleep, he had knelt down beside him on the mat with his knife in his hand, had shaken him by the shoulder: "Wake up, ya Abu Shaouish, for you have killed my father and the time has come for you to die," and had then cut his throat from ear to ear. He was taken to prison and kept there for a while, but nothing could be proved against him as twenty members of the Hamdan clan solemnly swore that he had spent the critical time in their company, discussing the weather.

That had been seven years ago. Again an *atwa* was arranged which expired three days after the murder, and was extended to three months against payment of fifteen pounds by the Hamdan clan to cover the expenses which the victim's clan had incurred by entertaining mourners, visitors and police. But the second *atwa* also expired, and despite the efforts of the dignitaries, Reformers and professional Arbitrators of the district, it was again found impossible to make the two clans agree on the amount of blood-money to be paid either in camels or cash. A third *atwa* was however arranged, which cost the Hamdans a considerable amount of money and which was to last "until Peace was concluded and forgetfulness obtained". As months and years passed and peace was still not concluded, it became a matter for new dispute whether the *atwa* was still in force or not. Several times during these years members of the two clans had come to blows which led to loss of limbs, teeth and eyes but not to the loss of life, as both families were careful not to complicate the main issue. Meanwhile Issa's father had been appointed Mukhtar in succession to the Old Man, and it was clear to everybody that the Abu Shaouish were merely waiting until he had reached the proper age, renown and wealth to avenge the honour of the family. Best of all knew this the Hamdan Mukhtar himself, and despite the elaborate precautions he took to protect his life he never really felt safe; and what with the additional worries about the Patriots in the mountains and the Hebrews on the Dogs' Hill, he felt like a man walking in the shadow of an evil cloud.

However, some six months ago a new, efficient District Officer had been appointed by the Government, a young man of ambitions named Jussuf Tubashi. This young man had studied at the University of Beyrout, was an admirer of the Roman dictator, and determined to make a career in the Government Service so that later, when the English and the Hebrews were driven out, he might become one of the leaders of the nation on the path from mediaeval backwardness towards the modern corporate state. Tubashi, who was naturally anxious to prevent a stupid murder in his district which would cast a blemish on his career, threw himself with youthful zeal into the task of mediation, and succeeded in a few weeks where the old dignitaries had failed in years: by mixing threats with persuasion, he induced the Abu Shaouish to settle the old feud against a reasonable amount of blood-money, and the Hamdans to pay it. This day was to be the day of his first triumph, and he had seen to it that the peace-making ceremony was given the proper publicity in the Arab Press and the higher circles of Jerusalem Society. When three days ago Mr. Newton, the Assistant District Commissioner, had informed Tubashi, his Junior District Officer, that the wife of Mr. Gordon-Smith, the Assistant Chief Commissioner, would herself be among the guests, Tubashi was convinced that henceforth his career was made.

Lady Joyce Gordon-Smith, who had lived for five years in

the country but had never been at an Arab peace-making before, had gladly availed herself of the opportunity to escape the boredom of Jerusalem by joining a party of Englishmen to Kfar Tabiyeh. She was in her early forties, tall and county-bred with regular features—a Wiltshire Juno as an admirer had once called her—with a preference for tweeds and flat-heeled shoes and a constant look of just-having-come-out-of-the-bath on her cool, aseptic skin. The rest of the party consisted of Cyril Watson, a dark and fidgety young man who lectured on Elizabethan Poetry for the British Council in Jerusalem, and Squadron Leader James Abdul Rahman Henderson who had embraced the Moslem faith, looked like a football professional and worked for Intelligence. There was also a third, elderly Englishman, a retired Lieutenant-Colonel named Wyndham, who did not belong to the party. He had fought during the first world war as a Battalion Commander in the Jewish Legion and had been known as a fierce disciplinarian among his men, who suspected him of an anti-semitic bias. However, as soon as the war was over Wyndham had published a book which was a passionate plea for the resurrection of the Hebrew State based on the prophecies of Isaiah, had retired from the Army and bought a small house on Mount Carmel where he lived alone, doing his own cooking and housework, and known to everybody as "the Colonel". He was rather unpopular among the British Colony because of his pro-Zionist views, and equally unpopular with the Zionist leaders whom he accused of cowardice for not having yet driven out the Arabs and proclaimed the Hebrew State. He was a short, dry and taciturn little man of a pronouncedly military bearing, with a rather fixed stare in his eyes and an aura of loneliness about him.

The Jerusalem party and the Colonel had arrived from different directions but almost at the same time in the morning, and had been directed by District Officer Tubashi to the house of the murderer's family, where according to custom the guests were to assemble. The Hamdan Mukhtar received them on the terrace of his house; he was beaming, and magnificent to look at in his new silver-spun agal. There were also two or three silent old men of the Hamdan clan who were ceremoniously introduced to the newcomers. Issa served sweet black coffee in thimble-cups, lowering his eyes before Lady Joyce Gordon-Smith's somewhat disconcertingly frank Junoesque stare, and they all sat down on the low wicker stools on the balcony. Squadron Leader Abdul Rahman accepted a water pipe and a rosary of yellow beads to play with, and the Mukhtar beamed delightedly. The conversation dragged on, Tubashi translating with great fluency.

Cyril Watson, who could not bear sitting still at parties for more than five minutes, strolled over to the parapet. "What's that village over there?" he asked, pointing with his coffee-cup towards Ezra's Tower. Tubashi translated with a knowing smile, discreetly lowering his voice as if to apologize for the tactless question. "Oh, that is the Hebrew settlement," the Mukhtar said in a non-committal tone.

"I see," said Watson. "Rather spoils the view, doesn't it?"

Tubashi translated with an even more delicate smile. The Mukhtar too smiled, non-committally. "That is as it pleases the Government," he said.

"Ask him where the murderer is," said Lady Joyce. Tubashi translated, reverting to his normal conversational voice.

"Ah, they want me to introduce the murderer to them?" the Mukhtar said, beaming again. He turned to Issa: "Call Abu Arkub, son."

Issa went into the house and returned a moment later with a shrivelled and seedy-looking little man, who remained standing at the door and touched his forehead and heart with an obsequious smile.

"Is that your father?" Lady Joyce asked, staring.

The Mukhtar laughed boisterously. "Oh, Abu Arkub, did you hear that? The lady thinks you are my father. Ha!" The little man smiled sourly. "No," the Mukhtar explained, becoming serious again. "He is my cousin. My father is in his room, slightly ill, and regrets to miss the great pleasure of being introduced to the guests."

Tubashi translated. "I thought somebody said the murderer was his father," said Lady Joyce.

"It has never been proved," Tubashi explained with his delicate smile. "Also, it would be inconvenient for the old gentleman to submit to the rituals of the ceremony. This man is a poor relative of our Mukhtar's and it has been decided that he should be the murderer."

"I see," Lady Joyce said drily. The vicarious murderer, seeing that people had lost interest in him, touched his forehead and withdrew.

"When is the show going to start?" asked Cyril Watson.

"Oh, soon. In an hour or two perhaps."

Watson sighed, wiping his face out of habit though it was not hot. He carried his handkerchief in his sleeve, but most of the time he held it in his hand crushed into a ball. "What's that growing over there?" he asked, looking down into the valley.

"Barley," Tubashi explained. "It is the winter crop coming up."

"And on the field to the right?"

"That is also barley."

"But why is the barley to the right so much higher than the other barley?"

Tubashi translated the question to the Mukhtar. "The barley to the right," he explained, "is grown by the Hebrews. They use fertilisers."

"I see," said Watson. "Why don't you use fertilisers too?"

Tubashi translated and the Mukhtar shrugged with a resigned smile. "We are poor," he said. "This is a very poor village. We even have to hire the tractor of the Hebrews at two pounds and a half per dunum."

"A peppery price, by Mohammed," Abdul Rahman Henderson remarked in Arabic, smoking his water pipe with an impassive face.

The Mukhtar gave no answer, smiling like a long-suffering man who bears his cross with patience.

"That is as it pleases the Government," he said.

"I think you people are having a bloody unfair deal," said Cyril Watson. Tubashi translated; the Mukhtar kept smiling blandly, saying nothing. He stood with his back to the parapet with arms folded, a tall and imposing figure. There was a silence, suddenly interrupted by the Colonel, who up to now had not spoken a word.

"That is all stuff and nonsense," he said sharply. "Ask him whether it is true that when he married his daughter three months ago he had the marriage room papered with pound notes."

Tubashi translated. The Mukhtar beamed.

"We have our customs of hospitality," he said modestly. "A man will ruin himself to do honour to his guests."

"Tell him," said the Colonel, "that one square yard of that wallpaper is enough to buy a tractor and fertilisers for the whole district."

"Ah no, Colonel," Watson intercepted, indignantly kneading his handkerchief. "I object. You can't ask them to change their traditions overnight. Next you will want them to open Woolworth branches and chemist's shops in the desert."

"Or synagogues," the Squadron Leader muttered half aloud, the pipe of the nargileh in the corner of his mouth.

The Colonel looked from one to the other with his parade stare, and subsided into silence.

"What did they say?" the Mukhtar asked Tubashi.

"They are arguing among themselves," Tubashi said, smiling.

"Tell our guests," the Mukhtar said measuredly, "that we are not of those who always bewail their misfortunes in the ears of the world, as certain people do. We have no propaganda offices in the capitals of Europe and no gold to buy newspapers and influential friends. We are a poor, simple and hard-working people who only ask that the earth which belonged to our fathers and fathers' fathers should not be taken away from us."

Tubashi translated with a certain solemnity, and there was another short silence, ended by the arrival of Assistant District Commissioner Newton and his wife. There were more introductions. Mrs. Newton wore a Mickey Mouse brooch, a Coronation scarf with the portrait of the Royal Couple, and a complicated hat which a Jerusalem modiste had copied from a Beyrout fashion paper. "Oh, we have met before," she said in her genteelest accent to Lady Joyce Gordon-Smith. "Have we?" said Lady Joyce. "On the boat," Mrs. Newton said. "Oh," said Lady Joyce, still staring incredulously at the hat, "one always forgets faces from a boat, doesn't one?"

There was more coffee handed round and they all sat or stood about not quite knowing what to do with themselves, in the paralysing atmosphere common to all social functions where the otherwise separate communities mixed. To make the awkwardness complete, Kaplan, the Hebrew District Officer, also turned up with his usual gloomy look. He was a native of the country—his grandfather had been one of the "Lovers of Zion" who, in the middle of the nineteenth century, came on foot from the Russian ghettos to settle in the Land. He was a tough, wiry and bitter man, whom years of struggle against biassed superiors had taught to distrust the government which he served. Between Kaplan and his colleague Tubashi it had been a case of mutual detestation at first sight. With his immediate superior, Mr. Newton, he got on relatively well because he shared the latter's passion for chess; but Mr. Newton resented Kaplan's efficiency, while Kaplan despised Mr. Newton's muddling ways. Besides, Mrs. Newton hated the Hebrew District Officer and had a melting weakness for Tubashi who took her out riding to Arab villages where all were nice to her.

There was another round of coffee. "Heavens," Lady Joyce remarked to Cyril, "I feel all scorched and black inside. Will they never start?"

"You must never refuse a cup—it's a deadly offence," said Cyril, who prided himself on his knowledge of Arab etiquette.

Tubashi, who had overheard Lady Joyce's rather audible remark, whispered something to the Mukhtar, who nodded consent. Tubashi clapped his hands and there was at once an expectant silence.

"Ladies and gentlemen," Tubashi cried, "as the ceremony will not start for a little while yet, our Mukhtar invites you all for a walk to show you the village."

They consented with relief and began descending the steps of the terrace in pairs, Lady Joyce leading the procession with Squadron Leader Henderson, and the Mukhtar with the silent elders of his clan bringing up the rear. Tubashi ran back and forth, explaining things with his obliging dragoman-smile. They followed the one cobbled serpentine road wending its way between the mud huts, with the gutter in the middle. "Would you like to see the interior of a hut?" Tubashi suggested.

The procession came to a halt in front of a small area of two or three square yards, fenced off by a row of stones which were meant to indicate a wall. In the middle of this area, in front of the mud hut, squatted a woman swathed in black, cooking the family dinner. Her cooking utensils were a rusty petrol tin poised on two bricks over a fire of twigs which gave out a thick smoke. She had blue dots tattooed on her forehead and chin and looked sixty, though she was probably not over thirty, to judge by the naked infant whom she had taken from her breast at the approach of the strangers. Three more children of various ages squatted round her on the stony ground charred all over by previous dinner fires. As the procession came to a standstill in front of her she made a move as if to run into the house, but remained sitting on the stones, her eyes cast down, stirring the brew in the petrol tin with a twig.

"What's that she is cooking?" asked Lady Joyce.

Tubashi questioned the woman. She muttered something, without lifting her eyes.

"It is a soup; they make it from a herb. I don't know how it is called in English."

Lady Joyce bent over the tin with its greenish liquid. "Sorrel," she pronounced.

"Yes. It grows everywhere around."

"Is that all they have for dinner?"

Tubashi asked the woman, and repeated the question rather harshly, as she did not answer at once.

"She says there will be bread too."

He led the way into the interior of the mud hut. The hut was a single room without windows. Half of the floor was covered with straw for the donkey which slept there. The other half was empty except for a torn mat on the earth, a big black goat's-hair blanket under which the family slept, and a board supported by two more petrol tins on which lay a few rags and a toothless comb, which made up all the possessions of the family.

"Please ask the Mukhtar what her husband's occupation is," said Cyril Watson when they were outside again, stuffing his handkerchief, which he had held pressed against his mouth, back into his sleeve.

The Mukhtar gave some lengthy explanations.

"He says," translated Tubashi, "that her husband is a railway worker. He has suffered several misfortunes; his roof fell in and he had to pay to have it mended. Also his first wife died a year ago and he had to buy himself a new one."

The Mukhtar added something, smiling contemptuously, and Tubashi translated:

"He says this one is of the cheapest sort—he got her for five pounds."

The woman, with eyes downcast, went on stirring the soup with the twig, her face expressionless as if she were deaf. One of the children began to cry. Its eyes were sticky with the Egyptian disease and flies were crawling over them in clusters. The guests stood looking on in silence. Suddenly the Colonel barked out:

"Ask your Mukhtar why they don't learn from the Jews how to co-operate."

Tubashi translated, his face impassive. The Mukhtar answered in a measured, polite voice. Tubashi translated:

"He says that they believe in the will of God and that they don't believe in socialism."

The procession moved on. They visited a second hut which looked a little more prosperous: there was a wooden partition separating the donkey from the family, and also separate mats for the children. In a corner sat a very old woman; the Mukhtar addressed some jocular remarks to her which she answered with a rapid torrent of words.

"They think she is a witch," Tubashi explained. "People here are still very superstitious. She sells marriage charms to young men before the wedding."

"What do they need charms for once they have secured the bride?" asked Lady Joyce.

"Oh—they are marriage charms, not love charms," Tubashi said elusively, with some embarrassment.

"I know what he means," said Cyril to Mrs. Newton as they walked on. "They are charms against impotence. You wouldn't believe how many of these village lads are impotent on their bridal night. It's perfectly frightful. A Jewish doctor in Tiberias told me about it. Sometimes several months pass before the marriage is consummated. It's of course because all these lads have to remain virgins until they can marry, and besides there is that most embarrassing ceremony when the mother rushes into the bridal chamber to fetch the sheet with the proofs of her daughter's honour with the whole village waiting outside, you know what I mean. It's perfectly disgusting, and of course any man would be impotent under the circumstances."

Mrs. Newton had turned first pink, then crimson, which Cyril didn't notice as he rarely looked at the person to whom he was talking. He chattered on, glad to show off his knowledge of Arab ways.

"There is also lots of homosexuality among them of course. As they have to wait for years until they have the money to buy a wife it's only natural. And their women aren't so very attractive, or are they? They are sometimes quite frank about it. You can often see pairs of good-looking lads walking along the road holding hands, or with their little fingers interlocked. In a way it's quite charming, sort of bucolic, if you see what I mean. And there is quite a lot of sodomy, too, of course. Most of their jokes are about sheep and nanny-goats and so on. . . ."

"Mr. Watson," cried poor Mrs. Newton, gasping. "I must ask you to stop at once. Nobody has ever dared to speak to me of such improper things."

Cyril looked at her flabbergasted, and his dark, restless eyes fastened for a second on the Mickey Mouse brooch and Coronation scarf. "Oh, I am frightfully sorry," he mumbled. "I didn't mean to. . . . It's only sort of—I mean folklore and all that, you know. . . ."

He gave it up, wiping his face with his handkerchief. Mrs. Newton walked on with lips compressed in silence, holding her chin up. While Watson was speaking she had kept looking back at her husband, with the idea of asking him to protect her outraged honour, but Mr. Newton had looked as usual hopelessly pacific and absent-minded. He was walking with Kaplan, to whom he had just remarked:

"I've now played through all the games but three of the New York tournament, and I am more and more inclined to believe that the Indian opening is just a mode which won't last."

"No," said Kaplan with his usual grimness of tone. "It is not just a mode, it is a new step in the evolution of the game. It's manœuvring under cover for position, which replaces the cavalry style of the old-fashioned King's pawn openings, just as in soccer the strategy of the low pass replaced the old kick-and-run technique. In both cases it is planned, co-ordinated, collective action succeeding to individual bravado. The style of all games is influenced by changes in the pattern of social life."

"I must think about that," said Mr. Newton. "You may have hit upon something there. . . ." He was, as usual, both impressed by, and resentful of, his District Officer's tiresome cleverness.

They came to a large open space at the lower end of the village. At the further side of it great activities were going on; women were busy round three open fires over which three whole sheep were suspended on spits, while two long deal boards on trestles, with a few wicker stools for the European guests, were being prepared as a banqueting-table. The smoke of the burning twigs mixed with the fragrance of slightly charred meat and burning herbs, and made everybody's mouth water.

"Doesn't it smell heavenly!" said Cyril. The Jerusalem party had been travelling since early morning, and now it was two hours past lunch-time. They all looked wistfully towards the other end of the open space.

"They are preparing the peace-making meal," Tubashi explained genially. "According to tradition it is the victim's family who prepares it and the murderer's family who pays for it."

"Let's go and watch how they do the sheep," proposed Lady Joyce.

"I am sorry, we cannot go to that part of the village before peace is officially made," said Tubashi. "Over there is where the Abu Shaouish live. We can't cross this space before the end of the ceremony. But our Mukhtar invites us to go back to his house and have some coffee."

With a sigh of resignation they turned back towards the Mukhtar's house. The Mukhtar pointed at a small, whitewashed stone building in the forbidden part of the village, out of which flocked a crowd of barefooted little boys. They were all in rags and had close-cropped hair, which made their brown heads look like billiard balls.

"That is the school," Tubashi translated the Mukhtar's explanations. "All little boys go there up to the age of twelve."

"He means ten," remarked Kaplan.

"All right, ten, Mr. Kaplan," said Tubashi with his imperturbable smile. "This is of course a very poor village. They cannot yet afford to give much education."

"Nonsense," the Colonel suddenly rapped out after having been silent for the last half-hour. "It's the Government who pays, and if the village would add its share they could have a proper school."

"Now look, Colonel, we are their guests, or aren't we?" muttered Cyril.

"Where's the girls' school?" asked Lady Joyce.

Tubashi translated, and for the first time he looked a little embarrassed.

"He says it is against tradition to send girls to school. . . . But this is of course a very backward village," he added in an aside. "Soon . . ."

". . . And a jolly sensible idea it is," the Squadron Leader muttered through his pipe.

"Don't be an ass, James," said Lady Joyce. "Let's go back."

While the procession marched back towards the Mukhtar's house, Kaplan said to Mr. Newton:

"When are you at last going to do something about it?"

"About what?" Mr. Newton asked, on the defensive.

"About this school business. The Hebrews pay for their own schools and the Government pays for the Arab schools. But the Government's revenue comes chiefly from the Hebrew taxpayer. If we have to finance Arab education we at least want it properly run."

"Since when have you taken Arab education so much to heart?" Mr. Newton asked, with an effort to be sarcastic.

"Since I've discovered that our only chance to come to terms with them is to have them properly educated. You can't come to an agreement with a fanatical horde of illiterates. I want to get some sense knocked into their heads so that we shall have a mentally grown-up partner to deal with."

"You've always got your colleague Tubashi," said Mr. Newton, resentful at being lectured to again. "Why can't you come to an agreement with Tubashi? He's been to a university, so there."

"A fat lot of good it did him," said Kaplan.

"Well, you can't have it both ways, my dear fellow—well, well . . ." said Mr. Newton, happy that he had at last scored a point.

They were back at the Mukhtar's house. During their walk more guests had assembled on the terrace: Arab dignitaries from other villages, two imams, a school teacher and a Beduin sheikh. There were also two young men in khaki shorts, the treasurer and the cobbler of the Commune of Ezra's Tower. They stood, leaning against the parapet, a little apart from the Arab guests, chatting together in Hebrew as if they were at home. There were more introductions and more rounds of coffee in thimble-cups. The Mukhtar greeted the young men from Ezra's Tower with solemn courtesy.

"I hear that you are expecting more of your friends to come to live with you," he said.

"So we are," said Moshe. "And there are even more to come in spring."

"They are welcome," the Mukhtar said blandly. "This is a poor country and a small country and soon there will not be land enough for anybody; but they are welcome. . . ."

". . . Look," said Cyril to Lady Joyce, "those Jewish settlers talk Arabic quite fluently."

"They would," said Lady Joyce. "They are all infant prodigies."

"I always wanted to live for some time in one of their settlements and find out about their social organisation and all that."

"Do," said Lady Joyce. "You'll have a lovely time eating kosher fish and sleeping with all the nice fat girls."

"I don't know," said Cyril, fidgeting. "I suppose one ought to go and talk to them. But they are so overpowering."

The Mukhtar, making solemnly the round of his guests, had moved on to the Beduin sheikh, and Kaplan joined the two young men at the parapet.

"How are things up there?" he asked. When he talked Hebrew his voice lost its bitterness and sounded almost warm.

"Everything under control," said Moshe. "Expenditure is going up, income is going down, twenty-two per cent are on the sick-list, and there is a new draft arriving next week."

"I know," said Kaplan. "They are refugees, mostly fresh from Europe, without any vocational training. You will have a bloody time until you get them assimilated."

"Everything will be under control," said Moshe. "Can't you use your authority as a Government official to get us some grub?"

"Patience," said Kaplan. "Patience; don't hurry; take your time, are the three commandments of a Government official and the common ground where the British and Arab philosophies meet. Ten years in His Majesty's Service have taught me that there is a deep affinity between the British and the Oriental outlook on life. The same detachment, the same traditionalism, the same mystic belief that somehow in the end everything will work out all right."

"Is that fellow with the pipe the famous Henderson?" asked Joseph.

"Yes, our pocket Lawrence in person. Last week he was again visiting in Arab costume the Mukhtars in my district, telling them that the Government doesn't like it if they sell land to us, and dropping the usual hints."

"And can't you do anything?"

"What? Protest to Newton? Nobody can touch Henderson's outfit. The right hand isn't supposed to know what the left hand is doing."

There was a movement in the crowd on the terrace. "It looks as if something's going to happen," said Joseph.

"Don't tell me it's the banquet," grunted Moshe.

". . . Ladies and gentlemen," cried Tubashi, and there was an expectant silence. "The peace-making ceremony is going to start now. Please form into pairs, and then we shall all walk behind the murderer and his family to meet the victim's family and rejoice at their reconciliation."

There was a general shuffling of feet and Abu Arkub, the murderer, appeared from inside the house. He had pulled the top part of his striped kaftan over his head so that he appeared hooded, and he wore his agal, the black head-cord, hanging round his neck as a symbol of accepting the yoke of bondage. He also carried a stick in his hand, at the end of which was fastened his kefiyeh, the white head-kerchief, the tassels of which were tied in knots.

The procession started moving down the terrace, the hooded murderer in front, bent under the symbolic yoke and carrying the kefiyeh on his stick like a flag of surrender. Behind him walked the Mukhtar leading his blind father by the arm; for just before the procession started the old man had suddenly hobbled out to the terrace, haughty and awe-inspiring, and apparently not at all sick. Behind them marched the silent elders of the clan, the Arab dignitaries, and the European guests.

The procession marched slowly along the cobbled road, with staring women and children clustering in the doors of the mud huts. A scraggy pariah-dog ran for a while alongside them, but a vigorous kick from Issa sent him sprawling on his back, with blood trickling from his muzzle.

"Isn't it simply fascinating?" Cyril said to Lady Joyce. "Everything in the ceremony has its special meaning which dates back to Mohammed's day. For instance the knots on the kefiyeh. They stand for the blood-money—each knot represents a certain sum, either ten pounds or thirty pounds, I forget which. Of course the blood-money was originally paid in camels; cash is a concession to the march of time."

"Why not in motor-cars?" said Lady Joyce. "A Ford for a simple murder and a Rolls for a dignitary."

"You can't take anything seriously," complained Cyril. "Have you got no feeling for tradition and all that?"

"I am hungry," said Lady Joyce.

They had arrived at the open space which divided the domains of the two Mukhtars, and the procession came to a halt. Tubashi bustled round, arranging them all into groups. The Hamdan family was lined up in a row, the guests stood in clusters a little distance away. The stick with the murderer's kefiyeh was planted in the earth. Meanwhile from the other end of the space the Abu Shaouish were advancing towards them in single file. They looked poorer than the Hamdans, except for their Mukhtar who led the procession. He was a tall, bony man with one eye conspicuously missing.

"That's the real stuff," Cyril whispered. "He looks like a brigand."

There was a great silence while the Abu Shaouish formed themselves into a row facing the Hamdans. "Looks as if they were going to sing an opera chorus," Lady Joyce said.

Henderson took his pipe from between his teeth. "Usually they don't make this fuss," he remarked. "Tubashi arranged it to show off to us."

"What's he declaiming?" asked Lady Joyce—for Tubashi, standing between the two rows and next to the white flag, had started on a speech.

"It's about peace and forgiveness and the common cause," said Henderson.

It was hot, and the afternoon breeze wafted the delicious smell of shashlik across the space. Presently Tubashi stopped. There was faint and dignified clapping, then silence. Suddenly the Abu Shaouish Mukhtar shouted something in a raucous voice which sounded like an insult, and there was clapping again, and Tubashi hurriedly untied one of the knots on the murderer's kefiyeh.

"What's that mean?" asked Lady Joyce.

"The victim's clan has just announed that in honour of the King they are reducing the blood-money by ten pounds."

The man standing next to the Abu Shaouish Mukhtar in turn shouted something, and there was more clapping and another knot untied.

"That's for King Farouk of Egypt," said Henderson.

"I thought the sum was agreed beforehand?"

"It is. And so are the remittances."

Another announcement was made and another knot untied. "Ten pounds for Mr. Chamberlain," Henderson translated. "Ten for President Roosevelt. Ten for His Excellency the High Commissioner. Ten for the District Commissioner. Ten for myself."

"You?" said Lady Joyce. "What about little me?"

"Women don't come in.—Ten for the Sheikh. Ten for Tubashi. That's the lot."

"They have given away a fortune," said Lady Joyce.

"Theoretically. It makes the sum look more important," said Henderson.

The Hamdan Mukhtar advanced and, wetting his thumb, counted a wad of notes into Tubashi's hands who, amid more clapping, handed them over to the Abu Shaouish Mukhtar. The remaining knots were untied on the murderer's kefiyeh which unfolded in the breeze.

There was a tense silence, while all eyes were turned on the murderer. Presently he detached himself from the Hamdan row and, humbly bent in his hood, advanced across the space which separated the two clans. When he arrived in front of the tall Abu Shaouish Mukhtar he stood still for a second, then lifted the Mukhtar's hand to his lips and kissed it. The Mukhtar drew the murderer up to him and kissed him on both cheeks. There was renewed clapping while Abu Arkub moved along the Abu Shaouish row, kissing each man's hands and being kissed on his cheeks. Then he righted himself and seemed to have suddenly grown a head taller. There was more clapping.

The murderer now having obtained formal forgiveness, it was the turn of the other members of his family to get reconciled. The first to advance was the Hamdan Mukhtar, leading his blind father by the arm. When the old man stood in front of the Abu Shaouish Mukhtar whose father he had killed, there was a last moment of tension. Then the Hamdan Mukhtar guided the blind man's two hands toward his enemy's right which hung limply by his side; but at the moment when their hands touched, the Abu Shaouish Mukhtar threw his arms round the old man's shoulders and kissed him prolongedly and with fervour. The two groups mixed, shouting, kissing and patting each other; some of the older men were seen crying.

"There is, after all, something to be said for tradition," Joseph said to Moshe, as the whole gathering was moving with alacrity towards the banqueting tables.

"Not if it's become a parody," said Kaplan who was walking next to them. "You should have heard the Bedu Sheikh's comments."

"What did he say?"

"He was so indignant, he almost got a stroke. He is the Sheikh of one of the Ruheiwat tribes who live mainly on smuggling hashish from Syria, and he's got all the contempt of the pure Bedu for the degenerate cross-breeds who live in towns and villages. He calls them mongrels, sons of bitches, and denies that they are Arabs at all. He is a great fellow. Would you like to meet him?"

"Is he a friend of yours?"

"He is my blood-brother," said Kaplan, grinning. "I once got him out of a mess—but that's a long story. . . . Oi, ya Sheikh!" he called to the tall figure walking a few steps ahead, who now stopped and with a quick swerve turned towards them.

"This is my brother, Sheikh Silmi of the Ruheiwat," Kaplan introduced in Arabic, "and these are my friends Jussuf and Mussa, two Hebrews from the settlement across the valley and very good boys."

"My brother's friends are my friends," said Sheikh Silmi, shaking hands with them. He was an elderly, dark and vivacious man, with a sparse black beard along the edge of his jaw which ended in an abrupt tuft on his chin.

"I was telling my friends that you did not like the ceremony," said Kaplan.

"It was a mockery," said Silmi. "It was like monkeys playing at being Arabs."

They arrived at the table, where the English party and some of the notables had already taken their places. "Will you tell my friends the Bedu legend which you just told me?" Kaplan asked Silmi when they were seated.

Sheikh Silmi smiled broadly, baring his teeth. "As you wish," he said. "At the beginning of the world there was nothing but a strong whirlwind in the desert, and God caught a gust of this wind and out of it he created the Beduin. This Beduin shot an arrow into the air and God caught it and made it into the camel. Then God bent down and picked up a lump of clay and made it into the donkey. And after that God saw that he had forgotten something, and he bent down again and picked up the dung which the donkey had dropped, and out of it he made the peasant."

The sheep were brought on enormous wooden dishes, surrounded by mountains of rice, and the meal took its traditional course. There were more speeches and more coffee, and at the end of the meal a fantasia, with the village youths galloping round the square on their small underfed horses and shooting their rifles into the air.

"*Habibi,*" Moshe said to Joseph with a discreet belch, "if we did that, they would confiscate the rifles as illegal arms and put us into jug. We are not picturesque."

"Shut up," said Joseph. "You have filled your belly with their food, so stop grumbling. I am enjoying myself."

"You go on enjoying yourself," said Moshe. "And I'll go on wondering where they got those new Mausers from."

"You must ask the Duce," said Kaplan.

"What are you a Government official for?" asked Moshe.

"To play chess with my superiors and collect taxes from you," said Kaplan. "And if you don't like it here you can bloody well go back where you came from."

At sunset the Jerusalem party set off.

"Did you notice," said Cyril Watson to Lady Joyce, "how those boys from the Hebrew settlement behaved? They looked as if they were making dirty cracks all the time, and it never occurred to them to come over and talk to us."

"What else did you expect?" said Lady Joyce.

"I thought you wanted to go and live with them to study Communism," said Henderson, lighting his pipe.

They were all tired, and walked for a few steps in silence.

"I don't know," Cyril said after a while. "One's got to be fair to them. Persecution and all that. But I must say, you can't call them encouraging."

"Never mind," said Joyce. "You go and study them and sleep with the girl comrades."

". . . Whereas these Arabs," Cyril mused, "whatever you think of them, they've got a certain style."

"That's it," said Joyce, getting into the car. "And now you've settled the problem I want to sleep all the way back from here to Jerusalem."

"Did you notice," Moshe said to Joseph as they were riding back, on horses borrowed from Gan Tamar, towards Ezra's Tower, "did you notice that not one of these English people said a word to Kaplan or to either of us?"

"I did," said Joseph. "Why didn't *we* go and talk to them?"

"Me?" Moshe puffed indignantly. "Crawl before that arrogant bunch of *Herrenvolk* number two?"

"They are less arrogant than shy," said Joseph. "Inhibitions are a national disease with them."

"What a misunderstood nation," said Moshe. "They had to grab an Empire out of sheer timidity."

Joseph patted the head of his horse. It was a small Arab horse and he thought of the pony he used to ride in the bygone days, and of the lawn in front of the spacious Elizabethan house, and of Mr. Watkins the gardener who preached on Sundays in the Methodist church.

"At home they are different," he said. "It is unfair to judge them by the type we meet out here. When people talk about the French, they mean the Frenchman in France. When they talk about the English, they mean the Englishman abroad—the tourist and the colonial. But you can live in England for years without seeing anybody of this type—except in the comic cartoons."

"I can only judge by those I know," said Moshe. "If they are so unrepresentative as you say, they shouldn't send them abroad. Don't try telling me that poor Henderson is pitting the Arabs against us because he's shy and has inhibitions."

Joseph gave no answer. He felt a little irritated by Moshe, as he often did. But after all it was not his business to defend the English. If they always appeared in the wrong light it was their own fault. Why could they never show themselves as they really were? Why did they disdain to give explanations and hold the judgment of the world in such sovereign contempt?

"You know it is more complicated than that," he said after a while.

"You don't say."

"It is a kind of double-decker sandwich. There is a crusty top layer of apparent arrogance, which in fact is just shyness, as I said. When you pierce that, there is a soft layer of jolliness and decency. But when you get through that too, you find the bottom layer of real conceit, which is the more unshakable as it is elastic, mumbling and incoherent. It is the arrogance of the under-statement, which is worse than boasting."

"*Tov, tov,*" said Moshe. "Whether it's a double-decker conceit or simple arrogance is all the same to me."

Having said his evening prayers and put on his blue-and-yellow striped pyjamas, the Hamdan Mukhtar voluptuously stretched his huge body in his bed. It was the first time for many years that he had gone to bed without the shadow of danger hovering over his dreams. He was too excited to go to sleep at once, and after a while called for Issa. Issa came in, his abaye hurriedly thrown over his underclothes.

"Well, son," said the Mukhtar with unusual geniality, "thanks to God it was a great day."

"Yes, Father," said Issa.

"With God's help there will be peace in the village now for ever," said the Mukhtar.

"So help us God," said Issa.

"Did it hit your eyes that the English and the Hebrews did not speak together?" the Mukhtar asked thoughtfully. "There must be something behind this. And Henderson effendi made a certain remark . . ."

"What did he say, Father?"

The Mukhtar looked at the pock-marked face of his son and didn't like it. But he had to talk to somebody.

"He made a remark about the Dogs' Hill. He said it was not certain that there would be more settlers coming to live there. He did not say anything clearly. Henderson effendi always talks in riddles."

"What does it mean, Father?"

"I don't know," said the Mukhtar. "But it is certain that they did not talk together. They are like cats and dogs, thank God. . . ." He laughed to himself, and added:

"If there are cats and dogs, what else is there? This is also a riddle, son."

"I don't know," said Issa.

"The stick," said the Mukhtar. He laughed to himself and would have liked Issa to laugh with him. But Issa only gave a sour smile, and the Mukhtar stopped laughing. "The stick," he repeated. "The stick beats both, the cat and the dog."

"Yes, Father," said Issa.

Outside in the hills, the moon was just rising over Ezra's Tower; the big, peaceful, orange-coloured moon of Galilee.

4

Pages from the chronicle of Joseph, a member of the Commune of Ezra's Tower

Sunday, November . . . 1938

Since last week our population has almost doubled. Ezra's Tower now counts 77 souls: 41 old settlers (including the five children), plus 11 newcomers who are to become permanent members of the Commune, plus 25 boys and girls who are to spend here six months of their vocational training.

The whole of last week was simply bedlam. All the sweet peace and routine wrecked, shattered, blown to smithereens. Oh our salad days, legendary days, days of youth and innocence.

The eleven new settlers were the first to arrive. They came on Tuesday. All we knew about them was that they were a mixed bag—Germans, Poles, Rumanians, and even an Egyptian—whom our Colonisation Department was to dump or rather graft on us, as a first instalment of further grafts which, within a year or two, should bring us up to our full establishment of two hundred adult workers. We further knew that they had only recently arrived in the country and were refugees—as distinct from us who, with the exception of Dina and Simeon, had all come before persecution in Europe had started in earnest and more or less out of our own free choice. Finally we knew that they were seven men and four girls, all unmarried so far, and our bachelors of both sexes were looking forward to their arrival with ill-concealed expectations. Particularly Gaby, our red-haired Viennese Messalina who, having a year ago left Max for Mendl, has now left Mendl too—(who, however, does not seem to care much, dividing all his time between the tractor and the string quartet).

Anyway, we rigged up our three disused tents from the early days, put up a streamer with "BLESSED BE HE WHO COMES" across the gate in the fence, and hoped for the best. They came from Tel Aviv in a truck and arrived during the midday break; so all of us except those working out in the fields lined up at the gate to welcome these newcomers with whom, for all we know, we are going to spend the rest of our lives.

As the big lorry jolted up the dirt-track with the eleven settlers standing upright in a bunch, and their bundles and possessions piled up messily around them, my first impression was that of a transport of survivors from a fire or earthquake who had saved whatever came first to their hands; there were mattresses, saucepans, a cuckoo-clock, a granny-armchair, a bicycle and even a bird-cage. But they were singing full blast "*El yivneh ha-galil*" and that improved things a little; though, as the lorry turned in through the gate, we all stared at them silently and dumbly, like an assembly of village yokels at the arrival of the summer guests. I too felt paralysed, and for a second I saw in a frightening flash our own crowd of heavy, slow-moving men and women, mute, wary and backwoodish as we had become during this first long hard year. . . . But then we began running alongside the lorry, escorting it to the Square, waving and shouting, and the spell was broken. The lorry stopped in front of the Tower and the new ones jumped down and started singing the anthem, standing nicely to attention; so we did the same, joining in. We hadn't sung the anthem for God knows how long, and it was all rather solemn. In the middle of it one of the new girls began to cry; she is very fat with a round pudding-face, and she went on singing the refrain with the tears streaming down her face:

Not yet dead is our hope, the ancient hope
To return to our Land, the ancient Land,
To return to our town, the town which David built. . . .

The second face which caught my eyes was the Egyptian's. He is swarthy to the point of being quite a Coloured Hebrew Gentleman, with the bluish-white eyeballs and the rubbery loose-jointed limbs of a negro step-dancer. He stood to attention in complete stillness of body—one of the things that Jews as a rule are unable to do—with even his pupils immobilised; they were turned upward, fixed on the topmost point of the Tower. The third one I noticed was a lean and gauche young man, the typical German Akademiker and future Dr. Phil. (subject: Neo-Kantianism). He had jerked to attention over-eagerly with all his muscles cramped and now stood looking as if his bones had been broken and re-set in the wrong way, trying to readjust them by little fidgets. I made a vow not to dislike him and had already broken it at the end of the first verse. Meanwhile Gaby's eyes had begun melting at the Egyptian (she seems to be capable of having an orgasm in her pupils), while Sarah's pinched little bird-face assumed that expression of primly indignant refusal which always comes over it when a man appeals to her starved senses. While we went on singing it occurred to me that, while with nine out of ten men Gaby would win hands down, in the case of the Egyptian boy it was just possible that the first impact of Adlerian psychotherapy would lay him out and make him forsake Gaby's more obvious charms. Then my eyes fell on Moshe, standing opposite me and singing full blast, while his gaze wandered with an experienced pawnbroker's appraisal over the goods and chattels heaped on the truck, which from to-morrow will enrich our Communal stores.

When the anthem was over we all flocked into the dining-hut, and the process of making friends with the new ones began. Max took the fat girl under his protection, his tapir-nose was fairly sniffing at her while he talked with great agitation (probably about the necessity of fostering Arab Trade

Unions). She listened, obviously not understanding a word and admiring him with her good big cow-eyes. Ellen was engaged in a serious and measured conversation with the Dr. Phil., now and then looking at me from the corner of her eyes. Dina took no part in the thawing-up proceedings. Contact with new arrivals from Europe always has a bad effect on her. She sat on the furthermost end of a bench, spooning her soup with a listless, withdrawn air. Since she is back from hospital the blue shadows under her eyes have deepened and she looks lovelier than ever.

On the whole we were doing our best; and yet it will be a long time until we make the new ones feel at home, and until we ourselves accept them. And even then, I feel, there will always remain a difference—hardly perceptible, unavowed, and yet implied in all relations. There will be memories of the early days which they do not share, allusions and jokes from which they will feel left out. They will always regard us as old-timers, the *Mayflower*-aristocracy of the place; and so shall we ourselves, in the secrecy of our hearts. (And, when all is said, we *have* built this place out of the wilderness, or haven't we?) But when the next graft arrives they will look up to both the older groups with awe and respect, unable to distinguish between them;—like the last arrival in the doctor's waiting-room who, unaware of the hierarchy previously established, lumps together all those present into one category of "those who were here before".

This little patrician arrogance will remain lingering about us and in due time we, the original seven-and-thirty, will become, as in Dagánia, Khefziba and Kfar Gileadi, a bunch of picturesque elders, with pipes and gout and prophetic beards —respected, legendary, and rather tiresome. . . . That is, those of us who live to see the day.

Later

The advent of the youth-group was less inspiring. To tell the truth, rather depressing.

It is not the first time that I have felt frightened by our new generation. These twenty-five adolescents of both sexes are fairly typical; they are all Sabras—born and educated in the country; they are all between sixteen and nineteen. The larger part of them are sons and daughters of farmers from Petakh Tikwa, Rosh Pina, Metullah and other villages of the old type, founded before the time of the Communes. The others come from the towns. School and the youth-movement brought them together and they formed a group with the aim of founding a Commune of their own. They will spend six months of their vocational training with us, and will be settled in about a year's time, on land promised to them by the National Fund in the Eastern part of the Valley of Jezreel, somewhere near Beisan. The group counts in all about a hundred and fifty youngsters who have been split up into smaller units for the period of their training.

So far so good. It is a good sign that many among the native youth want to go in for Communal life. This choice is of course made easier for them by our propaganda in the schools—our teachers are all Labour or I.L.P., and the Teachers' Trade Union sees to it that no right-wing heretics creep into the flock. With that too I agree—all education is propaganda for one way of life or the other; so why not propagate the way in which we believe? And yet, there is already a difference between us, who came from abroad groping for a new form of social and national existence, an experimental Order or Fraternity such as has never been tried before—and them, who slip into a ready-made form, guided by their elders. For us, the choice involved a revolutionary negation of our past—for them, it is an act of conformism.

That, however, would not matter so much. When a nebulous experiment solidifies into an institution, that only proves that it has succeeded. We do not want romantics and permanent upheavals. We want a stable pattern of life for our people. And if the new generation accepts the pattern which we evolved, there should be nothing but rejoicing.

And yet something inside myself, perhaps my innate scepticism, tells me that all this is too good to be true. The snag is not in the institution, but in the human quality of the new generation. I have watched them ever since they arrived —these stumpy, dumpy girls with their rather coarse features, big buttocks and heavy breasts, physically precocious, mentally retarded, over-ripe and immature at the same time; and these raw, arse-slapping youngsters, callow, dumb and heavy, with their aggressive laughter and unmodulated voices, without traditions, manners, form, style. . . .

Their parents were the most cosmopolitan race of the earth —they are provincial and chauvinistic. Their parents were sensitive bundles of nerves with awkward bodies—*their* nerves are whip-cords and their bodies those of a horde of Hebrew Tarzans roaming in the hills of Galilee. Their parents were intense, intent, over-strung, over-spiced—they are tasteless, spiceless, unleavened and tough. Their parents were notoriously polyglot—they have been brought up in one language which had been hibernating for twenty centuries before being brought artificially back to life. . . .

There, in the language, is the main rub. The revival of Hebrew from its holy petrifaction to serve again as the living tongue of a nation was a fantastic achievement. But this miracle involves a heavy sacrifice. Our children are brought up in a language which has not developed since the beginnings of the Christian era. It has no records, no memories, hardly any trace of what happened to mankind since the destruction of the Temple. Imagine the development of English having stopped with "Beowulf"—and even "Beowulf" is a thousand years nearer to us! Our Classics are the books of the Old Testament; our lyrics stopped with the Song of Songs, our short stories with Job. Since then—a millennial blank. . . .

To talk in an archaic idiom has of course its charms. We travel in a bus and offer a cigarette to a neighbour: "Perchance my lord desires to make smoke?"—"No, thanks. To make smoke finds no favour in my eyes."

But we are no longer conscious of this quaintness of our speech; where all walk on stilts nobody will stop to wonder. And so this young generation is brought up in a language which suffers from loss of memory; with only the sketchiest knowledge of world literature and European history, and only a very dim idea of what everything was about since the day when the Ninth Legion under Titus captured David's Citadel. They speak no European language except a little English on the Berlitz-school level; the not too numerous and not too competent translations of world classics strike no chords in them; the humanistic hormones of the mind are absent, no Latin or Greek being taught in our schools. As against this, they know all about fertilisers and irrigation and rotation of crops; they know the names of birds and plants and flowers; they know how to shoot, and fear neither Arab nor devil.

In other words, they have ceased to be Jews and become Hebrew peasants.

This of course is exactly what our philosophy and propaganda aims at. To return to the Land, and within the Land to the soil; to cure that nervous over-strungness of exile and dispersion; to liquidate the racial inferiority complex and breed a healthy, normal, earthbound race of peasants. These Hebrew Tarzans are what we have bargained for. So why am I frightened of them?

Perhaps because of the eternally conflicting values of creativeness and security. On one side the fever and the vision; on the other side the sluggish pulse of health. On one side of the scales persecution and otherness as spurs to spiritual achievement; hectic prophets and sick messiahs from Jesus to Marx and Freud. On the other side of the balance the price we had to pay for them; the smell of tons of burning flesh on the stakes of Spain; enough spilled blood to fill the Dead Sea; the stink and filth and claustrophobia of the ghetto; the deterioration of the hereditary substance through the survival of the nimblest, the humblest, the crookedest, into its final product, the flat-footed, shifty-eyed eternal tramp.

In Buchenwald they now hang people on hooks by their mouths, like carps. Who would not swap all the formulae of Einstein to take a single jerking wrench off his hook?

But who, having completed the transaction, would rejoice about it?

I almost forgot the episode which frightened me most. It was a story one of the young Tarzans told me with a grin when he saw me through the open door of my room working on Pepys. It was about a friend of his, born and educated in the Commune of Herod's Well. When that boy was thirteen, his father made him a gift of a fountain pen. When he was seventeen, he wrote a letter to his father which said: "Dear Daddy, to-day I have finished school. So I shall not need that pen any more and am sending it back to you."

That was an extreme case. But it is no use denying that these young Tarzans are a step backward and that it will take a series of generations until we catch up again. It is a deliberate sacrifice but that does not make it less depressing. Rousseau was lucky that the French did not take him seriously; had they followed his advice and all become shepherds and tillers of the soil, he would have hanged himself.

Wednesday

The Commission appointed by the British Government to work out suggestions for the partitioning of the country has published its report. According to their recommendations the Jewish State should comprise less than one per cent of the total area of Palestine—a rectangle forty miles long and ten miles wide—excluding most of our settlements, excluding the whole of Galilee, the Valley of Jezreel, everything. It is not a political report but a printed sneer of derision.

Together with the report, the Government has issued a White Paper rejecting partition—though not on the grounds of the monstrosity of the proposed frontiers, but because of the "political and financial difficulties involved". Instead, there is to be a Round Table Conference to decide the future of the country—a Conference to which not only the two interested parties, but all the Arab States are to be invited. This is an innovation. I have never heard of Britain inviting Iraq and Syria to take part in their discussions with Egypt. It can only mean one thing: they are looking for an excuse to get rid of their obligations to us and to bury the idea of our National Home. Our future is under its debris.

Thursday

Simeon is in hospital in Haifa with typhoid. I wish he were back. The indifference of our people here towards the political situation drives me crazy; they do not even seem to realise that something is wrong. Most of them only read the headlines in the papers. In the evening everybody is tired and can't be bothered; it is the old, honest and disastrous attitude: "we are doing our job; leave the rest to the politicians".

Last night there was a celebration; Judith, Moshe's wife and head of our laundry, has come back from the maternity hospital with twins—inmates number six and seven of the Children's House. There were sweet wine and cakes and the obvious jokes about Moshe's methods of rationalising production. As their room has just enough standing space for ten people we took turns to get in; Moshe stood at the door, sturdy like a prize bull, shaking everybody's hands with an earnest face and puffing with pride. As we drink wine only five or six times a year, even two small glasses of the revoltingly sweet stuff have an exhilarating effect; so there was a horra in the Square with Mendl doing his Pied Piper act and the new ones getting quite out of hand; the Egyptian dancing like a dervish, and the Dr. Phil. falling over his feet and breaking his glasses and generally making a fool of himself. The youth-group for a while looked on critically at us rapturous elders and then started a horra of their own among their tents, yelling and arse-slapping like a horde of Tarzans in the jungle.

Round midnight some of us had drifted into the kitchen for the traditional "cumsitz" with coffee and biscuits. There was the usual crowd—Reuben, Moshe, Max, Dina, Dasha and myself. I turned on the midnight news on the radio in the dining-hall, but of course there was nothing. I knew it would only lead to one of our usual sterile arguments but I couldn't keep quiet, so I started by asking the cumsitz-assembly what they thought should be done about the situation.

There was a hush of resentment, and at once I felt guilty for disturbing the celebration—we don't have so many of them. Then Reuben said cautiously:

"The Partition proposal was a scandal—but after all they have turned it down."

"Don't you see," I said, "that the fact alone of the publication of such a monstrosity is characteristic of their approach to the whole problem? One per cent of the country—think of it! It indicates the lines along which they search for what they call a 'reasonable compromise'. First they publish an insult with the comment that unfortunately for technical reasons it cannot be carried out; then they invite the representatives of the Moslem countries to decide upon our fate—having plainly hinted to them what the Government itself thinks should be done with us."

"Oh—you exaggerate as usual," said Dasha.

"Joseph's got under the influence of the Bauman-people," said Max. "He wants to throw bombs first on the Arabs, then on the English."

"Oh shut up," said Dina. "Bauman is no fool." When Dina talks about politics, her eyes assume the gravity of a child wondering whether it should eat its chocolates now or later.

"No fool?" cried Max. "When he's throwing in his lot with Jabotinski and his fascist terrorists?"

"Look, Max," I said. "Can't we keep internal party politics out of it?"

"No," said Reuben quietly, "you can't. These people are

fighting our Trade Unions and Labour Party tooth and claw. They have not created a single settlement of their own. They have split the *Haganah,* our defence organisation. They have no constructive achievements and nothing in their heads but shouting and playing at soldiers."

"In other words they are fascists. Hebrew fascists," said Max.

"You can't call Bauman a fascist," said Dina.

"Why not?" cried Dasha. "They throw bombs into Arab markets, killing women and children."

"They turn the heads of young fools like Benjosef," said Max, "inducing them to commit some idiotic outrage and get hanged for it. And Benjosef's accomplice was a lunatic whom they had to send to an asylum. That's symbolic. Fanatics and lunatics, the lot of them."

And so it went on. I was all the more furious because I knew that half of what they said was true. I let myself go and turned on Max.

"That fool Benjosef," I shouted, "was the first Hebrew hanged in this country since Bar Kochba's last stand against the Romans. You talk as if you hated that boy, who after all died for our cause, more than those who put the rope round his neck. God damn your objectivity. A race which remains objective when its life is at stake will lose it."

They were all silent for a second or two, but my anger didn't subside. Oh, what a relief it was to forsake objectivity and close my eyes to their point, to all the "buts" and "ifs" which I see as well and better than they do. And letting myself go I carried them—at least for a minute.

"Now, Joseph," said Ellen with all the seriousness of a responsible veg-gardener in a socialist rural settlement, "now, Joseph, let's be reasonable. . . ."

"But I don't want to be reasonable," I shouted. "I have had enough of being reasonable for two thousand years while the others were not. I was the reasonable fly running in zigzags over the window-pane because there was light on the other side and I had my legs torn out and my wings burnt off with matches. I am through with your reasonableness."

"So what do you propose to do?" Reuben asked coolly. Despite his calm voice I heard the warning undertone.

"I don't know," I said, feeling my rage change into impotence. "I only know that we have been offered one per cent of our country as a reasonable compromise. And I know that on that first night here when we were attacked in the open and could shoot back with a clean conscience and the blessing of God, I felt happy to kill. . . ."

"There you hear it—you hear the voice of fascism," cried Max in a high-pitched voice almost breaking into a crow.

"And you?" Dina asked suddenly, leaning across the table and breathing into Max's face. "And you, clever one? What do you propose to do? Sing 'The Red Flag', clever one?"

Max flinched back as if her breath had singed his face. It occurred to me that Dina, made impotent for love, had, perhaps alone among us, retained the chastity of hatred. Max must have felt something similar, for he grew pale in the furrows round his nose.

"If you still have the sense to listen," he said with surprising restraint, "I can tell you my idea of what to do. We have to win over the Arabs, whether you like it or not. You can call me any name you like and play anthems into my ear and dangle banners under my nose, you won't deter me from my creed. Proletarians of the world, the poor and humble of this world, unite. This is as sacred to me as the Ten Commandments or the Sermon on the Mount. The Arabs are the poor and humble and we are the poor and humble. There is no other way. This is my creed and I won't sell my creed for a mess of chauvinist pottage. . . ."

His big tapir-nose quivered, and his eyes with the constantly inflamed lids quivered too. I liked and hated him in the same breath. So I said:

"You should not have brought in that mess of pottage. It's a tricky parable—a boomerang."

"What do you mean?" said Max, blinking.

"Our ancestor, name of Jacob, got his blessing and the Land with it by cunning and crook. It's a disgusting story. He swindled the guileless Esau; he helped himself, so God helped him too. Had he been more scrupulous in the choice of his method, we wouldn't have got the Land—it would have fallen to the fur-skinned hunter of the deserts. . . ."

"Oh shut up," said Max.

"*You* shut up," I shouted. "You with your world-redeeming pacifist phrases. What if the Arabs won't be redeemed by you? They don't want your money, nor your hospitals, nor your Trade Unions."

"It's only the influence of the Effendis—the landowners and the priests," said Max. "They are frightened of losing their privileges. But once the people understand that we are coming as their real friends . . ."

"Once," said Dina. "Once, you clever one. Are you going to wait outside for that once? How long, clever one? How long are you going to wait, a hundred years or a thousand, tell me?"

"Nobody talks of waiting," said Max, who was visibly frightened of Dina. "I never said that. I only said that we have to meet them half-way in a spirit of goodwill and understanding."

"But they don't *want* to meet you, you blind idiot," I shouted. "They hate you because you are a stranger and because the priests told them to hate you and because they believe the priests and are illiterate and live in the thirteenth century and haven't read your Marx. So what do you do? You talk of goodwill and understanding, but in fact you elbow your way in, whether they like it or not. That's what you do, you bloody hypocrite."

"I can't argue if you yell at the top of your voice," said Max.

"Why don't you shout back?" said Dina. "Why don't you shout, clever one? It's because you don't shout that you will always be the loser."

"Really," said Reuben. "This is a bit unfair. A shouting match of two against one. . . ."

"Damn your fairness and your ideologies and all your Jewish bla-bla-bla," I said.

"That's a new one," said Ellen. "Joseph has become an anti-semite."

At that moment the steam-roller got at last into action. "This is not a discussion but a spiral nebula," puffed Moshe. "It is heated, vaporous, and has no beginning and no end. If I understood rightly Joseph has just discovered that the Government of Mr. Chamberlain would like to get rid of us. We know that. We also know that they can't. We have become too strong. We are no longer a promise on a piece of paper, but half a million men, one third of the country's population and more than two thirds of its economy. They let us down when the Arabs started shooting. We have shot it out with the Arabs and have proved that we are a match for them. We know our strength and have no need to get hysterical. We have built up what we have acre by acre and cow by cow. I for one know what my job is: to buy another acre and another cow. Good night."

Thus things were patched up—for the time being at least—and as there was no point in going on with the argument we all went to bed.

Shabbath

The early rains have started in earnest, and with them the second worst torture after the heat: *botz,* the mud. Next year, if we have the money, we shall build concrete pathways across the settlement; this winter we shall still have to live as marsh-dwellers.

If it were only a question of wading out to work and back home, that would be a trifle. The trouble is that our billets and living conveniences are scattered over an area of five acres. The communal showers and W.C.s are at a distance of 120 yards from the hut in which my room is; the Dining Hall is

80 yards away, the Reading Room 100, the Secretariat 150 in another direction. Thus all the routine functions of life become transformed into amphibious expeditions through the rain-beaten swamp, each necessitating a change from outdoor gumboots into indoor shoes and back, and the tedious paraphernalia of scraping, stamping and brushing one's footwear all day.

It is of course all a question of money. If we had enough money for proper sanitation, we could at least have running water and a W.C. for each living-hut. But this luxury not even the oldest and wealthiest Communes are so far able to afford. "The children first, then the cattle, then the workers. . . ." However, the first two concrete living-huts and three further blockhouses are nearing completion, and in a month's time everybody, including the youth-group, will have a roof over his head and the tents will be stored away for the next batch of newcomers.

The greatest plague during the rainy season is to have one's tummy upset—and it is a frequent one. To wade at night through the rain and gale and mud to the lavatory, possibly three or four times, is much worse than an Arab raid. But for these heroic achievements there are no laurels.

There is a water music by Haendel and an Alpensymphonie by Strauss; I wish Mendl would compose the Symphony of the Mud. It would have to be mainly written for double-bass—a slow, heavy, thumping, thudding, squelching, belching, squashing, splashing, atonal cacophony, to the accompaniment of the drumming of the rain on the roofs.

Sunday

The Arab unrest is petering out. Peter, leader of the *Haganah* in Chanita, our most exposed settlement on the Syrian border, visited us yesterday. He had a long hush-hush talk with Reuben, presumably about illegal arms. Later in the dining-hut he told us more stories about Wingate, who lived in Chanita for some time last summer; he was training them in offensive guerrilla-warfare and led them in various actions. They all worship him, even Peter who is a dry and cautious kind of fellow. Apparently he has the habit of working stark naked in his room, speaks little, has a laconic sense of humour, a romantic penchant for Hebrew History and seems to lack the faculties of fear and fatigue. Once he remarked to Peter: "You chaps learn more in a week than a Tommy in a month; but you can talk more in a day than he talks in a year. . . ."

That's all very well, but Wingate is an exception. He can't change the Government's policy, which is to accept our help against the Arabs and at the same time to prepare our Munich. And how indignant they are when the victim protests before having his throat cut. The Czechs at least have the consolation of having been sacrificed to save the peace of Europe. But we are let down without urgent need, simply because betrayal has become a conditioned reflex with this Government. The so-called Arab rebellion was a bluff, in which only about fifteen hundred hill-men participated actively. The Moslem world is split even more than the Christian; Wahhabis and Iraqis hate each other more than German and French; the desert tribes are busy with raids and blood feuds; the danger of a Moslem Holy War is about as real as the noble Sheikh of the movies. Our neighbours in the country are not even Arabs, but the descendants of Canaanites, Jebusites, Philistines, Crusaders, and Turks, with a good deal of Jewish blood. For all that they are charming people, naïve, cunning, quarrelsome, good-natured and cruel. The contradictions in their character are those of backward children: greed and generosity, cringing and pride, corruption and chivalry.

Of course they don't like us. They are slum-children in possession of a vast playground where they wallow happily in the dust. In comes another bunch of children who have nowhere to play and start cleaning up the place and building tents and lavatories with a horrible burst of efficiency. "Get out from here," they cry, "we don't want you."—"But there is plenty of room," says the clever lot, "and we've got permission to share it, and after we've improved it the place will be much nicer for you too."—"Get out, get out," they cry, having already pinched some of the new-comers' tools and toys; "get out, we don't want you. This is our place and we like it as it is."

They are a relic of the middle ages. They have no conception of nationhood and no sense of discipline: they are good rioters and bad fighters, otherwise none of our isolated settlements could have survived. As a political factor they have been negligible since the days of the Kalifs, except for their nuisance value. If treated with authority, they keep quiet; if encouraged, they make an infernal nuisance of themselves. The policy of the people who run the show here is to encourage them, so as to have an excuse to get rid of us. Two years ago when things began to stink to heaven they sent out a Royal Commission to investigate matters. "If one thing stands out clear from the record of the Mandatory Administration," says the Commission's report, "it is the leniency with which Arab political agitation, even when carried to the point of violence and murder, has been treated." If a cautiously understated official report goes as far as this, one can imagine how far our Hendersons have gone in their game. . . .

Oh, if at least I could hate as Simeon does! But after all I am half English myself. Spoiled and pampered by the safety of our island, uninvaded for a millennium while other countries served as battlefields, we could afford to muddle and bungle through the ages and develop the mystic belief that our bungling is some higher God-inspired wisdom. We will plunge ourselves and the rest of the world into a disaster worse than anything in history; and when we scramble out of it we will make humorous remarks about our own stupidity—blissfully unaware that, though we pay for our own mistakes, we shall never be able to pay for the horrors into which we have dragged the others, who are dead and buried and unable to share the joke.

Tuesday

More rain and more *botz.* It is not so much the dirt and bother which depresses one, but the sheer weight on one's boots. It drags you down, depriving you of all levity, makes you weary and earthbound. Stamping through the heavy mud I almost feel myself transformed, by force of mimicry, into a clumsy, dripping, melting figure of clay.

Thursday

Two new matches. Gaby has won the competition for the Egyptian (if he was ever aware of Sarah competing). They are shamelessly happy, his eyes bulging and hers melting. At least with them the oppressed territories of the flesh have attained full sovereign rights. She calls him "Ham" which in Hebrew means "hot", but could also signify Noah's second son from whom the Egyptians are descended, or else be understood in English as pointing to his hind parts. The other couple are Max and that very fat new girl from Rumania. Perhaps his sleeping with this gentle eiderdown will mollify his world-redeeming zeal. Both couples are going to move into the new hut which will be ready by next Shabbath; so I shall get rid of Max and have my room alone for the time being—though Ellen walks about with tight lips and hardly looks at me.

Poor Sarah is even worse off. Her chastity seems to have a corroding effect on her like a slow-acting acid. The bachelors of both sexes are a problem so far unsolved in the Communes. We have eleven of them. Those who have not become matched after a year or two become sexually allergic towards one another; the intimacy of life in the smaller Communes acts as a gradually materialising incest-barrier. As long as new grafts are still due, there is hope for them; once we have reached our full establishment there will be little hope left. Then some will resign themselves, some will break down and leave us—and probably come back after a year or so, defeated by their loneliness in the world outside for which they have ceased to be fit.

There is also the expedient of a year's leave. It works sometimes; but it can only be granted to one or two at a time, and people are reluctant to apply for it: partly because of a feeling of obviousness and ridicule attached to such a bridal quest, and partly because it has something of the pathos of the last chance about it, and they are scared of returning alone and defeated.

Sunday

I had hoped to enjoy a peaceful Shabbath afternoon with Pepys; instead, I had a two-hours talk with Reuben, which led to momentous consequences. Subject: myself (Joseph and his Brethren, or the Individual and the Community).

It was Reuben who provoked it. He came to my room and, with signs of mild embarrassment and a semi-official air, suggested a walk. I knew at once that something was up. Before, I had not fully realised how far I had worked myself into a crisis, and even less had I known that the others had noticed it. One is always apt to forget that the Commune has most sensitive antennae; taken one by one we are perhaps not very observant, but there is a kind of collective intuition operating as in an insect state.

The rain had stopped since the early morning and though the settlement was still a muddy mess, the slopes on the side of the wadi were already drying. Reuben suggested we should walk down into the wadi and then up the hill to the west to see how our new vines were getting on. So I put Pepys on the shelf and off we went. We passed the Tower and the Children's House; as always on Shabbath the children were all in their parents' rooms and the house was empty and still. The doors were open, showing the deserted beds and cots; at the end of the passage Dina sat all by herself on a stool, pretending to read. It looked as if she wanted to prove that she was still in charge of the house and of the children who were not hers.

The white house stood still and dead in the afternoon sun, submerged in the drowsy peace of the Shabbath, and strangely oppressive. As we passed, Dina looked up with a pathetically cheerful smile; she seemed to wait for an invitation to join us. Reuben nodded to her but said nothing, so I couldn't ask her either. "Reuben is taking me for a walk," I said to her, "and afterwards I am going to be thrown into the well." I saw on her face that she had guessed what it was about. We walked on without speaking and Reuben's silence told me that he in turn had understood why Dina was sitting alone in the empty Children's House.

We all know too much about each other.

Sometimes the air is overcharged like certain regions of the aether where too many transmitters operate on the same wavelength.

When we had passed the fence I said: "Well, let's have it out. What is it about—Ellen, or my fascist tendencies, or my general cynicism?"

Reuben took his time, walking steadily down the slope. At last he said: "It's about your attitude to the community in general. Everybody here has his problems and tries to simplify them. With you one sometimes gets the impression that you are deliberately complicating them."

"By what? By reading the newspapers? Or by refusing to live with a girl whom I don't love?"

Reuben paused again. "It is distasteful to me to meddle in your private affairs," he said. "But Ellen is in rather a bad way, and if things have gone as far as to upset the inner balance of a comrade and even her capacity for work, they cease to be private and become a concern of the whole community."

"Oh, God," I said. "Oh, Moses our rabbi."

Reuben kept steadily pacing down the slope. I would have hated him had I not known how much he himself hated the things he had to say.

"To cut a long story short," I said, "you can't force me

against my will to live with Ellen. There are limits to the community's claims on its members."

"If you were a Moslem," said Reuben, "you would regard it as natural that the community had the right to force you to marry a girl, or be stabbed by her brother with a dagger. If you lived in a town, you would also take it for granted that sexual relations entail certain responsibilities. It is a common mistake of most people to accept the limitations imposed upon them by traditionalist societies as matters of course, but to regard any interference on the part of a socialist society as intolerable."

"But of course," I said. "The whole point in a socialist society is to get rid of those traditional limitations and to reduce interference to a minimum."

"Quite," said Reuben. "The question is how you define that minimum. I believe that mutual respect for each other's feelings should be included in the definition."

"But what if there is incompatibility between those feelings?"

"Then there must be an adjustment imposed by Society which, to do a great right, must do a little wrong."

"And the 'little wrong' in my case would be an imposed union which I detest?"

"Either a stable union—or, if your detestation of it is really so strong and not simply egotism and emotional cowardice—then you should give up Ellen altogether."

"But I need her—and she needs me. And it all went quite well for almost six months."

"And after six months Ellen is beginning to feel the one-sidedness of your needs unsatisfactory and degrading."

"But Reuben," I moaned, "when will you all learn to understand that bodily relationships exist in their own right, and are neither more nor less degrading than intellectual ones? Is it degrading for my tennis partner if I don't play chess with him? To discuss politics in a frivolous small-talk manner is as obscene and shocking to me as a petting party with a half-virgin. But two people who give each other bodily satisfaction have a clean and healthy relation, which should be sufficient in itself."

"I don't agree with you," Reuben said. "I don't believe that sex can be isolated from the rest. But the point is not what you or I believe, but what Ellen feels. And she feels about it so strongly"—here he was looking down at his feet—"that she wants to bring the matter up in public at the next meeting."

"Oh, God Almighty," I said.

"Moshe and I tried to dissuade her, but we didn't succeed."

"I thought," I said miserably, "that we had got over that period of adolescent exhibitionism years ago."

"Well, there you are," Reuben said sullenly.

Despite my feeling of wretchedness I began suddenly to laugh. I had detected in Reuben's attitude a shamefaced masculine sympathy and solidarity, quite incompatible with his convictions and the part he had to play. At the same time memories came back to me of our early days and our comically embarrassing public confessions. . . .

"What's the matter with you?" asked Reuben.

"Do you remember," I said, "the time when Dasha solemnly confessed at a meeting that she was a vain, egotistic petty-bourgeois because she was afraid of getting fat?"

Reuben smiled. The afternoon sun was nice and hot, and we sat down on stones on the slope.

"And Max," I went on, "confessing that he was unable to rid himself of an 'irrational and antisocial' dislike of me, and asking the comrades to help him to get over it? And Sarah lecturing us on the virtues of chastity as a means of sublimating biological into social impulses? And the discussions about whether the smokers should give up smoking because the pleasure thus derived gave them a hedonistic advantage over the non-smokers? . . ."

"It was youthful nonsense," said Reuben, "and we soon stopped it."

He threw a pebble at a vulture perching at a few steps

from us, which rose flapping its heavy wings and emitting a sharp, protesting cry.

"Look, Joseph," he said, "we have been together almost six years. We were young fools when we came. Those confessions and sharings were the effusions of half-baked adolescents under the spell of the Essenes and the socialist mystics of Galizia. But now we have grown up, and if a mature comrade like Ellen feels driven to appeal to the whole community it is a quite different and serious matter."

"So there we are back again where we started," I said. "Exactly how serious is it, Reuben? You don't mean to say that there will be a motion to expel me? . . ."

Reuben kept on throwing pebbles though there were no more vultures about. As his silence became more prolonged, I felt my throat going dry. I had at last understood the danger in which I was, and felt the familiar pressure of fear in my heart and bladder. I had seen this kind of panic on a negro's face in a film, who was going to be lynched by a mob—a man accused of a crime he hadn't committed and who suddenly understood that the judges refused to believe in his innocence. All he did was to cry No! No! with a white-lipped mouth torn wide open like a gasping carp's, and knowing already that it was going to be yes! yes! solemnly, fatally, as in an irrevocable dream.

"So they are going to lynch me?" I said.

Reuben shrugged and kept throwing his pebbles with a distracted precision. A swarm of starlings circled over us and the sensation of the dream grew stronger. There were the hills before us, unchanged, and they would look just as still and unconcerned when they cast me out and I would have to go. In the declining sun they had begun to light up in a violet glow. It is a colour between silver and lilac, peculiar to our hills. Though barren, there is nothing rugged about them; they are soft and wavy, a great tide of undulating earth slumbered into immobility; a solid sea of silver limestone and terra rossa which combine into that unique, pale hue. They have an erotic fascination for people, and after the first showers in autumn when they begin to cover themselves with green fluff I sometimes dream at night that I lie on my belly and bite into the live throbbing flesh of the earth, sucking the milk of Galilee.

"So I am going to be lynched?" I repeated.

Reuben stopped throwing pebbles, but he didn't look at me.

"I don't know," he said. "If you remain stubborn, things look pretty nasty. There will be talk of unsocial behaviour, frivolity, disrespect for the female comrades, and so on. They cannot, of course, force you, and I don't think there is a sufficient case for expulsion. But they will all make unctuous speeches and then adjourn the whole thing, and after a while it will start again. And meanwhile the atmosphere will be poisoned. We have not had a scandal for years and everybody will enjoy it. It will appeal to the scavenger-instinct in all of us. And you will lose your temper as usual and provoke them even more. There is already a lot of feeling because of the sympathies you expressed for Bauman's dissidence and terrorism, and what one may call, not quite unfoundedly, your fascist inclinations. It will all be brought up and will make an even worse mess of it."

I said nothing. I thought of how I had boasted to Dina on the night when we occupied the Place: To approve and be approved of, to like and be liked—and how strangely she had looked at me when I had said that. I had a tugging, homesick feeling in my chest. Reuben went on in his groping voice:

"The trouble with you, Joseph, is that you are such a many-coloured bird. In a Commune the grey birds get on best—like myself."

I said nothing. It is true that Reuben is a grey bird, but I am terribly fond of him—perhaps just for that reason. And the reason for my panic was that I had suddenly lost the conviction that he was equally fond of me. And Moshe? And Max? And Dasha, Mendl, Simeon, Arieh, all of them? In what fool's paradise had I lived? What is the tie between us all? A kind of vague cohesion, habit, common interests—but is there any real friendship or intimacy? We hang together like a rubber belt which has lost its elasticity.

I wanted to be alone. I got up and started walking up the slope again. I said nothing to Reuben because I could not trust my voice. For a minute I thought I would go to see Dina, but then it occurred to me that when talking to her I would again forget myself and touch her hand, and she would withdraw it with a frightened little jerk. I stumbled over a stone and kicked it and went on climbing the slope as fast as I could until I lost my breath. Then I heard Reuben calling behind me and stood still.

When he caught up with me he laid his hand on my arm—a rare sign of affection with Reuben. It calmed me almost instantly. I felt as if my blood were, after a momentary stop, circulating again, starting at the place on my arm where Reuben's hand lay.

"Don't be a fool, Joseph," he said. "Though, in a way, it serves you right. At least you know now how Ellen felt all this time."

"Ellen?" I said. "It hadn't occurred to me."

"No—it had not occurred to you, because you were too preoccupied with yourself."

"That is not true. I pity her. It was a real wrench to me when the other day she started crying. Believe me, I have a feeling of great warmth and pity for her—but I can't help her."

"Pity is not the point," said Reuben. He smiled a little, his dim, resigned smile. "Your heart bleeds when she is there, and heals up at once when she turns her back. She is an object to you, not a subject. She only exists for you with reference to yourself. You are an emotional positivist. You only recognise observable phenomena of feeling. You love in abstractions. You are engrossed in Judaism but don't like the Jews. You love the idea of mankind but not the real man. You have lived with us for six years and still we are objects to you, not subjects."

"It isn't true," I shouted. "I am much fonder of you than you are of me."

Reuben's hand on my arm had gradually closed in a firm grip, and he was gently shaking me.

"That is sentimentality," he said. "You have emotions but no affections. You are fond of people as objects of observation and as projector-screens for your own feelings. That is how one is fond of a horse or a dog."

I felt hollow and exhausted. I wrenched my arm free and sat down on the damp slope. Reuben remained standing in front of me; I had never seen him so eloquent and commanding.

"Everybody carries with him a portion of loneliness," he said. "In a Commune more than outside. Outside, there is the family with its concentrated affections. Here there is only a diffuse, evenly distributed benevolence. It is not enough to satisfy people's cravings for intimacy, particularly not the women's. We have to supplement it by lasting personal unions."

"And so back to the holy family from which we thought we had broken away."

"Don't be absurd and unfair. We have liberated the child from parental tyranny, and the parents from economic tyranny. Don't you think that is quite a lot?"

"There remains the tyranny of monogamousness."

"Look," said Reuben, for the first time showing signs of impatience. "The idea of the Commune is to find a solution for pressing national and social problems. Do you not think it would be taking on rather too much if we tried to solve the biological and sexual problem as well? The difference between utopia and a working concern is to know one's limits."

I thought, and not for the first time during our argument, of Esther, Reuben's wife, a mousy, insipid little creature who, shortly expecting her first baby, looks like nothing but an enormous drum-belly with the rest attached to it as mere accessories. I have never been able to find out what Reuben's feelings towards her were.

"All right," I said. "We have argued enough. What do you expect me to do?"

"To conform to the unwritten law of the community—without which it could not exist, would, in fact, disintegrate within a year or so. To make the one final adjustment—or sacrifice, if you want to dramatise it. But what it all practically amounts to is that you share a room with Ellen instead of with Mendl and possibly the Dr. Phil. as a third. For, as you know, when the next graft arrives we shall have to put three bachelors into one room."

I had to grin. "If this isn't blackmail . . ."

"I haven't invented the Dr. Phil.," said Reuben. "And the bachelors have to live together."

"But even if I agreed, it would be a dreadful humiliation for Ellen that I should live with her because of outward pressure."

"Not if you switch on your proverbial charm and explain everything away as a misunderstanding. . . ." He smiled. "Besides, even sensitive women are surprisingly thick-skinned when it is a question of getting themselves married."

"You are the bloodiest Jesuit I have ever seen," I said.

"I am merely trying to discharge my duties as the elected one-year Secretary of the Commune," he said, with a quite serious face.

"And the alternative, if I refuse, is that I have to leave?"

He looked down at me with his faint smile.

"I never for a moment expected that you would choose it. After all, Joseph, you are one of our ancients."

I said nothing, but I knew that I had given in already. After the panic of a moment ago everything else was sheer relief—the relief of the candidate for lynching who hears his sentence commuted to life imprisonment. Life with Ellen even seemed suddenly to have its attractions—a nice, cosy prison-cell with books to read and plenty of exercise in the courtyard. . . .

This was the moment when Reuben, the communal Jesuit, came out with his surprise.

"Well, I take it that we are agreed," he said lightly. "Now there is another matter I wanted to discuss with you. The next graft is due in a fortnight. The Colonisation Department is speeding up the whole plan of our expansion. That means a lot of travelling about for the treasurer, to negotiate loans, buy new machinery and building material, and so on. Moshe is already unable to cope with both the outside and the local work. And now with this rush, and all our planning being upset, we shall need him here all the time. That means that we have to elect a new member of the Secretariat for outside work, who will have to spend five days a week in Jerusalem and Tel Aviv. Moshe and I have decided to propose that you should be elected for this job at the monthly meeting next week. . . ."

I gasped. "What is this—a bribe?"

"Think for yourself whether you can suggest anybody better qualified for the job. You are the best solution for our needs—and it is the best solution for yours."

Thus ended this memorable conversation. I have been cast into the well and pulled out again, and on Friday week I shall probably be appointed to the new job—as Joseph the Provider. Meanwhile I have to give a series of lectures to the Dr. Phil., called Introduction into the Elements of the Theory and Practise of Applied Shoe-making, with a view to turning him into my temporary deputy.

Marriage as a week-end institution won't be too bad either. I am almost looking forward to it; maybe one could do something about the National Birthrate. And I shall be in towns again and walk the solid pavements of Sodom and Gomorrha.

However, I am still too excited to see the consequences of it all. I had under-estimated Reuben, God bless him. I wish every Commune had a Jesuit like him. Some have in fact, or almost;—but then, what other place can stand comparison with Ezra's Tower? . . .

Wednesday

We had a break of a few sunny days, and yesterday during the lunch hour I climbed up the hill on the other side of the wadi to pay a visit to the Ancestor's Cave.

The Ancestor's Cave was discovered six months ago by Arieh the shepherd. The whole hill above the new vineyard is riddled with caves, about half a dozen of which served as burial chambers in Byzantine days. They have all been plundered countless times and even the bones have been scattered. The relatively best preserved is the one Arieh has found, the cave of Joshua the Ancestor. But his skull is missing; perhaps some Arab terrorist has pinched it to have one Hebrew less to cope with in the civil war after the Resurrection. They feel very strongly about this. To prepare for the coming campaign they have already buried four hundred Moslem heroes with their swords beneath the south-east corner of the Haram el Sheriff, whose task it will be to defend the Mosque of Omar against a post-apocalyptic attack from the Hebrew cemetery in the Valley of Josaphat.

Anyway, we like the idea of having the Ancestor's Cave, although it only contains a headless skeleton and the inscription with his name, and is an altogether modest affair compared to the antiquities discovered in other Communes—such as the Byzantine mosaic floor of the ancient synagogue in Beth Alpha, with its lovely picture of Abraham sacrificing Isaac, and various arabesques which look like draughts-boards. There is a story that when the Hebrew religion was made illegal after Bar Kochba's revolt, the believers would assemble in the synagogue and, when the watchposts signalled the approach of soldiers, would all squat down to play draughts.

I found Arieh with his sheep near the Ancestor's Cave; he

was lying as usual on his back, his fringed cartwheel-hat pulled over his face. Arieh is perhaps the only one of us capable of relaxing by lying on his back in the open air. When I go for a walk with Ellen or Dina or Moshe and we stop for a rest, they either squat on their haunches with knees pulled up, or lie on their stomachs kicking the earth with their toes; and always after a minute or two they become fidgety and change position. Living on the land has washed a good deal of restlessness out of our blood, but there is still something atavistic in us constantly on the alert. Our collective unconscious must be crowded with the hosts and ghosts of Legionaries, Inquisitors, Crusaders, Landsknechts and Cossacks. But our Tarzans, I believe, have got rid of them. Theirs the dreamless aseptic sleep without the fear and the vision—*chevaliers sans peur et sans rêves*.

Arieh is an exception; but then Arieh is simple-minded—to put it mildly. I am fond of him, and I think it is reassuring to have in at least one Commune a shepherd who is not an ex-professor of semantics but a moron.

I couldn't make out whether he was asleep or not. Guri, our giant sheep-dog, lay with his fore-paws across Arieh's chest. As I came closer he began to growl. Obviously Guri has taken over the element of suspicion from his master's subconscious. For though Guri is collective property, he regards Arieh as his real master, while for the rest of us he shows a kind of friendly condescension. We are all jealous of Guri and I wonder whether Sarah won't one day take the matter up in the General Assembly.

As Arieh did not stir, I decided that he was asleep and continued up the slope to the caves. I found the one I was looking for, and lowered myself through the narrow entrance-hole into the vestibule of the burial chambers. It was muddy and smelt of damp and urine. There are three small chambers opening from the vestibule—no more than niches hewn into the rock, each the size of a small coffin. But of course the ancestors were buried without coffins, just wrapped in a sheet and pushed into their niche. In the first chamber there are a few scattered bones, the others are empty except for the damp sand on the bottom of the niche. There is always a candle-stump in the first chamber; I lit it and went down the three slippery steps into the lower passage, careful not to bang my head against the rock. The lower vestibule contains three more niches, and the centre one is headless Joshua's. Engraved by a clumsy, childish hand into the hard lime-rock over the narrow entrance of the niche are the four letters *yod, shin, vaf* and *a'yin*: Joshua or Jeshu or Jesu. I looked at the bones embedded in the damp sand of the niche and tried unsuccessfully to work up some emotion; but I just couldn't believe that there ever was warm flesh round those pathetic bones, and strange clothes round the flesh, and ideas in the missing head. Least of all could I imagine what he may have looked like. However, according to the laws of probability, there must be a fraction in me which is directly descended from him. Inside my testicles there are some complicated but stable groups of molecules which were handed down to me from him with their pattern unchanged; and maybe some day I shall pass them on to Ellen and so down the chain. It is as if a long, long pipeline were laid out not in space but in time, and at every time-mile or so there is a tap attached to a pair of loins. Now and then the tap opens and the ancient stream mixes with other streams in other pipes. An elaborate system of irrigation, like our vegetable garden's, expanded over the dry crust of the globe. Well, well. . . .

Come to think of it, there are not even so many taps between old Joshua and myself: the length of the pipe is about seventeen centuries which equal no more than fifty-one generations. In other words, old Joshua was only about the twenty-sixth grandfather of my grandfather. Quite likely he was one of Bar Kochba's underground rebel army which fought the Legionaries in these same hills of Galilee, and his wife and kin were crucified or put to the sword, and his missing head, once bearded and warted and furrowed by yellow wrinkles, was buzzing with Things to Forget.

I climbed out of the cave, and who should be waiting for me outside the hole but Guri, whining with anxiety about the vanishing in the bowels of the earth of the one thirty-sixth fraction of his collective proprietor. As my head emerged from the hole he was howling with joy, and as I needed both hands to climb out of the hole he profited from the occasion to wash my face all over with his slobbering tongue. I was of course delighted; there is nothing more flattering than the attentions of a dog with a strong personality. People like you for this or that quality, but dogs pay homage to the very *Ding an sich* in you.

While walking down the slope I kept my eyes on the ground, looking for coins and surface-pottery. Coins abound here at this time of the year—the autumn rain washes them out of the soil of the decayed terraces. The other day the Dr. Phil. found a "Judaea capta" which is a rarity. He would. I only found some Constantines and Jupiter Ammons.

When Guri and I got back to Arieh, he was sitting up and smoking a cigarette with his great pal Walid, the Arab shepherd from Kfar Tabiyeh. Guri, who has strong racial prejudices, growled at Walid, but at a word from Arieh flopped his ears back and settled down in the classical Sphinx-pose, watching us with his tongue hanging out.

I shook hands with Arieh and Walid, and sat down with them for a cigarette. Walid is a quiet and very polite boy, so I went through the regulation question-and-answer ceremony.

"How are you, ya Walid?"

"I am well, thank God."

"So you are well, ya Walid?"

"I am very well, thank God."

"And your father is well too?"

"He is very well, thank God."

"I am glad your father is well, ya Walid."

"My father is well, thank God."

"And how is your older brother, ya Walid?"

And so on through the two younger brothers and the horse and the two mules and the cattle and the flock. The answer is always that all is well, even if the whole family is dying and the flock decimated by foot and mouth disease. It is a soothing, gentle ritual, of which the British lovely-day game is but a crude and simplified variation. When we got through with it, Walid, who had finished his cigarette and was chewing a halm of grass, said:

"I have just remarked to your friend that your young trees look very beautiful."

"Walid likes trees," Arieh said languidly, by way of explanation.

"I think trees are beautiful," said Walid.

"Why don't you plant some in your village?" I asked.

"Tzz!" said Walid, tossing his head up as a sign of violent negation. "That is impossible."

"Why is it impossible?"

"Tzz! The trees would not last."

"Why would they not last?"

"You have a quarrel with your neighbour and he cuts your trees down."

"That is very bad," I said. "Can you do nothing about it?"

"Tzz!" he said. "No. We can't grow trees."

We were quiet for a while, and just sat and watched the sheep and the clouds. Arieh offered cigarettes, but he had only two left, so he broke one into halves and he and I shared it. Walid twice politely refused to take the whole cigarette and accepted it the third time. After a while he said:

"You are very poor."

"Not very," I said. "And we have only just started."

"You have tractors and electricity but you have no cigarettes."

"We put all our money into tractors and machines, and later we shall be rich."

"No," he said. "When you have more money you will buy more tractors."

For some reason this irritated me, and I said to tease him: "Well, you have no tractors and no cigarettes either."

"But I am free," Walid said. "And you live like in prison."

"Walid thinks we work too hard," Arieh explained.

"Nobody tells us how much we are to work," I said. "We do it because we like it."

"You start planting trees and then you have to go on tending them. You always start something new and then you have to finish it, and when it is finished you have to start again something new. You are like prisoners. I am free. If I like I can go to-morrow to Egypt or to America or to England."

"You need money for that," Arieh remarked philosophically.

"*Ma lesh*—that doesn't matter," said Walid. "I can go wherever I like. Egypt or America or India. I am free and you are prisoners."

"Everybody who has set himself a task becomes a prisoner," I said. "But that doesn't matter. *Ma lesh.*"

"*Ma lesh,*" Walid agreed.

"*Ma lesh,*" said Arieh, lying over on his back and pulling his fringed hat over his eyes. . . .

Thursday

To-night I told Dina that I am going to marry Ellen. She said that she had expected it and made no further comment. We were standing together on the platform of the Tower, after dark.

We stood for perhaps five minutes in silence. Several times I wanted to speak, but each time I felt my voice thicken in my throat, and gave it up. I knew that we were both thinking of the same scene: that first morning when she had slept on my arm in the first-aid tent and we had climbed up the Tower to watch the sun rise over the hills.

Suddenly I had the wild idea that perhaps Dina's trouble was just fuss and hypochondria, and that by taking her by surprise I could break down the barrier. I silently counted ten to myself and then turned towards her and grabbed her by the shoulders with a hard grip. She did not shrink back, it was almost as if she had expected it; in fact I am convinced that she had expected it. She did not resist as I drew her towards me, but her body grew taut and unyielding; and she trembled so violently that I could hear the faint grinding noise of her teeth as she locked her jaws to prevent herself from crying out. By then I was terrified but I wanted to go through with it and I knew that Dina wanted me to go through with it, in the same desperate hope. Against her will her rigid body strained away from me; and at the second when I pressed my mouth against her tight dry lips, hardened by the clenched teeth behind them, she flung me away with the uncontrollable violence of an explosion. While we both stood panting on the dark platform, she managed to say in a kind of hiss: "Sorry, Joseph—please go away—quick"; and before I could make up my mind she was sick over the parapet. I did not even dare to hold her head.

After a while she got better and we climbed down the ladder. Again I did not dare to help her. In the faint light which came through the open door of the dining-hut she said good-night, contriving a kind of smile.

I walked out into the fields and threw myself down on the soft dewy earth. I closed my eyes and went into a day-dream about what I would do to the fellows who had done this to Dina if I could lay my hands on them. It was the first time in my life that a fantasy of this kind got hold of me, and when I pulled myself out of it I was all sweaty in my clothes and trembling. But sobering up was almost unbearable, so I began once more to dig my nails into the damp earth which became transformed into the liquid eye-sockets of Dina's torturer. When I sobered the second time, the attack was over.

Even now, in my full senses, I would accept the opportunity of physical revenge. This is against my reasoning and my convictions. But reasoning cannot satisfy either hunger or rut, and to-night I have learned that the thirst for revenge may become physiological reality. It would not help Dina, but it would help me.

I know a story of a Sicilian peasant who had spent five years in prison for the attempted murder of his wife's seducer and who, the day he was released, went straight to the seducer's house, killed him, and went contentedly back to prison for the rest of his life. The Italian Communist who told me the story, said that after ten years in prison the peasant seemed perfectly happy and knew no regret. At the time I could not believe this; now I understand that under certain circumstances a life-sentence or the gallows may appear as a reasonable price to pay for regaining one's peace of mind.

The Arabs seem to know this. And some of Bauman's youngsters too, like that boy Benjosef who went on singing the anthem until the cord choked his voice. That isn't so easy as it sounds. The climate, or the contact with this earth riddled with ancestors' caves, seems to reopen certain taps in the pipe which had better remain sealed.

Now that I have written it down I have exorcised the headless Joshua. Articulateness is the death of instinct. But have I not said before that the trouble with us is that we have become too articulate? . . .

Friday

Ran into Dina first thing in the morning outside the shower-baths, and walked with her to the dining-hut for breakfast. Her hair was still damp from the shower and faintly steaming in the cold morning air. The contrast of the fresh cold-water-gloss on her face and the blue shadows under her eyes made her look more attractive than ever. At breakfast she chattered with unforced gaiety. She seemed to have forgotten all about yesterday, and after the first plate of porridge I too felt much better.

Anyway, yesterday has settled it: Ellen is moving into my room to-morrow.

Sunday

Simeon has been transferred from the "infectious" ward, so yesterday at last I could go and see him in the Hadassah Hospital in Haifa.

With his face flat on the pillow he looked more than ever like a sick falcon. His black eyes fastened on me as soon as I entered the ward and seemed to pull and steer me on my way round the other beds to his side. His face is emaciated and so are his long, loose-fingered, nicotine-stained hands. The blanket on his bed was neatly tucked in and his pyjamas buttoned up to the neck; there was nothing undressed about Simeon in bed. The blanket, bedside locker and even the pillow were littered with papers and newspaper cuttings.

I sat down on a chair by the bed, and grabbed his hand which lay flat on the blanket.

"One shouldn't touch me—I may still be infectious," he said, but I could see that he was pleased. "Well, how are things on our ivory tower?"

"I am to marry Ellen and to be made treasurer for outside work," I blurted out.

"No!" he exclaimed in frank and naïve amazement. He seemed excited by my news like a schoolboy being told what had been going on in the class during his absence. Simeon did after all look more human in bed.

"You don't say. . . ." He laughed, but after one or two chuckles started to cough. "By God, Reuben has got his dialectics right. . . . But it is a good thing," he continued. "You are the best person for the job. And otherwise you would have quitted—sooner or later."

So Simeon too had noticed how much adrift I had been. They all seem to have noticed it—except myself.

It was visiting hour, and each of the four patients in the room had one or two relatives sitting at his bedside. They were all absorbed in their own conversation and created a neutral, relaxed atmosphere in which each bed with its locker, chair and screen formed a little island of privacy. Simeon lay on his back, his eyes gazing at the ceiling. "Tell me more about our ivory tower," he said.

"Gaby is marrying the Egyptian and Moshe has twins—but this you probably know already."

He nodded. "What else?"

"We bought a mare from Ein Hashofeth for twenty pounds."

"How old?"

"Three years. Ash-coloured. Rather nice, but showing too much rib."

"What is she going to be called?"

"*Alliyah.*"

He gave a short, bitter chuckle. "Immigration," he repeated. "Symbols, symbols and nothing behind it."

An old fat nurse waddled past carrying a bedpan. Despite her neat uniform she looked more like the wife of a rabbi disguised as a nurse.

Simeon was silent for a while, then he cleared his throat and asked in a casual voice:

"And the saplings?"

"Judith is looking after them. Since the rains they have grown almost an inch."

"Any duds?"

"Not as far as I know."

"The last row towards the corner of the veg-garden needs some extra watering."

"I'll tell Judith."

He gazed at the ceiling and gave a shrug. "What's the difference, anyway. . . ."

"When will they let you out?" I asked.

"In about a week."

"You'll have to share a room with Mendl and the Dr. Phil."

"I won't."

"It will be difficult to find another arrangement. We are expecting a new graft in a fortnight."

Simeon said nothing, and after a while I asked:

"They'll send you first for convalescence to Sichron?"

"I expect so."

"And when will you be back home?"

"Never."

I stared at him and he looked at the ceiling, then slowly turned his head to me.

"It doesn't really surprise you, does it?"

My heart was thumping.

"*Habibi,*" I said at last. "No. No, I won't believe it."

He smiled. "The funny thing is, I can't yet really make myself believe it either."

More than anything that he could have said, this convinced me that arguing was useless. Without Simeon the image of the Place in my mind's eye had suddenly become a shade darker and greyer—like a scene on the stage with the lights gradually being shut off. It was perhaps even worse than if we lost Dina. A Commune is not simply a crowd—it is a pattern, a mosaic figure, and if a piece breaks loose it leaves a gap for ever.

"But why, Simeon?" I asked.

His smile became ironical. "Ask yourself and you will find the answer."

I kept silent, for Simeon made me feel not only miserable, but guilty—just as during our last talk in the tree-nursery. I had avoided him ever since and, to tell the truth, his illness had been rather a godsend to me. But there it was now—and I could no longer escape it; just as I could not escape that other question centred round Ellen.

It is no good running away from things—they move slower and steadier, and in the end they always catch up with one.

Simeon had propped himself up on his elbow, searching among his papers. He was very weak, and his thin neck with the skinny Adam's apple trembled slightly with the effort. The fat nurse waddled excitedly towards us. "I told you you are not allowed to sit up," she cackled.

"Go to hell," said Simeon quietly. She gaped at him but

he went on searching among his papers, ignoring her completely, and after a few seconds she turned on her heel and walked off, with a red face, and without another word.

"Read these," said Simeon, thrusting the bundle of newspaper cuttings into my hand and letting himself fall back on the pillow. The cuttings were neatly labelled and held together by a clip. I read:

"According to a statement issued by the Government of Northern Rhodesia, the elected members of the Legislative Council have unanimously opposed any immigration of Jewish Refugees. The acting Governor, therefore, felt unable to advise the Secretary of State that the matter would be proceeded with further at the present time. . . ."

"It is stated that mass immigration into Portuguese colonies is strictly forbidden. . . ."

"President Vargas of Brazil has issued a decree . . . fixing the annual quota of immigration at two per cent of the total number of immigrants of the same nationality during the last fifty years. . . ."

"A memorandum urging the prohibition of foreign immigrants into Cyprus has been submitted to the Municipal Council by local professional corporations. . . ."

"Refugees from European countries will not be encouraged to emigrate to New Zealand, according to a statement made last week by Mr. Nash, the Minister of Finance. . . ."

"It is understood that the Government of South Africa is unwilling to contemplate any modification in the stringent provisions of the Aliens Act, which makes Jewish immigration virtually impossible. . . ."

"It is reported that the Uruguay Government has instructed its Consuls to refuse visas to Jews who are emigrating for racial or political reasons. . . ."

Simeon looked at me with his bitterly hypnotic eyes. There was a fluid poison in them and I understood why the fat nurse had not answered back.

"Observe," he said, "that these are cuttings taken from one English newspaper only, and that they all appeared during the last three months. I have the decrees of about twenty more countries on my list—decrees prohibiting admittance of the lepers with the yellow spot. And now read this. . . ."

"It is reported from reliable sources in Germany whose origin cannot be disclosed, that for some time experiments have been carried out in state orphanages for the painless physical liquidation of children incurably crippled, insane, or of undesirable racial heredity. The methods applied are phenol injections into the aorta, intra-venous air injections to cause thrombosis, and lethal chambers filled with carbon monoxide gas."

Simeon watched me. "It may be exaggerated," I said after a while.

"You think so? No, you don't. It's the Englishman inside you trying to close the shutters. And now read this."

It was the previous day's paper, which had not reached us yet in Ezra's Tower. I read:

"LONDON, *December 8.—The Marquess of Dufferin and Ava, Colonial Under Secretary, appreciated the moving appeal for the admission to Palestine of 10,000 Jewish children whose parents had become victims of persecution in Germany, but pointed out that His Majesty's Government was unable to accede as they must consider the danger of prejudicing the Round Table Conference on Palestine which is shortly to assemble in the capital.*

. . . It was further pointed out during the debate in the House of Lords that the Government's decision to turn down the Palestine Hebrew Community's offer to receive the children was equivalent to robbing them of the prospect of escape."

I handed the cuttings back. "What are you collecting this stuff for?"

"I have been asked to edit a pamphlet."

"By whom?"

He paused, then said, looking at me with an ironic smile:

"By the Bauman Group—and those connected with it. Don't pretend again that you are surprised."

"No," I said. Then I added:

"So that's why you are going to leave us."

Simeon wiped the sweat from his face, unfolding a neatly pressed handkerchief.

"Is that all your comment?" he said. "I thought you were going to call me a fascist, a killer, an outcast and whatnot."

"No," I said. "I won't."

For a while none of us spoke, but all the time Simeon was watching me and I knew that every expression on my face would be stored away in his memory as if on photographic records. Then he said:

"Things are moving quickly now. In a few months or weeks our group will have to go underground. The Government will start arresting and deporting us. Then we will start to shoot—and believe me, we'll do it more efficiently than the Arabs. We have a few technical surprises ready for them."

He spoke with the self-assurance of a man with an army behind him.

"Where will the stuff come from?" I asked.

"The arms? We have plenty, and there is more coming."

"Where from?"

"From abroad. You will hear about that in due time. You will hear a lot more to surprise you."

I said nothing. Everything Simeon said sounded boastful and fantastic—everything except the way he said it. The lure was in his self-assurance. It sapped the resistance of my judgment. His contact always acted on me in the way of communicating vessels: it emptied my critical faculties and filled me up with faith. It was an immensely comforting sensation. All that was needed was to take the plunge and one would be rid of all doubts and filled with inner certainty and the boons of blind obedience—like on the first night when I was shooting under Reuben's orders.

". . . But the time for you has not come yet," said Simeon, and I felt as if he had deliberately cut the contact. "They need you at our ivory tower. Moshe is right about carrying on with the job as long as there is a possibility. When we need you we shall let you know."

"I haven't said yet that I agree," I said. But Simeon merely smiled:

"Do you think I would have told you the things I did, if I didn't know that we can trust you?"

The visiting hour was drawing to its end and all over the ward people gathered themselves up and lingered by the beds in the elaborate process of leave-taking. Simeon seemed to shrink again to a sick man in a hospital bed dreading to be left alone. I felt pity for him—the pity for the strong which is more painful than pity for the weak.

"Oh, Simeon," I said, pressing his damp yellow fingers, "why can't we stay on in our ivory tower? You with your saplings and I with my old boots and Pepys. Is that too much to ask?"

He withdrew his hand. "Ask from whom?" he said drily. "From God or from the British?"

"Time, please," called the fat nurse—but she dared not come close to Simeon's bed.

"What will you live on in the town?" I asked; and only now did it occur to me that after altogether six years' work with the Commune, Simeon was to leave us without a shilling or a spare shirt of his own.

Simeon shrugged. "I shall be a professional killer," he said. I couldn't even make out whether he was joking or not.

"Time, please," called the nurse, looking at us.

"Remember one thing, Joseph," said Simeon. "A phrase which you yourself once said to me. 'It is the deed which counts and not its inner shadow.' Each of our acts goes on record. It is weighed on objective scales and not on the individual balance."

"Time, please," called the nurse. I was the last visitor in the ward.

DAYS OF WRATH

(1939)

"Ireland, they say, has the honour of being the only country which never persecuted the Jews. Do you know why?"

"Why, sir?" Stephen asked.

"Because she never let them in," Mr. Deasy said solemnly.

JAMES JOYCE, "Ulysses'

DAYS OF WRATH (1939)

1

"And the king of Babylon smote them, and slew them at Riblah in the land of Hamath. So Judah was carried away out of their land. And they burnt the house of God, and brake down the wall of Jerusalem, and burnt all the palaces thereof with fire, and destroyed all the goodly vessels thereof. And them that had escaped from the sword carried he away to Babylon; where they were servants to him and his sons until the reign of the kingdom of Persia."

(Kings and Chronicles)

2

"Now in the first year of Cyrus king of Persia, the Lord stirred up the spirit of Cyrus king of Persia, that he made a proclamation throughout all his kingdom, and put it also in writing, saying: The Lord God of heaven has given me all the kingdoms of the earth; and he has charged me to build him an house at Jerusalem, which is in Judah. Who is there among you of all his people? his God be with him and let him go.

"Now these are the children of the province that went up out of captivity, and came again unto Jerusalem and Judah. And they set the altar upon his bases; for fear was upon them because of the people of those countries. And when the builders laid the foundation of the temple of the Lord, they set the priests in their apparel with trumpets, and the Levites with cymbals, and they sang together by course in praising because

the foundation of the house of the Lord was laid. But many of the priests, who were ancient men, that had seen the first house, wept with a loud voice; and many shouted aloud for joy: so that the people could not discern the noise of the shout of joy from the noise of the weeping.

"Now when the adversaries of Judah and Benjamin heard that the children of the captivity builded the temple, then they troubled them in building, and hired counsellors against them to frustrate their purpose all the days of Cyrus king of Persia, even until the reign of Darius king of Persia. And in the reign of Ahasuerus wrote they unto him an accusation against the inhabitants of Judah and Jerusalem. And in the days of Artaxerxes wrote Rehum the chancellor and Shimshai the scribe and the rest of their companions a letter against Jerusalem. This is the copy of the letter that they sent unto Artaxerxes the king:

"Thy servants the men on this side of the river, and at such a time. Be it known unto the king, that the Jews that came up from thee to us are come unto Jerusalem, building the rebellious and the bad city, and have set up the walls thereof and joined the foundations. Be it known now unto the king, that, if this city be builded, and the walls set up again, then will they not pay toll, tribute, and custom, and so thou shalt endamage the revenue of the kings.

"Then sent the king an answer unto Rehum the chancellor, and to Shimshai the scribe, and to the rest of their companions: Peace, and at such a time. The letter which ye sent unto us has been plainly read before me. And I commanded, and search has been made, and it is found that this city of old time has made insurrection against kings, and that rebellion and sedition have been made therein. Give ye now commandment to cause these men to cease, and that this city be not builded, until another commandment shall be given from me.

"Now when the copy of king Artaxerxes' letter was read before Rehum, and Shimshai the scribe, and their companions,

they went up in haste to Jerusalem unto the Jews, and made them to cease by force and power."

(From the Book of Ezra)

3

The desk of the Hon. Patrick Gordon-Smith, O.B.E., Assistant Chief Commissioner to the Government of Palestine, was an ordinary polished mahogany desk such as one might see in any department store. As if to compensate him for the desk's lack of history and tradition, the tall windows of the temporary Government offices in the Hospice of St. Paul opened on the noble sight of the wall of the Old City of Jerusalem, built by Soleiman the Magnificent of huge, ochre-coloured squared stones, some of which betrayed by their relief-work Roman origin and had once formed the outer wall of Herod's Temple. Bending to the left in his armchair, the Assistant Chief Commissioner could also obtain a partial view of the bustling life in front of the Damascus Gate—a dusty and smelly but extremely attractive medley of donkeys, camels, and Arabs in all kinds of attire, which, despite the noisy cries of lemonade vendors, the roar of the cracked gramophone on the terrace of the nearby Arab coffee-house, the occasional tinkling of sheep-bells and the constant hooting of motor-cars, had a strangely dream-like quality, as if a scene from a mediaeval etching, illustrating a pilgrim's tale, had come to life. It was one of the few parts of Jerusalem as yet unspoiled by the vulgarity of modern Hebrew architecture, and one to which Jews rarely ventured these days as the whole Arab quarter north of the Old City Wall was considered unsafe for them.

The A.Ch.C. was reading with a harassed air the topmost document of this morning's yellow in-tray, concerning a protest of the Armenian community against an alleged infringement of the *status quo* in the Basilica of the Nativity in Bethlehem, said to have been committed by Greek Orthodox priests by attaching the curtain of their chapel to the upper nail No. 1 on the pillar south-east of the left-hand set of steps leading to the Manger.

It was the A.Ch.C.'s habit to read in the morning the papers in the non-urgent yellow tray first, before turning to the urgent blue and so to the top-urgent red tray. As the years passed, this habit had grown such firm roots that to adopt the opposite procedure now appeared to him as an eccentricity of doubtful taste. Once, when pressed for an explanation—though he disliked explanations of a personal character which smacked of psychology—he had tried to improvise one.

"I suppose," he had said in his halting, groping manner, "I suppose it's one of those things you can't explain. However, if you come to think of it, it's rather obvious. The so-called urgent matters get attended to in any case, whereas the other ones are apt to fall into neglect. It's rather like mothers trying to get their plain daughters married first—a kind of compensatory social justice, if you see what I mean."

The girl who had asked the question—a pretty little Jewess employed as a translator and apt to take liberties with a kittenish air—had looked rather puzzled. She had meant to taunt him and had been defeated by her own weapons, that kind of logical feint they were all so fond of. Hovering over the short plump girl from the lean height of his six feet two inches, the A.Ch.C. was having his quiet fun. For he knew of course that the explanation he had given was at the best a first approximation to the truth. A closer examination, however, would have led back to the A.Ch.C.'s early school days and would have proved far too embarrassingly "psychological" to be discussed. It would have led back to the commandment, implanted during those early days, that it was bad form to be too "keen" on anything except on games, and to the conditioned reflex to restrain one's rash impulses—established to a degree where the suppression almost preceded the impulse itself and second thoughts came before first. Now the A.Ch.C. was in truth rather keen on his job, a weakness which he successfully hid behind a discreetly bored and harassed air; hence it seemed to him all the less permissible to rush into one's office, throw one's hat down and jump at the urgent entries like a shopkeeper tearing open his envelopes to see what orders had come in overnight.

To turn to the yellow tray first and leave the red one to the last was thus not only a matter of sheer common sense, as he had pointed out to the intrusive translator, but also a question touching upon things which one did not mention explicitly for fear of sounding pompous and a prig: tradition, dignity and form. The value of the ritual became enhanced by the fact that it was performed while the A.Ch.C. was alone in his room. In the presence of a subordinate he occasionally even went so far as to reverse the order; for courtesy demanded that one should sometimes adapt good manners to bad ones so as to avoid giving offence—like eating with one's fingers at an Arab meal pretending that one enjoyed it, or arguing with Jews about legal niceties pretending that they mattered.

The A.Ch.C. rang the hand-bell on his desk, a wrought-iron camel-bell whose touch gave him each time a sensuous pleasure, and ordered his private secretary, Miss Clark, to search among the files relating to the division of rights and duties among the various communities at the Holy Places, for the one concerning the *status quo* in the Basilica of the Nativity in Bethlehem. Before he had finished reading the next document, which was a vigorous protest of the orthodox Rabbinate of the anti-Zionist Agudath faction against alleged unorthodoxies occurring in the ritual slaughter-houses controlled by the orthodox pro-Zionist Mizrakhi faction, Miss Clark had come back with the required document. It was a report by an Arab Sub-Inspector addressed to the then Governor of Jerusalem, Sir Ronald Storrs, in 1920, and containing an admirably concise definition of those contested privileges, infringements of which led, at an average twice a year, to blows and bloodshed among the clergy of the various denominations. Under the heading "*Basilica of the Nativity, cleaning thereof*", the record stated:

(1) That the Greek Orthodox Community may open the windows of the Basilica throwing Southward, for the time of cleaning only.

(2) That the Greek Orthodox Community may place a ladder on the floor of the Armenian chapel for cleaning the upper part of this chapel above the Cornice.

(3) That the Armenians have the right to clean the North face of the pillar on which the Greek Orthodox pulpit is placed, up to the Cornice only.

(4) That by mutual agreement the following has also been arranged:

(*a*) That the Greeks should attach their curtain tight to the lower nail No. 2 at the foot of the pillar which lies South East of the left hand set of steps leading to the Manger.

[This paragraph the A.Ch.C. underlined with a blue pencil.]

(*b*) That the Latins should have their curtain fall naturally down the same pillar, leaving a space of 16 cm. between it and that of the Greek Orthodox.

(*c*) That nail No. 1 be left unused by any of the communities.

[This the A.Ch.C. underlined twice.]

(5) That whenever the Government is to clean any part of the Basilica, the necessary implements should be Government's.

(6) That the above arrangement, however, is subject to alterations in case of any official documents in favour of any of the above communities being produced before next year's cleaning.

"Look," the A.Ch.C. said to Miss Clark, " 'No. 1 nail to be left unused by any of the communities.' A nice, clear-cut case. I wish they were all like that."

Miss Clark gave one of her fervently affirmative little gasps. She had an unlimited admiration for the A.Ch.C., always harassed by those beastly native sects and communities and whatnots, and yet always patient, polite and kind. She tried to alleviate his burden by her quick, silent, self-effacing diligence, and expressed her opinions mainly in the form of that affirmative sigh or gasp consisting in a sudden sharp catching of her breath, in which all her repressed and disciplined feelings were exploded. At first the A.Ch.C. had been a little startled by these recurrent inhalatory reports, but he soon became accustomed to regarding them as a time-saving equivalent for "Yes, Mr. Gordon-Smith", while the emotional implications he chose quietly to ignore.

He dictated two short notes to Dunby, the Junior Secretary, who was to draft an answer to the Armenian protest, and to promise an inquiry (the sixth or seventh) into the ritual slaughter business; then turned to the next entry. It consisted of about a dozen letters, pinned together with translations attached, from various Arab notables and village mukhtars adhering to the moderate Nashashibi party, who expressed their loyalty to the Government and asked for protection from the Arab terrorist bands. Two of the letters contained the naïve question whether the rumour was true that the Government approved of terrorism as a means of getting rid of the Hebrews; and if so, would the Government tell the terrorists to stop extracting money from Arabs and leave their property alone.— This, however, concerned the Military and the C.I.D. While handing the letter to Miss Clark, the A.Ch.C. permitted his thoughts to dwell for a second on his nephew Jimmy who served as a junior officer in the Black Watch, and who had had his leg amputated last week after an engagement with terrorist bands attacking a Hebrew settlement. But it only lasted for a second; with a slight feeling of guilt for letting personal emotions creep into public business he turned to the blue, semi-urgent tray.

The first document in it bore the familiar Hebrew heading of the Zionist Executive and the familiar signature of Mr. Glickstein, requesting an interview with His Excellency *re* admission of the 10,000 children from Germany. Across the top was written in H.E.'s pithy handwriting: "No. Matter definitely settled by statement Col. Sec. Hse. Commons Nov. 24

and Hse. of Lords Dec. 8." The A.Ch.C. turned to Miss Clark with his worried smile.

"He is an insistent fellow, our Mr. Glickstein, isn't he?"

Miss Clark uttered her little gasp. It was tinged with commiseration for her chief whom H.E. had left once more to hold the baby, and with disapproval for the insistent Mr. Glickstein with his gold-toothed smile.

"Write that His Excellency regrets he is unable to see him, but that I shall be glad to have a talk with him Monday next at 11 A.M."

Turning to the next item in the tray, he thought that H.E. went indeed a bit far in demonstrating his dislike of the Hebrew community. For the last year or so he had persistently refused to see Glickstein, and at this year's official Garden Party practically none of them had been invited. Glickstein was a trying person, and his insistence on pushing a matter which had been settled at Cabinet level was both unpolitic and in deplorable taste, but equally deplorable was H.E.'s demonstrative rudeness to them. It put one in the wrong with an otherwise perfectly good case and laid the Administration open to tiresome attacks in the House and in Geneva, which Mr. Glickstein and his friends were so clever at staging. However . . .

The next item was a digest of yesterday's Hebrew and Arabic Press, teeming as usual with gross inexactitudes and venomous attacks on each other, on dissenting factions in each party's own camp, and mainly on the Government. He skipped the leader columns with their ever-repeated emotional tirades and concentrated instead on the shorter notes with some factual content.

"We hear", wrote the leading Hebrew paper, "that there is at present no permanent Hebrew physician to attend to Hebrew patients at the Government Hospital in Jerusalem. We are also informed that the Government Health Department does not employ a sufficient number of Hebrew officials. Arabic reigns supreme in that Department. The British heads of the Department prefer

talking Arabic to the Hebrew officials rather than Hebrew. One of the heads requested to be greeted in Arabic and not in Hebrew. . . ."

To this page efficient Miss Clark had attached on her own initiative a typewritten note which said: "Facts ascertained from Health Dept. In Government Hospital Jerusalem 4 out of 10 doctors on the establishment are Jews. So are 21 out of 53 nurses. The three members of the Hospital clerical staff are all Jews. Out of 75 medical officers in the whole Department at present 31 are Jewish and of 331 nurses 38% are Jewish."

"Excellent," said the A.Ch.C. "We'll send them a rectification."

He leant back for a moment in his chair, both arms resting on the supports, his tall, lean upper body bent over the desk in a curve. He looked out at Soleiman the Magnificent's wall, behind which ran King Solomon's Street through the shuks to the Temple Area with the Dome of the Rock (whose main preacher, Sheikh Abdul el Khatib, had just been murdered by extremists of the Mufti's clan).

"The pettiness of it all," said the A.Ch.C.

Miss Clark gave her little gasp. "One sometimes wonders whether they will ever become really civilised," she ventured.

Miss Clark would have been at a loss to give an exact definition of the word "civilised", yet she had a vivid image of its meaning: it meant lunching at the Strand Corner House on tea, two rolls and butter and a slice of cheese, to the accompaniment of the uniformed women's orchestra playing Liszt's Hungarian Rhapsody.

The A.Ch.C. seemed to-day in a relaxed mood; he was leaning back in his chair, pursuing his thoughts.

"Too much sanctity in the air—don't you think, Miss Clark? It poisons the atmosphere. Holiness is only bearable in mild solutions, like bath salts. The concentrated essence is venom."

The absence of the usual gasp made the A.Ch.C. realise that he had shocked Miss Clark. Confident, however, of her imminent forgiveness, he turned to the urgent tray, of which the main item was a lengthy confidential report from the C.I.D. Political Department, Branch for Hebrew Affairs, on the activities of the *Irgun Z'wai Le'umi* or "National Military Organisation". This extreme nationalist para-military body had considerably increased in strength since the affiliation of the so-called Bauman Group. There also seemed to be a marked change in their policy. Up to now the *Irgun* had been mainly engaged in smuggling in illegal immigrants from Eastern Europe and in acts of retaliation against the Arabs. During the last week, however, it had succeeded in establishing a secret short-wave transmitter operating on wavelength 37.3 for about two hours a dav. The station was apparently ambulant as the direction of the beam had been traced on different days to locations varying from Tel Aviv to Lower Galilee. The main announcer was a Hebrew girl with a Sephardi accent and a pleasant contralto voice. The contents of the broadcasts were divided about equally between attacks on the Mandatory Power's alleged anti-Zionist policy and attacks on the passivity of the *Haganah,* the leftist Defence Organisation controlled by the official Zionist bodies. The broadcasts began and closed with a recorded chorus of the Hebrew national anthem and were interspersed with the slogan "Your kin is murdered in Europe. What are you doing about it?" monotonously repeated every five minutes. The switch in emphasis from anti-Arab to anti-British propaganda was marked, and seemed to point to intended terroristic action against the Administration. A supplementary list of suspects (List III B) was attached. It contained about thirty names, among others that of a certain Simeon Stark from the Communal Settlement of Ezra's Tower.

". . . Well, well," said the A.Ch.C. "What do you think of that?"

"I think it is a shame," Miss Clark said primly, her pale cheeks faintly flushed with indignation. "We let these people in and defend them against the Arabs, and instead of gratitude we get this."

"Quite," said the A.Ch.C., and it occurred to him for the

first time that Jimmy would have to cancel his entry for the Sports Club's tennis tournament. "Quite so, Miss Clark—though not entirely so."

He leaned back in his chair and for a moment stared at her absentmindedly. Miss Clark, lowering her lids, thought that the A.Ch.C. looked to-day even more harassed than usual. He will kill himself, what with all those beastly sects and communities, she thought. And yet, she confessed to herself with a little flutter of the heart, that harassed look somehow increased his indefinable air of distinction. She knew nobody so distinguished-looking as her chief—not even H.E. Everything about him contributed to the effect: his slimness and height, the delicate slope of his shoulders which was a result of his always having to bend down when talking to others; the grey strands in the dark hair and even the slight irregularity of his eyes, one of which was a shade darker than the other, giving his glance a certain impersonal fixity as if he were wearing a monocle.

Gradually the A.Ch.C. seemed to come to life again, as if a battery gone flat inside him were being re-charged. 'Quite so, Miss Clark, but not entirely so,' he repeated to himself, wishing that one could see things in such a simple, straight-cut, black-and-white manner as Miss Clark did. Alas, one could not. And alas, the way one saw them made little difference to the final outcome.

He at last turned to the top-urgent tray with a suppressed grimace of reluctance. It contained only one memo, and he had known all the time what it was: H.E.'s request for the draft of the Suggestions for a Statement of Policy by H.M. Government, to be submitted at London's request. And he also knew the main points of H.E.'s Suggestions, as summed up in the pithy handwriting on the memo.

"Thank you, Miss Clark," the A.Ch.C. said. "I shan't need you any more this morning." And, craning his back in a gothic arch over the desk, he began to draft out the paper in his small, punctilious hand.

"Shall I remind you of the time?" Miss Clark asked him from the door. "You have guests for luncheon."

"Yes—call me at a quarter to one, will you?" he said without looking up from the paper.

It was one of the habits of the A.Ch.C. which increased Miss Clark's respect for him that, when immersed in his work, he regularly forgot the time.

4

A year and a half after his first trip, Dick Matthews had arrived for a second visit to the Middle East. His last book, *Has Democracy Lost Its Guts?* published a few months before, had been a success, which enabled him to drop newspaper work and concentrate on magazine pieces. He had been commissioned to do a series which would cover his expenses and were later to form the backbone of a new book.

As he walked down the street of the Prophets with his heavy, lumbering gait and with the pleasant sensation of a double-arrack consumed at the King David Bar slowly mounting inside his head, he saw a hatless young working man, wearing shorts and the zipped leather jacket of the Communal Settlements, coming towards him. He had a kind of humorous monkey face which Matthews thought he had seen before, and he was walking in the middle of the dusty road talking to himself, his lips moving and his eyebrows grown together over the saddle of the nose, jumping up and down.

Matthews halted at the edge of the pavement. "*Sh'mana Bakhur,*" he called in a throaty Michigan-Hebrew with a half-choked flourish after each vowel, "*amod,* stop, I know you from somewhere."

The young man stopped, looked at him blankly for a second, then smiled.

"Joseph—from Ezra's Tower," he said in ringing public-school English. "So you have come back to us and have learned Hebrew as well."

"Yepp—a few words," said Matthews. "I grew to like your bloody country."

"Which half of it—ours or the Arabs'?"

"For God's sake," said Matthews. "Can't you lay off it even for the first thirty seconds?"

"No," said Joseph. "You couldn't either if you lived here."

"What were you reciting to yourself when I wakened you? A manifesto?"

"No—our monthly deficit. I am now a kind of treasurer of the Commune, you see."

"Is that why you are in Jerusalem instead of tilling the soil in Galilee?"

"Precisely."

"And where are you going now?"

"To the Settlement Department of the Executive. Trying to get them to guarantee a six months' promissory note for a hundred pounds on the Workers' Co-operative Bank, of which sum I shall pay fifty pounds as a token of goodwill to the Agricultural Co-operative Institute, where a bill of ours for two hundred and fifty pounds was due yesterday."

"Christ," said Matthews. "And what are you going to do with the remaining fifty?"

"Lend it to the Treasurer of Commune Dalia, who in exchange promised me a promissory note of three hundred pounds guaranteed by the Dairy Co-operative 'T'nuva', out of which I hope to get at least seventy-five cash from the W.C.B., for which I hope to buy a second-hand tractor engine which was advertised in *Davar* by a farmer in Rekhovot."

"And when are you going to be bankrupt?" asked Matthews.

"Never. On the contrary, we are quite prosperous. We have discovered a new spring which will give us enough water to irrigate another sixty dunums. But we have got a credit-inflation in the country and no cash, so one has to juggle along."

"I want to hear more about that," said Matthews. "Now I've got a luncheon date with your honourable what's-his-name. What about dining with me at the King David to-morrow?"

"Like this?" said Joseph, pointing to his leather jacket and shorts. "I haven't got any other clothes here." (Nor anywhere else, he thought.)

"Who cares?" said Matthews. "Got some complexes about it?"

Joseph smiled, shaking his head. "All right, I'll come," he said after a moment's hesitation. "Good-bye."

"So long," said Matthews. But after a few steps Joseph turned and walked back towards him.

"Listen," he said with some hesitation. "You come from abroad and know what's going on there. We here know nothing. What do you think our chances are—I mean politically?"

Matthews looked at him steadily for a second.

"Bad," he said. "Mr. Chamberlain is selling out on you."

Joseph gave no answer. He stood for a moment or two, his eyebrows raised, then turned to go.

At ten minutes to one the A.Ch.C. turned through the gap in the stone wall into the cactus garden in front of his house. It was an old converted one-storey Arab building, from the outside nothing but an austere stone cube with thick walls and small windows; but inside it was cool and dim and comfortable with the slightly musty atmosphere of a vault. The entrance door opened into a large hall with a stone-tiled floor and a few Persian rugs. It was sparsely furnished with sofas and easy-chairs along the walls, low inlaid casual tables and a huge fireplace of bricks which, though rather incongruous, fitted pleasantly into the general picture. In the centre of the room stood, somewhat statuesque, Lady Joyce, offering her forehead to the ritual flamingo-kiss. From the quality of her smile the A.Ch.C. gathered that his wife was indisposed with a touch of migraine. Like many barren women, she tended to pay exaggerated attention to her periodic indispositions and the climate made it all the worse.

The Arab man-servant brought the tray with drinks and three letters. One was an invitation to a painter's exhibition in Tel Aviv printed in English and Hebrew, the second an invitation by the Jaffa citrus growers printed in English and Arabic, the third a short typewritten letter on ordinary foolscap with no heading and no signature, in Hebrew only. The A.Ch.C.'s Hebrew being rudimentary, he was on the point of pocketing the letter to have it translated later, when a word typed in capitals caught his eye: it was MA'VET, death. He fetched the dictionary from the shelf, and sinking into his armchair, his legs crossed, began to decipher it while sipping his arrack.

"Why do you bother?" asked Joyce.

"It's something rather quaint," the A.Ch.C. said, looking up a word in the dictionary. After a couple of minutes he had finished.

"Now listen to this," he said, holding the letter carefully at its edges between outstretched fingers.

"The Assistant Chief Commissioner, Jerusalem.—Repeated warnings were sent to the Police Informer and Agent Provocateur Itzhak Ben David of 133 Bukhara Street in Haifa, to stop his treacherous activities.

"These warnings having been of no avail, the High Command of the Hebrew National Military Organisation, after hearing the evidence submitted, has found Itzhak Ben David guilty of High Treason towards the Nation, and passed sentence of death on him.

"The sentence will be carried out at the first available opportunity. . . ."

"Rather funny," said Joyce.

"I don't think it is. These fellows mean business. They have killed in what they call reprisal actions quite a lot of Arabs."

"Killing Arabs is different," said Joyce. "They won't dare touch a man working with us."

"I wonder," said the A.Ch.C., replacing the dictionary on its shelf. His further comments were interrupted by the servant announcing the first guests, Professor Shenkin of the Hebrew University and his wife.

Professor Shenkin was an elderly little man with a goatee, who advanced towards the mistress of the house with a deep bow and an outstretched hand. His wife Rebecca was short, fat and swarthy; she came from one of the old Jewish families in Jerusalem who had lived there under Turkish rule for well over a hundred years. Her father, a baker in the Old City, had amassed a fortune by real-estate speculations and owned several houses in the ancient quarter of the Hundred Gates. He was an orthodox Jew and fiercely opposed to political Zionism. In the old Turkish days the few thousand Jews in the country —mostly saintly old people who had come to die in the Land— had been tolerated by the Moslems except for an occasional pogrom hardly worth mentioning; whereas now that the Zionists had come with their talk of a Hebrew State, the Arabs had become hostile, the National Fund made land speculation almost impossible, the heathen youth in the Communes were desecrating the Land, and the workers in the bakery were organised in trade unions. Mrs. Shenkin inwardly shared her father's convictions, but she never argued about them with her husband who had come from Bucharest and was a Zionist, though of the most moderate wing. She was very proud of being married to a university professor. She was aware of the fact that her father's money had been a decisive factor in the match but found this not disturbing; how could one expect a learned savant to marry a baker's daughter if she had not even money? She had gratefully borne him five children, and on the whole their marriage had been very happy.

When the greetings were over, Mrs. Shenkin found herself standing in the uncomfortable presence of Lady Joyce Gordon-Smith at the fireplace, while the two men had drifted away towards the other end of the room. The servant offered her a drink, and Mrs. Shenkin violently shook her head. "I drink not. I am not a modernish woman," she said in her terrible English.

"I do," Joyce announced languidly. Leaning with her back against the fireplace she looked down at the top of Mrs. Shenkin's head, trying to find out whether she wore a wig. Joyce had been told that all orthodox Jewish women had their hair cut when they were married and had to wear a wig for the rest of their lives. But through the thin, greyish strands on Mrs. Shenkin's crown she could see the pale shimmer of her scalp; she wore no wig.

"We just come back from Tel Aviv," Mrs. Shenkin said conversationally. "We were visiting my second son who studies in the Gymnasium. Tel Aviv is a beautiful city. You go often there?"

"Never," said Joyce. She had only been to Tel Aviv once, and the dreadful architecture of the Hebrew town, its broiling streets lined with lemonade shops, teeming with a sweaty, noisy crowd, had made her feel that she had fallen into a semitic ant-heap. She loved to walk through the Arab shuks, though they were even more crowded and smelly; but then, they were the Orient—whereas Tel Aviv was only a Mediterranean East End, a cross between Whitechapel and Monte Carlo.

"Why not?" asked Mrs. Shenkin. "Do you not like to swim in the sea?"

Mrs. Shenkin never swam in the sea but she rightly assumed that Joyce did.

"It is too crowded," said Joyce.

"Yes—what crowds!" cried Mrs. Shenkin. "Soon Tel Aviv will have hundred fifty thousand people. And twenty years ago—nothing." Though rather anti-Zionistic, Mrs. Shenkin shared in the general Jewish pride in Tel Aviv.

Joyce said nothing. She sipped her dry Martini with an inward-turned look, preoccupied with her indisposition. These fat Jewish women were supposed to know about herbal teas and things. But then it was of course impossible to ask her.

"This is my son," announced Mrs. Shenkin. Left to bear

the brunt of the conversation, she had produced a photograph from her bag.

"Nice," said Joyce after a fleeting glance, without taking the photograph from Mrs. Shenkin's hands. However, she had to admit that the slim, fair boy looked remarkably attractive. How these two ugly people had succeeded in producing him, beat her.

"He is a genius," Mrs. Shenkin remarked matter-of-factly. "He translates Pushkin's poems into the Hebrew language."

"How clever," said Joyce.

"Yes. He translates Pushkin and he knows not one word of Russian."

Lady Joyce suddenly started coughing into her cocktail. She made a mental note of the story for the Club: the Jewish infant prodigy who translates Pushkin without knowing Russian. She put her glass down.

"Then how does he do it?" she asked with, for the first time, a certain warmth in her voice.

"Oh, it is quite easy," said Mrs. Shenkin. "A friend of his who is Russian tells him the contents and then he makes it rhyme."

"How very clever," said Joyce.

The servant announced Mr. Richard Matthews, and the American lumbered into the room, looking rather untidy, somewhat absent-minded and slightly tight. Joyce had met him at a luncheon party which H.E. had given during Matthews' first visit, and had instantly disliked him. He was clumsy, uncivil and conceited in a kind of vulgar-democratic way—typically American. However, he had made himself quite a reputation during the last two years, and as the A.Ch.C.'s wife one had to entertain all sorts of people. This party was in his honour, and the Shenkins had been produced because those American papers always complained that one was not nice enough to the Jews. To restore the balance she had also asked Kamel Effendi el Shallabi, the editor of a moderate Arab weekly, but he was late as usual.

They stood around the fireplace, holding their glasses, with the dull feeling of pointlessness which is the ritual atmosphere of all Jerusalem parties. Professor Shenkin was holding forth with some involved story about excavations on the Dead Sea, and why they had gone wrong. Now and then the A.Ch.C., with an air of friendly approval, put in an unobtrusive question which showed up the professor's ignorance of archaeology. However, Shenkin was not an archaeologist but a professor of philosophy, though nobody knew what exactly he philosophised about. In a lifetime he had only published two short papers in Hebrew periodicals, one on "Spinoza and the Neo-Platonists", the other on "Talmudic Influences on German Mediaeval Mysticism". There was a rumour that he had obtained his chair at the University because some relation of his was on the Board of Curators in America from where the money came.

At last Kamel Effendi arrived, red-faced, buoyant, elegant, and carrying a bunch of roses for the hostess. He greeted the Shenkins with effusive heartiness though they had met only once, eight years ago at an official garden-party. There were more drinks. Matthews had a huge whisky and soda, Kamel Effendi an arrack which he sipped rather daintily with his little finger sticking out, while the Professor nursed a glass of sweet, sticky local vermouth. Watching him, Joyce remembered with a shudder the one dinner-party at the Glicksteins' which she had been forced to attend, and where they gave you sweet Carmel wine in liqueur glasses with your fish.

At last the party moved into the dining-room. A slight odour in the air informed Joyce that the Arab cook had once again burnt the pilaff—he always did it when there were Jewish guests, though how he knew beforehand remained a mystery. However, she felt too fed-up with all of them to care.

Kamel Effendi was holding the stage. Prompted by a question of Matthews, he had launched into Arab politics:

"Ah, the Mufti, the Mufti!" he cried. "He and his family are the ruin of the country. How often have we warned our

English friends against the machinations of the Husseini clan! We told them how the Mufti used his position and the religious funds entrusted to him to finance his terrorist gangsters. In each little village he had his agents. In each mosque the mullah preached hatred and murder by his orders. Alas—you did not believe us. . . ." He turned to the A.Ch.C. with a waggishly accusing finger. "No, you did not believe us, so you supported Hadj Amin until he betrayed you and the country was flowing with blood. And then you let him escape under your nose to Syria from where he continues to make trouble with Italian money."

The A.Ch.C., smiling, applied himself to the burnt pilaff. He looked like a tolerant schoolmaster at a picnic whose pupils have got slightly out of hand, pretending not to notice it.

"Is it true that he escaped from the Omar Mosque in women's clothes?" asked Mrs. Shenkin's piping little voice.

"Bbah!" cried Kamel Effendi. "I care not how he escaped. I care that his paid bandits have killed my cousin Mussa Effendi, and Fakhri Bey Nashashibi, and Sheikh Abdul Khatib the great preacher of the Omar Mosque. Hadj Amin is a curse. All the Husseini family and their National Party are a curse. They kill and blackmail everybody opposed to them and drive us to bloodshed."

The arrack and the heavy burgundy-type wine from Rishon le Zion were beginning to tell on Kamel Effendi. His face had grown even redder and he spoke in a rather loud voice.

"You talk almost like a Zionist, Kamel Effendi," said the A.Ch.C., who was having his quiet fun.

"A Zionist—bbah!" said Kamel Effendi. "We don't need the Husseinis to fight Zionism. All Arabs are united against the Zionist danger." Suddenly remembering the Shenkins, he turned with a broad smile to the Professor. "It is not personal," he said affably. "Friends remain friends. We are talking about principles."

The Professor, who had tucked his napkin under his grey goatee, smiled back eagerly.

"We each have our extremists and trouble-makers to cope with in our own camp," he said unctuously. "You have your Mufti and his followers, and we have our young fanatics. Without them, Arabs and Jews could live as happily together as they did a thousand years ago in Spain."

"Quite so," said the A.Ch.C. "The question is of course on what terms," he added innocently.

"Terms—bbah!" cried Kamel Effendi, and he unexpectedly turned to his hostess who sat in a cramped erect position in her chair, waiting for that faint tide of pain to return. "If you, madame, honour me with an invitation to your house, do I ask you for terms? And enjoying the privilege of your hospitality, do I ask to be master of the house? No, madame, I do not. It is the same with our Jewish friends. They enjoy our hospitality —*ahlan w'sahlan,* you are welcome. We will be like brothers. We will receive you with open arms as our guests. . . ."

"Yeah—paying guests," murmured Matthews, but fortunately Kamel Effendi did not hear him. The A.Ch.C., who did hear, helped himself to more pilaff.

". . . like brothers," concluded Kamel Effendi. "Just as in the glorious days of the Spanish Caliphate, as our friend the Professor said. But terms—bbah! If they want our house—never!"

"Well, Professor?" said Matthews with a heavy wink of his eyes. "It's your turn now."

Shenkin was stroking his goatee.

"Of course," he said. "Personally I see our friend's point. I was always opposed to this provocative talk about a Hebrew State which only upsets our Arab friends. For me, Zion is a symbol. A state! What is a state? A selfish, old-fashioned prejudice. . . ."

"*Aywah!*" nodded Kamel Effendi. "This is very true."

"Our young fanatics," the Professor went on, "want a Jewish majority. What is this talk? A provocation. What are numbers? What are quantities? It is the spirit which counts. We must come in a spirit of friendship and understanding to our

Arab friends. The Jews abhor violence. It is our historical mission . . ."

"Boloney," Matthews said suddenly and audibly. They all looked at him, but he was absorbed in his pilaff.

"Won't you have some more?" Joyce asked with a ringing voice through the silence. "Though I'm afraid it's rather . . ."

"Yes," said Mrs. Shenkin earnestly, "it is burnt. Our cook also does it. It is because of the Primus stoves."

"Yes—aren't they awful?" Joyce said icily.

"Look," said Matthews, having swallowed the last bite on his plate, and turning to the Professor. "Have you people come to build a country or just another ghetto?"

"I came," said Professor Shenkin who was squirming on his seat, "I came to teach at the Hebrew University."

"Damn your University," said Matthews. "People must have security first, and some income, and some leisure, before they can think of a university. You do everything the wrong way round."

"This is a matter of opinion," said Shenkin.

"It isn't," said Matthews, emptying his glass. "You people drive me crazy. One wants to help you and you make it so hellish difficult."

Kamel Effendi chuckled. "That is a very true remark, Mr. Matthews. We are in the same position. We want to help these poor people, and how do they thank us? They want to take our house away."

"Aw, chuck that talk about your house," said Matthews. "For the last five hundred years it wasn't yours but the Turks'."

Kamel Effendi went red again, while Shenkin relaxed in his chair, dabbing his head with his napkin.

"The majority of the population has always been Arab," cried Kamel Effendi. "Take myself. My family is descended directly from Walid el Shallabi, Muhammed's conquering General. We are the most ancient family in Palestine. . . . The Husseinis and Nashashibis are mere parvenus," he could not refrain from adding.

"My father is a Cohen," Mrs. Shenkin piped suddenly. "And the Cohens are the descendants of the Kohanim, the priests in the old days."

"Shall we go?" Joyce said to her, rising rather abruptly. She had been impatiently waiting for Matthews to finish his last spoonful of ice-cream and now felt that she wouldn't be able to stick it a minute longer. Seeing the Shenkin woman's bewilderment and ignorance of English custom, she explained: "The gentlemen will join us later for coffee." And with a contrite smile she sailed out of the room, followed by the short, waddling Mrs. Shenkin, a queen with inadequate suite.

The four men stood for a second, and as they sat down again the A.Ch.C. said, to turn the conversation:

"There seems to be a khamsin in the air. My wife usually feels it twenty-four hours in advance."

"That's your local variety of the sirocco?" asked Matthews.

"Yes—only more pernicious."

"Ah—the khamsin!" cried Kamel Effendi. "In a real khamsin everybody goes crazy."

"Then this country must be living in a permanent khamsin," said Matthews.

Kamel Effendi laughed stertorously. The Professor stroked his beard.

"When the east wind breathes, the pastures of the shepherds mourn and the head of Carmel withers," he quoted from somewhere in the Bible.

"Quite," said the A.Ch.C. "But the same scorching east wind is also called 'the breath of the Lord'. So if we are all mad, it's holy madness, you see."

"I reckon," said Matthews, "that God Almighty has less to do with it than your Colonial Office."

"*Aywah,*" said Kamel Effendi. "And your Lord Balfour."

"There we go again," said the A.Ch.C. "Who would like some port or liqueur?"

They all refused except Matthews, who took a balloon-glass of brandy. "What was wrong with old Balfour?" he asked, thrusting his big untidy head towards Kamel Effendi.

"He gave our house away," said Kamel Effendi, who liked to stick to the same metaphor.

"More boloney," said Matthews, tasting the brandy and finding that it was good. "There never was a house here. There was a desert and a stinking swamp and pox-ridden fellaheen. You were the pariahs of the Levant and to-day you are the richest of the Arab countries. Your population was on the decrease for centuries because half your babes were dying from filth in their cradles, and since the Jews came it has doubled. They haven't robbed you of an inch of your land, but they have robbed you of your malaria and your trachoma and your septic childbeds and your poverty. . . ."

"Come, come, Mr. Matthews," the A.Ch.C. said, putting on his harassed air, though secretly he was enjoying himself. "This is rather strong language, and a bit unfair too."

Kamel Effendi had jumped up from his seat. He was gasping for words.

"Bbah!" he brought out at last. "Now we know where we are. You come here as our guest, saying you are a journalist from America—but you are just one of those people whom they . . ." He made a frantic gesture of rubbing his index against his thumb, and his face underwent a rather unpleasant change.

"Yeah," Matthews said calmly. "I am one of the Elders of Zion—huh?"

"I think it is time we joined the ladies," said the A.Ch.C., and the Professor obediently got to his feet, but Kamel paid no attention to him.

"I care not who you are," he shouted. "You come here as our guest and then you abuse us. This is what we receive for our hospitality. . . ."

"Come off it, Mr. Kamel," said Matthews. "I am not your guest, I am paying my keep, and I haven't asked your permission."

"I care not whether you pay," cried Kamel Effendi. "And I care not for their hospitals and their schools. This is our country, you understand? We want no foreign benefactors. We want not to be patronised. We want to be left alone, you understand! We want to live our own way and we want no foreign teachers and no foreign money and no foreign habits and no smiles of condescension and no pat on the shoulder and no arrogance and no shameless women with wriggling buttocks in our holy places. We want not their honey and we want not their sting, you understand? Neither their honey nor their sting. This you can tell them in your America. If they are thrown out in other countries—very bad, very sorry. Very, very sorry—but not our business. If they want to come here—a few of them, maybe thousand, maybe two thousand—*t'faddal,* welcome. But then know you are guests and know how to behave. Otherwise—to the devil. Into the sea—and *hallass,* finished. This is plain language. You tell them."

There was a painful silence while Kamel Effendi wiped his forehead and the A.Ch.C. stood hovering over the group like an unhappy flamingo. Then Matthews said unexpectedly:

"Yeah—I see your point, Mr. Kamel. I guess you are wrong, but wrong in your own right."

The A.Ch.C. gave him a curious little stare with his two-coloured eyes; he seemed on the point of making a remark, and on second thoughts didn't. But Kamel Effendi laughed stertorously and without transition.

"Ho!—ho!" he shouted. "Wrong within your own rights. It is a profound saying, my friend—very profound." He appreciatively clicked his tongue, and spontaneously grasped Matthews' hand, pumping it. "No offence, Mr. Matthews," he said. "Here we all get a little heated sometimes. It is our climate, you know—the khamsin."

And so they all repaired to join the ladies in a fairly jolly mood—except for the Professor who slunk along the corridor with his head on one side and trailing his finger along the wall.

5

The Shenkins soon left—they had to visit a daughter-in-law who had just given birth to her third child in the maternity clinic of the Hadassah; Kamel Effendi followed a few minutes later. Matthews, having asked the A.Ch.C. for a quarter of an hour's off-the-record talk, stayed on. Joyce retired to lie down in her room; the khamsin was getting worse and so were her nerves.

"Cigar?" the A.Ch.C. asked when they were alone. He sank into his favourite armchair and let the harassed look slowly fade from his face. "Well, Mr. Matthews," he said, "to-day you had a taste of the peculiar atmosphere of this little country. And they were both moderates, mind you. . . ."

"The Professor sure was," said Matthews. "I reckon the matching of the teams was pretty unfair."

The A.Ch.C. smiled. "Possibly," he said. "But you can't expect me to invite for fairness' sake a Hebrew terrorist. Mind you, I would enjoy it, but my wife is rather fond of her furniture."

Matthews filled up his half-empty brandy glass with soda. "Christ," he said. "Your khamsin takes it out of a guy." He emptied the glass and put it down on the inlaid table with a slight clank. "And now tell me straight, Mr. Chief Commissioner," he said, shifting his heavy body forward in the chair, "why are you selling out on them?"

"I am afraid . . ."

"Aw, come off it. Don't be afraid. This will be strictly off the record, Mr. Chief Commissioner."

"Assistant," corrected the A.Ch.C. Though he kept smiling politely, the difference in colour between his two eyes became accentuated, a sign that he was angry. "May I ask what exactly you mean by 'selling out'?"

"Aw, come off it," Matthews repeated, drawing out each vowel into a lingering flourish. It was as if a massive bull deliberately tried to excite the slender matador. "You have read the League of Nations reports. They say plainly that you have been inciting the Arabs against the Hebrews so that you should have an excuse to let Zionism down."

The A.Ch.C. tipped the ash from his cigar with the circumspection of a clinical operation. It occurred to him that he couldn't go to see Jimmy in the hospital on Sunday as he had promised to open a Horticultural Exhibition in Tel Aviv.

"My dear sir," he said, "I am a sincere admirer of the Jews. They are the most admirable salesmen in the world, regardless of whether they sell carpets, Marxism, psychoanalysis or their own pogromed infants. It is child's-play for them to get around well-meaning people such as Professor Rappárd and other members of the Geneva Mandates Commission—or members of both our Houses if it comes to that. If those fantastic accusations were true, how would you explain the fact that we had two hundred British soldiers killed fighting the Arab revolt? Don't you think the fact that they were defending Jewish life and property deserves to be mentioned when certain rash criticisms are made?"

"That's so much sob-talk," said Matthews, filling up his glass uninvited.—I'll drive this smug guy mad, even if he calls his Ahmed or Mahmed to throw me out, he thought. "A year back," he went on, "when I was here the first time, I saw a gang of your Mufti's Arab cut-throats throwing stones at a couple of old Jews and yelling at the top of their voices: *'Eddaula Ma'na,'* 'The Government is with us.' Will you deny that, Mr. Chief Commissioner?"

"Assistant," the A.Ch.C. corrected. "I shall certainly not deny it. The trouble-makers make the crowd believe it, just as they make them believe that Jews are throwing dead pigs into the Mosque of Omar. But it would be a bit unfair to make us responsible for each rumour in the shuks, wouldn't it?"

"No, you won't get away with that," said Matthews. "The Arabs believed that you welcomed the killing of Jews because your whole attitude encouraged them to believe it. You backed the Mufti during twenty years though you knew about his doings. I have read your Royal Commission's Report, all the four hundred pages of it, which accuses your local administration of condoning Arab terrorism. This isn't Jewish sales-talk—it's printed in your Majesty's Stationery Office. I know one of your Intelligence guys who toured in his car the Arab villages near Nazareth, telling them not to sell land to the Jews because your Government is against it. I know of others who smuggled arms to the Syrian rebels. I know this isn't your personal responsibility, but you should have raised hell to stop those romantic young pansies from your universities being let loose to chase about in Beduin dress and stir up trouble. I have met a few of these hush-hush guys, and if I had a say in your Government I would spank their arses and send them back to college. Aw, let's talk straight, Mr. Chief Commissioner. You've been asking for trouble and you've got it, and now you complain because English soldiers are killed. You had to crush the Arab gangs, not for the sake of the Jews but for your own sake, because this country is the strategic centre of your Empire, and you need it. Even so, you did bloody little to defend the Hebrew settlers who were left to look after themselves and sent to jail for possessing rifles with which to defend themselves and their women-folk. . . ." He pulled a dog-eared notebook from his pocket. "Here, your Royal Commission's Report, page 201: '*To-day it is evident that the elementary duty of providing public security has not been discharged. If there is one grievance which the Jews have undoubted right to prefer it is the absence of security.*' . . . No, Mr. Chief Commissioner, you won't get away with it so easy. Your gratitude-talk may go down with your phony professor and his like, but it won't go down with an impartial observer."

He puffed and finished the rest of his glass. 'Christ,' he thought, 'if he doesn't rise to that he's a dead fish.'—The A.Ch.C. looked at him thoughtfully.

"The impartial observer referred to is doubtless yourself, Mr. Matthews?" he asked quietly.

"I guess I am," Matthews said. "I am not a Jew, and back home I disliked them as much as anybody else did."

"But you seem to have undergone a conversion."

"Yea. You can call it that if you like."

"Doubtless our persuasive Mr. Glickstein had a strong influence on you."

"Glickstein be damned. He's the same type as your Professor. They stink of ghetto."

"Then what made you change your mind in this rather—violent way, if I may ask without being unduly curious?"

"You may. I've seen their settlements. I've been down the Jordan Valley and up in Galilee and in the Jezreel Valley and in the Huleh swamps. Those are some guys. They're a new type. They've quit being Jews and become Hebrews."

"I share your admiration for them. But after all, don't you think you are being a little romantic about it—just as some people whom you dislike are being romantic about the Arabs?"

"Nope. I haven't seen the Arabs producing anything worth showing off, except cabarets and filthy postcards, from Tangier to Teheran—not for the last thousand years."

The A.Ch.C. smiled.

"Has it never occurred to you that a race may cherish and preserve certain values or a way of life, which are not expressed in spectacular achievements?"

"Maybe," said Matthews. "But that isn't the point we were discussing. I am not so easy to side-track, Mr. Commissioner. It's not the philosophy of life we are discussing, but the policy of your Government which is selling out on the Jews."

The A.Ch.C. gave a mock-distressed sigh.

"No, you are not easily side-tracked, Mr. Matthews. I had the privilege to admire your singleness of mind in your book 'Has Democracy Lost Its Punch?' "

"Guts," Matthews corrected. "Guts, guts, guts. But that too is beside the point."

"Not so much as it seems," the A.Ch.C. said mildly. "Your book is, if I may say so, a brilliant and pungent attack on what is termed by a popular though nebulous catch-word our policy of appeasement in Europe. Well, Mr. Matthews, I must confess I am an inveterate sinner in your and your friends' eyes. I am in favour of coming to terms with the Arabs—of appeasing them, if you like. In other words, I believe that all policy, past, present and future, has to be based on reasonable compromise."

"Yea," said Matthews. "The question is what you call reasonable."

"Let's see," said the A.Ch.C. "I thought the term self-explanatory. But that may be a national prejudice. So we had better consult the dictionary. . . ."

He emerged from his armchair and crossed with his gentle flamingo-stoop to the bookshelf.

"Now let's see," he said, visibly regaining the mood of quiet fun. ". . . Rear-arch, rear-vault, reason, *reasonable*. Here we are: *"Sound of judgement, sensible, moderate, not expecting too much, ready to listen to reason; agreeable to reason, not absurd, not greatly less or more than might be expected; inexpensive, tolerable, fair.* . . . That's about all the Concise Oxford Dictionary has to say. If this doesn't satisfy you, I've also got here the Shorter Oxford Dictionary in two volumes, and the Oxford Dictionary in twelve."

Leaning against the bookshelves, he politely smiled down at Matthews who once more filled his glass with soda, conscious of the poisoned absurdity of this dialogue. It may have been the khamsin—which gave him the sensation that the rubbing of his shirt drew sparks from his skin and raised the fluff on his chest in tingling irritation; or perhaps it was just the general atmospheric poison of the country. As his eyes met the A.Ch.C.'s double-coloured gaze, he asked himself from what source that guy derived his arrogantly modest self-assurance. What's he got to be so modest about? he asked himself, his head slightly swimming. And suddenly he had an absurd vision of the A.Ch.C. as a boy walking along that narrow passage of the via dolorosa with its twelve stations from the Lower First to the Upper Sixth. At its beginning stood a trembling little boy in a cricket cap, thin-limbed, sensitive, and rather too imaginative, rather too keen on poetry and all that; past the fifth or sixth station stalked a completely transformed person with a jutting Adam's apple and a breaking voice, in the painful process of having his sensitivity derided and his reflexes conditioned so that repression came before impulse and second thoughts preceded firsts; at the end emerged the striped-trousered finished product of that exclusive passion lane, that distinguished torture-chamber and soul-tannery—encased in a supple and resilient crust, a tanned hide impermeable both to outside influences and the sealed-off pressure from within; an adhesive armour the more impregnable as it was not something put on, but the crustification of formerly living tissue transformed into supple callousness. . . .

Matthews yawned and stretched his legs out. "Aw, Mr. Chief Commissioner, let's come to the point."

"Help yourself to another drink," the A.Ch.C. said, crossing back to his armchair. "The whole matter is simpler than it appears. From the beginning the Husseini clan had the strongest following among the Arabs; and among the Husseinis Hadj Amin, the later Mufti, commanded the greatest authority. Hence the smoothest way of dealing with the Arabs was to deal through him. We would naturally have preferred to deal with the Moderates; just as we preferred dealing with Dr. Brüning to dealing with Herr Hitler. In both cases we were accused of 'backing' the extreme wing whereas in fact our policy merely endorsed, and adjusted itself to, the regrettable but undeniable course of events. Arab Nationalism here is growing rapidly and inevitably as in Egypt, Iraq and Syria. There may be individual sympathisers with this trend in some of our Departments, just as we have individual admirers of Herr Hitler—though I may point out in parenthesis that I am not one of them; however, I can assure you that these personal inclinations have hardly any influence on our basic policy. Nationalistic movements necessarily follow an irrational trend; hence it is useless to argue with Arab nationalists, even of the more moderate brand, about the indubitable benefits they derive from Jewish immigration. They want to be masters in a country where they form the majority; and they are afraid of and opposed to Jewish domination, regardless of any material benefits. . . ."

"Then why do they sell their land to the Jews whenever they get a chance?"

"My dear sir—individual greed and patriotic feeling are antagonists as old as the world. The desire to eat one's cake and have it is a general human characteristic."

"And so you are going to make it your business to check this greed and foster patriotic feelings by prohibiting the sale of land to the Jews. . . ."

"We may indeed have to enforce legislation to that effect," the A.Ch.C. said casually, while wondering where this confounded American intruder got his inside information from.

"You realise, Mr. Chief Commissioner, that such a law, prohibiting the free sale of property to Jews, would be unique in the world—except for National Socialist Germany?"

"I know that if we bring in an Ordinance to that effect—though I wish to point out that nothing has been officially decided yet—the Zionists will raise their usual hue and cry, using precisely your arguments, Mr. Matthews. But the analogy in fact is purely extraneous. Germany has an old-established Jewish population, whereas here such a law would merely aim at protecting the native population against the foreign influx."

"I thought your Government was pledged to establish a National Home by means of a 'close settlement of the Jews on the Land'? But I guess I have come to the wrong country."

The A.Ch.C. looked at his watch. It was the first sign of annoyance he had permitted himself, and he at once effaced this self-indulgence with a charming smile.

"Well—we won't start a legalistic argument, Mr. Matthews. The simple truth of the matter is that we have to balance the conflicting interests of the two communities. We are extremely sorry for the Jews, and it may not be irrelevant to point out that in aiding Jewish refugees Great Britain has played a larger part than any other country in Europe—or outside Europe, if it comes to that. There is, for instance, good reason to believe that a considerable proportion of the Jewish children in Germany whose transfer to this country proved not feasible, will shortly be admitted to the United Kingdom itself. However, we cannot afford to antagonise the Arab world for the sake of the Jews, just as we could not afford to start a world war for the sake of the Czechs. You may say that we have sacrificed the Czechs, and I shall answer you that in order to avoid a world-conflagration this small sacrifice was justified. We have quietly faced the wrath of well-meaning but somewhat hot-blooded young men like yourself, and we were called names and had a very bad Press—but that was a small price to pay for ensuring Europe's peace for our lifetime. You may say and write, Mr. Matthews, that we have no 'guts'—personally I rather dislike the term—but you will have to admit that we never lacked the courage to incur momentary unpopularity in the interest of lasting good. Our task in this country may be ungrateful, but be assured that we shall carry it through. We have come to terms with Egypt and Iraq, and we have to come to terms with the Arab population in this country, on the basis of a reasonable compromise which will fully safeguard the rights of the Jewish minority. That is the whole issue in a nutshell—and everything else is propaganda and rhetorics. . . ."

There was a short pause; then Matthews heaved himself into an erect position.

"Thank you, Mr. Chief Commissioner," he said. "That's all I wanted to know. Now we are fixed. I've listened to your reasonable reasoning which will bring the world greater disaster than the ravings of lunatics. So long."

He lumbered towards the door. The A.Ch.C. affably accompanied him. Then he went back to his armchair. He thought it would perhaps be better if he himself wrote to the organisers of the tournament to cancel Jimmy's entry.

—Well, old man, he thought, to have one leg cut off defending Jewish settlements doesn't seem to satisfy Mr. Matthews. What about the second one? Otherwise he will keep on saying that you have lost your guts.

6

Answering Colonel Wedgwood's question, the Colonial Secretary, Mr. Malcolm MacDonald, said that 1220 *illegal immigrants have been prevented from landing in Palestine between February* 15 *and April* 15, 1939.

On March 21, 269 *Jews from the steamer* Assandu *had been ordered to return on March* 25 *to Constanza, their port of departure.* 710 *Jews, of whom* 698 *were from Germany, were prevented from landing from s.s.* Astir *on April* 2, *and ordered to return.* 250 *Jews were prevented from landing from the ship* Assimi *on April* 11, *and the vessel was detained with its passengers at Haifa port and ordered to return.*

The Colonial Secretary was then asked by Mr. Noel-Baker whether, since the Jewish refugees had suffered appallingly, they had been returned when refused permission to land.

Mr. MacDonald said that they had been returned to their ports of embarkation.

Mr. Noel-Baker: "Does that mean to concentration camps?"

Mr. MacDonald: "The responsibility rests on those responsible for organising illegal immigration."

The Minister added that the Government had the fullest sympathy with Jewish refugees, but if they allowed one shipload more would follow.

(From the debate in the House of Commons,
April 26 and 27, 1939)

Any commanding officer whose ship or boat has hoisted and is carrying the proper ensign or appropriate flag may pursue any vessel within the territorial waters of Palestine which he believes to be carrying intending immigrants and which does not bring-to when signalled or required to do so. He may also, after having fired a gun as a signal, fire at or into such vessel to compel her to bring-to.

(Amendment to the Immigration Ordinance, *Gazette Extraordinary,* Jerusalem, April 27, 1939)

7

According to his new routine of life, Joseph had spent the week-end—that is, Friday afternoon and the Shabbath—at home in Ezra's Tower, and had set out on Sunday morning to his customary round of duties.

He got up at half-past three, jumped noiselessly over Ellen's sleeping body with his child inside it, ran the hundred yards past tower, dining-hut and children's house to the shower-bath, ran back, got dressed, took the imposing dispatch-case which went with his office (it had once belonged to the Dr. Phil.), and was just in time to catch the milk-truck to Haifa. David the driver was surly and unshaven as usual—he suffered from the national disease, duodenal ulcers—so Joseph settled down to sleep in the seat next to him and only woke from time to time when a jolt sent his head bumping against the side frame of the driver's cabin. But the jolts ceased as they reached the metal road, and for a couple of hours there was nothing to disturb his sleep.

He woke, however, as he had intended to, at a particular curve a few minutes past Nazareth, where the road emerging from the lower Galilean hills opened on a sudden, breath-takingly lovely view over the Valley of Jezreel. To the south the valley broadened into a plain about twelve miles wide and flat, glistening in the new-born sun—a brilliant chess-board with squares of cultivation in dark and lighter green, lemon yellow and sienna. The main Afuleh-Jerusalem road cut sharp and straight across the plain, a white arrow in flight, pointing at the silvery chalk hills of Samaria which embraced the valley in a sweeping semicircle like the walls of an amphitheatre. To the west, this distant and hazy wall ended in the darker pine slopes of Carmel, falling into the pallid sea; to the east, in the aggressive bulk of Mount Gilboa.

But the distant hills were merely the frame of the picture; the feast for Joseph's eyes was the green Valley of Jezreel itself, the cradle of the Communes. Twenty years ago a desolate marsh cursed with all the Egyptian plagues, it had now become a continuous chain of settlements which stretched like a string of green pearls across the country's neck from Haifa to the Jordan. It was the proudest achievement of the Return, the nucleus of the Hebrew State, the valley of valleys. A battlefield throughout the ages, it was grandiose even in its geological features, for its eastern part sloped down into the deepest inland depression of the earth, four hundred feet under sea level. This eastern part was a broiling tropical underworld with temperatures surpassing a hundred degrees in the shade, and it seemed perverse that the oldest of the large Communes—Herod's Well, House Alpha and Josef's Hill—had been set up just in this infernal, swampy, disease-ridden and robber-haunted spot. But twenty years ago land in those savage marshes had been cheap and each square yard of the country had to be bought for hard cash; and the National Fund's only sources of income were charitable donations and the blue collecting-boxes which the jet-eyed, curly-haired children of the race jingled in the East-Ends from Warsaw to New York;—begging-bowls for the purchase of a kingdom. The race proverbial for its financial genius had to buy its national home by acres on the instalment plan, and native speculation soon drove the price of an acre of desert marsh up to the level of a building plot in an industrial town. If this was Jehovah's punishment of the money-changers, the old desert god had once more proved his vindictive ingenuity. But this time the Colonial Office had outwitted even old Jehovah. No more waste land was to be sold to the homeless. The wooden plough had to be protected against the noisy tractor, the thirsty earth against the artifice of irrigation, the stones on the fields against impious removal and the helpless mosquitoes against the cruel draining of their breeding marshes. For behold, there was still justice in the world which looked after the feeble.

—A jerk of the lorry woke Joseph from his brooding and sent his head straight against the roof of the driver's cabin. He was grateful for the pain which cut the bitter stream of his thoughts and his cramp of impotent hatred. During the last few days it had become almost an obsession. At night, when he tried to settle down to sleep, the stream began its turgid flow. At first it was only a trickle of phrases, of arguments to convince an invisible, impersonal, dumb and almighty opponent. Sometimes this opponent appeared as the copper-faced Police Major who had visited them on the first day; sometimes it was the whole House of Commons whose stilted antics had once enchanted him from the Visitors' Gallery; sometimes the bear-skinned automaton banging his stiff legs down on the gravel in front of Buckingham Palace. But he could never catch the Speaker's eye nor stop the leg-throwing six-footer marching past; and as his plea remained choked in his throat, its pressure increased and the trickle swelled to a torrent, which expanded through his whole body until his stomach contracted in a spasm and he spat green bile into his handkerchief. I shall either get a stomach ulcer, he thought, or join Bauman's terror gang. This is the real alternative. One can reach a point of humiliation where violence is the only outlet. If I can't bite, my wrath will bite into my own bowels. That's why our whole race is ulcerated in the bloodiest literal sense. Fifteen hundred years of impotent anger has gnawed our intestines, sharpened our features and twisted down the corners of our lips.

When at last he fell asleep he had no real dreams, only half-conscious images of torment. He was sitting in the Visitors' Gallery and shouting down to the Speaker with his white wig, but nobody heard his voice and he could never catch that beautiful and dignified figure's eye. He tried to bar the bear-skinned Guard's way, but the six-footer marched through him with his banging legs as if Joseph were transparent air. And once he seemed to hear a suave, cultured voice with the accents of his own University: "In the interest of peace and order, the honourable Members are invited to sit on the drowning men's heads."

—The nights were bad. But in the morning, instead of trying to get in touch with Bauman or Simeon, he would get on with his complicated duties as a roving Treasurer of the Commune of Ezra's Tower. The Commune was growing rapidly; a third graft had arrived and Joseph knew that for the time being he was indispensable. He longed to have a talk with Simeon but both he and Bauman had gone underground, and though Joseph knew one end of the chain through which he could get in touch with them, he was instructed only to do it in case of urgency. He envied them for having burnt their bridges, and admired them as a little clerk admires the gambler who plays for all or nothing. Oh, for the supreme gift of irresponsibility, the gift to translate feeling into direct action! Oh, for the relief of having one's wrath exploded with a good, home-made bomb! The act of killing already appeared to him divested of its flesh-tearing, physical aspect, free from the angle of death and pain, as an almost platonic act. It was no longer the tactile sensation of the mush which had replaced Naphtali's eye, but the clean, impersonal act of aiming at a spark in the night. What a luxury to press one's finger on a hard metal trigger and get hanged singing the anthem and have done with it—done with the Things to Forget which refused to be forgotten and were being repeated on an ever-increasing scale with ever more lurid details; growing on one, growing into one, clawing at one's brain and bowels, while the waving hands of the drowned failed to catch the Speaker's eye. There was only one hope of arousing his attention: by the report of the bombs which Bauman's people threw. But that was not his, Joseph's, job. He had to wangle a loan from the Settlement Department for a pump to irrigate two hundred more dunums; and two hundred more irrigated dunums meant a haven for fifty more families.

There was only one relief: his week-ends at home. In the shadow of Ezra's Tower the tragedy became almost unreal and the only problem was whether the new chicken-house should be built first, or the new shower-bath. And there was Ellen, a mainstay of the vegetable garden and mother of his future child; and there was Dina.

The lorry slowly descended among the foothills of Zebulun into the valley. To their left stood the young Balfour Forest with rows of silvery Aleppo pines. They too had been planted by the National Fund and were thus intruder trees, Jewish trees, each slender stem a thorn in the native patriots' eyes who organised raiding parties at night to cut the young trees down and dig the saplings out of the earth; so that during the riots bloody battles were fought between the Hebrew forest-watchers and the killers of trees. What a country, Joseph thought, what a country where each stone and tree is bristling with a high-tension charge and cursed with archaic memories. Your eye rests on a peaceful Arab stone house, but suddenly your brain draws a spark; for lo, you have noticed that one of the stones is part of a Roman column broken by the rebel Maccabeans, or the lintel of a Byzantine synagogue from Bar Giora's days.

—And yet the morning was of a lovely freshness and the air sweet with the taste of young apples like the Shulamite's breath. Patterns of wild tulips, iris and cyclamen lay spread beneath the slender pines like carpets under young princes' feet. Nestling in the woods shone the red roofs of the Communes "Ginegar" and "David's Hill";—the latter drawing another painful spark of association, for the David in whose honour the Commune was named was not the dancing king, but the Welsh statesman under whose premiership the promise of the Return, now broken, had been given.

As at each turn of the road more fields and pine woods came into sight, the fresh blades of the wheat sparklingly aquiver with fat drops of dew, Joseph's mood rose again and his delight with the beauty of the resurrected valley got the upper hand. This delight was in him each time he travelled through the valley, together with a childish pride. Look, he told himself, there is another Hebrew cow munching the pasture irrigated from a Hebrew well, and a Hebrew hen brooding over her Hebrew eggs—which will doubtless become infant chicken prodigies. But his self-mockery could not erase that jubilant pride of ownership, the joyously insane feeling that everything around here was his own private and exclusive creation—including the sows, the hens and the flock of sheep coming down the slopes of Ephraim.

After Nahallal the road drew nearer to the massif of Carmel, its soft slopes patchy with tufts of scrub, green firs and silvery olive groves. They passed through another cluster of Communes with their square white concrete blocks and red roofs. There were also some Beduin camps and one or two small Arab places in picturesque decay—amidst their modern surroundings they looked like reconstructions of native villages in some colonial exhibition.

As they approached the western gateway of the valley, there was another wrench for Joseph. To their left, perched on a hill, stood the ruins of the great Galilean necropolis and onetime seat of the High Court of Israel, the town of Beth Shearim, where the survivors of Bar Kochba's revolt had hidden. It was a lonely and nostalgic place, strewn with broken columns and honeycombed with burial chambers. But the hallowed site was now named after some obscure Moslem saint called Sheikh Abreik, whose shrine happened to be in the vicinity. . . .

Come now, Joseph nudged himself, we are getting rather like the Irish—or the Welsh who deplore that all cities on the isles haven't got names with fifteen consonants on a string. But then, nationalism is only comic in others—like being seasick or in love. Oh, well, he thought, a people fighting for survival can't afford a sense of humour. That's perhaps why we lose our renowned wit when we return to the Land. To think that we have over a hundred Hebrew periodicals and dailies, but not a single comic paper! This is an essentially humourless country. Hebrew doesn't lend itself to stories about two Jews in a railway compartment—it is an angry tongue.

The road was now closely hugging the slope of Carmel; to their right opened the plain of Acco, littered with factories and oil refineries; beyond it, one could catch glimpses of the yellow dunes and the glassy expanse of the sea. The nearness of the great port made itself felt in the dense traffic on the road in spite of the early hour; there were Arab buses loaded like Noah's Ark, and Hebrew buses shabby and workmanlike, and camels and donkeys and petrol trucks. At last, shortly after seven o'clock, they passed the old railway station in the Arab suburb of Haifa, where one of Bauman's bombs had killed forty people a few weeks ago.

8

Topmost in Joseph's dispatch-case lay the weekly shopping list for his household of a hundred and fifty people.

The wholesale offices of the Co-operative were down-town in the new business centre and were more like a debating club than a shop. Joseph placed his orders for a sack of sugar and the required quantities of spaghetti, rice and tea, then took an autobus which took him uphill to the Hebrew quarter "Glory of the Carmel". As it climbed the steep serpentine road, the view over the sparkling bay expanded, and the edge of the sea widened its circle and was lifted higher, keeping level with the ascent of the bus. The harbour shrank and the yellow dunes with their wavering white surf-line stretched out to the horizon. The curved massif of the Carmel was hugging the bay in its protecting elbow; near its bend the breakwater jutted out and the glassy sea was dotted with steamers and fishing boats. A little further out a single ship with a black hull rode at anchor, isolated from the rest. It was the Rumanian cattle steamer *Assimi* with two hundred and fifty refugees on board, who had been refused permission to land.

Half-way up the Carmel, Joseph got out of the bus and continued his shopping. He had discovered a cheap grocer of Lithuanian origin, a bearded little man wearing a skull-cap, who had located the ten lost tribes of Israel in the Caucasus and found each week a new proof for his theory, so that it took Joseph half an hour to buy a hundredweight of dried apples, which, Dasha maintained, were essential for the vitamin diet of the under-nourished arrivals in the new draft. The rest of the morning went on the acquisition of ten cubic metres of timber for the Commune's carpentry shop (they were now producing their own furniture at Ezra's Tower), three sheets of leather for the shoe shop, whose smell gave him a nostalgic pang for the good old days, and various tools and spare parts for the tractor.

He lunched heretically in a small Arab eating-house where the food was cheap, dirty and tasty, and whose fat proprietor confidentially informed him that Hitler, Protector of Islam, would soon destroy the British Empire, restore the country to the Arabs and drive the Jews into the sea—except Joseph himself who, being the proprietor's friend and an educated person, would be spared and might even get a job in the establishment, provided he brought some capital with him.

He lingered over the sweet, strong coffee, striking off the finished tasks from his crammed notebook; then, in the damp midday heat, started once more on his rounds. He bought plywood and shoe polish, sun-glasses and contraceptives, toothbrushes and insecticides for the Communal stores, took the Dr. Phil.'s spectacles to an optician, and as a special treat visited Ringart's bookshop from which he emerged, after an hour's browsing, with a three-piaster pamphlet on combating tomato pests for the Communal Library. By then it was dark and his jangling nerves told him that there was a khamsin in the air. For some unknown reason he was worried about Dina, though when he had last seen her she had been neither better nor worse. Perhaps it was only because he knew how badly the spring khamsins affected her. And anyway, there was nothing to be done about Dina.

He had supper in the Workers' Club, listened to a lecture on the new Russian theatre, and went, very tired, to the cheap lodging-house where he always stayed in Haifa. It was a dirty, bug-ridden place run by an orthodox Polish Jew. Here he had to share a room, with no furniture except the beds in it, with three others. However, his room mates were not yet in, and by the time they arrived he was asleep.

The next morning he took a couple of hours off to attend the hearing of a case of illegal immigration in the Magistrate's Court, about which there had been some talk in the Co-operative Office.

He had never been to a Magistrate's Court before and was surprised by the lack of ceremony in the proceedings, the bleakness of the court-room and the informal, almost familiar atmosphere prevailing in it. There were about twelve to fifteen rows of benches, on which policemen and civilians, Jews and Arabs sat mixed together, with the sleepy expression of schoolboys when the sun shines outside. Facing them on a dais sat the Magistrate, Mr. Wilmot, a dry, elderly man with an absent-minded air. The dais was only a few inches high, but the table in front of the Magistrate had a marble top, which was the only solemn thing in the room. To the left of the dais were two separate benches at right angles to the others, representing the dock.

When Joseph entered the room, an old, bleary-eyed Arab with a red tarbush was standing in the dock and making an excited speech to the Magistrate, who stared dreamily at his nails. In front of the dais stood an English Police sergeant listening to the Arab's speech with a righteous and sour smile. Gradually it became clear that the sergeant had charged the Arab with cruelty to his mule. The mule was covered with sores caused by a skin disease and the sergeant had obtained a previous injunction against the Arab prohibiting the use of the mule until it was cured from its disease; however, at the date specified in the charge, the sergeant had seen the mule standing before the Arab's cart, which was heavily loaded with durra, near the Arab's hut up on Mount Carmel. The Arab, on the other hand, offered to bring ten witnesses who would swear that the mule had not worked for the last three weeks; and nobody in the audience doubted that he would be able to bring them.

When the Arab paused for breath, Mr. Wilmot, the Magistrate, seemed to wake up. "Ask him," he said in a small, dry voice to the interpreter, "whether he thinks that the sergeant was telling lies." The Arab raised both arms in protest; he had never said such a thing.

"Then he admits that he used the mule with the cart?" asked Mr. Wilmot. Again the Arab protested. "But that's what the sergeant says," said the Magistrate. The Arab was silent for a while, then he burst into a new torrent of speech.

"He says," the interpreter repeated grinning, "that it is true that the mule stood before the cart, but he says it wasn't harnessed to the cart."

"Then why did he put it there?" asked Mr. Wilmot.

"He says," said the interpreter, "that this is a free country and he can put the mule where he likes."

"Fifty piasters or two days," said the Magistrate. The sergeant smiled contentedly and the Arab was led out, protesting.

The next case was that of a young Beduin from Transjordan, charged with contravening the Traffic Regulations by persisting in riding his camel on the wrong side of the road. He was fined ten piasters and produced contemptuously a five-pound note which the Clerk could not change; they walked out of the court, shouting at each other.

Mr. Wilmot fumbled among his papers.

"Brod–etsky, Wilhelm," he read out. "Illegal immigration. . . . Where is he?"

In the row in front of Joseph there was a stir. An Arab policeman rose and nudged a thin little man with an ear-trumpet who was sitting beside him. He had already aroused Joseph's curiosity by fidgeting incessantly with his trumpet and craning his neck to hear what was going on. His neck was long and thin like a scrofulous child's. He rose hurriedly, squeezed past the Arabs sitting in his row and walked with quick, jerky steps behind the policeman to the dock.

"Is he represented?" asked the Magistrate.

A tall, pale man had risen in the front row. "I am representing him, your Worship," he said.

"Ah, Mr. Weinstein," the Magistrate said drily. "As usual."

"As usual, your Worship."

For a silent second the Magistrate and Weinstein looked at each other. Mr. Wilmot's eyes were vague. Weinstein's were equally expressionless; he looked haggard and ill. Brodetsky in the dock craned his neck and held the trumpet to his ear.

"Was ist los?" he cried suddenly. *"Was will man von mir?"*

"Tell him to wait until he is questioned," the Magistrate said, turning over his papers.

Weinstein crossed to the dock and spoke loudly into the trumpet:

"Sie müssen warten, Herr Brodetsky. Geduld."

Brodetsky nervously jerked his shoulders. "*Geduld, Geduld,*" he repeated, probably to himself.

After establishing the defendant's name, age, place of birth and profession—questions which Brodetsky answered readily, even eagerly—Mr. Wilmot proceeded to read out the charge, according to which the accused person had, on the date specified, arrived in territorial waters on board the Rumanian cattle ship *Assimi* carrying two hundred and fifty-one persons without immigration permits. The vessel had been intercepted by coastal patrol and ordered to return with its passengers to its Rumanian port of origin, but permitted to take food, drinking water and medical supplies, as epidemics had broken out on board. Under cover of night, while the detained vessel was riding at anchor in Haifa port, the accused person had jumped overboard and swum ashore, thereby entering the country without permission contrary to the Immigration Ordinance of 1933. He had been found lying unconscious on the beach by an Arab watchman and handed over to the Police.

"Does he plead guilty or not guilty?" the Magistrate asked.

"Not guilty—as usual," said Weinstein. He looked at the Magistrate with the same look of cool, concentrated hatred which Joseph had often seen in Simeon's eyes.

During the evidence of the night watchman and the Police witnesses, Brodetsky kept on fidgeting. He alternately held the trumpet to his ear and tried to arouse the attention of his lawyer, who stood with his back to the dock. His eyes were shifting restlessly along the rows of the audience as if asking for support, but seemed unable to focus on any single face. In the momentary pause when the Police witness had finished his deposition, he suddenly pulled his lawyer's sleeve and explained something to him with frantic gestures.

"What does he say?" asked the Magistrate.

"He says he has been boxed on the ear and cannot hear well."

"By whom?"

"By a guard in Dachau."

"I don't see the connection with the charge."

"No, your Worship." Weinstein looked as if he were going to add something, but did not.

The defendant again explained something in great agitation.

"What is it now?"

"He says the battery of his hearing apparatus slipped from him while he swam in the sea and he asks to be provided with a new battery."

Brodetsky hopefully held out his battered ear-trumpet towards the Magistrate, with a shrug to indicate that it was useless. The Magistrate met his eyes for a second, then reverted to the papers in his file. "Tell him that will have to be dealt with later," he said without looking up.

The barrister turned to the defendant who obediently replaced the trumpet to his ear. *"Später,"* he shouted into the trumpet.

"Später, später," Brodetsky repeated to himself, shrugging.

"Ask him whether he wants to make any statement bearing on the case."

"Wünschen Sie etwas zu sagen?" Weinstein shouted.

"Sagen? Sagen? Ich will zu meinem Neffen. Was ist hier los?" Brodetsky said nervously.

"He says that he wants to see his nephew and he keeps asking for what reason he has been brought to this room."

The Magistrate looked at Weinstein.

"You have explained the charge to him?"

"Repeatedly," said Weinstein.

"He was mentally examined and found in a state of nervous tension, but sane," said Mr. Wilmot, turning over his papers.

"Yes, your Worship." Weinstein hesitated for a second, then said in a flat monotone: "The desire on the part of a person escaping from danger of life to find refuge with the only surviving member of his family can hardly be interpreted as a sign of mental insanity."

After a moment's silence the Magistrate said:

"The nephew referred to lives at . . . ?"

"He is employed by the Potash Company on the Dead Sea."

"Is he in the audience?"

"No. He is in hospital with malaria."

"Everybody always seems to be in hospital with malaria," Mr. Wilmot said in a mutter. He suddenly closed the file with a determined gesture and leant back in his chair.

"Well, I am listening to the Prosecution."

The Prosecutor, a tall, well-groomed Christian Arab who

had so far taken little part in the proceedings, began to talk before he had completely risen to his feet, and had finished within two minutes. He summed up the evidence, quoted the text of the Immigration Ordinance, and demanded that the accused person be sentenced to six months' imprisonment with a recommendation to be subsequently deported. He spoke a careful English and gave the impression of repeating a daily routine performance.

After him it was Weinstein's turn. He spoke in a deliberately colourless voice. He referred to the known facts of persecution in Germany, Austria and Czechoslovakia which gave those who succeeded in escaping no choice but to cross as quickly as possible any frontier they could reach. However, even if they managed to evade the frontier patrols, they found no safety on the other side, as most European countries had brought in legislation against this undesirable influx, and they remained under the constant threat of arrest and expulsion. It was thus inevitable that they should try by any means to reach the shores of the country which by international agreement had been granted to them as a National Home, and which was their only remaining hope. Hunted by the Police, without passports or legal residence, it was materially impossible for them to follow the regular procedure, that is to apply for an immigration permit and wait for probably a year or two until their turn on the quota came. Under these circumstances to distinguish between "legal" and "illegal" immigrants became a mockery.

"If I have a madman at my heels," he went on in his colourless voice, "and I see an autobus passing, I shall jump onto the platform regardless of traffic regulations. I leave it to your Worship to decide whether the bus conductor would be right in pushing me off the platform because I boarded the vehicle outside the prescribed stop."

He paused, wound up with the plea that these aspects of the case should be taken into consideration by the Court, sat down and swallowed two pills from a little box in his waistcoat pocket, looking iller than ever.

Brodetsky bent in great excitement over his lawyer's shoulder. *"Was ist los?"* he asked.

Weinstein cleared his throat and bent to the trumpet. *"Geduld,"* he said.

"Was, was?" said Brodetsky, looking questioningly to the audience.

After some more technicalities Mr. Wilmot rose, patiently waiting until Brodetsky had been persuaded to keep silent.

"As always in these cases," he said, looking at nobody in particular, "I say again that it is my duty as a Magistrate to use the penalties which I am empowered to inflict in order to restrain, as far as may be, those who are contemplating similar offences."

He looked at the accused man, who was now bobbing up and down on his toes in soundless excitement; then again averted his eyes.

"I am sensitive to the truth of what Mr. Weinstein said," he went on, looking at the barrister, "that the conditions in certain countries in Europe have caused what one may call a stampede of the mass of the persecuted out of those territories, and that in these circumstances deterrent punishment can have little effect. However, it is incumbent upon me to endeavour to exercise my discretion so that, if possible, such deterrent effect may be produced."

He made a pause, cleared his throat and went on, speaking with a marked deliberation:

"It is possible that I am wrong and that such cases should be dealt with differently. I hope this case will be taken to appeal and I should like to have a direction in this matter from a higher court."

He had been looking at Weinstein, but now turned deliberately to the defendant, who was craning his neck with the trumpet to his ear.

"For the above reasons I sentence the accused person to three months' imprisonment from the day of arrest, and shall recommend to His Excellency the High Commissioner that he be deported."

There was a silence, and then once more Brodetsky's voice ringing out:

"Was ist los? Was ist los?"

Weinstein talked to him while the Court rose, trying to persuade him to follow peacefully his escort. But Brodetsky refused to budge and shouted more and more loudly that he could not wait any longer and wished to go at once and live with his nephew. He finally was half dragged, half carried out by two Arab policemen, trying to hang on to his lawyer's sleeve and yelling in a shrill, sobbing voice:

"Was ist los? Was ist los? Was hab' ich getan?"

Joseph walked out of the Court. Downstairs at the gate Weinstein passed him with an unlit cigarette between his lips which was moving up and down from a nervous tic. He was absent-mindedly fumbling in his pockets for a match. Joseph gave him a light, addressing him in Hebrew.

"Thank you," said Weinstein. His face was yellow and his hands slightly shaking.

"Are you going to appeal?" Joseph asked.

"What?" said Weinstein. "Oh, yes, as usual." His eyes, which again reminded Joseph of Simeon's, focussed on Joseph's dispatch-case.

"Are you a clerk?" he asked.

"No—I am from a Settlement."

"Settlement," Weinstein repeated. His cigarette was still twitching up and down. "And what are you carrying there?"

"Papers," said Joseph.

". . . Papers," Weinstein repeated. "We are all carrying papers. Perhaps we should be carrying revolvers."

He smiled distractedly and walked off with a slightly limping gait, clutching his dispatch-case to his side.

Luckily Joseph had so much to do that he found no time for brooding. His tasks as a communal purveyor having been finished the previous day, except for those items which he could only get in Tel Aviv or Jerusalem, he now had to embark on his more tedious duties as a money-raiser, diplomatist and wangler. They included a protracted argument with the District Manager of the Workers' Sick Fund to get the people of Ezra's Tower graded into a higher health- and lower premium-category; negotiations with the Workers' Bank for the prolongation of a promissory note; and making a row at the Committee of Culture and Education about the inferior quality of the last three lecturers they had sent.

To appease Joseph, the Secretary of the Committee gave him a free ticket to the Eden Cinema. It was a rare treat, for living on the Communal purse, Joseph could not find it in his heart to go to a show, though he was entitled to do so once a fortnight. He arrived at the cinema after the performance had started, watched the entry of the German troops into Prague, followed the first stages of a young heiress' tragic struggles to become, against her parents' wish, the world ice-skating champion, and fell asleep. When he woke, the heiress had just broken an ankle and was being carried away in an ambulance, so Joseph pushed his way out and walked back to his lodging-house.

This time his room mates were already in their beds. One of them snored and a second, apparently a new arrival from Europe, kept on begging in his sleep, in a high, piping voice, that somebody should stop doing something to him: after which he counted up to ten, each number followed by a jerk and a groan. Joseph woke him and gave him a glass of water; but after a while the man again fell asleep and again started counting. Joseph resigned himself to watching the plaster flaking from the ceiling and the cockroaches creeping over the floor, in the yellow light of the shadeless electric bulb. From outside came the slow beat of the tide in the harbour where the *Assimi* rode at anchor with her two hundred and fifty passengers on board, including eighty women and children.

At last Joseph fell asleep. He was woken again after a few hours by the wailing of the *Assimi's* siren. He was angry, for just at the moment of being woken up he had been on the point of making his voice heard and catching at last the white-wigged Speaker's eye. The room was dim; it was still very early. The snorer in the next bed snored, but the man who had counted to ten had calmed down; he lay on his stomach with one arm hanging over the side of the bed, his open mouth burrowed into the pillow. The fourth bed, which had been occupied by an old man with a beard, was empty.

The siren wailed a second time and Joseph jumped from his bed and crossed to the window. Under the window there was a shapeless crouching figure wrapped in a black-and-white praying scarf which he had drawn hood-like over his head, with the tassels hanging over his eyes. He was balancing on his heels, forward and back in the traditional rocking movement of prayer, while his fist rhythmically beat his chest. Through the window, down in the harbour, the mast-tops of the *Assimi* could be seen slowly moving past the long breakwater towards the open sea, followed by a swarm of circling seagulls; carrying its passengers towards the sunny Mediterranean and the various forms of death awaiting them. The hooded figure was mumbling and swaying on his heels; the crown of his head was littered with small black flakes: he must have burned some paper to obtain ashes as befits the occasion of the prayer for the dead.

9

The first intimation of the impending disaster reached the Hebrew Community on Sunday, February 26. According to London agency reports published by the Hebrew and Arabic Press, the British Government had submitted to the delegates of the Round Table Conference its proposals for the transformation of Palestine into an independent Arab state, and for further prohibitive measures against the immigration of Jews, who were for all time to remain a minority not exceeding one-third of the total population.

The Round Table Conference had opened in St. James's Palace on February 2, 1939, with an address of welcome by Prime Minister Neville Chamberlain. The Palestine Arabs, the majority of whom belonged to the fugitive Mufti's party, refused to sit at the same table with the Hebrew delegation. The British Government, endorsing their attitude, split the conference into two parallel Anglo-Arab and Anglo-Hebrew conferences. The Hebrew delegation demanded the continuation of the British Mandate and of Jewish immigration according to the country's economic absorptive capacity. The Arab delegation demanded abrogation of the Mandate and of the Balfour Declaration, the banning of Jewish immigration and the prohibition of the purchase of land by Jews. After about a fortnight's deadlock the British Government was now reported to have issued its proposals which accepted in substance the Arab demands.

On the same day the London newspapers also reported that the Government had endorsed the Spanish insurgents' demand for immediate recognition. Certain sections of the Press commented that the British Government trusted General Franco's generosity and his promise to avoid reprisals against the Loyalists. The same newspapers expressed the opinion that Arab generosity was to be the best guarantee for the rights of the Jewish minority.

Coincident with these reports came the news of the erection of a concrete security wall round the Jewish quarter of the Old City of Jerusalem, of the murder of a popular Hebrew teacher in the vicinity of Solomon's Pool, of the explosion of yet more bombs in the Hebrew centres of Haifa and Jerusalem, and of jubilant Moslem demonstrations hailing the Mufti and Mr. Chamberlain.

While the usual terror acts continued, the Jewish representative bodies issued their usual protests against "the planned liquidation of the National Home and its handing over to the rule of the gang leaders"; and their President, the aged and venerable Professor of Organic Chemistry, urged as usual restraint in the face of disaster. However, a considerable section of the Hebrew youth had by that time become convinced that restraint was not the proper answer to disaster. For twenty years they had practised loyalty and restraint, and were now on the point of losing everything; whereas their opponents had practised rebellion and violence, and were to be rewarded by the granting of all their demands.

The controversy over the question of the use of violence had already some time ago led to a split in the ranks of the Hebrew defence organisation. The old organisation, "Haganah", controlled by the Jewish official bodies and socialist in outlook, adhered to the principle of passive defence; it was tolerated by the Government to whom it had given valuable help in crushing the Arab rebellion. The new organisation, "Irgun", was numerically smaller and organised on the conspiratorial lines of a terrorist underground movement. Its members were extreme nationalists in outlook, derided the impotence of the Jewish official bodies, were denounced as fascists by their old comrades of the "Haganah", and hunted by the Police. They had secret wireless transmitters and printing presses, a considerable stock of arms, and sympathisers in all layers of the Hebrew population including the Police Force and Government Departments. Their leaders were two students of the Hebrew University in Jerusalem, both in their twenties: "Razi", alias David Raziel, a Bible scholar, later killed in action serving with the British Forces, at that time interned in the concentration camp of Sarafand; and "Yair", alias Abraham Stern, a poet, later killed by the Police while trying to escape arrest.

On Monday, February 27, twenty-four hours after publica-

tion of the British Government's proposals, the "Irgun" struck.

In the early morning hours of that day, the secret wireless transmitter, "Voice of Fighting Zion", announced that "punitive military actions are being carried out at this hour simultaneously in all the bigger towns and on the roads of the country. These punitive actions of our forces should serve as a warning to Arab terrorists who committed atrocities during the last thirty-two months against the Hebrew community; to the British Government, which has broken its solemn pledges and closed the gates of the Land of Israel; to the world at large, which has so far done nothing to prevent the slaughter of our kin."

It was not an empty boast. Simultaneously at the indicated hour, bombs and land mines exploded and volleys were fired in the Arab quarters of Jerusalem, Jaffa, Haifa and Sarafand; cars were assaulted, rails blown up and trains derailed all over the country. Arab casualties during that one hour equalled the Hebrew casualties during the last three months.

The action had started everywhere at 6.30 a.m. and was over by 7.30 a.m. No member of the "Irgun" was caught by the Police. At 8.30 a.m. General Bernard Montgomery, Commander of the Haifa District, had the streets of the town cleared by armoured cars with loudspeaker vans who ordered everybody home. A daylight curfew was imposed until the next morning.

A few hours later the Colonial Secretary, Mr. Malcolm MacDonald, made a statement in the House of Commons. In lieu of the expected official confirmation of the Government's proposals as released to the Press the day before, the Colonial Secretary appealed to the public in "England and Palestine . . . to withhold judgment until an authoritative statement could be made". The Colonial Secretary also regretted that "incomplete and in some important respects misleading reports of the Government's intentions had gone to Palestine where they had been the cause of serious incidents". Pressed by the Leader of the Opposition for a statement "to prevent further misleading ideas", Mr. MacDonald said that "after what had taken place in Palestine any further statement would be undesirable."

It looked as if, for the moment at least, disaster had been averted. The bombs and land mines had spoken in the only language which, anno domini 1939, *the world understood. A few hours later the Prime Minister confirmed the unconditional recognition of General Franco's Junta as the legitimate government in Spain. His announcement was received with cries of "shame"; one member shouted: "You should be impeached as a traitor to Great Britain."*

10

The khamsin is a hot, dry, easterly wind blowing from the Arabian desert. The name is of Egyptian origin and signifies "fifty"—the fifty days between Easter and Pentecost on which the khamsin is said to be particularly frequent.

As with its kin: sirocco and foehn, bora and mistral, the khamsin's effect on the humours of man is violent and mysterious. Its intensity varies from a tepid breeze, importunate like an unwanted caress, to the scalding whiff from an open boiler. But it is not the surface effect of the moving air which counts; nor its heat; nor the thirst, the irking dryness in throat and nostrils. What matters is the khamsin's nervous effect, and the things which it does to those functions of the body which are beyond voluntary control.

There are no statistics on the increase of suicide, manslaughter and rape on khamsin days. Its influence on the nervous system cannot be expressed in measurable quantities.

Measurable are only the physical changes in the atmosphere. It is known that the temperature close to the ground may jump upward during a khamsin by 35 degrees and pass 110 degrees in the shade. The relative humidity of the air may drop to one-seventh of the normal and come within 2 per cent of absolute dryness. The electrical conductivity of the air may increase to twenty times its normal value, while its radioactivity may increase two- to three-fold. But what do these measurements reveal? Not much, except perhaps the fact that man is subjected to the moods of Nature in more and subtler ways than he is wont to imagine. His apparent dominion over her is purely external; as Gulliver was tied in his sleep by the Lilliputians, so he remains attached to the blind forces by a web of thin, invisible threads tied to his solar plexus, the para sympathetic ganglia, the electrical charge of his nerve-sheaths, the vaso-regulators of his endocrine glands. A clumsy slave who imagines himself master because his chains have been replaced by a silken strait-jacket.

The sky on khamsin days over Ezra's Tower is leaden grey with high vapour and desert dust. On the slope facing Kfar Tabiyeh the twigs of the young pines move in a soft, rain-heralding way in the mute air; but there will be no rain. The liberating thunder seems on the tip of Nature's tongue; but she sticks her tongue out at you and there will be no storm. There is a protracted expectation and frustration in the sulphuric air; like Messalina's long, tormenting embrace it excites but refuses relief; a panting, suffocating ascent which never reaches its climax. A storm is brewing within arm's reach, brewing inside people's ears and ribs, which will never discharge itself.

The day after Joseph had left for Haifa, the khamsin was particularly bad. Dina had spent the evening trying to read, while Sarah, with whom she shared her room, was discussing with Max an article in the Hebrew I.L.P. paper about how to help the emancipation of the Arab woman. Sarah thought that the best way was a frontal attack on religion. Max thought that the question of the Veil and birth-control should come first. Sarah thought that the main obstacle was the Arab fear of Hebrew domination. Max thought that they should renounce any claim to dominate in a solemn declaration. Sarah thought that Bauman's gang were Fascist criminals. Max thought that they were discrediting the whole movement and should be handed over to the Police. Sarah thought that it was the human approach to the Arabs which counted. Max agreed that the human approach had not been carried sufficiently far. At this point Dina unexpectedly started to scream. Max looked at her, bewildered, along his drooping tapir-nose. "Oh, go away," she screamed, stamping her feet, "go, go away all of you and leave me alone. . . ."

She tried to control herself, biting her lips and pushing the hair out of her face. "Are you ill?" Max asked, bending towards her, and sniffing sympathetically. But Dina suddenly hit out at his chest with her fist, and while Max stumbled back, she ran out of the room.

It was hot and there was nobody outside. The khamsin caught her from behind; it felt as if somebody were blowing on the nape of her neck with a hot, foul breath. Behind the tower the rust-coloured moon hung motionless on a greyish gauze of mist; it looked like a clot on a soiled bandage. She hurried across the Square and past the dining-hut where some meeting was on; the hum of the all too well-known voices came out floating on the hot breeze like a swarm of insistent flies. She hurried on through the married living quarters with its square white concrete blocks. The door of Joseph's room stood open and the room was brightly lit. On the bed, facing the door, Ellen, Gaby and the Egyptian were sitting side by side. Ellen, with her swollen belly, was leaning back on the bed and reading out something from a magazine, and they all three laughed. The Egyptian had his arm round Gaby's shoulder; her leg was pressed against his from knee to ankle.

Lifting her eyes from the magazine, Ellen saw Dina's slender figure silhouetted against the darkness; she called out to her, but the figure moved on as if frightened.

Once outside the circle of light, Dina hesitated for a second whether she should turn back and join the company of the others. But the idea of sitting still in that cramped, narrow cubicle with its stuffy air and the odour of Joseph and Ellen's copulations lingering on the bed, made her hurry on again. It seemed to her that she knew not only all their voices by heart but also the individual smell of their perspirations. There was an itching dryness inside the hot shell of her nostrils; for a while the world seemed to consist of smells alone, floating in the air like threads of various colour. There was the greasy whiff of tepid dishwater from the communal kitchen, the sour-milk smell of the nursery, the acid smell of the sheep-pen, the biting ammonia of the men's urinary, the sickly-sweet odour of indisposed women. When a small child she could always tell when her grown-up sister or her friends were unwell. She closed her eyes and scratched frantically with her sharp finger-nail in the dry cavity of her nose. At last she had discovered what she was going to do; sobbing and biting her nails, she burst into the stable-shed and groped her way in the hay-warm darkness towards Salome's box.

The brown mare was asleep, but as soon as Dina's hand touched her flank she scrambled to her feet with a docile and plaintive neigh. Dina found the stable lantern and a box of matches; while she put the saddle on the horse she felt suddenly quite cheerful. She had gone out on night rides several times before when a similar mood had come over her; and though lately snipers had again taken occasional pot-shots at the settlement in the dark, wounding two people, and it was not considered safe to walk alone outside the entrenchment at night, this only gave an additional thrill to her undertaking. She extinguished the lantern and led Salome quietly out of the shed and past the rows of tents of the youth camp. A moment later she had reached the barbed wire and passed through the gate. She looked round, but there was nobody to see her; she gave Salome a pat on the flank, planted her left foot firmly in the stirrup and, with an elastic jump, mounted. She would have liked to go for a wild gallop but the moon was not bright enough, and if she broke a leg of the communal mare she might as well commit suicide at once. They had a way of unctuous forgiveness in such cases which made one feel a leper for weeks. It delighted her that she was doing something definitely "asocial" and naughty; and that, as Salome couldn't tell tales, nobody would know a thing about it.

As she walked the horse down the slope on the farther side of Kfar Tabiyeh, the hills around her looked as if dipped into a silver bath. Their silence gave her an unearthly feeling. From the height of Salome's back even the khamsin felt like a warm, impersonal caress. She decided to ride straight down into the wadi, follow its course and then take the path up the opposite hill to the Ancestor's Cave.

However, as she reached the bottom of the slope and rode through the narrow, twisting bed of the wadi strewn with boulders and dry thistles and tufts of scrub, a sense of oppression came over her. The slopes now rose on both sides over her head; she could no longer dominate them with her view. Salome was carefully picking her way among the rubble and could not be induced to go quicker. There was no sound except the dry crunching of her hooves and the occasional screech of her slipping on a stone. Dina thought longingly of the noises in the far-away dining-hut and of the bright light streaming through the door of Joseph's room. The hills had withdrawn into themselves; there was an air of refusal about them, the exhalation of an immense loneliness. She was on the point of admitting defeat and turning Salome's head, when at a sudden twist of the wadi she saw a man in Arab dress walking steadily towards her.

Something in his gait and clothing told her that he was one of the villagers from Kfar Tabiyeh. At the first moment the man seemed as startled as she was and stopped uncertainly about twenty yards in front of her; then, probably perceiving that she was a woman, he resumed his walk and came steadily closer. To turn back now would have meant admitting that she was scared; she pressed her heels into Salome's flank and rode on. She could not induce the horse to walk quicker on the slippery rubble, nor did the man hasten his steps, so that the few yards which were still between them seemed to drag on for minutes. She now saw that he wore a kefiyeh with a black cord and a striped Arab skirt with a checked European jacket. When at last they were level he stepped aside and looked up at her, silent and open-mouthed. She could see the gap of two missing front teeth in the dark cavity of his mouth and the blind, milky pupil of one eye destroyed by trachoma. When she had passed him he said something which she couldn't understand in a hoarse voice and, after a moment's hesitation, turned and began to follow her. But now there was a clean stretch of path before her, and Salome, suddenly frightened, broke of her own accord into a gallop. When Dina turned her head after a minute, there was nothing behind her but the empty wadi, deserted between the silver hills.

Her heart-beat became normal again as soon as she found herself on the ascending path to the Ancestor's chamber; only her thighs, locked round Salome's warm flanks, went on trembling for a while. She told herself that she was a coward and a fool to be frightened by a harmless villager. The words he had spoken to her had probably been just a greeting, and her riding past in silence must have offended him. There was after all something in what Max had said about the human approach. She should have given him a friendly and firm "*marhaba*" and not betrayed her fear. That was what Ellen or Dasha would have done in her place. But then Ellen and Dasha had never known—anyway, she was all right now and quite cheerful again. Only her legs in the stirrups went on trembling; for her flesh knew better, and knew that what the man had said had not been just a greeting.

The caves in the moonlight were rather a disappointment. There was no tree or pole to which she could fasten Salome, so she had to drag the horse after her up and down the slope while she searched for the entrance which at night was not easy to find. Twice she thought she had found it, but each time it was only one of the empty smaller caves. The moon was already fairly low and it must have been pretty late in the night, but the sky had cleared, so its light shone brighter.

At last she found the little mound and behind it the steep narrow hole leading to the vestibule. She pulled Salome's head down so that she could weigh the end of the reins with a stone, then, lying flat on her stomach, put her feet into the hole and let herself slide down. Down in the vestibule the smell was terrible—some Arab shepherds must have used the hole as a latrine. She groped nervously in the pockets of her shorts for the matches she had brought with her from the stable, broke one, lit the second, and found the candle stump which was always left lying about in the first burial-chamber. In the yellow light of the candle the cave looked friendlier, but her apprehensions had been correct: the sand on the ground of the passage was littered with dried excrement. Covering her nose and mouth with her free hand and stooping under the low ceiling, she descended the three stone steps to the lower vestibule. There were the three niches, and the middle one was Joshua the Ancestor's.

The bones were still there all right and the skull was still missing; no miracle had happened since her last visit. The bones lay in a disorderly heap on the damp sand of the narrow chamber. "Hallo, Ancestor," Dina whispered, squatting on her heels. She scratched a little with her nails in the sand, in the exciting hope of finding a coin. But the chamber had been plundered God knew how many times and by whom: Roman Legionaries, Arab shepherds, Crusaders, Turks, until they had even pinched the Ancestor's head and strewn his bones about so that his left tibia lay upside-down across his ribs, like a ballet dancer's leg thrown up in a high kick. She wanted to replace the tibia in its proper position but couldn't get herself to touch it; and while she hesitated, her bust squeezed into the chamber, a trickle of liquid tallow dropped from the candle, into the sand just beneath Joshua's pelvis and glinted there, an obscene jelly-blot. It was as if even the Ancestor derided her by spilling his semen under her face. She flinched, and as she hurriedly withdrew her body from the niche, knocked her head against the low rock ceiling.

Biting her nails and feeling sick, she scrambled out of the passage. She put the candle back into the first chamber of the upper vestibule and crawled out through the hole, lifting herself up by her elbows. Salome was patiently waiting for her outside the entrance, her head bent under the pull of the reins; but instead of the fresh night air for which she thirsted, there was once more only the hot, foul breath of the khamsin.

With trembling lips she mounted the horse and began her descent down the steep path. The moon was almost gone and the hills were no longer silver-smooth and aloof, but dark, hulking silhouettes. She dreaded riding once more through the wadi but there was no other way home. She wished Joseph or Reuben were here with her but they slept far away in their beds unaware of her doings. She said a prayer, forgetting even to be ashamed. At some distance in front of her rose two dark round hillocks, almost symmetrical, side by side; " the Giant's Buttocks" Moshe had once called them. She had thought it funny then, but now she saw the naked giant lying flat on his stomach, his hind-part lifted in monstrous blasphemy to the sky.

She had reached the wadi. This was the smooth end of it; she dug her heels into the tired horse's flanks until it broke into a jerky gallop. But they soon came to the narrow, twisted stretch choked with rubble where the horse could only advance step by step; and as they turned the corner she saw the Arab with the gaping teeth standing in the middle of the gorge; but this time there were two others behind him, waiting for her.

11

Having finished with this week's business in Haifa, Joseph early next morning took the autobus to Tel Aviv. He slept for most of the three hours' journey through the orange and lemon groves of the Maritime Plain of Samaria of which the strip along the coast was in Hebrew, the next, parallel inland belt in Arab possession. Whenever Joseph, waking, looked through the window, he saw not the landscape but an unprotected flank. When they arrived in Tel Aviv, the khamsin had just reached its peak.

Each time Joseph came to Tel Aviv he was torn between his contrasting emotions of tenderness and revulsion. Tenderness for the one and only purely Hebrew town in the world with the lyrical name of Hill of Spring and the jostling vitality of its hundred and fifty thousand citizens; revulsion from the dreadful mess they had made of it. It was a frantic, touching, maddening city which gripped the traveller by his buttonhole as soon as he entered it, tugged and dragged him round like a whirlpool, and left him after a few days faint and limp, not knowing whether he should love or hate it, laugh or scorn.

The whole adventure had started less than a generation ago, when the handful of native Jewish families in Arab Jaffa decided to build a residential suburb of their own, on what they imagined to be modern European lines. Accordingly they left the molehill of the Arab port with its labyrinthine bazaars, exotic smells and furtive daggers, and started building on the yellow sand of the Mediterranean dunes the city of their dreams: an exact imitation of the ghetto suburbs of Warsaw, Cracow and Lodz. There was a main street named after Dr. Herzl with two rows of exquisitely ugly houses each of which gave the impression of an orphanage or Police barracks, covered for beauty with pink, green and lemon-coloured stucco which after the first rains looked as if the house had contracted smallpox or measles. There was also a multitude of dingy shops, most of which sold lemonade, buttons and flypaper.

In the early nineteen-twenties, with the beginnings of Zionist colonisation, the town had begun to spread with increasing speed along the beach. It grew in hectic jumps according to each new wave of immigration—an inland tide of asphalt and concrete advancing over the dunes. There was no time for planning and no willingness; growth was feverish and anarchic like that of tropical weeds. Each newcomer who had brought his savings started to build the house of his dream; and woe to the municipal authority who tried to interfere. Was this the promised land or not? For a decade or so, while the Eastern European element predominated among the immigrants, the source of inspiration of all these petrified day-dreams remained the stone-warren of the Polish small town. The Hill of Spring became a maze of stucco, with rusty iron railings along narrow-chested balconies and an Ionic plaster-column or Roman portico for embellishment.

However, life in Tel Aviv in those early days owed its peculiar character not to the people who had houses built, but to the workers who built them. The first Hebrew city was a pioneer city dominated by young workers of both sexes in their teens and twenties. The streets belonged to them; khaki shirts, shorts and dark sun-glasses were the fashionable wear, and ties, nicknamed "herrings", a rarity. In the evening, when the cool breeze from the sea relieved the white glare of the day, they walked arm in arm over the hot asphalt of the new avenues through whose chinks the yellow sand oozed up and which ended abruptly in the dunes. At night, they built bonfires and danced the horra on the beach, and at least once a week they dragged pompous Mayor Dizengoff or old Chief Rabbi Hertz out of their beds and took them down to the sea to dance with them. They were hard-working, sentimental and gay. They were carried by a wave of enthusiasm which had a crest and no trough. They were touchy only on one point, the Hebrew language. They fought a violent and victorious battle against the use in public of any other tongue; the slogan "Hebrews talk Hebrew" was everywhere—on buses, shops, restaurants, hoarding-posts; speakers from abroad who tried to address a meeting in Polish, German or Yiddish were howled down or beaten up. There were few cafés in those days but many workers' clubs; the cheap cafés sold meals on credit and got their supplies on credit; landlords let rooms on credit in their houses which were built on credit; and yet the town, instead of collapsing into the sand on which it was built, waxed and grew. . . .

—Ah, those were the good old times, the legendary days of ten years ago! As Joseph walked through the noisy crowd in Eliezer Ben Yehuda Street, of the two emotions battling in his chest revulsion got the upper hand. This cheap and lurid Levantine fair had ceased to be the pioneer town he had known and loved. One noisy café followed the other with flashy decorations, dance-parquets and microphones and blaring loud-speakers through which crooners from the suburbs of Bucharest and aged artistes from Salonica poured out their Hebrew imitations of American imitations of Cuban serenades. There were beauty parlours and antique shops and interior-decoration shops; and in the harsh white blaze of the sun it all looked like a noontide spook—the oppressive dream of a sybarite who has overeaten at lunch. This was the newest quarter of the town, built since the recent immigration from Germany and Central Europe had started, and the stucco-idyll of the older parts had been defeated by the aggressive cubism of the functional style. The houses here looked like rows of battleships in concrete; they had flat oval terraces with parapets jutting out like conning towers, and they all seemed to shoot at each other. The streets had no skyline and no perspective; the eye jumped restlessly along the jagged, disconnected contours without ever coming to rest.

Last week Joseph had run into Matthews, and Matthews had asked him for luncheon to-day at the Café Champignon on the beach. As Joseph crossed the over-crowded terrace in the noise of the orchestra playing the "Merry Widow", people turned their heads to look at him; he was the only person here in the traditional Commune dress. He felt a sudden homesickness for Ezra's Tower; it seemed to him that he had left it not two days, but weeks ago.

Seated at a table near the railing, overlooking the sea, he saw Matthews, who was arguing with a waiter. Joseph felt a sudden relief at the sight of the heavy-jawed face with the squashed boxer's nose—it was so obviously gentile in these sharp-featured semitic surroundings.

"Listen," Matthews was explaining to the waiter as Joseph sat down, "I've ordered a bottle of Chablis. This is syrup."

The waiter, dressed in a white jacket whose sleeves were too short for him, lifted his shoulders. "But please—it is written on the bottle: Chablis."

"It is muck," said Matthews. "Taste it."

"But please: here it is written on the bottle. Perhaps it should be sweet—I don't know. I have been a teacher before in Kovno, Lithuania."

"Taste it," said Matthews.

"But I don't drink--ulcers, sir, please."

"Then take this away and get me some beer."

"We have no beer, please, only wine."

"Then call the manager."

"But the manager is busy."

"Listen," said Matthews. "How would you like it if I bashed this bottle on your head?"

The waiter looked at him doubtfully, lifted his shoulders, and carried the bottle away. A minute later he returned with two jugs of iced beer, smiling all over his crumpled face.

"Well, how do you like Tel Aviv?" asked Joseph.

Matthews took a deep draught and put his glass down, sighing with contentment. "Swell," he said. "If you were allowed to punch somebody's nose once a day, it would be the swellest city with the swellest people in the world."

"Particularly the waiters," said Joseph.

"Maybe the poor guy was really a teacher in Kovno, Lithuania, and got his ulcers in a concentration camp."

Joseph looked round the terrace and sighed. The khamsin lay on people's faces like a spasm. The women were plump, heavy-chested, badly and expensively dressed. The men sat with sloping shoulders and hollow chests, thinking of their ulcers. Each couple looked as if they were carrying on a quarrel under cover of the "Merry Widow".

"I can't blame the gentiles if they dislike us," he said.

"That proves you are a patriot," said Matthews. "Since the days of your prophets, self-hatred has been the Jewish form of patriotism."

Joseph wiped his face. The khamsin was telling on him. He felt sick of it all: Judaism, Hebraism, the whole cramped effort to make something revive which had been dead for two thousand years.

"It is all very well for you to talk as a benevolent outsider," he said. "The fact is, we are a sick race. Tradition, form, style, have all gone overboard. We are a people with a history but no background. . . . Look around you, and you'll see the heritage of the ghetto. It is there in the wheedling lilt of the women's voices, and in the way the men hold themselves, with that frozen shrug about their shoulders."

"I guess that shrug was their only defence. Otherwise the whole race would have gone crackers."

"I know. That's what I keep repeating to myself. But sometimes one gets fed-up and wants to run away to a country with a moderate climate and moderate people, who don't live in absolutes. Here even the sky conforms to the all-or-nothing law: nine months of scorching sun without a drop of rain, and three months of deluge. . . ."

He leant back and drank some beer. "This is nice," he said. "Reminds me of a certain country pub back home. It was dim and smoky and the men said one word each in half an hour."

"It's always the same story," said Matthews. "If you are a dumb ox you want to be a chatty parrot. If you are a parrot, you wish you were a dignified ox. Drink your beer and take it easy with your Dostoevski."

Joseph drained his glass, smiling. "Of course," he said, "the crowd at a dog race at home isn't a much prettier sight than this one. But the flaws in other races are diluted, while with us you get them in concentration. It's the long inbreeding, I suppose. They called us the salt of the earth—but if you heap all the salt on one plate it doesn't make a palatable dish. Sometimes I think that the Dead Sea is the perfect symbol for us. It is the only big inland lake under sea level, stagnant, with no outlet, much denser than normal water with its concentrated minerals and biting alkaloids; over-salted, over-spiced, saturated . . ."

"They extract a lot of useful chemicals from it," said Matthews.

"Oh—quite. Marx and Freud and Einstein and so on. They are the crystallised products of the brine. But for all that the water doesn't get more palatable. . . ."

"How about some grub?" said Matthews. "Waiter! The guy won't listen. I guess this one was an opera conductor in Danzig."

"The trouble with this town is," Joseph went on, "that ten years ago the immigrants were mainly volunteers with an ideal in their head, and now they are mainly expatriates with a kick in their pants. Oh, you should have seen it ten years ago! Now it has become a town of refugees—the saltiest stratum of the Dead Sea."

Matthews had at last succeeded in getting hold of the waiter and gave his orders. He seemed bored with the discussion.

"Stop worrying about your Dead Sea," he said. "These shipwrecked folk don't matter. What matters is your new native generation and they're O.K."

"Yes—but they are on the other extreme. No salt at all. No intellectual passion, no sensitivity."

"Christ—you can't have it both ways. Maybe for fifty years you'll have to stop producing Einsteins and give other people a chance."

"You know," Joseph said, smiling, "you are the best Hebrew propagandist I've seen. The gentiles always are. Ours are all like Glickstein."

"Yeah," said Matthews. "An Arab gent accused me the other day of being paid by him. The fact is I've seen your Maccabi team beat the English Police three to one at soccer, and when they had to carry off the referee on a stretcher I became a Zionist. Here, let's buy a paper."

A newsboy had entered the terrace, shouting out the early afternoon editions. Matthews bought all of them and pushed them across the table to Joseph.

"They're all printed the wrong way round," he said. "Tell us the news about Mr. Hitler's latest doings."

Joseph unfolded *Davar,* the Labour daily, and after a glance at the headlines automatically turned to the back-page column with the local news from the Settlements in small print. His face suddenly turned ashen.

"What's the matter?" said Matthews. "Has Chamberlain done a Munich on the French?"

"No," said Joseph. "They have only killed Dina."

12

"There is only one chair, so you must sit on the bed," said Simeon.

His room, in the old Florentine quarter of Tel Aviv, looked more like a prison cell. It contained a narrow camp-bed, a table with a Primus cooker on it and one rickety chair. Instead of a wardrobe or chest there was a cardboard box under the bed which contained all Simeon's belongings. Nevertheless the room looked clean and tidy.

He took the Primus cooker from the table and put it carefully in a corner of the floor where a dark rim on the stone tiles indicated its usual place.

"As I can only go out when it is dark," he explained, "I have to cook for myself. The flat belongs to an old man who keeps a second-hand bookstall and is out all day."

Joseph sat down on the creaking bed which sagged under him until he almost sat on the floor. Simeon sat upright in the chair, facing him.

"You'd better tell me all the details," he said.

"There isn't much to tell," said Joseph. "The doctor says there were at least two at her. She must have put up a strong fight for her finger-nails were broken and there was blood and bits of skin under them, and there was also blood and bits of skin between her teeth. They counted twenty-seven stabs on her, none of which could have caused instantaneous death. Her nose was broken and some of her hair torn out with shreds of scalp. That is all. They also stole Salome."

He spoke in a flat voice as if giving an account to the weekly meeting in Ezra's Tower.

"And the Police?" asked Simeon.

"The Police came next morning. They brought blood-hounds. The Major did all he could. There were two separate scents which both met at the quarry behind Kfar Tabiyeh. Underneath the quarry there is a pool and there they lost the scent. Then one dog led on to the Mukhtar's house. They questioned the Mukhtar and some of the villagers, who all knew nothing."

"And so that's that?" said Simeon.

"As far as the Police is concerned, more or less. There is hardly a villager who hasn't been to the Mukhtar's house at one time or another."

They were silent for a little while. Joseph lit a cigarette and offered one to Simeon. By the way Simeon inhaled the smoke Joseph could see that he had not been able to afford cigarettes for some time.

"What about Reuben and the others?" Simeon asked.

"When we got back from the funeral I argued with Reuben and Moshe half through the night. I reminded them that this was the fifth case and that the Police never found anything and never will find anything. They said they were prepared to retaliate if they could find out who did it, but refused to take life for life indiscriminately. . . ." He paused. "I hope you don't want me to repeat the argument," he added.

"No," said Simeon. "I know it by heart: self-restraint, ethics and the purity of the cause—the whole menu. . . . What came of it in the end?"

"I told them that I was through with arguing and was going to quit. They were quite decent about it and gave me a month's leave to think it over."

He was crouching on the bed, yellow and shrivelled like a sick monkey.

"So that is how matters stand now with you," said Simeon reflectively. After a while he asked:

"Supposing you decide to leave, what about Ellen?"

"She will get over it. And to the child it won't make any difference. . . ."

He made a pause, then suddenly jumped up.

"The only question for me is," he said vehemently, "whether your crowd is willing and able to settle this, or not. Everything else doesn't matter."

Simeon gave him a cool look and said carefully:

"I have to report the matter to Bauman and he has to take it up with the Command."

"I want to speak to Bauman myself," said Joseph.

"That can probably be arranged. But it will take some time."

Joseph sat down again, as if the effort had exhausted him. He leant back against the wall and looked vacantly at the ceiling through his yellow sick-monkey eyes. There was a faint but insistent whistling from the street.

"Somebody to see me," said Simeon. "You must go now. Come and see me the day after to-morrow at the same time. I may have news for you by then."

Joseph obediently rose and walked to the door. As he opened it, he felt Simeon's grip on his arm.

"Pull yourself together," said Simeon. "In parenthesis, I was also once in love with Dina. But that isn't the point. The point is that these things are happening to our kin in Europe hour by hour."

"I don't care," said Joseph.

"Then go and drown yourself," said Simeon, giving him a hard push out onto the landing and banging the door after him.

Joseph reeled against the banister, stood limply for a few seconds, then wiped his eyes and began slowly to descend the narrow stairs.

13

A week after Dina's last excursion to the Ancestor's Cave, around midnight a heavy car jolted up the dirt track to the sleeping village of Kfar Tabiyeh. It halted at the Hamdan Mukhtar's house and two men in Beduin dress got out of it and walked up the outside flight of stairs leading to the balcony. It was new moon and from the balcony they saw the searchlight of Ezra's Tower slowly milling round the dark hills. The door from the balcony to the Mukhtar's room stood open; across the doorstep a servant lay on a mat, asleep. They shook him gently by the shoulder and the servant sat up with a jerk.

"*Marhaba,*" one of the men said in a throaty dialect. "We have been sent to talk to the Mukhtar."

"Welcome twice. Who sent you?" the servant asked, startled.

"One whose name should only be mentioned in a whisper. . . ." The two men pushed their way into the room, followed by the dazed servant. From a corner of the room they heard the Mukhtar's snore, then the snoring suddenly ceased. "Who is there?" he asked in a wakeful, imperious voice.

The servant lit the oil-lamp on the floor, under Mr. Chamberlain's portrait with the blue beads against the Evil Eye. The two men touched with their finger-tips forehead and heart.

"*Marhaba,*" said the one with the throaty voice. He was small, dark and wiry, with a sparse beard along the edge of his jaws and a tuft on the point of the chin. "We have been sent to fetch you, ya Mukhtar. We have come in a motor-car."

"Who sent you?" asked the Mukhtar. He was sitting up on his bed in his blue-and-yellow striped pyjamas. The centre button over his stomach was open, disclosing a fluff of black hair. The dark little man looked meaningly in the direction of the servant. "Go," said the Mukhtar, whose face had grown dark. The servant withdrew.

"Fawzi el Din is back in the hills, ya Mukhtar. He sent us for you. Get dressed, ya Mukhtar."

The Mukhtar looked from one to the other with a flicker in his eyes.

"They said Fawzi had surrendered to the English."

"They say many things. Get ready, ya Mukhtar, we have little time."

The Mukhtar looked at them without budging. "Where is he?" he asked.

"You shall know when you get there. Fawzi likes not to be kept waiting."

"I shall send Issa to him, as before."

"He sent us for you, not for Issa. Get dressed, ya Mukhtar."

The Mukhtar looked at him, then at the other man. They both stared at him hard, and the flicker in the Mukhtar's eye became more pronounced. "Ya Mahmud!" he called. The servant appeared. "Get my clothes."

While the Mukhtar dressed, the two men waited outside on the balcony with their backs to the open door of the room. They did not speak to each other. In the distance, the thin beam of light from Ezra's Tower slowly circled the night.

The Mukhtar emerged from the room, fully dressed, followed by the servant. His white head-cloth floated majestically to his shoulders, held by the coil of spun silver threads. He was a head taller than the little bearded man. The other man was of medium height, dumpy, and of lighter colour.

"I wish to take Issa with me," said the Mukhtar.

"We have been told to bring you alone," said the little man.

On the top of the stairs the Mukhtar hesitated for an imperceptible moment. The two men stood behind him. "I shall be back in the morning," said the Mukhtar over his shoulder to the servant. "There is no need to talk."

The servant bowed at the Mukhtar's back. "Peace with you, ya Mukhtar."

They got into the car; the Mukhtar and the man with the beard sat in the back, the other man took the wheel. They drove in silence down the bumpy dirt track. As they approached the bottom of the hill, the Mukhtar asked:

"From what country do you hail?"

He could not make out the dialect the little man spoke. His Arabic was throaty and pure, but foreign. At first he had thought he recognised the accents of some of the poorer tribes of Sinai, but it wasn't quite that.

"From Hadramaut."

So he was a Yemenite. That's why he had not recognised the dialect, the Mukhtar thought. He had never met a Yemenite before—except a Yemenite Jew from whom he had once bought a silver arm-ring in the shuks of Jerusalem. He remembered that he had been surprised at the pure Arabic that dark, wiry little Jew had spoken to him. . . . A sudden deadly suspicion flashed through the Mukhtar's mind. He bent forward to the driver, who had so far not spoken a word. "And you?" he asked.

"From Beyrout, ya Mukhtar."

Of course, he was a typical Syrian mongrel. They had all shapes and shades there—God alone knew the ancestry of a Syrian from Beyrout. But the Sephardi Jews in Beyrout were mongrels too, and many of them went to Arab schools. . . .

Bbah—donkey thoughts, the Mukhtar reassured himself. Was he a son of death, to think of such absurdities? It was only because the sudden return of Fawzi had shaken him. He had hoped to be rid for good of the Patriots. And then there was that matter with that Bastard, Issa. He would after all have to send him away, to Beyrout, to be on the safe side. Issa had not told him, but the Mukhtar had seen the scratches on his face and the deep gash on his hand, as though from a dog-bite. He had fallen from the horse, Issa had said, but the Mukhtar knew; and he also knew about the others, Auni and Aref. However, she had been asking for it, the shameless bitch, riding a horse alone at night with naked arms and legs. . . .

The car had reached the entrance to the wadi at its smooth end. Somewhere just round here must be the place where it had happened. Once more that shrill suspicion flared up in his brain, more insistent this time. The car stopped near a heap of boulders in the dry stream-bed.

"From here on we must walk, ya Mukhtar," said the Yemenite.

"Where to?" asked the Mukhtar, without budging from his seat.

"You will see, ya Mukhtar."

The driver switched the headlights off. He got out and stood at the door on the Mukhtar's side of the car. The Mukhtar looked from one to the other, but he could not make out in the darkness the look in their eyes. Puffing and mock-clumsily to indicate that he felt perfectly at ease, the Mukhtar climbed out of the car.

"Walk straight ahead, ya Mukhtar," said the Yemenite. The Mukhtar got slowly going, and the two men followed behind. His white head-cloth shone in the night three steps ahead of them, and by the curve of his shoulders they could tell that his right hand was clasped on the knife in his belt. They turned round a sharp bend in the wadi; at some distance to the left they saw the soft curved silhouette of two twin hills, the "Giant's Buttocks".

"Stop," said the Yemenite. "Stand still and drop that knife, ya Mukhtar. We have arrived."

The Mukhtar swerved round with an alacrity they had not expected from his heavy bulk. The two automatics were pointed from a distance of three yards straight at his stomach. He hesitated, then let the knife drop; it fell with a sharp clink on a stone. "How much money do you want?" he asked in a thick voice.

"Stand against that rock," said the Yemenite, and the Mukhtar retreated two steps until he stood with his back against the rock. "Who killed the Hebrew girl?" asked the Yemenite.

Ah, so they did not know, the fools. Of course—had they known they would have taken Issa and the two others, instead of him.

"What Hebrew girl?" he asked; his voice sounded genuinely surprised.

"Don't play the fool, ya Mukhtar. Either you tell us who they were, or you will die in their place."

"I heard there was an accident with a Hebrew girl, but I know no more."

The man from Beyrout suddenly jumped forward and hit him with the butt of his automatic across the face. The Mukhtar did not budge. He slowly passed his hand across his nose and mouth, looked at the blood on it and let it slowly drop; then he spat out the broken teeth.

"Who killed her?" asked the Yemenite.

"Whom?" said the Mukhtar.

The Syrian hit him again with the revolver butt, twice and with full force on the face and skull. The Mukhtar supported himself with the palms of his hands against the rock, then slowly slid down onto his knees. He remained thus for a few seconds, breathing heavily, then sat down on the rubble, his back against the rock.

"The English will hang you," he said with an effort.

"If you don't tell us who killed the Hebrew girl, you will die, ya Mukhtar," said the Yemenite.

The Mukhtar panted. "I don't know," he said. "What is she to you? You are not from her village."

"She was from our tribe, ya Mukhtar. Therefore we must kill one of your tribe to wash out the shame."

Through the mist and haze which surrounded his brain, the Mukhtar dimly realised that the Yemenite was talking sense. "We will pay blood-money," he panted. The upper half of his body swayed and had a tendency to slump down, but he supported himself in an erect position by the flat palms of his hands on the rubble. The world around him grew confused, he was back in the days of his youth, haggling with Beduins over a blood feud. "We will pay you forty camels," he panted. He began to recite like a litany the traditional list of camels to be paid:

"*Raba w'rabaiah,* male and female, four years old. *Hag w'hagga,* male and female, under four years. *Jeda w'jeda,* two smaller ones. *Marbout w'marbouta,* male and female, even smaller. *Libne w'libnieh,* two yearlings. *Mafroud w'mafrouda,* two small ones being weaned from their mother. . . ."

"Who killed the Hebrew girl?" asked the Yemenite.

"She was a whore," the Mukhtar panted. "Who can blame them? You are strangers—bringers of whores and corruption—strangers. . . ."

His heavy body suddenly slumped over. The Yemenite picked up the Mukhtar's knife from the stones.

"Wake up, ya Mukhtar, for you are going to die now," he said.

The Mukhtar raised himself and, panting, tried to crawl away on all-fours. For a minute or so the Yemenite watched him crawl blindly round in circles among the scree; then he stabbed him between the shoulders. The Mukhtar groaned and tried to crawl quicker, while the Yemenite went on stabbing him, until he collapsed on his stomach.

They found him the next day on exactly the same spot where Dina had been found, with twenty-seven stabs in his body, and a typewritten note in Arabic pinned to it: "*Akhaza assar w'nafa ellar*—revenge has been taken and the shame done away with". It was the ancient Beduin phrase which the tribe chants in triumph when a blood-guilt has been avenged.

Investigation by the Police established that the murderers had come in a motor-car from a different part of the country, that there was no evidence of their having any connection with the settlers of Ezra's Tower, and that they were persons originating from Arab countries, one of them a Yemenite. The Police further assumed that the killers belonged to Bauman's notorious *"Plugath ha-shakhorim"* or Black Squad, recruited from among the coloured Jews from Iraq, Kurdistan, Yemen and Bokhara; but they were unable to produce any decisive clues.

After the Mukhtar's funeral a crowd of villagers from Kfar Tabiyeh marched up the slope of the Dogs' Hill and threw stones at Ezra's Tower, but they were dispersed without serious incident by the reinforced Settlement Police. For a few days there was considerable excitement in the village, and rumours circulated to the effect that Fawzi's gang would return and burn down the whole of the Hebrew Settlement. These rumours were discussed with mixed feelings, as the Patriots had drawn heavily on the village's cattle and sheep; besides, the harvest of the winter crop was at hand, and if trouble broke out again most of the harvest would be lost.

The basic reason, however, of the villagers' half-hearted reaction to their Mukhtar's death was that they regarded the matter as a private blood feud between the Hamdan clan and the Settlers. They called the Hebrew girls whores and bitches, but they had disapproved of the hideous deed of Issa and his accomplices. Issa was anyway disliked throughout the village, and the two others were known as thoroughly bad lots, both of them having been previously jailed for theft. After the murder of the Hebrew girl the villagers had expected to find one at least of the three with his throat cut any morning, and would have regarded this more or less as a matter of course, a logical development of the blood feud. That the Hebrews had picked on the Mukhtar instead of Issa was an unexpected and sensational turn of events, but nevertheless strictly in conformity with blood law, according to which the injured party is entitled to take its revenge on the first near relative of the murderer they can lay their hands on. The fact that they had chosen the most important member of the Hamdan clan even rather impressed the villagers. The issue now clearly rested between Issa and the people of the Dogs' Hill. It was Issa's duty and privilege to avenge his father, and it would have been grave presumption on anybody else's part to interfere in the matter.

However, Issa appeared in no hurry to take action, except for the dropping of occasional hints to the effect that he was making elaborate plans and would soon be on the murderers' track. Meanwhile he made preparations for a journey to Jerusalem, allegedly in connection with his planned revenge, in fact because there was some business to settle with the Arab Bank about his father's heritage, and also because he wanted to have a look round the capital, to which he had never been before.

With the approach of the harvest, the excitement in Kfar Tabiyeh began to ebb. For some weeks there was still tension between the two villages; the people of Kfar Tabiyeh ceased to hire the tractor from Ezra's Tower and to send their children to the dispensary—until the other Mukhtar's first grandchild had its arm bitten through by an enraged mule. The child was saved, and after that relations were gradually resumed. The death of Dina and of the Mukhtar were never referred to, and for some years to come no further acts of aggression were committed by the people of Kfar Tabiyeh against the settlers of Ezra's Tower.

14

Pages from the chronicle of Joseph, a member of the Commune of Ezra's Tower

TEL AVIV, *Monday,* May . . . 1939

The eternally surprising thing after a shock which at the time seemed to unhinge the world is that the earth keeps turning and one's stomach digesting. It is this benevolent indifference of Nature pedantically sticking to her routine which keeps us sane. But as we are parts of Nature, her indifference is also at work inside ourselves. Our heartbeat has only stopped for a moment. Once it has resumed its regular ticking we have already surrendered to the universal law of indifference, and its total assertion will only be a question of time. At this stage our suffering undergoes a change of colour; the original pain turns into a secondary feeling of guilt. For to go on living is already a betrayal, a breach of solidarity towards the dead.

This is the stage when the transformed pain becomes almost unbearable. Up to now we were dazed, floating over the border between the two realms. Now the day has come when the line between them is drawn; and only now do we realise the finality of the division and the callous surrender of making it. By returning to life we have made a frontier and condemned the dead to permanent exile.

Then comes the second change. We no longer suffer with the dead, but from the void she left behind her. The person has been replaced by her hollow mould. It is impressed upon all the objects that surround us, and on everything we do. The more we suffer from the aggression of these petrified traces, the guiltier we feel. Live memories become fossilised. We don't pity the dead but ourselves for the loss suffered—those parts of us which were shared, and have been torn off. It is a loss of property, a depreciation in value of all our activities. It is an egotistic pain, as all pain is. This, if any, is the meaning of "let the dead bury their dead".

To surrender to life and yet to try to preserve the full integrity of the pain is a hypocrisy born of guilt. Once the choice is made there is no going back, and the task is to adapt oneself to a changed and impoverished world. The constant mourner lives in the magic hope that it may become again what it was before. It never will. The world has lost some of its warmth which it will not recapture. A solar spot has burst and expanded its heat into the great pool of entropic indifference. Its spectrum has undergone a change which affects everything I experience or do. Ezra's Tower will never be the same. Triumph will be less triumphant and defeat less stinging. Everything has become a little less important, a little paler, a little greyer. That is all. After a year this general impoverishment will be all that remains of Dina, who rode with me on a truck on our first night, and always wore a blue shirt open at the neck, and whose hair was blown over her face when we climbed to the top of the Tower, by the soft wind of Galilee. . . .

Tuesday

The death of the Mukhtar makes everything only more final. It was as if Dina had been buried with an undrawn cheque in her fist. Now the account is settled and the file closed. There is nothing more to be done. Yesterday there still was.

Perhaps if they had allowed me to take part in the action it would have been different. I wonder. I remember that night, after I had tried to kiss her dry lips with the clenched teeth, how . . .

GOD, GOD, THE THINGS THEY MUST HAVE DONE TO HER. . . .

Later

I have to go through with it. Words are the only magic to exorcise the pain.

. . . I remember that night, after I had tried to kiss her

dry lips with the clenched teeth—how I lay in the field, biting the earth and raving of revenge. It was the same during the whole week before I learned about the Mukhtar's death. I implored Simeon to let me take part in it and I demanded in all earnest that they should not only kill but torture—screaming at him until he threw me out. And now it means nothing to me, except a hideous anticlimax;—and the knowledge that the file is closed and nothing remains to be done.

An eye for an eye would be a wise rule if the victim could regain his sight by the culprit's eye. I have experienced that the desire for revenge may become a physical yearning like thirst; but its consummation is like drinking salt water. Some men adrift on the sea go on drinking it until they lose their reason. Some killers go on kicking their dead victim in the rage of their impotence. But the dead is always triumphant and the living is always defeated.

Wednesday

If I had emotions to spare I would perhaps even pity the fat Mukhtar. Nevertheless I believe that this action was necessary and justified. Whether we like it or not, all social life is based on the implicit assumption of collective responsibility for individual deeds. Jesus was denounced not by one Caiaphas but by "the Jews" who carry the blame to this day; the first Parliament was instituted by "the English" and every Englishman is proud of, and seems to participate in, this act; the same goes for the Rights of Man which "the French" gave the world and the concentration camps in which "the Germans" murder us. In war we act on the principle that the blame is homogeneously distributed among the individuals who constitute the enemy nation and hence that it makes no difference which particular individual is killed. Civilised warfare is as promiscuous in the choice of its targets as an Arab blood feud—which Europeans regard as a barbarity; and in three-dimensional war even discrimination between ages and sexes disappears completely. The only remaining difference is that the laws of the tribal blood feud are more honest and explicit in treating the adversary as a homogeneous, collectively responsible unit.

"The Arabs" have been waging intermittent tribal war against us for the last three years; if we want to survive we have to retaliate according to their accepted rules. By throwing bombs into Arab markets the Bauman gang performs exactly the same inhuman military duty as the crew of a bomber plane; the only difference is that the latter do it from the comparative safety of a few thousand feet in the air. To throw a hand-made bomb in a crowded bazaar needs at least as much courage as to press a button opening the bomb-trap. And yet pilots are called heroes and the Bauman gang are called gangsters and terrorists and what have you.

Of course, to press a shining metal button high up in the air is a more hygienic business than to plant a knife into a fat Mukhtar. What the public resents is not the killing but the detail and the mess. To sign a declaration of war is an act of statesmanship; to bump off the man before he can sign is a crime. Our ethics are but an elaborate form of schizophrenia.

But all this has nothing to do with Dina. I do not wish to avenge her any longer. If I decide to quit and join Bauman, it will not be for this reason. Dina, you are out of this. "Into thy hands I commend my spirit." Ah, if it were as simple as that. Into thy hands with the broken nails and bits of torn skin under them. . . . My spirit yes—but my reason I deny you. And if my heart is burnt to ashes, my reason I shall keep on ice.

Sabbath

More than half of my month's leave has gone. If I look back at this last fortnight, the days and nights seem to melt into one dim, shapeless smudge. It has the ambiguity of being both a very short and very long time—like a single flash fixed on a film where one can only afterwards measure its length. Most of the time I spent in my room working on Pepys or brooding and day-dreaming. I don't know what I would have done had Moshe not given me the money to take a room by myself. I have spoken to nobody except Simeon. Once I went swimming in the sea; but I remembered the last time I had gone swimming with Dina, so I went home and it was worse than ever. I feel constantly hungry but am unable to eat the things which she liked. At first I re-lived all our memories; now I try to avoid everything that reminds me of her. I move about like an invalid with a bandaged wound anxious to avoid rubbing against the furniture and walls. It is a kind of tight-rope walk where one always falls off the rope.

I know that I have a decision to take, but if I try to think it out I get nowhere. Instead of arriving at a result, I find myself lost in a day-dream. I try to straighten out the coils of my brain but they keep slipping from my grasp and curling up again. Perhaps real decisions are never thought out; they mature by themselves as a tree grows. So I have postponed the whole issue until after I have spoken to Bauman. Simeon says it will be some time next week. They have to be careful, as a whole bunch of them were arrested a few days ago.

The trouble is, I don't seem to care either way. I haven't been home since the funeral, and I rather dread seeing the Place again. It appears to me empty, changed and hostile. The Tower is like a threatening memento. A new disease: turrophobia.

But the alternative holds no lure either. To bump off somebody and get caught and hanged would probably be all right. But one doesn't get oneself hanged as easily as that. Nothing is easy in this specialised world of ours. They didn't even let me take part in the killing of the Mukhtar. You have to start from scratch, and work your way with patience and perseverance until you earn your cord. Simeon took some pains to explain this to me. And I haven't got the patience to take a course in terrorism as if it were practical gardening or rabbit-breeding. For one thing, it tastes too much of the cinema. For another, I have no patience left for anything. To hug a phantom in one's arms night after night doesn't leave one much vigour for the day.

No watchmaker can mend a broken spring; he has to send for a new one. Where can I look for a new spring?

Words, words, words. The trouble is that the whole issue upon which I have to decide has lost its reality for me. I no longer care a damn about Round Table Conferences, Arabs, Hebrews and National Homes. I wonder whether I ever did.

There was of course the Incident. But what a squalid little incident to decide a man's fate—even if the man was only an over-sensitive boy. Simeon's, for instance, is quite a different case. Simeon has all the Roman virtues; he loves his people and hates their enemies. I do not even love my people. I rather dislike them. Self-hatred is the Jew's patriotism, Matthews said.

Sunday

Before my father died there was a time when he took me every Sunday to the slums. There I learned that the poor were not the nice superior people which they appear in fairy stories, but wretched, illiterate and drunk; the women were hags with shrill voices and the children had nits. So I became a socialist not because I loved, but because I hated the poor. They were what conditions had made them, and therefore conditions had to be changed.

After the Incident I began to frequent those whom I had decided to regard henceforth as my people. They were as disappointing as the poor had been. I was attracted by their keenness, their intensity and their brains, but their achievements were spoiled for me by their ostentation. I hated their acid analytical faculty, their inability to relax. I hated their lack of form and ceremony and breeding, their shortcuts from courtesy to familiarity, their mixture of arrogance and cringing. They were the slum race of the world: their slums were the ghettos, whether the walls were made of stone or prejudice.

Constant segregation would thwart the healthiest race; if you keep slinging mud at people they will smell. Persecution has not ceased for the last twenty centuries and there is no reason to expect that it will cease in the twenty-first. It will not cease until the cause is abolished, and the cause is in ourselves. With all the boons we have brought to humanity we are not liked, and I suspect the reason is that we are not likable. If the poor were as idealised propaganda paints them, it would be a crime to interfere with their happiness; if the Jews were as the philosemites describe them, there would be no reason for this Return. But Jewry is a sick race; its disease is homelessness, and can only be cured by abolishing its homelessness.

I became a socialist because I hated the poor; and I became a Hebrew because I hated the Yid.

Monday

On Simeon's advice I have been re-reading the chapters in Flavius Josephus about Massada, the last Hebrew fortress which, after the fall of Jerusalem, held out against the Romans. When the Romans set fire to the inner wall by means of catapulted fire-brands, and Massada had become untenable, the Commander of the Fortress gave orders to the garrison to kill first all the women and children and then themselves. In his last speech he explained to them what fate awaited those who fell alive into the hands of the Romans; then he went on:

"But I find that you are such people as are no better than others either in virtue or in courage, and are afraid of dying, though you be delivered thereby from the greatest miseries. For the laws of our country and of God himself have from ancient times continually taught us that it is life that is a calamity to man and not death; for the union of what is divine and what is mortal is disagreeable. . . ."

He must have been a personality of remarkable powers to persuade his men to cut the throats of their women and children and afterwards their own; and it was a long and protracted business for there were nine hundred and sixty-two of them; and only two women, who had hidden themselves in an underground cave, escaped to tell the tale. Each man slew his own family; then they chose ten men by lot who slew all the other men; then they cast lots again and the one to whom it fell killed the remaining nine and finally himself. The name of this last man, the last free Hebrew to live, has not been recorded, nor any other names of the garrison, except that of the Commander, one Eliezer Ben Yair; and Yair is the alias adopted by the spiritual leader of the Bauman gang: Abraham Stern.

It is a savage tale, this story of the last Hebrew fortress, and yet strangely soothing. "The union of what is divine and what is mortal is disagreeable. . . ." There is an unmistakable Christian accent, and yet neither Ben Yair nor his chronicler Josephus seems to have had any knowledge of the new sect. But it was a time of howling and gnashing of teeth, and the new religion with its emphasis on immortality and resurrection was in the air. "Who is there," Yair asks referring to the mass slaughter of Hebrews by the Romans, "who is there that revolves these things in his mind and yet is able to bear the sight of the sun, though he himself might live out of danger? . . ." I believe there is a similar reason for the religious trend among our terrorists. The Hebrew underground began as a purely political movement and has developed more and more mystic accents. Simeon showed me yesterday some of Yair-Stern's poetry. It has a strange archaic fervour—quite untranslatable:

My teacher carried his praying-scarf in a velvet bag to
the synagogue:
Even so carry I my sacred gun to the Temple
That its voice may pray for us.

Or the refrain of the anthem he wrote for the underground movement:

These are the days of wrath, the nights of holy despair:
Fight your way home, eternal tramp,
Your house we shall repair
And mend the broken lamp.

Though he tries to hide it, Simeon has an almost religious admiration for Yair-Stern. He seems to regard him as a kind of gunman-messiah.

Tuesday

At last—to-morrow I am going to see Bauman in Jerusalem. Apparently that is where he lives, or at least, where he is at present. Curious—all the time I imagined that he was here in Tel Aviv; and though Simeon never directly said so, I was under the impression that he lived somewhere just around the corner. This somehow strikes me as a particularly neat piece of deception, though properly speaking there was no deception at all. Simeon never gives himself conspiratorial airs, and yet he is completely wrapped up in a shroud of elusiveness. Conspiring has become such a routine with him that it is invisible. I believe he hardly ever lies to me; he just automatically omits every reference to relevant facts. The closer I come to these people's world the more I feel as if I were running into a dense bank of fog inside which all is muffled and dim, and full of deceptive echoes.

To leave this room where I have been hiding since I came back from the funeral is like breaking up another link with Dina. There has never been such intimacy between us as within these solitary walls. Her picture hangs over the bed; I shall take it off the last minute before we leave. It was her room as much as mine; the scene of our bitter honeymoon.

To-morrow she will become homeless again and have to look for another exile and suffer another betrayal. The law of universal indifference will have stolen another victory, and will go on ticking in my flesh.

There is one alone, and there is not a second.

If two lie together then they have heat: but how can one be warm alone?

15

The city of Jerusalem is a mosaic of religious and national Communities, more or less neatly divided into separate residential quarters competing in holiness and mutual hatred.

Its sacred core, the Old City, is surrounded by Soleiman's Wall and divided into a Moslem, a Christian, an Armenian and a Jewish quarter. Outside the Wall there is the German Colony, the Greek Colony and the Commercial Centre; the rest of the town is part Arab, part Hebrew. The latter part is again subdivided according to the origin and period of the immigrants who built it, from the ancient slum ghetto of the quarter of the Hundred Gates to ultra-modern Rechavia, non-Aryan offshoot of the Weimar Republic complete with glass, chromium, Goethe, Adler and Thomas Mann. Each of these separate worlds lives at no more than a ten minutes' walk from the others. They stare and sniff at each other without mixing, rather like camels sniff at the exhaust pipes of motor-cars, and derive about as much satisfaction from it.

The night after their arrival in Jerusalem, Joseph and Simeon walked through the badly lit Arab quarter of Musrara, almost deserted at this late hour, then turned into Me'a She'arim, the Street of the Hundred Gates. The "Hundred Gates" is the oldest of the Hebrew quarters outside the confines of the Old City; it was founded in the eighteen-seventies, and its first inhabitants were the ancient and pious who came to the Land not to live but to die. They brought with them their savings of a lifetime, which they handed over to the Kehillah, the Jewish Community, in exchange for a monthly pittance to the day of their death. While waiting to die they prayed, quarrelled, studied the Book and made souvenirs of the Holy

Land—albums with pressed flowers from Mount Scopus, sachets of velvet filled with holy earth, pen-holders of olivewood with a tiny inlaid lens through which one could see a micro-panorama of Jerusalem. These souvenirs were sent abroad to be sold to other Jews, and their proceeds were the main income of the Community. In between these godly occupations the elders of the Hundred Gates fought their family feuds, cheated, begged, got drunk once a year to celebrate Esther's triumph over Haman, fasted on the day of the Temple's destruction, ate bitter herbs to commemorate the exodus from Egypt, blew the ram-horn which brought down the walls of Jericho, expected Messiah's arrival from week to week, and while waiting to die begot children at a patriarchal age. As the years passed younger people too began to inhabit the Hundred Gates, men in black kaftans and fur hats, women with shorn heads and wigs, pious and prolific. A dozen children to a couple were no rarity in those days, the younger ones sleeping in their parents' beds, the others on the floor; they lived in holiness and squalor, in tenements with labyrinthine courts and long narrow iron balconies teeming with toddlers and vermin. Unlike the Moslem slums which were fragrant with spices, horse-dung and charcoal, the Hundred Gates smelt of oil lamps and Primus cookers, damp washing and hot beans in grease. However, underneath all this variety of smells lay as an ever-present foundation the odour of Jerusalem: the odour of the sun-heated rocks and of the white chalk dust in the streets, product of the decaying stone on which the city stands.

"If you bandaged my eyes," said Joseph, "I could still tell the Hundred Gates by their holy stench."

They had walked in silence for the last few minutes and Joseph spoke mainly to ease his own tension. But while he spoke he remembered Dina's obsession about smells, and instantly he knew that Simeon remembered it too. The lines of transmission from Ezra's Tower, from their common past, were still functioning, though they trailed loosely like telegraph wires damaged by a storm. He still felt the old affection for

Simeon, but they had both changed, and so had the quality of their relationship.

"That is one way of looking at the Hundred Gates," said Simeon. "I will tell you another way. A few weeks ago two elderly rabbis of the Chassidic sect contacted the Command. They were brought with the usual precautions before Bauman. I was present at the interview. When they were led into the hide-out they were literally trembling with fear. Bauman asked them what they wanted. The older rabbi asked him after some humming and hawing whether it was in our power to occupy on a given day the Mosque of Omar for two hours. Bauman asked for what purpose. The rabbi explained that the two of them were kabbalists, students of the Zohar, and that they had established beyond doubt the conditions under which the advent of Messiah can be brought about. This year was the propitious one and it was only necessary to perform a certain sacrifice accompanied by a certain ritual on the Sacred Rock where Abraham offered Isaac, where the First Temple stood and where the Mosque of Omar now stands. Seven Kohanim of the rabbi's choice, direct descendants of the priestly aristocracy of Israel, were already undergoing the prescribed rites of purification, and the animals for the sacrifice had been chosen and bought. All they needed now was that we should occupy the Mosque of Omar on the given day, and hold out for two hours.

" 'Do you realise, rabbi, that it would cost us many dead and bring immediate civil war over our heads?' said Bauman.

" 'Yes, there would perhaps be some people killed,' said the rabbi, 'but they would only be dead for a few hours because Resurrection would follow immediately. And as for civil war'—he smiled—'well, well, Messiah will look after that.'

"So Bauman told them he would look into the matter, and as they left, the younger man, who was one of the chosen Kohanim, kissed his hand, and the older one kissed him on the mouth.—I am glad you did not laugh at the story," Simeon concluded.

Joseph knew that a few months ago he certainly would have laughed. Even now he listened to the story with mixed feelings. He envied Simeon for whom it was easy not to laugh—Joseph actually could not remember ever having seen Simeon laugh, and his rare smile was confined to the lower half of his face. Once, Joseph remembered, he had asked Dasha, who for a time had been in love with Simeon, why she did not live with him. "One does not embrace a razor," Dasha had said.

They left the labyrinth of the Hundred Gates and turned into the Bokharian Quarter. It was plunged into darkness except for an occasional window lit by a candle or oil-lamp. In the thin light of the crescent moon the chalk dust of the decaying rock shimmered white on the unpaved road. The houses here were more spacious; it was a poor quarter, but of austere dignity. Its inhabitants had come towards the end of the last century from the Emirate of Bokhara in Central Asia. Their ancestors had begun their Eastward migrations after the destruction of the Temple by Titus. They had first gone to Mesopotamia where Hebrew culture flourished for a while at the universities of Sura and Pompedita; then, when the usual happened, they had wandered on to Kurdistan and Turkmenistan and Bokhara. After the Moslem conquest they formed small indestructible islands in the Islamic Sea; cut off as they were from the rest of the world, the Bokharian Community gradually became convinced that they were the only surviving Jews on the earth. For about fifteen hundred years nothing happened to shake their conviction. They lived in segregation; their shops in the bazaars had to be two feet under street level so that their heads should not reach over the Moslem customers' shoulders; in the streets they had to wear a rope round their waist so that an instrument of punishment should be handy if they gave offence.

In 1866 a Russian army under Suvorov entered the Emirate of Bokhara. Among the Russian soldiers was a Jew. He brought the incredible tale that there were millions of Jews left in the world, and was called a liar. Challenged to name a town in Europe where such alleged Jews lived, he named the Warsaw suburb Nalewki. The Jews of Bokhara went into council and finally produced a letter which was duly stamped and addressed "to the Venerable Jews in the Town of Nalewki on the Continent of Europe". The letter arrived; and in due time an answer reached the Chief Rabbi of Bokhara. It began with a rather cool confirmation of the soldier's tale, the Jews of Nalewki obviously resenting the doubt cast upon their existence; while the rest of the letter was devoted to a detailed analysis of the grammatical offences against the Holy Language contained in the letter of the Bokharian Jews.

Simeon and Joseph turned into a narrow side lane. It was dark and steep; the part of the lane behind them ended abruptly in a field of stones. They were near the outer confines of the city, where Jerusalem ended and the Judean desert began. Somewhere on that dark stony slope were the tombs of the Judges with seventy burial shafts hewn out the rock, supposedly the graves of the Sanhedrin, the High Court of Israel. Joseph had visited them a few weeks before; the closely packed, narrow burial chambers looked much the same as the Ancestor's Cave at Ezra's Tower and the countless other rock-graves all over the country. The land was honeycombed with them; wherever one travelled they looked at one like tiny black windows in the white surface of the rocks. And yet there were no ghosts or haunted houses anywhere. Perhaps the dead hereabouts were too old and intimate with God to indulge in such clumsy manifestations.

"I am sure that Dina went to see the cave that night," Joseph heard himself say without knowing why, or remembering his intention of saying it.

"How do you know?" Simeon asked in a curious voice.

Joseph gave no answer. They walked past a window lit by candle-light inside. Joseph saw a bare room, a little under street level. It was furnished with one iron bed, straw mats on the stamped mud floor and one large piece of Bokhara tapestry —red sun-disks on black silk—hung on the whitewashed wall. On the bed sat a young woman in a coloured head-cloth giving her breast to a child. The man was lying on his stomach full length on the floor, with two candles in front of him, studying the Book in a thick-papered folio print yellow with age; around him on the floor lay the various Commentaries in equally bulky editions. He was in shirt-sleeves, had a black beard and wore a coloured skull-cap on the back of his head. He read rapidly, marking the line with his finger and nodding his head; from time to time he turned to one of the Commentaries and then back to the Book. The woman was slowly rocking her body forward and back, her gaze fixed on the candle. The lips of the man moved in a steady murmur and he kept on nodding rapidly with his head and shoulders. The two rhythmic movements were like two pendulums out of step.

—They walked on and turned another corner. There were no lights showing anywhere, but it was not completely dark, as it never is in Jerusalem, the stars being numerous, bright and close. There was a faint odour of chalk dust, burnt logs and thyme—in the Bokhari Quarter, Arab and Hebrew smells became fused. In one of the barrel-vaulted doorways stood a boy and a girl in shorts, their arms round each other. They looked closely at Simeon, apparently resenting the disturbance. Simeon said something which sounded like a password. "*B'seder,*" said the boy, "All clear." Again they turned a corner and almost stumbled over a Yemenite beggar asleep with his head on a doorstep. He woke and put his hand out, drowsily wailing his litany. Simeon gave the password and the Yemenite waved them on, flashing his white teeth over the scant black beard.

"Is he sleeping on his tommy-gun or what?" Joseph could not refrain from asking.

Simeon walked on a few steps before he answered; then he said:

"If you think this is a comedy there is still time to turn back."

"I am sorry," said Joseph.

The street was as dark and quiet as before, but suddenly there seemed to be something uncanny about its silence. Joseph felt as if eyes were watching them from behind each of the dark windows. They arrived in front of a large stone building whose massive front was broken up by vaulted windows and gates and some thin columns, which gave it a vaguely oriental look. It had a flat roof, and Joseph saw the silhouette of a man bend over the parapet to peer down at them, and then withdraw. A relief inscription over the main gate told him that this was a House of Prayer and Learning, built by one Ephraim Ben Huda, a native of Bokhara, who had arrived in the Land with his wife, nine children and five brothers, in the year 5672 from the creation of the world; which, Joseph worked out, was roughly fifty years ago.

They passed the main gate and a second gate, and halted in front of a side door where Simeon rapped out a signal on the panelling. After a few seconds it was opened by the *shamash* or door-keeper. He was a short and very thin old man in a kaftan reaching down to his feet, and with a black skull-cap from which two long plaited side-locks emerged like pigtails and hung down to the edge of his jaw. He closed the door behind them without a word. They were in a dark corridor from which opened the door to the *shamash's* lodge, lit by a candle. On a mat on the floor lay the *shamash's* wife under a large, striped quilt cover. She had a round face framed by black plaits which gave her a youngish air, and a terribly fat body which shaped the quilt into a hillock. The *shamash* shuffled into his room and closed the door from inside, leaving them in darkness. Simeon pulled an electric torch from his pocket and in its light Joseph saw that they were walking over a floor of stone mosaic in a chess-board pattern. They came into a hall which, judged by the echo of their steps, must be vast and empty.

"This place is called 'The Palace'," said Simeon in a voice only slightly lower than normal. "You will have to learn to find your way in the dark, as on the ground and upper floors we can use no light. In the cellars it is safe."

Later on Joseph learned the history of "the Palace". It was a building originally meant to serve as a synagogue and Bible seminary, and also as a residence for the rich Bokhari who had built it. The synagogue and seminary had been on the ground floor; upstairs there were a large, now derelict, banqueting-hall and a great number of bedrooms. The old Bokhari was still alive and said to be over a hundred. His wife had died, his brothers and children had gone out into the world; he lived alone in a small room with a painted glass door opening onto a landing, which had once served as a pantry. There he sat all day and night smoking his water pipe and studying the Book, hardly ever emerging from it. The *shamash* who was almost as old as he and whom he had brought with him from Bokhara, and the *shamash's* wife who was about half a century younger than her husband, were looking after him. From time to time his children and grandchildren came to see him, and once a year on the eve of Passover the whole tribe assembled in the banqueting-hall, cleared for this occasion of the cobwebs and the plaster flaking from the ceiling, to eat the meal of bitter herbs and unleavened bread, and listen to the recital of the exodus from Egypt.

Underneath the ground floor there was a labyrinth of cellars, vaults and rooms. Here had once lived the servants, the servants' relatives, the servants' friends and the servants' guests. It was said that since the building was finished the rich Bokhari had never been down to the cellars. A year ago one of his great-grandsons had joined Bauman's organisation and had asked the old man for permission to use the cellars at night "for purposes of teaching and learning". He did not say what was going to be taught and learned, but the old man consented without asking; he was not interested in the cellars, and he was not interested in anything any longer—except his water pipe, the Book, and playing kabbalistic patience by shuffling the letters which make up the Name to derive new meanings from each chance permutation.

The *shamash* asked no questions either. Though the sounds of the rifle-range installed in the thick-walled cellars reached him only as muffled thuds, he presumably understood that the friends of his young master were preparing to fight the Moslems; and he wholeheartedly approved of fighting the Moslems, who, when he was a boy, had cut off three fingers of his right hand for the theft committed by another boy of three apples. The *shamash* knew his place; he never spoke a word to the members of the organisation, nor was ever spoken to by them.

As to the *shamash's* young wife, she had once asked her husband what those nightly goings-on meant, and had received such an unusually terrible beating with the rope from the withered little elder whom she over-towered by a head's length, that she never committed the sin of curiosity again.

They crossed the vast empty hall, their steps faintly resounding; the yellow circle of Simeon's torch moved over the floor like a puddle of light in front of them. They had passed a young sentry in khaki shorts and shirt at the end of the corridor; a second one grew suddenly out of the darkness as they reached the staircase leading down to the cellars. The sentries saluted, clicking their heels and lifting the right forearm bent at the elbow, with the open palm facing forward. No words were exchanged. They walked down the steps into a passage in the cellars, lit by oil-lamps. Joseph was glad of the light; the dark hall with its silent sentries had been rather distasteful and oppressive. Three boys stood together in the corridor, talking; at their approach they sprang to attention, saluted, and stood rigid until they had passed them. It was an intimation to Joseph that Simeon must hold a relatively high rank in their organisation.

They passed a door with another very young sentry in front and a muffled voice faintly audible from inside. It was a female contralto voice with a Sephardi accent, which was repeating a slow text in a monotone:

This is the voice of Fighting Zion, the voice of liberated Jerusalem. Your kin is murdered in Europe; what are you doing about it? This is the voice of Fighting Zion. They send them back in swimming coffins; what are you doing about it? This is the voice.

"Recording," said Simeon. "The transmitter is mobile."

It was the first bit of inside information Simeon had ever given him and Joseph couldn't help feeling thrilled. There were intermittent short bursts from some automatic weapon, but though they must have been fairly close to the range, the sound of the firing was muffled. Simeon, who guessed Joseph's unspoken question, smiled with the lower half of his face.

"We have got a fellow who was an expert in sound-isolation with a German aircraft firm," he explained with suppressed pride in his voice. A man with a portfolio hurried past them who, while saluting, smiled at Simeon—a sight which gave Joseph a feeling of relief after the pathetically earnest faces of the young sentries. They stopped at a door. "Wait here for a moment," said Simeon. He knocked and entered; but almost on the doorstep he collided with Bauman coming out with brisk steps.

Instead of his battered black leather jacket Bauman wore a newish brown one, but otherwise he looked less changed than Joseph had for some reason expected. He greeted Joseph, smiling all over his broad, comfortable face. Joseph felt relieved to see Bauman holding his hand out instead of giving the bent-arm salute.

"Funny to see one of the old faces again," said Bauman. "It doesn't often happen since I've turned Fascist." He spoke with good-humoured irony, without bitterness. "Simeon has told me a lot about you," he added, surveying Joseph with smiling but attentive eyes.

"He didn't tell me much about you," said Joseph with a grin. Bauman noticed that this grin was different from what it used to be. He remembered Joseph's face always ready to crumple into a smile along certain fixed creases. Now it was a rather laborious process—as if the smile were searching for new folds in the skin along which to break.

"Listen," said Bauman, "I want a long talk with you, but first I've got to take a look at some new recruits. Or would you like to see for yourself? They are *yeshiva bochers*."

"It will be fun for you," said Simeon. "I must get along to my meeting; see you later." He saluted Bauman and walked down the corridor.

"Come along," said Bauman. "Let's have a look at the *bochers*. Afterwards we'll talk."

Yeshiva bochers were pupils of the Orthodox Talmud schools in the Old City—relics of the Middle Ages. Joseph experienced a faint revulsion whenever he saw one of those awkward adolescents with love-locks slinking through the streets of Jerusalem—a prayer-book in one hand, the forefinger of the other trailing along the walls, muttering to himself, blind to his surroundings. Sometimes a boy of eighteen, dressed in short black trousers and black cotton stockings, would walk on his father's hand, trailing behind him like a small child. Sometimes there were two of them walking hand in hand, bumping into people like blind men, while arguing about scholastic subtleties.

They walked along the corridor and entered a vaulted room which had once served as a wine-cellar to the owner of the house. A small barred window opening on the back area of the house was barricaded with sacks of cement to isolate sound and avoid suspicion. The bags had to be fitted and removed each night—a tiresome fatigue for the recruits.

The room was lit by an oil-lamp on the stone floor, and next to the lamp squatted a youngster, studying in a book with moving lips. When Bauman and Joseph entered the room he shoved the book carefully into a blue velvet bag and scrambled to his feet. He wore a black skull-cap and a grey felt hat on top; his long side-locks dangled like corkscrews parallel to his cheeks which were covered with reddish down. His black cotton stockings were held by garters of string tied above the knees, and hung in loose wrinkles along his shins.

"Where are Gideon and the two others?" asked Bauman.

"They have gone to the r-ange," the boy said in the traditional sing-song of the Orthodox. The range, installed in an ancient boiler-room, had space for only three people at a time.

"Stand to attention when you talk to me," Bauman said in an even, not unfriendly tone. The boy pulled his shoulders up until they came almost level with his ears and made him look like a hunchback. His thick moist lips tried an ingratiating smile which gradually faded away; his large brown eyes, like an Alsatian pup's, hesitated between fear and devotion.

"What is that book you were reading?" asked Bauman.

The boy gingerly handed him the blue velvet bag. The Star of David was embroidered on it in gold threads; it was the traditional kind of bag in which the Orthodox carry their prayer-books and scarfs to the synagogue. Bauman opened it and took the book out. It was the *Short Arms Manual,* by D. Ras—the first Hebrew military manual, printed illegally by the organisation. The author's pen-name was composed of the initials of the two leaders of the Command who had written it in collaboration, David Raziel and Abraham Stern. The book was a marvel of linguistic ingenuity, as Hebrew had as yet no words for fire-arms and even less for the two-hundred-odd parts of a modern automatic weapon. Raziel and Stern had undertaken the task with the twofold enthusiasm of Hebrew scholars and expert gunmen. The Language Board of the peaceful Hebrew University had unwittingly assisted them by giving advice to the alleged editors of an alleged technical dictionary. At the bottom of the dark-blue linen cover stood the only words in Latin characters which the book contained: "Printed in Geneva". That was a private joke of the authors —the book had been printed on an illegal press installed in the ghetto-warren of the Old City.

Bauman fingered the book with a book-lover's tenderness

for a first edition. "Well, how far have you got with it?" he asked. "I haven't said 'At ease' yet," he added sharply.

The boy's shoulders jerked up again. "You may examine me, sir," he said. "What page, plea-se?"

Bauman looked at him. "You mean that you are learning the whole book by heart?"

"What pa-age plea-se?" the boy asked, with the self-assurance of an infant prodigy.

"Page seventeen," said Bauman.

The boy passed his fingers before his eyes and after a few seconds his body began to sway forward and back in the rhythm of reciting a prayer:

". . . And the butt. If the ca-atch is forced do-own," he recited, rocking himself, "the small spring under the tri-igger blocks the mo-ovement of the second lever, and unless the le-ever is well oiled our weapon will ja-am. . . ."

The oil-lamp stood next to the boy's feet and threw his magnified shadow on the wall. The tall shadow swayed forward and backward like a mocking echo of his movements, the cork-screw side-locks flapping like pendulums across the ears.

"That will do," said Bauman. He pulled with a quick movement his gun from the holster under his armpit and emptied the magazine into his palm. The boy watched him fascinatedly, peering down along his nose, his angular shoulders drawn up.

"Here," said Bauman. "Hold it."

The boy took the gun and held it pointing downward with a stiff arm, a little away from his body. Suddenly Bauman struck out at the boy's wrist and the gun dropped to the floor. Bauman jumped one step back and forcefully slapped the boy in his face, first right then left, his arms swinging like flails. The boy stood with lifted shoulders, without defending himself.

"That will teach you to hold fast to your gun," said Bauman evenly. "Take it again."

The boy picked up the gun from the floor. For a second he hesitated how best to hold it, then he took a step back and, holding the gun tight to his hip with elbow drawn back, pointed it at Bauman. His long yellow teeth were biting into his lip and there was a flicker in his brown eyes. One could see how the mere gesture of pointing the gun began to do things to him. A current seemed to flow back from the trigger and expand through his whole body, thawing its rigidity and giving it a tense, feline suppleness. His eyes narrowed and were steadily fixed on Bauman.

"That's better," said Bauman.

The boy's body at once relaxed, and his awkwardness returned. He put the gun into Bauman's out-stretched hand.

"Well?" said Bauman.

The boy swallowed. "I have deserved it, sir," he said.

"Right," said Bauman. "You may carry on." He turned on his heel and left the room, followed by Joseph.

The boy, standing to attention, followed them with his eyes. He stood rigid until the door had closed and remained so for another second. Then he sighed, pulled his stockings up, tightened the strings above his knees and sat down on the floor by the lamp. He scratched his head, smiled uncertainly and took the book out of the prayer-bag. After a minute the world around him had faded once more while his lips went on mumbling, his body swaying, his side-locks flapping across his ears, his mocking giant-shadow rocking behind him in deep and solemn bows.

16

"How do you like our Palace?" Bauman asked when they were back in his room. Like the other rooms, it had cement bags blocking the window and contained a deal table, a lamp and three chairs. "Sit down," he said, pushing a packet of cigarettes across the table to Joseph.

"It's a highly effective setting," said Joseph, feeling that this was the wrong kind of tone, but unable to find the right one.

"The trouble with you is," said Bauman after a short pause, "that you are a romantic; and being ashamed of it you distrust anything which smacks of romantics—like darkened rooms and sentries in the street, which for us are elementary precautions. You are so determined not to take yourself seriously that you will persist in thinking it's sheer make-believe even when they put a rope round your neck."

Joseph sat with his head bent and the sick-monkey smile on his face. "Knowing me so well," he said, "do you still want me in your crowd?"

"Don't be an ass," said Bauman, looking at him across the table.

Joseph wanted to pull himself together but found it difficult to do. He had expected so much from this meeting with Bauman, and now he felt like ringing the bell at the dentist's when the tooth has already ceased to hurt. The tension had gone out of him and this whole interview seemed pointless and unreal. From time to time the muffled rattle of the range sounded through the wall, but that too seemed meaningless and dreamlike.

"I suppose I am too old to become a terror-boy-scout," he said.

"Who expects you to?"

"Simeon gave me some hints about the procedure of joining —six months' apprenticeship, going through tests, taking the oath and so on."

"Simeon is a pedantic donkey," said Bauman, smiling broadly. "If you come over to us you'll have more important jobs to do."

"Such as?" said Joseph.

"We haven't got anybody who's been to an English university. You are a rare bird in Israel."

"I loathe everything connected with propaganda."

"Even speaking on an underground radio transmitter and turning out illegal leaflets, when you know that instead of a fee you get five years in jail if they get you?"

Joseph smiled.

"A moment ago you promised me a rope, and now it's only five years."

"It isn't quite as funny as that," said Bauman. "They have started third-degreeing our boys. The Police here is riddled with former Black and Tans who know this kind of job."

"Simeon told me something about that," Joseph said doubtfully.

"And you thought that he exaggerated," said Bauman with a touch of sharpness. "Actually Simeon doesn't know yet all the details. One of our fellows, name of Benjamin Zeroni, escaped yesterday from Jerusalem prison. How he did it is quite a story which I shall tell you one day. I have spoken to him. Both his thumbs were dislocated as a result of being suspended by them for two hours. He was also beaten on the genitals, bastinadoed, and questioned while having water poured into his nostrils."

Bauman wiped his cheek with the palm of his hand and Joseph remembered the gesture—product of Bauman's experiences with the humorous jailor in Graz.

"So far this only seems to happen in isolated cases," Bauman continued, "and it is possible that their high-ups are unaware of it. The man responsible, in all the four cases of which we know, is a certain Inspector C. We have sent him two warnings to stop. He has ignored them, so now we have to punish him. It will be the hell of a job, for since we sent the warnings he drives about with a bodyguard of two men armed with tommy-guns."

He spoke in his usual good-humoured voice with the broad Viennese accent. Joseph looked at him rather incredulously, noting the euphemism "to punish" which Simeon too had repeatedly used when referring to the murder of the Mukhtar.

"I am telling you about this," Bauman went on, "because it is one example of where you come in. I know little about England, except that it has the most influential and the worst-informed public opinion in the world. Its ignorance seems to grow in proportion to the unpleasantness of the facts. They know nothing about Hitler, or India, or their own slums. When they are forced to take notice there is a public outcry, but then it is usually too late.

"We here are ruled by a discreet department of their discreet Colonial Office. If their public knew what's going on here, they would be horrified and perhaps do something about it. But they don't. And the high-pitched voices of our Glicksteins will never reach their ears."

He lit a cigarette, threw the match on the floor and went on:

"You have probably noticed that, unlike Simeon, I don't hate the English. You know better than I that the type one meets in the Colonies is not representative. When I got out of Austria I spent six months in their country. They were kind and sympathetic, and had no idea what it was all about. They live on the moon, a gentle moon with green pastures and tennis-courts. When they touch our hot earth they lose their balance. But likes and dislikes aren't the point. The point is that we need them and they need us. We need them because this country is under their control. They need us because the Arabs naturally want their independence and will double-cross them in an emergency, as they have done before. A Jewish State, tied to them by common European tradition and mutual interest, would be of much greater value to them than a standing garrison in a hostile native population. They had to withdraw step by step under pressure from Egypt and Iraq; if Palestine becomes an Arab State they will sooner or later have to withdraw from here too; if it becomes a Hebrew Dominion, it will be a solid and permanent bridgehead to the East. The more far-sighted of their statesmen knew this, hence their pledge to us. But their giants are dead or sulking, and their Empire is in a state of Wagnerian Götterdämmerung; St. George has become tired of fighting the dragon and is trying to bribe it. They've put their island under an umbrella and we are left to swim in the drink. . . ."

Joseph had never heard Bauman so eloquent. Bauman squashed his cigarette with the determination of crushing a harmful insect, and went on:

"It follows that we have to do two things if we want to avoid drowning altogether. One is persuasion: proving to them that no dragon can be bribed, regardless of whether it's a Teutonic, Roman, Arab or Jap dragon. Two is making a hell of a nuisance of ourselves. Driving each argument home with a bang. Otherwise they won't listen. That's where our Glicksteins go wrong. They squeak. They keep on piping what good boys we are. Result: a pat on the shoulder and a kick in the pants. A nation of conscientious objectors can't survive. We have to force them to take us seriously, then they'll do business with us. But to achieve that we have to speak the only language they understand. . . ." He patted with his fist the gun under his leather jacket. "That's the new Esperanto," he concluded. "Surprising how easy it is to learn. Everybody understands it, from Shanghai to Madrid."

He leant back in the armless chair, his forearms with closed fists on the table, waiting for Joseph to speak. What he had said was not new to Joseph; it was the logically unassailable doctrine of the post-Genevan world. Whether the doctrine was propounded by the strong aiming at conquest, or by the weak aiming at survival, was merely a difference in degree, not in kind. For ultimately the strong too was animated by fear and insecurity, and ultimately the weak had to resort to the same violent and detestable means. It was a global infection against which the only defence was to get contaminated oneself.

But these were theoretical considerations. The reality was Mr. Brodetsky with his ear-trumpet crying *"Was ist los?"* and the wailing of the *Assimi's* sirens. Before these all moral scruples were but different forms of escape.

"Of course I have to agree with you," said Joseph. "But it would be dishonest to pretend that I do it with enthusiasm. You and I, Bauman, grew up in a different tradition."

"So we did," said Bauman. "In the 'twenties. That was when

Briand and Stresemann discussed the United States of Europe and King Feisal of Iraq welcomed the future Jewish State. So what?"

"Oh, I know," said Joseph. "It was a world of pink mirages and now we have entered the age of the New Realism. But it startles me that its up-to-date, stream-lined power logics should be accompanied by all this maudlin opera stuff—Wotan and Blood and Soil and Roman Fasces. And it's the same among your arm-lifting terror-scouts. They think they are the heirs to young David and the Maccabeans. Between you and me, Bauman—if the Maccabeans hadn't been such bloody heroes, our ancestors would have become Hellenised and would probably have escaped the ghetto. . . ."

"Oh, go to hell," Bauman said abruptly. "You've got that intellectual squint which makes you see both sides of the medal at the same time. You are more Jewish in spirit than that Talmud student with his love-locks. . . ."

He got up and began pacing up and down the room.

"To see both sides is a luxury we can no longer afford. We are moving into a political ice age. We have to build our Eskimo huts and national fires, or perish. . . ." With his hands in his pockets and head thrust forward, he looked as if he were going to charge the wall with his skull.

"You still cling to the 'twenties when it looked as if it was going to be spring and frontiers and classes were to melt away in the red sun. Well, that's finished. As far as I am concerned it was finished when little Dollfuss shot our big red Vienna into shambles. Up to that day I thought Jewish nationalism just as bloody as any other, and the Return a romantic stunt. When they locked me up I had time to think it over and decided that the moment had come for us to stop redeeming the world, and to start redeeming ourselves. We can't wait until socialism solves all racial problems. That will perhaps happen one day, but long before that day we shall have been exterminated. There is a time-lag we can't jump over. Oh, if we had time, if the others would only wait. . . . You know, Joseph, you are the philosopher, not I—but it seems to me that time is a dimension of politics, and that idealists always forget to reckon with this dimension; that's why their picture seems so flat. If time allowed for jumps we wouldn't have to wade through all this mud. . . ."

He stopped short in the middle of the room.

"There we are back to fundamentals. I thought you had thrashed that out with yourself some six or seven years ago when you decided to come to this country."

"I had," said Joseph. "But at that time we hoped that this nationalism of ours would be different, and that we were going to build a socialist model State. Not an Eskimo hut—but Ezra's Tower. And to some extent we have succeeded."

"I have no quarrel with Ezra's Tower," said Bauman, regaining his good temper. "But those lovable idiots think they have a quarrel with me. They are working hard and have no time for politics, so their roots are still in the 'twenties and their heads in the clouds. They are pacifists and legalists like all honest-to-God Social Democrats, and if we left it to them we should share the fate which befell their comrades in Austria, Germany, Italy and so on—who all lived in their own Ezra's Tower. I love them, but I hate their muddled thinking."

"I have often wondered," said Joseph with a grin, "whether I don't prefer Rousseau's muddle to Robespierre's clarity."

"Oh, shut up," said Bauman. "Of course you don't. Your pals in Ezra's Tower need the British, but they object to British Imperialism. They want to build a nation, but they object to the paraphernalia of nationalism. . . ." He resumed his pacing up and down the room.

"It can't be done without the paraphernalia. That's the answer to your quibbling about our opera stuff. Our boys have to run greater risks than ordinary soldiers. If caught they are not treated as prisoners but tried as criminals. They need discipline; and there is no discipline without a ritual. . . . It is against reason that a man should walk into machine-gun fire because another man tells him to. But soldiering is based on the irrational assumption that he ought to do so. Therefore every army must have its tradition and its myth. That's where the Bible and the Maccabeans come in with us. Whether you and I like it or not makes no difference. There is no contradiction between what you call the New Realism and the New Mythology. You can't lead a high-pressure movement through rationally controlled channels, and you can't freeze up emotion. In normal times emotion finds normal outlets, but in a political ice age it bursts out in volcanic myths.

"You once said to me that we are nationalists *faute de mieux*. That's true enough of you and me, but you can't expect my boys to work up much enthusiasm for it. Nobody will choose to die *faute de mieux*. . . ."

There was a silence, and the muffled rattling through the wall. At last Joseph said:

"You win, Bauman—as usual. I have to agree with you, *faute de mieux*. . . ." He grinned wearily. "So what's the next step?"

Bauman had wandered back behind his desk and resumed his seat.

"You are quite decided to take the plunge?" he asked.

Joseph nodded. Bauman looked at him doubtfully.

"You didn't sound it," he said.

"It was only a kind of rearguard action," said Joseph with an apologetic grin. "I like to have my *i*'s properly dotted."

Bauman looked unconvinced. "In your present mood it is difficult to talk business with you. Simeon told me you were shaken by Dina's death, but I didn't realise to what extent. This *faute de mieux* talk is a disparagement of your own past—as if you bespattered everything you've done during the last six years."

Joseph shrugged. "I asked you at the beginning of our talk whether you still wanted me. You told me not to be an ass. I cannot pretend. At present I don't feel particularly enthusiastic—about anything. I suppose that will improve with time. Meanwhile what precisely do you want me to do? My leave expires next week and I have got to tell them at home what I've decided."

"Oh—there is no need to tell them anything," Bauman said with some reluctance.

"So you don't want me?"

"Of course we do."

"Then what?"

Bauman began marching up and down again.

"Naturally we have discussed you—in the Command," he said, even more hesitatingly than before. He sounded as if he were talking against his own conviction. "We have even worked out a kind of plan how to make the best use of you. It is roughly this. You tell the fellows in your Commune that you have changed your mind and won't have any truck with us bloody Fascists. You carry on with your present job. It will give you the best cover towards the Police—much better than going underground. People from the Settlements are all on the side of the angels. In your spare time you do a bit of subversive propaganda for us. Twice a week—in Tel Aviv or here—you meet someone from us; once to discuss and deliver the written stuff—leaflets and so on; once for recording. We have the means of making your voice sound different on the air so that you won't be recognised.—That's about all. . . ."

He eyed Joseph rather anxiously. While he spoke Joseph had looked as if he was going to interrupt and protest, but he hadn't. He felt the need to digest the opposing emotions roused in him. The first had been a violent revulsion at the idea that he should deceive Reuben, Moshe, Ellen and all the rest of them at home. The second was a sudden and glorious flash of relief at the thought that he wouldn't have to leave them. It was the same overwhelming emotion he had experienced during that memorable talk with Reuben when he had also thought at first that he would be cast out. But on that occasion he had been fully conscious of what Ezra's Tower meant to him, whereas this time he had deceived himself into believing that he was through. Only now that he saw a chance to avoid the breach did he realise the unbearable wrench which it would mean.

"Well," Bauman said, "what do you think of it?"

"I'll have to think it over," said Joseph.

"Moral scruples?" said Bauman. "They would be justified if your private activities would be damaging to them. In fact, the contrary is true. Your first contact with us led to the action against the Mukhtar, and I am convinced every one of your saintly hypocrites secretly rejoiced about it. Besides, no community should have the right to control the political activities of its members, as long as these are broadly in keeping with its aims."

"You are a bloody Machiavelli," said Joseph.

"It's the logic of the ice age," said Bauman. "We have to use violence and deception, to save others from violence and deception."

Joseph gave no answer. Already his momentary elation was followed by a new wave of disgust at choosing that easy way out. Reuben had showed him the way out of that first crisis—had enabled him to eat his cake and have it—and now Bauman was doing the same. But he was too weary to argue about Ends and Means—for that was what the whole question finally boiled down to. This was no time for soul-searching. Who was he to save his integrity while others had their bodies hacked to pieces? In the logic of the ice age tolerance became a luxury and purity a vice. There was no way to escape the dilemma. To wash one's hands and let others do the dirty job was a hypocrisy, not a solution. To expose oneself was the only redeeming factor. . . .

"Oh, damn it all," he said helplessly. "I wish to God you would let me take part in an action—even if only one. Then at least I wouldn't have the feeling that it's all been made easy and cheap for me. . . ."

"If you think five years for a broadcast is cheap . . ." Bauman began wearily—then suddenly he checked himself in the middle of the sentence, swerved round and with a broad grin took two steps towards Joseph. He laid his hands heavily on Joseph's shoulders, pressing him against the wall.

"You want action?" he said. "You are sure you really want it?"

Joseph looked at him with a sudden hope. Looking into Bauman's face from so close, he saw the yellow malaria colour as a foundation under the taut, dry, brown skin. Bauman squeezed his shoulders, then took his hands away.

"All right," he said. "I have an idea. . . ."

He didn't tell Joseph his idea—which was that Joseph was going to pieces, and that the best remedy for a man going to pieces was to give him a dangerous job, in the course of which he would either get killed or cured. It was a drastic kind of psychology but it had worked once or twice on Bauman himself and so he assumed it must work on others as well. He was quite electrified at the prospect of the magic cure he had found for Joseph.

"Listen," he said in an excited schoolboy whisper. "If you must have action, you shall have it. We are preparing a job where I could fit you in. It's a highly irregular thing to do, but I am going to take a chance. The condition is that afterwards you work with us on the lines I told you. . . ."

"All right," Joseph said quickly, infected by Bauman's excitement. He felt as if his pulse had been abnormally slowed down during the past weeks and was returning at last to its habitual rhythm. His heart went out to Bauman. "You are a prop," he said.

"I am a bloody Fascist," said Bauman. He looked at his watch. "I've got to go," he said. "We're swearing in a new recruit. More opera stuff. Do you want to see it? That's irregular too, but the Command knows about you. You just have to look as if you belonged."

17

They walked along more corridors, past the room where the girl was still recording in her monotonous voice, then stopped at a door with two sentries outside. The sentries saluted and so did Bauman; Joseph had to follow his example. Reluctantly he confessed to himself that he did not really dislike it; the sudden tightening of the body and the precise, mechanised gesture was a shake-up and pull-together. In every man there is a little cadet who wants to click his heels, he thought, suppressing a grimace.

He followed Bauman into a room lit by candles. Facing the door, two men were sitting behind a table with a third empty chair between them. They rose as Bauman entered and there was more saluting. Along the wall stood some more men, who also snapped to attention. They were all between twenty and thirty, and had the air of young men from good families—with keen but reserved faces, well-groomed hair and the slightly self-conscious courtesy of an officers' mess. Bauman introduced Joseph as a "guest" without mentioning his name and without further comment. They all shook hands with him, polite and unsmiling. Then Bauman sat down on the empty chair at the table, and the men on either side of him followed his example. The one on Bauman's right was a sharp-featured intellectual with rimless glasses and a tense, aggressive face. The man on his left was tall, slim and elegant, and looked like a professional gambler. The table behind which they sat was covered with a blue-and-white national flag in silk. In the centre of the flag an old parchment map of the country was spread out. To the right of the map was placed a leather-bound Bible; to its left a revolver. Five blue burning candles stood upright in a silver *menorah,* the five-branched candlestick, emblem of the Maccabean dynasty.

"Let's begin," said Bauman. He was the only one in the room with an easy and informal manner. Joseph took his place among the other young men standing lined up with their backs to the wall. He had gathered that they were junior officers of the organisation, while Bauman and the two others seated behind the table were members of the Command. There was a tense silence in the room, emphasised by the flicker of the candles.

Bauman read out from a piece of paper the name—which was an alias—of the candidate, and at a sign from him the young officer standing next to the door opened it and gave an order to the sentry in the corridor. The sentry called out the name, and presently a young boy entered through the door, which closed behind him. He saluted and advanced three steps until he stood in front of the table. He must have been told beforehand what to do, for there was no hesitation about him. He might have been about seventeen and had blue eyes and smooth fair hair parted in the middle, and looked the type of boy who in school is called "babyface" and resents it. At this moment he gave the impression of being in a trance. Standing rigidly to attention, his wide-open eyes were fixed for a second or two on the flame of the candles, skirted the Bible and stuck fascinatedly on the revolver.

"Kiss the Bible and touch the gun," said Bauman, rising to his feet followed by the other two behind the desk. The boy did as bidden. It was so still that one could hear the small, damp noise of his lips touching the leather cover of the book.

"Now speak the words after me," said Bauman. *"In the name of the All-present who brought Israel out of the house of bondage in Egypt . . ."*

"In the name . . ." the boy repeated in a dreamy voice, looking with puckered brows into the candle.

" . . . not to rest until the Nation is resurrected as a free and sovereign State within its historic boundaries, from Dan to Beersheba. . . ."

" . . . from Dan to Beersheba."

"To obey blindly my superior officers . . ."

" . . . officers . . ."

"*. . . not to reveal anything entrusted to me, neither under threats nor bodily torture; and that I shall bear my sufferings in silence.*"

"*. . . in silence.*"

The candles flickered and one could hear the boy's breathing. In a dreamy, entranced voice he repeated the last words of the oath:

"*If I forget thee, Jerusalem . . .*"
"*If I forget thee, Jerusalem . . .*"
"*. . . as long as my soul resides in my body.*"
"*. . . in my body. Amen.*"

For the full length of a minute Bauman said nothing and let everybody stand to attention. In the tense silence one could feel how the significance of the moment sank into the boy's soul, to leave its indelible mark there. Every nerve in Joseph's body craved to cry out at them to stop, that they had no right to do this to a child. He tried to evoke Dina's mutilated face in the open coffin, but it did not help and did not connect. We shall never be forgiven this, he thought, for we know what we do.

And we should never be forgiven, he answered himself, if we omitted to do it.

"Dismiss," said Bauman.

The boy turned about and marched out of the room, with the precise movements of an automaton.

Later, when Joseph took his leave from Bauman in the corridor, Bauman asked him:

"What did you think of it?"

"I thought," said Joseph, "that I did not envy you. I would rather obey than command."

"Who would not?" said Bauman.

The yellow malaria colour of his cheeks seemed more pronounced now, but perhaps it was merely the pallid light of the oil-lamp.

THE DAY OF VISITATION

(1939)

". . . And indeed that was a time most fertile in all manner of wicked practices, in so much that no kind of evil deeds were then left undone; nor could any one so much as devise any bad thing that was new, so deeply were they all infected."

FLAVIUS JOSEPHUS, "The Wars of the Jews"

THE DAY OF VISITATION (1939)

1

The uncertainty about the country's future was brought to an end on May the 17th. On this day the British Government issued a Statement of Policy, known as the White Paper of 1939, *which was meant as a final settlement of the Palestine problem.*

"It has been urged," the Statement ran, "that the expression 'a National Home for the Jewish people' offered a prospect that Palestine might in due course become a Jewish State or Commonwealth. His Majesty's Government therefore now declare unequivocally that it is not part of their policy that Palestine should become a Jewish State."

It was an unusually candid political document. For the next five years a last batch of Jews, numbering seventy-five thousand in all, was to be allowed to scramble in before the doors were closed; then, from June 1944 *to the end of the world, no further Jews were to be allowed to enter Palestine. By that date, the document reckoned, the Hebrew community would have reached one-third of the total population of the country. From then onward, owing to the disparity of birth-rates and unrestricted Arab immigration, it was condemned proportionally to fall to a smaller and smaller minority. To prevent any economic expansion of this minority, the High Commissioner of Palestine was further empowered to prohibit the purchase of land by Jews. Making use of these powers, the Land Transfer Acts of February* 1940 *restricted the zone in which Jews were free to buy land to five per cent of the total area of the country.*

The National Home had become transformed into one more cramped Oriental ghetto with sealed gates.

In the Parliamentary debate which followed a few days later, the Right Hon. Winston Churchill (Conservative) called the White Paper "a plain breach of promise, a base betrayal, the filing of a petition in moral and physical bankruptcy, a new Munich and an act of abjection". Sir Archibald Sinclair (Liberal) declared that "the arbitrary prohibition of Jewish immigration without any corresponding restriction of Arab immigration, introducing an element of discrimination against the Jews on grounds of race and religion—these things are grave departures from the terms of the Mandate, and they call in question our moral right to continue to hold it". Mr. Herbert Morrison (Labour) declared that his Party regarded "this White Paper and the policy in it as a cynical breach of pledges given to the world"; and that he "would have had more respect for the Colonial Secretary and his speech if he had frankly admitted that the Jews were to be sacrificed to the incompetence of the Government in the matter, to be sacrificed to its apparent fear, if not indeed its sympathy with violence and the methods of murder and assassination".

According to the terms of the international Mandate, the White Paper could only gain legal validity if endorsed by the League of Nations. The League's Permanent Mandates Commission met on June 16 *and found unanimously that the new policy contradicted the terms of Britain's trusteeship. The last word now rested with the League's Council. It was to meet in September* 1939. *It never met, and the White Paper never acquired legal validity.*

Its provisions however were implemented point by point: the sale of land to Jews was prohibited in 94.8 *per cent of their homeland, access to it was refused to survivors of the great massacre and shiploads of them drowned in* 1941 *and* '42 *in the waters of the Mediterranean and the Black Sea. Those who succeeded in getting ashore were sent to prison or deported to Eritrea, the Sudan or the Island of Mauritius; helpers in the work of rescue were treated as criminals and given long sentences of imprisonment. A document with no legal validity became the legal guide of Government, Law Courts and Police; lawlessness reigned as the supreme law in the Holy Land.*

2

The reign of lawlessness began on the very evening of the new policy's inauguration. It began at precisely 8 P.M., the hour at which the Palestine Radio was to broadcast the official text of the White Paper in Arabic.

At that hour, Issa, son of the late Mukhtar of Kfar Tabiyeh, was sitting with two newly won acquaintances on the terrace of the little Arab coffee-house near Bab el Mandeb, the Damascus Gate, waiting for the broadcast to begin. The proprietor of the coffee-house, who had once been a follower of the moderate Nashashibi clan, and whose establishment had been burnt down by the Mufti's followers during the riots of 1937, had specially installed a loudspeaker for the occasion to prove his patriotic feelings.

Issa had come to Jerusalem to arrange with the Arab Bank certain matters in connection with the Mukhtar's death. He wore a cream-coloured suit with pink stripes, patent leather shoes with white suede inlays, and a black armlet as a sign of mourning. It was his first visit to the capital, and he successfully hid his excitement under a mask of blasé boredom. The circumstances of his father's death had caused a certain stir and had helped Issa to gain access to circles of high Arab society not usually open to an obscure village Mukhtar's son. His two companions he had only met the day before, at one of the weekly "at homes" of Mme. Makropoulos, widow of Josef Makropoulos, the author of *Pan-Arab Renaissance*. Mme. Makropoulos had a political salon where the higher British officials and visiting celebrities met the Arab intelligentsia in an easy and civilised atmosphere—and where they could relax from the strain of intense and purposeful Jewish hospitality where Banquo's ghost kept cropping up from under the dinner-table. Issa had been taken to the party by a Director of the Arab Bank and was also armed with a letter of introduction from District Officer Tubashi. He had been received with kindly sympathy which helped him to overcome his shyness and assume the rôle of a martyr of the Cause, which from that moment onward he genuinely felt himself to be.

The two other young men, seated on low wicker stools and sipping black coffee while waiting for the broadcast to start, belonged to the new Arab intelligentsia. Farid, a dark, lanky young man, had the untidy and romantic appearance, the tweedy nonchalance and languid air of an Oxford undergraduate. He came from one of the oldest Arab families in Jerusalem, had been educated by an English private tutor, wrote English poetry, and articles against English Imperialism in the Arab *El Difa*. Salla, his best friend, was a round-faced dandy with a clipped blond moustache. The two of them had been planning for over a year to launch the first Arab literary weekly, but had so far been unable to find the necessary financial backing.

Issa, anxious to show his lights, had just told them a smutty story from Beyrout but had met with cool disapproval; to ease the silence he hummed the popular jingle: *Falastin baladna, Yahud kalabna,* Palestine is our country, the Jews are our dogs —but that did not cut much ice either. There was still about a quarter of an hour left before the broadcast was to start, and Salla ordered more coffee. "Would you like a nargileh?" he asked, turning politely to Issa. Issa longed for one but thought that smoking a water pipe would be considered provincial and boorish. "No, thank you, I only smoke cigarettes," he said. Salla offered his silver case and they both lit cigarettes, but Farid refused, shaking his head with the dark, wavy hair which had a tendency to fall over his brow. "I shall have a nargileh," he said. Then, with one of his sudden changes from languidness to enthusiasm, he turned briskly to Issa.

"When we start our magazine you must write us an article about Arab village life," he said.

Issa grinned, half flattered, half incredulous. "Village life?" he said. "What is there to write about? The fellaheen are stupid, backward and filthy."

"This is just the point," said Salla, his chin propped on the silver knob of his walking-stick. "We must rouse the fellah from his apathy. Look at the Hebrews."

"Ah, the Hebrews," said Issa. "They use tractors and fertilisers and imported livestock. They've got the money."

"Surely you must have enough money in Kfar Tabiyeh to buy fertilisers and even a tractor," said Farid, with the mouthpiece of the water pipe between his teeth.

"Ah—but we lack co-operation," said Issa.

"But that is just the point," cried Salla. "Lack of co-operation. Jealousy and blood feuds. Ignorance. Superstition. A mediaeval economy. That is what we have to fight." He was thumping his chin after each phrase with the walking-stick.

"Ye-es," said Issa. "But the younger ones all want to run away to the towns where they get wages and can go to the cinema."

"And sell the land to the Jews," said Salla.

"Ah—so it is," Issa agreed. "The Jews have the money. And the prices they pay! I could tell you stories . . . "

He hastily checked himself, and his eyes shifted round the tables in the neighbourhood. They were mainly occupied by small shopkeepers from the shuks, with a sprinkling of villagers and Beduins from Transjordan. The terrace was more crowded than usual because of the broadcast and the historic events, but the men all sat peacefully sucking their nargilehs or playing tauleh, the ancestor of backgammon, with an air of laziness and content.

Farid sat with his legs stretched out, elbows on knees, sucking at the tube and watching the bubbles in the glass bowl.

With his high forehead, dreamy eyes and sensuous lips he looked attractive and he probably knew it. He was a frequent guest at the rather dull parties of the English colony and, having had some of his poems printed in the *Jerusalem Mail,* was a favourite with the middle-aged and intellectually inclined among the English women. Young Farid, who was twenty and a virgin, allowed himself to be spoiled with a languid and blasé air. He knew from one painful experience that all European women were sex teasers, and he was careful not to expose himself to humiliation. Besides, he was in love with his three years older cousin Raissa, daughter of a Syrian patriot who had escaped being hanged by the Turks in 1916 and was shot by the French in 1926.

"It is a curious thing," he said dreamily. "These Jews come from the towns of Europe to become peasants—and our peasants all want to run away to the towns."

"Ah!" said Issa. "It is very bad."

"Well, what about that article for our magazine?" asked Salla.

"I don't know," said Issa. "I have never written poetry before."

"Poetry?" asked Salla, arching his eyebrows and lifting his chin by means of the stick.

"There you see," Farid said gloomily. "Even our youth still identifies writing with poetry. And what poetry! 'My beloved's lips are red corals, her teeth are shining pearls, her haunches like a cedar tree', all over again."

"I did not really mean it," said Issa, who had grown copper-red. He particularly resented being placed in the category of "our youth" by this badly-dressed town boy who was probably younger than he and did not know what a woman is. Ah, if he could only tell them about that Hebrew bitch.

"Anyway," said Salla, in a tactful attempt to turn the conversation. "All this is going to change now. Once the Hebrews are prevented from buying up the land and tempting the fellah, the rush to the towns will stop. By God, it was time the English did something about it."

"Do you believe they did it for our sake?" said Farid. "They don't want more Jews to come in because they are even more afraid of the Jews than they are of us; that is all."

"Falastin baladna, Yahud kalabna," suggested Issa, trying to regain the lost ground.

Salla ignored him. "For whatever reason they do it, I can only say *hamdul'illah* and praise God for it," he said, knocking his stick for emphasis against the floor.

"You will soon put on a tarbush," said Farid, and they both laughed. The red tarbush had been the emblem of the moderate Nashashibi party, and since their leading members had been bumped off by the Patriots, it had practically disappeared from the country. On the terrace everybody wore either Arab headgear or was bareheaded as they themselves were.

"But seriously," said Farid in a changed voice. "I admit that this White Paper is the first fair move of the British for twenty years—since they so generously promised our country to the Jews without asking us. . . ." He made a pause: when Farid talked seriously he was very careful in the choice of his words. "But this much admitted, you have still to see that it does not go far enough to repair the fantastic injustices of the past. All Arab States have their Parliaments—we are denied it because it would give us a majority over the Jews. Egypt and Iraq have attained independence—but though Iraq is a country of savages compared to us, they ask us to wait another ten years until we are granted the same international status. Who knows how often they will change their minds in these ten years, as they did in the past? It is all or nothing—and now."

Issa looked at him open-mouthed. He had never before heard anybody speak so cleverly and with such a beautiful choice of words.

Salla nodded, silently acknowledging his friend's superiority. "It is almost time," he said, looking at his watch. At the same moment the proprietor of the café switched on the wireless and the loudspeaker on the terrace began to crackle. It was a few minutes early and the Hebrew Children's Hour was still on. For a few seconds a warm, husky, girl's voice spoke in an amplified whisper to the mute crowd on the terrace. She spoke the words of a Hebrew nursery rhyme; her voice sounded so close that they thought they could feel her warm breath exhaled through the loudspeaker. They listened with expressionless faces, their eyes on the bubbling pipes, to the rhymed words of a language so kin to their own. " . . . And the sailors stuffed wax into their ears," Farid quoted to Salla, who smiled appreciatively, while rapping the silver knob against his teeth. Issa wondered what sailors they were talking about but did not really care. He thought of the Hebrew girl, and the fury of his unappeased desire for her paled the pock-marked skin of his face.

"Peace with you, children," the voice whispered, fading away in a smile; and for about twenty seconds there was silence. Then a male, factual voice announced the next item on the programme: a summary of the Government's Statement of Policy for Palestine, in Arabic. The faces on the terrace grew a little tenser. They waited in silence. A sharp and very loud crack came from the loudspeaker;—then nothing. The silence continued for an entire minute, then for a second and third one; the only sound on the terrace came from the tauleh players slamming down their disks.

"Have you killed your radio, ya Ahmad?" a fat man shouted at the proprietor. Some men laughed. "It is in order, by God, but it has gone dumb," the proprietor said in an anxious voice. He was frightened lest the Patriots should make him responsible for the trouble and burn his awnings and wicker stools for the second time.

Suddenly the loudspeaker spoke again. It was a different announcer this time and he sounded rather flustered. He explained in Arabic, and then repeated in the two other languages, that for technical reasons the broadcast of the Statement of Policy had to be postponed for an hour and a half. Meanwhile the station would send recorded Arab music.

A low murmur went over the terrace; then the players resumed rolling their dice and slamming down their disks with the mechanical movements of a lifetime's routine.

Salla rapped the floor furiously with his stick. "Oh, the hyenas, they have changed their minds again," he cried.

"Idiot," said Farid quietly. "You heard the broadcast from London. They can't change a Government Statement in an hour."

"But what happened? what happened, in the name of God?"

"Most likely the Jews have blown up the radio station in Ramallah."

"Ah! perhaps," said Salla, regaining hope. "Yes, surely that is it," he added, already convinced. "But that won't help them."

"No," said Farid, stirring the live coal in the small metal cup on top of the glass bowl.

"But all the same—they have courage, those children of death," Salla said, twisting his moustache in reluctant admiration.

"They have learned from us," said Farid, who was practising English equanimity.

Issa looked at them with gloomy dislike. He thought of the two dark figures who had come at night to fetch his father, and once more that icy ripple of fear ran through him, receded, and swept through him again, with the pitiless monotony of the tide.

3

The cable connecting the broadcasting studio in Jerusalem with the transmitting station in Ramallah had been cut at 8 p.m., precisely at the minute when the broadcast was to start, by members of the "Haganah". A convoy of armed cars carrying the Director of Programmes and his staff was at once dispatched to Ramallah.

At 9.30 p.m., by the time the broadcast was resumed, a crowd had assembled in front of the District Commissioner's Offices in Tel Aviv; they sang the anthem, stormed the District Offices, tore up the records of the Immigration and Land Registry Departments, threw the furniture through the windows, hoisted the Zionist flag and set fire to the building.

At 10 p.m., by the time the British Police had succeeded in dispersing the rioters, the Central Immigration Department in Jerusalem was burning too; when the fire brigade arrived the building was gutted and the files containing the lists of illegal immigrants earmarked for deportation had been destroyed.

At 11 p.m., by the time the Jerusalem fire had been put out, a new demonstration marched down Allenby Road in Tel Aviv and clashed with reinforced British Police. The Military Commander of the District imposed a curfew upon the town, and for the remaining hours of the night the country slept an uneasy sleep, until the Day of Visitation dawned.

This was the name given to the day by the National Council of the Hebrew Community, who had chosen it from Isaiah:

And what will ye do in the day of visitation, and in the desolation which shall come from far? to whom will ye flee for help?

To whom indeed? For a few days the Press and public opinion in Britain denounced the strangling of the National Home; American public figures protested against the "tearing up of a pact with the conscience of mankind"; there was the usual hue and cry as in the case of the Chinese, the Spaniards and the Czechs. Then all grew tired and quiet, and the law of universal indifference had its way; for the conscience of mankind is a diffuse kind of vapour which only rarely condenses into working steam.

And so the Day of Visitation dawned.

From early in the morning groups of boys and girls marched in military formation through Jerusalem. The Hebrew National Council, led by Glickstein, had proclaimed that it should be a day of protest with (orderly) processions, (peaceful) demonstrations and a complete stoppage of work (in all but the essential Government services). There was also to be a national registration of volunteers who were to pledge themselves to be ready for any emergency. The street walls and hoardings were plastered with posters bearing slogans like "We were here before the British and shall be here when they are gone" and "For Zion's sake will I not hold my peace and for Jerusalem's sake will I not rest".

The formations converged towards the football ground of the Hebrew Secondary School in the new residential quarter of Rechavia. All wore khaki shorts, and their political affiliation was only expressed in the colour of their shirts. For once all hostile factions were marching together. They paraded on the football ground, before a blue-and-white national flag at half mast. Glickstein made a speech calling them to fight the new policy to the last drop of their blood, but without violence and disorder. Nobody quite knew what he meant but it did not matter. There were several thousands of them, tightly packed between the two goals of the football ground with its cropped dry grass burnt yellow by the sun; the heat, emotion and perspiration fused them together into one coloured lump with a collective odour, voice and impulse, ready for anything. At the end of the meeting the order was given out to march in close formation down Ben Yehuda Street to Zion Circus; but on leaving the stadium they found the street barred by a cordon of Police. At once the formation broke up and merged again into an amorphous clot, as when the molecular structure of a solid is melted down to a thick, semi-liquid mass; and as its internal heat increased this seething mass began to throw out bubbles which burst and disintegrated against the firm wall of the Police; it could be foreseen that in a minute or so the whole mass would boil over. Shouts went up and soared in shrill flutterings over the heads of the dense crowd of adolescents; behind them the smaller children pushed and shrieked in hysterical elation, ready to throw themselves upon the rifles and tommy-guns, which for them were but magnified models of tin. The hard-jawed policemen looked expressionlessly at this strange and vocal Eastern crowd which they over-towered by a head's length and the like of which they had never seen before; then, at an order of their Commander, who had been calmly parleying with an agitated Glickstein, they gave way and watched the unruly crowd pass by—most of them with considerable relief and a few with regret. Behind their broken line the procession re-formed with cries of triumph and contempt; the blue-and-white streamers floated once more over their heads in the blazing sun, asking for refuge for their murdered kin, and for the Hebrew State.

About the same hour, still before noon, a different crowd had assembled in the Synagogue of Yeshurun, the largest and most modern of the many prayer-houses in Jerusalem. They were all old or elderly people, about five thousand of them. Wrapped in their gold- and silver-spun praying scarves, the men stood in rows between the ascending grades of pews, alternately beating their chests and performing series of quick little bows, according to the text of their murmured prayers. The women, sitting apart in the gallery, looked down red-eyed and sobbing. While they mechanically recited the text, their thoughts roamed the brooding expanse of distant Europe, fastened on a brother's house in Warsaw, a daughter married in Vienna, on children and grandchildren whom they would never see. For there were six millions of them caught and writhing in the rapidly tightening net between the Dniester and the Rhine; and now the Government had said that only seventy-five thousand of these would be allowed to escape—the rest, if they tried to jump, were to be thrown back into the net.

"Blessed be the All-present, blessed be He; blessed who gave the Law to His people, blessed be He."

The aged rabbi conducting the service threw open the carved doors of the Holy of Holies at the back of the altar. Inside the shrine stood six tall, doll-shaped figures clad in heavy velvet tunics with lace embroidery. In place of the head each figure showed, emerging from the tunic, two pointed sticks hung with small silver bells. The rabbi bowed his knee, kissed the hem of the first figure's velvet covering and took it into his arms. After him his aged attendants advanced one by one to the shrine, repeated the same ceremony and each lifted up one of the figures. Led by the rabbi, they formed into a procession and walked in single file round the synagogue. The silver bells tinkled thinly through the silence and the crowd pressed towards the procession to kiss the figures' velvet hems; the women on the gallery and those men who could not get close enough blew kisses with their finger-tips. When the procession had completed its circle, the ram-horn was blown three times and the congregation answered in chorus the traditional words. Then the six figures were laid alongside each other on the altar and the rabbi and his attendants proceeded to undress them. When the bells were dismantled and the tunics taken off, each figure was seen to consist of an ancient and voluminous parchment scroll. Each scroll contained the handwritten text of the five books of Moses; they had been rescued, complete with their traditional velvet drapings and silver bells, from burnt-down synagogues in Germany. Each parchment was mounted in the traditional way on two parallel wooden spools about four feet long. The sticks on which the bells hung were the handles of these spools; by turning both in the same direction the parchment was wound from one spool to the other and could be read like a moving screen.

The six aged men now proceeded to the altar and read in turn one specially selected verse from each of the saved scrolls. To find it some had to re-wind twenty or thirty yards of parchment, but they did it without hesitation, and found the verse with the ease of opening a book on a marked page. When the reading was over, the scrolls were dressed again and carried once more round the synagogue, the bells faintly audible over the sobs of the crowd; then they were replaced in the Holy of Holies and its door was closed.

There was a silence while the congregation waited for the next canonical prayer, as laid down in the rigid rules of the service. But instead of intoning it the priest suddenly swerved round to face the crowd, and, lifting both arms above his head, in a thundering voice cried out the words of David's psalm:

"Blessed be the Lord my strength, which teacheth my hands to war, and my fingers to fight. Bow thy heavens, O Lord, and come down: touch the mountains, and they shall smoke. Cast forth lightning, and scatter them: shoot out thine arrows, and destroy them. Rid me, and deliver me out of great waters, from the hand of strange children; whose mouth speaketh vanity, and their hand is falsehood. That our sons may be as plants grown up in their youth; that our daughters may be as the polished columns of a palace. . . ."

Facing the audience with his arms lifted up and tears running down his face, he stood in the poise of the ancient High Priests of Israel. Two attendants moved up to him from the right and the left, one holding the five-armed Maccabean candlestick with the candles aflame, the other a printed copy of the White Paper. He took the paper first and with a wrathful gesture of his narrow hands tore it up; then held the candles to it and let it go up in flames.

It was an unorthodox and unheard-of thing to do; a roar broke from the crowd, which, after a few reverberations, shaped itself into the old incantation "Hear Israel, the Lord is God and God is one". They said it thrice; then, as if a miracle had just been performed under their eyes, the men in the crowd fell into each other's arms, shouting and crying with joy.

They left the synagogue comforted, happily convinced that now all would be well. They clung to symbols as their fathers had done whose faith alone had enabled them to survive; and like their ancestors not so long ago, they believed in the power of the symbol to smite Pharaoh's hosts and bring their children and grandchildren safely across the sea.

Proudly carrying their flags and streamers, the other procession marched from the football ground to the centre of modern Jerusalem; when they reached Zion Circus they were disbanded by their leaders and told to go home. They were disappointed with this peaceful anticlimax, for all morning they had been exhorted to fight without being told whom or how; but it was luncheon-time and very hot, and they were tired and hungry, so they went home without demurring.

In the afternoon, however, when it became cooler, they began to flock back. By five o'clock the crowd had become so dense in Zion Circus that all traffic had to be diverted.

Zion Circus is a white, hot and dusty expanse of asphalt at the intersection of the town's main artery, Jaffa Road, with the shopping centre of Eliezer Ben Yehuda Street. The houses are in concrete or Jerusalem stone, white or sulphur. When the sun is high, people without sun-glasses cross it with eyes narrowed to slits. There are two cafés and a cinema. It is mainly frequented by Hebrews and on this day no Moslem ventured near it, except the Arab shoeblacks sitting in a row in the narrow shadow of the façades, and using their brushes as drumsticks on their wooden boxes to attract customers.

The crowd shouted slogans and milled round the square between the Café Europe, Café Vienna and Zion Cinema, aimless, angry and frustrated. The Police had thrown a cordon across Jaffa Road to protect the District Commissioner's Offices which were about a hundred yards down the road from the square, and this provoked the crowd whose only aim now became to break through the cordon and march to the District Offices. They pressed forward, were pushed back by the Police and re-formed, more defiant than ever.

By 6 P.M. the Police had to make use of their batons and a score of people had to be carried across the square with blood-covered faces. This incensed the crowd even more and they began to throw stones and bricks at the Police, a few of whom were injured. The Police charged. For hours they had obeyed the order to stand put and face the jeering crowd with restraint; now they obeyed the order to charge, and they let fly. They attacked the crowd in groups, hitting out right and left, blind to age or sex, and the screams of their victims seemed only to increase their fury. As always when the jovial guardians of peace and order are turned loose, they were more savage than the mob, for in them brutality was paired with a good conscience. Where the crowd thinned out towards its fringes, they gave chase to single men and women running for shelter into side streets; but when they succeeded in grabbing one, a ring formed round them which tore the screaming victim from their hands, and they had to beat their way out of the ring to rejoin their panting colleagues. Several of them had their uniforms torn to shreds and a few lost their helmets and batons to the crowd.

By 7 P.M. the crowd was smashing shop windows, among them those of a German restaurant and a British department store in Jaffa Road. The whole square was now a boiling cauldron with scuffling groups moving across it like bubbles. Then, with the fall of dusk, came a temporary lull.

The first line of the Police had been broken, but the second stood firm, protecting the District Offices. They stood astride Jaffa Road at its intersection with a narrow side street called Queen Melisande Lane. They were armed with rifles, and though so far they had not been ordered to make use of them, the ominous dark hole of the muzzles kept the front of the crowd at a distance of about fifteen yards. Most of them had only arrived in the country a few weeks before and were rather bewildered by what they saw.

Second from the right in the line stood young Constable Turner, a fair, good-looking lad from a village in Suffolk. Holding his rifle with a firm grip in the at-ease position, he looked at the undulating crowd before him with his wide-open, slightly bulging eyes. He had never before seen a mob behave like that and he did not know what all this shouting was about, except that one of the fellows had said that the Jews here wanted Independence, and he had added that if British rule wasn't good enough for them, all they had to do was to buy their tickets and go home where they came from and see whether Hitler was better. That was fair enough. Not that he had any grudge against Jews, queer fish though they were; he had known one in the Force, from Whitechapel, who had been a very decent, regular fellow. And back home in Suffolk on embarkation leave he had listened to a sermon by the vicar against Hitler and Race, and how the poor blighters had their synagogues burnt down; so he had arrived in this country with pity for them and open-minded like.

But on the other hand there was what the sergeant had said when he had given them a talk after debarkation—a regular eye-opener it had been, for the sarge knew what he was talking about, what with five years in the country and knowing the lingo and the ropes.

"You'll have to look out sharp," he had said to them, "for this is a hot country. If there is no trouble with Johnny Arab, there is trouble with Moishe Jew. Johnny Arab is easy enough to get along with but he is excitable like, and when he gets excited he does a bit of shooting. He is a clean fighter though, who does most of his shooting in the open hills. Moishe Jew is a different customer, all smiles into your face but sly. He likes planting time-bombs which go off when you don't expect it, and ambushing in dark streets, gangster fashion. He's also got helpers everywhere. Johnny Arab is quiet just now, but the Jew has something up his sleeve; so watch your step. . . ."

Constable Turner had been watching his step ever since, and if a Jewish shopkeeper or waiter talked to him, all smiles and "please" and "thank you", he would just look at him and think that he knew what he knew.

Just now they were all screaming again on the square like a lot of monkeys in the zoo. Having finished with the shop windows they were now smashing the telephone-boxes and street lamps. One after the other the lamps went out; then there was a flash like from a short-circuit and the rest of the lamps went out together. The square was plunged into sudden twilight, and as it grew darker the yelling and screaming increased. Young Constable Turner confessed to himself that he didn't like it.

In the first row of the crowd, directly opposite him, Turner had remarked an oddly dressed boy with black love-locks and black cotton stockings fixed with strings. He was pressing a velvet bag to his hips, the like of those they always carried on their way to the synagogue. The boy looked and behaved like a devil, yelling and gesticulating, and jumping up and down. Several times he was pushed forward by the pressure of the crowd almost into Turner's arms, and then he elbowed himself back into the crowd, but he didn't seem to be frightened. On the contrary, he was pulling faces at Constable Turner. Turner tried to look the other way, but for some reason his gaze had always to return to the boy's face. Just now the boy was sticking his tongue out at him—there could be no doubt about it though it was almost dark—and what with his dangling side-locks framing the dark-eyed face, and the long, pointed tongue sticking out, it was an ugly sight which almost gave one the creeps. Presently the boy started yelling at him, or rather chanting something in their lingo which Turner did not understand; nor did he guess that he, Turner, had sung those very same words himself, though in translation, back home in church. *"Cast forth lightning and scatter them,"* the boy yelled, dancing in a frenzy on his toes, *"shoot out thine arrows, and deliver me from the hand of strange children."* Turner wished he could collar that boy, and give him a good shaking maybe, to teach him some manners. But just to stand and stare and dodge the stones thrown at you, with that grimacing devil under your nose, it kind of got you down. Well, that's how it is, the policeman's lot, always—or nearly.

Now they'd started singing again, all together—their anthem or whatever it was—it sounded as if they meant to bring the houses down. And as they sang, they advanced. One could not properly see the crowd moving forward from the square, but one could see the pressure increase on those in front. They tried to hold their place, butting back with elbows and buttocks, but the pressure was too strong for them and a few lost their balance and fell, squirming on the asphalt while others tumbled over them; there were now less than ten yards of open space left and it was almost completely dark. Turner squinted at the faces of his fellow policemen; they stood rigid as if the whole show didn't concern them. The mob was throwing stones again, not from the front, of course, but from further back where it was safe; Turner had to dodge a brick which came hurtling at him like shrapnel and missed his head by inches. And all the while the singing went on—part seemed to do the singing, part the throwing; now it swelled even more and there was a new violent push forward. Those in front were swept forward by a big wave, the whole dark mass was moving; then there was a shot followed by two others and the second man to Turner's right gave out a yell and went down in a queer kind of spiralling slow-motion.

Almost at the same second the sergeant yelled out a command and Turner felt his rifle fly upward and dig its butt firmly into his shoulder, as if the rifle had obeyed of its own accord. The next command followed immediately and Turner pulled the trigger—whether he felt regret or relief for having been ordered to fire only over the heads of the crowd he couldn't say, for simultaneously with the flash he saw a dark and supple mass, like a jumping wild-cat, fly at him, and felt a hot stinging pain in his left knuckle. He screamed and let go of the rifle; then he saw as if in a crazy dream that the boy with the grimacing devil's face was hanging on to his neck and biting into his knuckle, holding fast with his teeth. Crazed with fright and frantically trying to wrench his hand free, young Constable Turner suddenly remembered the words of the psalm: *De-*

liver me from the hand of strange children; then he lifted his right fist and gave the devil a whacking blow on the head.

The boy tottered and let go, but before Turner could grab him some of the mob had torn the boy back, and Turner's rifle had gone too. He looked round with dazed eyes and saw that there still was a number of separate skirmishes going on in the street, but the mass of the crowd was floating back and the cordon had re-formed. The volley had after all had its effect. and a minute or so later there were again about twenty yards of free space in front. "Order arms," the sergeant shouted; but Turner had no longer any arms to order. "I'll pay them back for this," he muttered under his breath; then he saw the blood trickling from his hand, and reported for permission to fall out.

4

Later in the same night Joseph was walking home to his dingy hotel in the Street of the Prophets, chuckling to himself. A week ago the utter futility of this demonstration would have filled him with despair; since the action last Friday he did not mind. But how like the Glicksteins that this day of days should end in such a contemptible and humiliating manner! Bauman's organisation had taken no part in it; they believed in action, not in demonstrations. The official leaders had all made speeches about "deeds and not words" and "resistance to the last drop of blood"; the only thing they had forgotten to say was what deeds they expected from the people and what form their resistance should take. The crowd, keyed up and then left without a lead, had acted under its own confused impulses; and to-morrow the Glicksteins would issue a statement against rowdyism and for order and discipline, and everything would go on as before.

Why could the Irish, the Serbs, the Indians with their ninety per cent of illiterates, find the proper form and expression for their struggle—and this proverbially clever race be so utterly helpless every time a disaster befell them? It was not cowardice—the story of each of the Galilean settlements was an epic in itself. But the nation as a whole had lost its self-confidence in the centuries of dispersion. Its leaders came from the small towns of Poland and Tsarist Russia, where authority was represented by a corrupt police sergeant, usually drunk, and where the only way to deal with authority was to bribe or cringe. They could argue and protest and write brilliant memoranda to the League of Nations; when it came to action the ghetto in their blood began to tell, and they were helpless. . . .

The street was deserted and littered with broken glass. As he turned into Jaffa Road, plunged into darkness, he ran into a Police patrol armed with tommy-guns. There were two of them and they shouted at him to put his hands up; while one held him at the point of his gun, the other began to search him for weapons. Their manner showed that they were frightened and expected him to throw a bomb at them at any moment; and this fact filled Joseph, who was unarmed, with an ironical satisfaction. "What's the matter with you two?" he asked in English with a careful drawl. "Got the wind up?"

Their manner changed instantly. The one who had been patting his pockets stopped doing it, the other lowered the barrel of his gun.

"Sorry, sir," he said. "We are under orders, and thought you were a . . ." He looked doubtfully first into Joseph's face, then at his clothes. Accent and appearance did not fit and the man looked somewhat puzzled.

". . . a Jew?" Joseph asked helpfully.

The policeman became even more confused.

"It's all right, sir, we were only acting according to instructions," he said.

"But I *am* a Jew," Joseph said, childishly enjoying himself. "Good night, officer."

"Good night, sir," said the constable, completely taken aback.

Joseph walked on, grinning in the dark. He had gone about a hundred yards before he asked himself what reason he had to be so pleased with himself. After all, one couldn't expect the Glicksteins to acquire that certain accent. And when all was said he had only got away with being of the Race by the fact that he was not entirely of it. . . . He suddenly stopped grinning. It struck him that, hypocrisy apart, this was the real reason why the Race was persecuted in the East but tolerated in the West. They were tolerated to the extent that their substance became diluted. No normal people could endure the undiluted substance—that extreme and exposed condition of life which had crystallised in it.

Oh, damn, he thought, there we go again. And he had believed that since last Friday he had got over this kind of thing. Perhaps last Friday night had been just a trifle too easy. The Arab night watchmen on the beach had become gentle as lambs once they saw the muzzles of the automatics point at them, and the rest had been almost incredibly smooth going. The boat had turned up in the deserted bay near Natanya only half an hour after the appointed time. Directed by Morse signals from torches on the beach, it had anchored just outside the shallows so that the lifeboats with the cargo had had no more than fifty yards to row. The crates with the guns and ammunition had been safely loaded onto the milk-trucks within an hour. Most of the two hundred passengers were able to wade ashore from the lifeboats themselves; only the children and some old people, among them one with a wooden leg, had to be carried. When they came out of the water they all kissed the earth and most of them wept. Had they not been firmly told to shut up, they would have started singing hymns. Long before dawn they had all been put into trucks and dispersed in safe places; the action was over. The night watchmen were found, gagged and tied, three hours later by an Arab shepherd in the hills of Samaria. . . .

The only hitch had been that they were unable to finish refuelling before daylight came, and just as it was lifting anchor for the return journey, the boat had been sighted by a coastal patrol launch and seized by the authorities. However, they only got the Rumanian captain and his crew, who couldn't give away much as all their dealings had been with straw men under assumed names. The old tramper was lost—but there were two others on their way with eight hundred illegals this time; and after these there would be yet others with fugitives and arms. . . .

Joseph walked along the dark Jaffa Road, carefully picking his way among the broken glass and fragments of bricks. Without being aware of it, he was whistling under his breath the tune of "We shall rebuild Galilee". Since last Friday he felt a changed person—a patient who has undergone a magic cure after a long, toxic disease. His only regret was that he would not be allowed to take part in any more actions. Bauman was firm on that point; and with Bauman, unlike Reuben or Moshe, arguing was impossible. On the other hand, Bauman had taken him to a certain extent into his confidence and had given him certain explanations connected with last Friday's action—that is, he had told him as much as Joseph ought to know to get the background right when he started doing propaganda for them.

The people and the arms came from various countries, but mainly from Poland, via Rumania and Greece. The boats were old Greek or Rumanian cattle ships, coastal tramps or Turkish smuggler ships which could not be found on Lloyd's register. They had to be chartered by the Organisation's middlemen at a high price to cover the risk of their being seized by the British. For the time being the Organisation had plenty of money, mainly from rich American Jews to whose imagination this kind of thing appealed more than the subscription lists of the National Fund for the planting of trees or of the Hebrew University for the creation of a chair for Mathematics. There was, for instance, a certain Rumanian millionaire who had made his money by trafficking in arms and who, having lost his daughter in a pogrom of the Iron Guard, had given half his fortune to the Organisation on condition that it should be used for buying arms. Others gave a fixed amount for the smuggling of a fixed number of refugees into the country. There were many such sources which the law-abiding Glicksteins had never been able to tap.

The arms came mainly from Poland. The Polish Government was anxious both to get rid of its Jews and to make trouble for the British. Official Zionism had been too scrupulous to make capital out of this opportunity. The Bauman organisation had as few scruples as Mr. Chamberlain's Government. Its leaders, Raziel and Stern, had gone to Warsaw and made contact with a certain branch of the Polish General Staff. They had been received with open arms and come back with more positive results than they had ever expected. The Poles were providing as many Jews with passports and were sending as many arms as the Organisation could transport. The only difficulty was to find ships whose owners were willing to run the risk. For the time being they could not bring in more than five hundred people a month, plus a few tons of arms. But this was only the beginning. By the end of the year they hoped to reach a monthly five thousand; and by the end of 1940, if there was no war . . .

"Boy, oh boy," Bauman had exclaimed at this point, pacing up and down the room, head thrust forward, hands in his leather jacket. "Give me five years and we shall have another half-million in, and with it the majority in the country. Once we have the majority the rest is easy. Five years, man—if they would only wait five years with their bloody war, our problem would be solved. . . ." He had stopped in front of Joseph, looking at him with wild eyes.

"Do you think there will be no war until 1944?" he asked, putting his hands on Joseph's shoulder. "Listen," he went on, talking in a fever, "we are only just beginning. But we have got our start. Man, is it too much to ask for five years, having waited for two thousand? Tell me, is that too much?"

He was shaking Joseph by the shoulders. Last Friday's had

been the seventh transport to arrive since the Polish action had started, and so far all had arrived without a hitch, only two ships having been seized after unloading. Bauman was wild and drunk with hope. A precarious hope has a more unbalancing effect than despair. He suddenly took his hands from Joseph's shoulders and looked at him as if he were a stranger.

"Dismiss," he said, for the first time treating Joseph as a subordinate.

5

It was curious, Joseph reflected as he continued his walk towards Zion Circus, now dark and deserted, it was strange indeed that political imaginativeness was nowadays only to be found among extremist movements of the tyrannical type. Nazis, Fascists and Communists seemed to hold the international monopoly of it. It was not due to their lack of responsibility, as the envious democracies pretended, for these movements remained equally imaginative in their methods after they had ascended to power. One would have expected that a democratic structure would leave ampler scope for the display of originality than these rigidly disciplined bodies; and yet the opposite seemed to be true. Apparently submission to discipline and boldness of vision were not as incompatible as was generally assumed. Those who denied the freedom of ideas were full of ideas and ingenuity; while the defenders of free expression were dull and pedestrian with hardly an idea worth expressing.

—Well, obviously these were symptoms of the political ice age. Exposed to temperatures approaching absolute zero point, all matter displayed a curious and irregular behaviour. Even in physics different laws seemed to operate on different climatic levels. . . .

Joseph heard the bell of an ambulance car coming down Ben Yehuda Street, and as he was too keyed up to go to bed he decided to have a look at the Hadassa Hospital, just off Jaffa Road, to get an idea how many people had been injured in the day's riots. He turned back, and after a few yards turned into the steep, narrow side street leading to the hospital. As he approached the old drab building he saw that there was already quite a crowd—all anxious relatives, and all arguing at the same time with the British policeman and the Hebrew nurse guarding the entrance gate. The harassed nurse kept disappearing into the building to inquire about the names given to her, and the constable tried to persuade the crowd to form a queue, but without success. They kept on pushing towards the gate and shouting over each other's heads whenever the nurse came back; the nurse kept plugging her two thumbs into her ears, yelling at them to keep quiet and to speak one at a time. Joseph watched the scene with disgust—a homely disgust which he experienced at least once a day when watching similar scenes at bus stops and office counters. As usual he told himself that these people acted under the pressure of their past. He had trained his mind to apologise for what his senses perceived; but it had little power over that momentary revulsion which was also a pressure-product of his own past and couldn't be helped, just as the crowd's reactions couldn't.

He turned to go home when he noticed the boy with the lovelocks whom Bauman had slapped, coming out of the gate. The boy had a bandage round his head but wore his skull-cap and the greasy black felt hat on top of it; he was smiling uncertainly with his thick lips and held the blue velvet bag pressed under his arm. It occurred to Joseph that members of the Organisation had been forbidden to take part in last afternoon's demonstrations so as not to expose themselves unnecessarily, and that the boy had no business to get mixed up in a scrap. He waited until the boy had got clear of the crowd and was walking down the street, then caught up with him. "What have you been doing there?" he asked.

The boy gave a start, then recognised Joseph and smiled, reassured. He had only seen Joseph twice in the Palace, and though he didn't know what or who Joseph was, he knew by instinct that he was a kind of outsider, not part of the hierarchy of his superior officers, and therefore safe.

"Ooh—I have been hit by a policeman," he said in a triumphant sing-song. "But I took his rifle away."

"Did you?" said Joseph. "Just like that?"

"No—I bit him in the ha-and."

It was too dark to see the expression in the boy's face. In his sagging black cotton stockings and the long black kaftan he looked like a scarecrow.

"You know you had no business to go there," said Joseph. "And particularly not carrying *that*. . . ." He rapped with his fingers on the bag under the boy's arm. "If they had caught you, you would have got yourself into a bad mess—and others too."

The boy opened the bag and pulled the book out of it. They were close to a street lamp which had been out of the crowd's reach, and he held it up to the light. It was an ordinary, tattered prayer-book. "What is wrong with tha-at if they caught me?" he asked mockingly. "I was on my way to the synago-ogue. What is wrong with going to the synago-ogue?"

Joseph gave no answer. He hated meddling, but he had made up his mind to mention the matter to Bauman or Simeon. The boy was stuffing the book into the bag. They were standing near a hoarding plastered with posters from the eve. The ornate, loud-mouthed protests and threats of the official Hebrew bodies were torn and smeared with caricatures. On the heavy-lettered slogan "To the Last Drop of Blood", quoted from a speech by Glickstein, the word "blood" was crossed out and replaced by "ink". Another poster with the words "If I Forget Thee, Jerusalem" had been half torn off, so that the words were hanging upside-down showing the dry glue on the back of the paper.

The boy was looking at the posters in the dim light of the street lamp. Joseph could see him smile mockingly. He was curious to find out what went on in the boy's head.

"What do you think of all this?" he asked.

The boy lifted his shoulders.

"Do I know?" he said. "It is written: A wolf in a sheep's skin is a great danger; but a sheep in a wolf's skin is an object of laughter."

"Where is that written?" asked Joseph.

The boy smiled, twisting his side-plaits round his finger.

"You have made it up," said Joseph, and for the first time the boy was not entirely repulsive to him. "Why have you joined the Organisation?" he asked.

Again the boy shrugged. "Why not?" he answered in a sing-song, with his half-humble, half-superior infant-prodigy smile. Somewhere beneath his cringing and gaucherie that boy was quite sure of himself, or of something encased in the very core of himself. It was as if he accepted the awkwardness of his own body and manners as something of no consequence, as a mere accident which could not touch that inner certainty.

"Can't you answer properly?" Joseph said. The boy reluctantly turned away from the hoarding and faced him. Under his black kaftan he wore a white, soiled, cotton shirt buttoned up to the neck but without a tie. Instead of a stud the shirt had a white thread-button which was broken, showing its wire frame. His face, between the two spiral braids hanging down to his shoulders, still had the bi-sexed ambiguity of adolescents and the coarser cherubim. His eyes and lips were moist, and the lips always moving.

"Why do you ask a question to which you know the answer yourself?" he chanted, with a certain hostility.

"Because your reasons may be different from mine," said Joseph. "Well, why have you joined?"

"Ooh," the boy complained. "They have asked me that at each of the tests."

A camel rocked past them, occupying with its load almost the whole width of the lane. They had to flatten themselves against the wall. The Arab, riding on a heap of sacks, was asleep. The camel passed them with measured sullenness, its hooves whirling up a cloud of dust as it reached the unpaved end of the lane.

"And what did you say when they asked you?" Joseph pressed the boy. It had become of a sudden importance to him to know what the reasons were which had got him and this boy into the same boat.

"What I said? I gave them Exodus 20:1, and Deuteronomy 19:21 and 25:19 and 32:41 and 32:42. . . ."

"Meaning?" Joseph asked; but already his curiosity was extinguished.

"Meaning," said the boy, with mocking triumph in his voice, "meaning: Blot out the remembrance of Amalek from under heaven. Thine eye shall not pity, but life shall go for life. I will render vengeance to mine enemies and will reward them that hate me. I will make mine arrows drunk with blood, and my sword shall devour flesh. . . ."

He had begun hopping up and down on one foot, clapping his hands, his side-locks flapping round his ears. He looked like a big clumsy child in an outgrown coat skipping a rope.

Joseph watched him with fascinated disgust. "That will do," he said.

"Now you know," said the boy, coming to rest. His eyes resumed their former expression of timid mockery. In a different voice he said, as if trying to comfort Joseph:

"It is also said: In much wisdom there is much grief; he that increaseth knowledge increaseth sorrow. And how dieth the wise man? as the fool."

He made a deep, mocking bow at Joseph and made off in a hurry, hop-skipping along like a schoolboy, his side-locks flapping, the velvet bag tightly pressed under his arm.

It was almost morning, and the sky a transparent, silky grey, preparing for the sun to rise over Mount Zion.

"There goes your undiluted substance," Joseph thought, following the boy with his eyes.

THIEVES IN THE NIGHT

(1939)

"To have one's heart with God is not the same thing as having one's head in the clouds."

THE REV. FATHER P. N. WAGGETT, S.S.J.E.,
in a sermon on the Mount of Olives, 1918

THIEVES IN THE NIGHT (1939)

1

In May the sky over Ezra's Tower is a blue lava field. The earth looks as if Jehovah had thrown a carpet down on Galilee; the air bubbles caught under the carpet are the hills, and the creases the wadis. Seen from Kfar Tabiyeh, the red-roofed white houses of the Settlement look like a colony of mushrooms spreading over an ever wider area of the hill. There were five and twenty on the Dogs' Hill when they came, and now after two years there were almost three hundred. And the God of the Hebrews had blessed their cattle and multiplied their flocks.

The happiest days for Joseph during this spring of 1939 were the Fridays and Shabbaths he spent at home. Ezra's Tower was a lotus-land untouched by the gales of the ice age which were shaking the world with increasing fury. He had fallen in love with the hills all over again, and he had a theory that the Song was written by Solomon during a Galilean spring-excursion. Its counterpart, the sermon of vanities, was a product of the glum hills of Judaea where the royal pessimist resided; but the Song clearly belonged to Galilee:

. . . *The fig tree putteth forth her green figs, and the wines with the tender grape give a good smell. Take us the foxes, the little foxes, that spoil the vines.*

The world was invaded by the barking little foxes, but Ezra's Tower still held its own. The saplings which Simeon had planted threw their lattice of thin shadows on the grass as a token of the future forest's shade. It was curious that the memory of Simeon's sharp, bitter personality should survive in the form of this baby forest of firs. Simeon the heretic was dead to the Commune, but already a different, legendary Simeon grew in the forest's roots. And in the minds of those who had come after her death there was a mythical Dina, an image of purity and perfection from the early legendary days.

With the growth of the Commune its fraternal homogeneity had transformed itself into a more articulate structure. As in a mature organic cell there was now a clear distinction between core and periphery. The periphery was made up of concentric layers according to their age, though the division between neighbouring layers became blurred with time. But the core retained its peculiarity and distinction. They were the founders, the Old Ones: Reuben, Moshe, Dasha, Ellen, Arieh the shepherd, Mendl the pied piper; Sarah, who since Dina's death was in charge of the children's house; Max, who was still in the opposition. At the last General Meeting most of them had been re-elected to the administrative posts they held, and though the Secretariat contained some new blood from the outer layers, it was easy to foresee that for the next few years they would continue to monopolise all key positions—until the periphery, in growing frustration, produced its own leaders, and captured the Secretariat in turn. This was how it had happened in the older Communes, and the same would doubtless happen in Ezra's Tower. The absence of privileges for the bureaucracy prevented its crystallisation; they had no army, police or party apparatus to support them, their actions down to the minutest detail were under constant public scrutiny, and the principle of total economic equality, outlawing money and barter, made it impossible for them to bestow favours or bribe the electorate. Their only satisfactions were increased responsibility, a more direct influence on the development of the Commune, and the sensation of power derived from it. It was but the shadow of power, without substance and stability, and yet for those who yielded it real enough to be cherished more than they were prepared to admit, even to themselves. The instinct to dominate had not been abolished, merely tamed and harnessed; but that, Joseph thought, was as much as anybody could hope for.

Of course, the model society of the Commune was limited both in size and by the necessary selection of its human material. Repeated on a large scale and by compulsory means it was bound to collapse. Oases are not expandable. But it had proved that under certain conditions a different form of human life could be attained; and that again was as much as one could hope for. . . .

On this particular Friday, the last in May, Joseph was lying in the field near the Ancestor's Cave under the blue lava sky, chewing a grass halm. On his way back from Jerusalem he had been to see Ellen and the child in the maternity clinic at Gan Tamar. She had looked very happy and almost pretty in the white bed with the red poppies on the bedside table. Joseph had brought them, and she had been so grateful and overjoyed that he in turn had felt moved by a mixture of pity, fondness, physical desire and the guilt of not being able to feel more for her. However, if one did not analyse this mixture too closely, it could almost pass for the real thing. And what, after all, was the real thing? So many emotional compounds passed under that name, that this one might claim it as well as any other. Who knew whether what he felt for Dina was more real? Perhaps if Ellen had been the unattainable one and Dina the mother of the child, his feelings, too, would have been reversed.

Anyway, the child was a girl and it was to be called Dina. It had been Ellen's suggestion, and it was one of those things about Ellen which went into the compound and made it more solid and adhesive.

—Leaning on his elbow and chewing the sweet halm of grass, he saw Reuben strolling towards him. Reuben had grown even more quiet and self-effacing during this last year; he for one was immune against the temptations of power. Or was he? What if his reserve and modesty were only a subtler, inverted means of deriving satisfaction from it? Oh, the fallacy of those simple words which people used to describe each other, as if the qualities expressed by them were irreducibles and not highly complicated mixtures! "Modesty" was believed to be an irreducible element like nitrogen; and lo, neither of them was. . . .

"How does it feel to be a father?" Reuben asked, settling in the grass at Joseph's side in the relaxed, lazy mood of the Shabbath eve which descended over the whole Commune after the traditional hot shower-bath.

"God knows," said Joseph. "I was just trying to work it out. I am busy convincing myself that there is no cause for loin-pride, that the fact that the thing was born with some fluff on its head is no merit of mine, and that others have equally small pink nails on their fingers and toes, the opening and closing of which is a rhythmical reflex and no certain sign of early genius."

Reuben smiled. "What a rabbi you are," he said. "Your thinking proceeds in a kind of mirror-writing—from right to left like the Hebrew letters. Sometimes you give the impression that you live altogether in a mirror."

"And what of it?" said Joseph. "People shoot themselves in front of mirrors and make love before mirrors. It is an old prejudice to think that self-awareness destroys the power for emotion, and that feeling must be dumb and innocent. The dog while eating enjoys himself, but he doesn't know that he enjoys himself, otherwise he would eat slower and leave the best bits to the last; and thus by lack of self-awareness enjoys himself less. 'Innocence' means the opposite of *nocentem,* hurt. To be *nocent* is more human, and it hurts more. . . ."

"Go on, Rabbi Joseph, I am listening. Where does the chosen race come in?"

Reuben was in an unusually happy mood. The reason was that to-night a new settlement was to be founded in the District, and that Ezra's Tower was to serve as godfather to the new colonists, as Gan Tamar had once served to them. The trucks with the new settlers and their equipment had arrived in the morning, and to-night there would be a celebration before they set out.

Joseph turned over on his belly. He grinned at Reuben with an affection that was increased by the fact that he was now hiding half his existence from him—the half connected with Bauman and the gang. But then, did not a well-meaning cheat always increase affection? Husbands never felt more affectionate than after the casual adultery so indispensable for happily balanced matrimony. Which went to prove that sincerity was just another compound, like affection.

"Where the chosen race comes in?" he repeated. "I will tell you a parable. Once upon a time the most perfect product of creation were the fish. They were swimming happily the seven seas, and apart from the occasional accident of being eaten by the bigger ones, all was well with them.

"Then came the time when some force drove some fish to creep ashore and become amphibious. Those who did had a terrible time of it. Instead of drifting with streamlined grace through the water, they had to waddle and wobble painfully on their bellies through swamp and muck, and gasp piteously for air with a new and imperfect contraption specially evolved for this purpose. It took ages until these new, ugly, awkward creatures began to appreciate the compensations for their debasement and sufferings: the sun, sound and form, copulation, hot rocks and cool winds."

"Is that all?" said Reuben. "Where do the Jews come in? Did the amphibians get circumcised?"

"Don't you see?" said Joseph. "The Arabs are the fish. They are happy, they have tradition and beauty and self-sufficiency and lead a timeless, care-free, lackadaisical life. Compared to them we are the graceless amphibians. That's one of the reasons why the English love them and dislike us. It is not political. It is their nostalgia for the lost paradise—a kind of eternal week-end—and their detestation of the 8.35 to the City. For behold, we are the force that drives the fishes ashore, the nervous whip of evolution."

"That was beautiful, Rabbi Joseph," Reuben said, smiling.

"It was merely a digression to settle, once for all, this irksome Arab question," said Joseph modestly. "However, in my present happy mood I can't be bothered with Arabs and shall return to my original text, which is concerned with that mirror-writing of the mind that occurs on the higher levels of self-awareness. I wish to point out to you that it is sheer philistine nonsense to associate introspection with morbidity. *Cogito ergo sum* is the classic introspective statement which started modern philosophy and shaped our attitude to life. The theme-song of all evolution is the trend towards greater articulateness. Romeo loves as passionately as your dumb Arab shepherd, but his emotion has become articulate and introspected, and is therefore on a higher level. It has become *nocent*—that is, both its hurt and its bliss are sharpened, have a finer and keener edge. But that is just the opposite of morbidity. It means one rung up the ladder of living."

Reuben smiled. "If I am not mistaken, I once heard you rave against the 'curse of knowingness' on our race. And there was a time when you admired Bauman's terrorists who refuse to see the other side of the medal."

Joseph looked at him, rather taken aback for a second. "What a snake in the grass you are," he said. "In fact there is no contradiction—except the old one that you have to use your fist to protect your block in which the thinking takes place; which paradox is not of my making but inherent in the human condition and particularly noticeable in a moral ice age. You pacifists have always to drop your principles in an emergency because you refuse to acknowledge that basic antinomy of nature. Keep your gun oiled and your mirror clean. There is no contradiction in that."

"Well, well," said Reuben, rising to his feet. "I liked your parable better. . . . I must be getting back. Come along,

Moshe is waiting with the accounts. He wants to kiss you for getting the cash advance from the Co-operative. That certainly was a triumph of your articulateness. . . ."

Joseph sighed, but got to his feet obediently. They walked back together, discussing the preparations for the evening. Joseph had decided to go out with the settlers' convoy to the new Place to-night and come back with the returning lorries the next day. Reuben, too, would have liked to go, but he had a meeting of the Education Committee on the Shabbath morning. Joseph pitied him.

"I wonder whether we shall ever grow out of this meeting-itis," he said. "It's the measles of democracy."

"But harmless," said Reuben. "Fascist pox isn't."

Joseph, for a change, agreed. Amicable, they discussed the location of the new cowshed and the extensions to the children's house, which had become too small for its thirty-seven inmates—and, with Joseph's daughter, thirty-eight.

2

As a send-off for the advance party of the new settlers, a special meal had been prepared in the dining-hut. The tables had been put together to form a long double horseshoe covered with a white tablecloth and decorated with flowers; the hut was transformed into a solemn banqueting-hall. This happened only three or four times a year, on the eve of Passover, on New Year's Day, at the Feasts of the Maccabeans and of the Planting of Trees. In the monotony of communal routine the white, glittering tables and the festive atmosphere were highlights of the season whose memory lingered on for weeks.

The advance party consisted of only twelve people—eleven boys, and one girl called Rachel who seemed to play an important rôle among them. She was very short, under five feet, with short-cropped black hair, quick movements, and such a high-voltage charge about her dominating little person that one was afraid to touch her lest one get an electric shock. She came from Rumania, and her boy friend, who was secretary of the group, from Germany. His name was Theo; he was blond and tall, with an awkward stoop, timid and slow in gesture. He was obviously the ideal type for a communal secretary, a lightweight junior edition of Reuben; what he lacked in vitality Rachel would supply. The two of them sat together at the top part of the banqueting-table between Moshe and old Wabash, who never missed an opportunity to be present at the founding of a new settlement.

There were few Helpers this time and only a small advance party, partly because the Arabs had been calmed by the White Paper, and had left the rioting for a change to the Jews, and mainly because the advance party was for some time to live in an abandoned Arab house which stood on the site of the future Settlement and would give them reasonable protection while they prepared the ground for the main group, to follow a few weeks later. The Settlement was to be called Tel Joshua, or Joshua's Hill; it was to be built on a hill at twelve miles' distance from Ezra's Tower and to serve as a strategic link between the Upper Galilean Communes and the Valley of Jezreel. The land had been bought by the National Fund a few years ago but had been thought unfit for colonisation as it had no water, which had to be carried on donkeys from a place four miles away. This group of fifty young people, recent arrivals from Germany and Rumania, still at the bottom of the queue for land, had applied for Joshua's barren hill, and after a long struggle with the Hebrew Colonisation Department, had got their way. They had left Europe much later than the crowd of Ezra's Tower, and their load of Things to Forget was accordingly heavier and more lurid in detail. Half of them had arrived without a visa; they were illegal immigrants with faked papers, liable to be deported if caught. They did not care how long they had to bore until they found water, nor about the malaria rate; these were trifles compared with the things they had experienced where they came from. They were hungry for land, hungry for stability, hungry for the smell of cattle-sheds, of donkeys and horses; hungry above all for a life that made sense, sustained by the warmth of a fraternity where every boy and girl had been tested, was liked and approved.

The dining-hall was bright, looked much brighter than usual with the light reflected from the white tablecloth; it smelled of the fresh salad and herbs in the big wooden bowls and was saturated with that convivial buzz produced by the vibration of plates, voices and glasses. There were speeches; old Wabash, white-bearded and blue-shirted and looking more than ever like a slightly gaga Prophet from the Bible, told with gusto the tale of the first Twelve in Dagánia and of the suffering *milliohnim;* he was followed by Moshe dispensing some good horse-sense advice to the new settlers, and by Max with quotations from Glickstein and Lenin. But except for the awestricken and solemn debutants of Tel Joshua nobody paid much attention to the speeches. As on each of the rare occasions when they drank wine, the people of Ezra's Tower revealed themselves in a light normally dulled by routine and fatigue. Putting their emptied glasses down on the white tablecloth with a show of recklessness, their faces shone like mirrors from the lumber-room with the cobwebs and dust wiped off.

Joseph's gaze travelled the round of faces of the old guard, trying to discover the changes they had undergone since that night when they had set out for Ezra's Tower. Moshe had grown fatter, with a touch of baldness, and looked a little like a successful stockbroker. Hunchbacked little Mendl had grown even quieter, the listening look in his eyes had become more pronounced, and his sudden transformations into the pied piper rarer; he had recently finished his Galilean Symphony and there was some talk of the National Philharmonic Orchestra producing it. Gaby, the communal Messalina now in charge of the dressmaker shop, was beginning to develop a puffed and tartish look; instead of fluttering her eyelashes as she once used to, she had now taken up quivering nostrils. Six months ago she had caused another scandal by being unfaithful to the Egyptian—and, of all people, with the Dr. Phil. Ham, the dark savage, had threatened to kill poor Fritz and could only be dissuaded from it by the whole matter being thrashed out in the General Meeting, where Max had delivered a much-admired speech on sex and society, Gaby had cried, Fritz publicly confessed his unsocial behaviour, and Ham, moved almost to tears, had solemnly forgiven them all and was stopped just in time by Sarah from singing the Anthem. After that, Sarah had used her pedagogic talents to comfort the Egyptian by opening spiritual vistas for him, and three weeks later the Egyptian had suggested that they should get married and live together on a higher plane. Sarah had made a terrible fuss, asking each member of the Secretariat separately for advice and accusing herself of being unfair to poor Gaby. Ham got so ashamed of his base desires that he told Sarah he was ready to renounce her and to agree with her higher view of the matter, whereupon Sarah got hysterics, and it had taken all of Reuben's diplomacy to bring the affair to a happy conclusion.

Almost from the first week they were married, a change began to occur in Sarah. Her pinched little face with the hungry-virgin eyes began to fill up into matronly softness and she put on weight at a fantastic rate. Since Dina's death she had been in charge of the children's house but without being officially confirmed in her office—all major decisions resting with a committee of three—and this had been the second great frustration in Sarah's life. Three months after her marriage Reuben had proposed to the General Meeting that the committee should be reduced to an advisory capacity and Sarah be made a member of the Secretariat with full responsibilities. The meeting, though with some doubts and hesitations, had voted for the proposal, and this had completed Sarah's transformation from a skinny, frustrated little squirrel into a rotund and efficient matron. It had taken her seven bitter years of detours and self-deceptions to find the form of life she was made for;

but at last she had found it. In the world outside, without the sustaining warmth of comradeship around her, she would probably have gone to pieces. . . .

Becoming conscious of Joseph's gaze, Sarah turned her head. He gave her a friendly grin and continued his silent survey of the old guard. Dasha, fat and pretty with her round face and high slavonic cheekbones, was just coming back from the kitchen, flushed and triumphant at the success of the meal. Arieh the shepherd was chewing his shashlik in contented rumination; the Dr. Phil. was holding forth on the merits of bootmaking to an admiring girl from the youth camp. He, too, had lost his nervous fidgetiness and looked broader and more self-assured. Joseph contrasted in his mind's eye the men and women around him with the crowd in the cafés of Tel Aviv, the crowd with the frozen shrug about their shoulders, and he felt a deep satisfaction, a conceitless pride which was close to humbleness, at being one of the founders of Ezra's Tower. This was right and good and made sense. Here something broken was being made whole again: men were recovering their lost integrity.

His eyes met Reuben's, and Reuben gave his snake-in-the-grass smile and said: "Speech". Joseph shook his head but others had heard, and a minute later the whole table was clamouring for a speech. It came almost as a shock to Joseph that, despite his unbalancedness and contradictions and the sense of his own futility, these people liked him. As he stood before them and they looked at him with curiosity and expectation, the mirror in his mind revolved and he asked himself how he, always unable to see himself as a whole, was reflected in their eyes. Oh well, they would just see the old monkey face with one or two grey strands over the temples, eyebrows meeting in the middle and lifted in the usual grin. He decided to tell them the parable of the fish.

"*Chaverim,*" he said, savouring the mellow archaic taste of the word, born in the hard desert, which had given a new turn to the history of man; "*chaverim*—comrades . . ."

3

The engine roared and the truck swayed like a drunkard as the convoy entered the dry stream-bed of the wadi. They had passed the Giant's Buttocks and were now following the wadi's course towards the south, away from the familiar country of Ezra's Tower and Gan Tamar, into new, strange hills, deserted but for a few wretched mud villages perching on the slopes of desolation. In front and behind, the other trucks crept cautiously forward with dimmed headlights.

Joseph lay stretched out on the canvas cover of the truck, his arms folded under his head. This time he had a truck all to himself, for there were few Helpers needed. It was a comfortable one, loaded with crates of farm implements and some sacks of flour on top.

On the truck in front the new settlers were singing "God will rebuild Galilee". On the truck behind, which carried some of the Helpers, they were arguing over the White Paper. As the truck of the Helpers came closer or fell back, Joseph caught fragments of the debate and lost it again, while the singing in front swelled and faded. The stars over his head displayed all their Galilean brilliance, the Great Bear sprawling on his back and the Milky Way clotted into a luminous, branching scar.

The truck behind was pulling close again. They were still arguing. A girl's voice said:

"Once we have irrigated the southern desert we can bring another four millions in."

"That still leaves twelve millions out," a man said.

"It doesn't matter," said the girl. "Half of them will be killed anyway. The other half will be all right for a while. . . ."

The truck receded, but the girl's voice lingered on in Joseph's ear: "Half will be killed, the other half will be all right for a while." She had said it as soberly as if checking a household account. What a grandiose arithmetic history had taught this race. Their population chart, instead of moving in a curve, looked like the zigzag of lightning.

The truck gave a jolt and slowed down; the singing in front became weaker, and from the truck behind came once more the girl's voice arguing in the dark:

". . . Nationalism? Nonsense. It's homesickness."

"How can people be homesick for a country they have never seen?" said a man's sceptical voice.

"It's in the race. Homesickness is endemic in the race. . . ."

Joseph's truck accelerated and the rest of the argument was lost. How they always harped back to this question of "race"—as if it explained anything. As if some biological variation could explain this phenomenon of the lightning zigzag trace of their fate—that jagged scar across the face of human history.

He lay back on the canvas, glad to have the truck to himself. To the south he saw a very bright planet, perhaps Mars or Jupiter, he didn't know. He remembered that first night, walking back after the shooting to Dina's tent, when he had seen this same planet rising, and had decided that if other stars were populated they must doubtless have their own kind of Jews. For Jews were not an accident of race, but simply man's condition carried to its extreme—a branch of the species touched on the raw. Exiled in Egypt, in Babylon, and now over the whole globe, exposed to strange and hostile surroundings, they had to develop peculiar traits; they had no time nor chance to grow that hide of complacency, of a specious security, which makes man insensitive to and forgetful of the tragic essence of his condition. They were the natural target of all malcontents, because they were so exasperatingly and abnormally human. . . .

Made homeless in space, they had to expand into new dimensions, as the blind develop hearing and touch. The loss of the spatial dimension transformed this branch of the species as it would have transformed any other nation on earth, Jupiter or Mars. It turned their vision inwards. It made them cunning and grew them claws to cling on with as they were swept by the wind through countries that were not theirs. It increased their spiritual arrogance: deprived of Space, they believed themselves chosen for eternity in Time. It increased the protective adaptability of their surface, and petrified their inner core. Constant friction polished their many facets: reduced to drift-sand, they had to glitter if they wanted to avoid being trodden on. Living in bondage, cringing became second nature to their pride. Their natural selector was the whip: it whipped the life out of the feeble and whipped the spasm of ambition into the fit. In all fields of living, to get an equal chance they had to start with a plus. Condemned to live in extremes, they were in every respect like other people, only more so.

—A nationalist? I?—Joseph echoed the girl's voice.—Nonsense. Our nationalism is homesickness for normality.

The singing swelled up, receded. They were singing one of the popular horras, a folk-song with a passionate, almost hysterical tune.

—Nationalism? Nonsense . . . —Joseph repeated to himself.—This earth means something different to us than Croatia means to the Croats or America to the Americans. They are married to their countries; we are searching for a lost bride. We are homesick for a Canaan which was never truly ours. That is why we are always foremost in the race for utopias and messianic revolutions, always chasing after a lost Paradise. Defeated and bruised, we turn back towards the point in space from which the hunt started. It is the return from delirium to normality and its limitations. A country is the shadow which a nation throws, and for two thousand years we were a nation without a shadow. . . .

The wadi narrowed to a gorge; the starlit rocks on its flanks seemed to meditate the law of universal indifference. The convoy moved along them, a dark caravan of pilgrims. On setting out on their long pilgrimage they had left a house and garden behind; all that had been swallowed up by the desert and now they had to start building again. They were returning to a Canaan of thistles and thorns. Half of them were illegal immigrants: they survived without official consent. How those with the complacent hides and solid shadows grudged them even this waste of scrub and stones!

—Ay, don't give in to bitterness, Joseph told himself; oil your gun but keep your mirror clean. We shall always be betrayed because something in us asks to be betrayed. There is this urge in us for the return to earth and normality; and there is that other urge to continue the hunt for a lost Paradise which is not in space. This is our predicament. But it is not a question of race. It is the human predicament carried to its extreme.

Far off in the night a light had begun to blink; it looked like a red spark suspended in the air. Straining his eyes, Joseph discovered the pale silhouette of the hill on which Tel Joshua was to stand.

—Good, Joseph thought. We have occupied another acre of space. The hunt will go on and the stakes will keep burning, but a few hundred will live here; and the wilderness shall be glad for them.

The truck stopped abruptly. The whole convoy came to a standstill; the drivers switched their headlights on and hooted wildly into the night. The distant spark went rhythmically on and off, flash and darkness, flash, flash and darkness, flash and flash, dot and dash.

—They have gone crazy, Joseph thought, reading the message. They are sending Isaiah in Morse:

And they shall build houses and inhabit them; and they shall plant vineyards, and eat the fruit of them.

—They should send it in code, Joseph thought. It is a subversive message, opposed to official policy and against the law.

The truck had started to move again. The argument in the truck behind continued. The drivers, sobered, dimmed their lights and the convoy resumed its journey, stealthily like thieves in the night.

THE END